Every Hour *until* Then

Books by Gabrielle Meyer

Timeless

When the Day Comes

In This Moment

For a Lifetime

Across the Ages

Every Hour until Then

"The drama builds with each page, and I could not wait to see how it would all turn out. Fans of history, romance, or time travel will adore this book."

Julie Klassen, bestselling author, on *When the Day Comes*

"Gabrielle Meyer merges epic moments in history with personal themes of romance, faith, and self-sacrifice."

Mimi Matthews, *USA Today* bestselling author, on *In This Moment*

"A breathtaking journey through time and history! Prepare to be entranced!"

Sarah Sundin, bestselling and Christy Award–winning author, on *In This Moment*

"With rich historical details and a riveting conundrum, *When the Day Comes* had me glued to the pages, the story tugging at my heart and lingering with me long after the last page. A triumph of a story!"

Susan May Warren, *USA Today* bestselling author, on *When the Day Comes*

"A seamless blend of choices and chances celebrating the enduring spirit of a woman faced with a remarkable future, this first book in the TIMELESS series is a lovely and memorable time-crossing feat."

Laura Frantz, Christy Award–winning author, on *When the Day Comes*

"A fresh and innovative twist on time travel, each book of the TIMELESS series features clever heroines, emotionally charged love stories, and unpredictable twists that will keep readers engrossed until the last page."

Elizabeth Camden, RITA Award–winning author

"Meticulous research, intriguing characters, sweet romance, and an evocative dual-time setting make this one of my favorite reads of the year."

Lisa T. Bergren, bestselling and award-winning author, on *When the Day Comes*

TIMELESS • 5

Every Hour *until* Then

GABRIELLE MEYER

BETHANYHOUSE
a division of Baker Publishing Group
Minneapolis, Minnesota

Published by Bethany House Publishers
Minneapolis, Minnesota
BethanyHouse.com

Bethany House Publishers is a division of
Baker Publishing Group, Grand Rapids, Michigan

Printed in the United States of America

Library of Congress Cataloging-in-Publication Data
Names: Meyer, Gabrielle, author.
Title: Every hour until then / Gabrielle Meyer.
Description: Minneapolis, Minnesota : Bethany House Publishers, a division of Baker Publishing Group, 2025. | Series: Timeless ; 5
Identifiers: LCCN 2024041944 | ISBN 9780764243011 (paperback) | ISBN 9780764244032 (casebound) | ISBN 9781493448128 (ebook)
Subjects: LCGFT: Thrillers (Fiction) | Christian fiction. | Historical fiction. | Novels.
Classification: LCC PS3613.E956 E94 2025 | DDC 813/.6--dc23/eng/20240906
LC record available at https://lccn.loc.gov/2024041944

Unless otherwise indicated, Scripture quotations are from the King James Version of the Bible.

This is a work of historical reconstruction; the appearances of certain historical figures are therefore inevitable. All other characters, however, are products of the author’s imagination, and any resemblance to actual persons, living or dead, is coincidental.

Cover design by Jennifer Parker

Published in association with Books & Such Literary Management, www.booksandsuch.com.

Baker Publishing Group publications use paper produced from sustainable forestry practices and postconsumer waste whenever possible.

25 26 27 28 29 30 31 7 6 5 4 3

To my younger sister,
Andrea Skoglund,
the first person willing to come with me
on make-believe adventures.
Some of my best memories are made with you.
I love you.

TIMELESS FAMILY TREE

Theodosia
B. 1733 & 1973

Libby
B. 1755 & 1895
(book 1)

Maggie
B. 1841, 1921, & 1981
(book 2)

Grace
B. 1667 & 1887
(book 3)

Kathryn
B. 1865 & 1915
(book 5)

Hope
B. 1667 & 1887
(book 3)

– *cousins* –

Rachel Howlett
B. 1672 & 1862

Anne Reed
B. 1692 & 1892

Caroline
B. 1706 & 1906
(book 4)

There is a time for everything.

Ecclesiastes 3:1 NIV

1

OCTOBER 31, 1887
LONDON, ENGLAND

A cold wind rattled the window frame in my bedroom at 11 Wilton Crescent as the edges of a tree branch scraped across the glass. I burrowed deeper under the thick cover of my bed, unable to take my eyes off the book in my hand. *The Strange Case of Dr. Jekyll and Mr. Hyde* had been published last year by Robert Louis Stevenson, but it was my first time reading it, and I was both enthralled and terrified. I had to remind myself that the story was just that—a story—and there was nothing to be afraid of. There was no madman terrorizing London.

My candle flickered and then died out, leaving only the soft glow of embers in my fireplace to light the room. I'd been reading for so long, the wick had burned to the bottom and would need to be replaced.

As the wind continued to howl, I lay for a moment in the darkness, wondering if I should set the book aside and go to sleep or if I should get up and look for another candle. It was after midnight, so if I went to sleep, I would wake up in my other life in 1937, and I would have to wait for an entire day to return to 1887 to finish the story. I was working on an important exhibit at the Smithsonian

Institute with personal items belonging to George Washington, but not even that fascinating project could hold my attention if I couldn't finish Dr. Jekyll and Mr. Hyde's story tonight.

It was the strange reality of my existence, living two lives at the same time. When I went to sleep tonight in 1887, I would wake up tomorrow in 1937. After I spent the day there, I'd go to sleep and then wake up in 1887 again, without any time passing while I was away. I had two identical bodies but one conscious mind that traveled between them. It had been this way since I was born and would continue until my twenty-fifth birthday in less than three years. On that day, May 20, 1890, I would have to choose which life I wanted to keep and which one I would forfeit forever.

But I wasn't thinking about my choice tonight. All I could think about was how the book would end.

With a sigh, I pushed aside the covers and set my bare feet on the thick rug.

The wind suddenly calmed, and the unexpected stillness allowed another sound to capture my attention.

I moved to my door and pressed my ear against the panel, the terrifying story of Dr. Jekyll and Mr. Hyde too fresh in my mind for me to find the courage to walk into the hallway without a candle.

Until I realized someone was crying.

My sister's room was next to mine, and my parents' rooms were on the floor below us. There should have been no noise outside my bedroom—yet I heard it again.

Slowly, I opened my door and stepped into the hallway. "Mary?" I whispered into the void. "Is that you?"

My younger sister's bedroom door was ajar.

"Where will you go, Miss Mary?" Sarah Danbury, Mary's lady's maid, asked in a desperate voice. "Especially on a night such as this?"

Concerned, I walked to Mary's room and opened the door a little further. A lone candle offered a bit of light as Mary stood near an open satchel, dressed in a dark travel suit, filling her bag with a few items of clothing. She wiped her wet cheek with her shoulder but kept packing.

Danbury stood nearby, helpless, as she wrung her hands together. When she saw me standing at the door, her young face looked relieved, if only a little.

"What are you doing?" I asked Mary.

My sister looked up quickly, clearly surprised to see me. She had just turned nineteen, but she was delicate and appeared much younger, especially when she cried. Her dark red hair, the same shade as mine, was caught back in a low chignon with tendrils falling around her pretty face. When her gaze met mine, her green eyes glistened with fear.

"What are you doing?" I asked again as I walked into the room. "Why are you packing?"

Mary glanced at her maid and nodded for her to leave.

Danbury bit her bottom lip and looked like she might try to protest, but she knew it wasn't her place to debate with her mistress. With a slight curtsy and a pleading look in my direction, Danbury left Mary's room, closing the door behind her.

"Now can you tell me?" I asked.

My sister wiped away her tears as she went to her bureau and pulled out several pairs of stockings before returning to her satchel to stuff them inside. "I'm sorry, Kathryn. I can't tell you where I'm going."

"This is absurd," I said as I investigated the satchel to see what she was packing. "Where are you going?"

She sniffed and swallowed hard. "It doesn't matter."

I frowned, truly perplexed. Our father was Sir Bernard Kelly, a renowned physician and respected author. Our mother was Mrs. Agatha Kelly, a leading member of Victorian society and a patron of the arts. Mary and I were rarely allowed to leave the house without a proper chaperone during the day, much less in the middle of the night, alone. It wasn't safe, nor was it wise. And my sister had never been reckless or careless. She was a rule-follower and loved to please my parents.

I took Mary's forearms, stopping her from packing her bag, forcing her to look at me.

Her eyes were swimming in more tears, and the anguish on her face broke my heart.

"What's wrong, Mary?" I asked gently, trying to remain calm. "You've been acting strange all week."

With a soft cry, she threw herself into my arms. "Oh, Kathryn," she wept bitterly. "My life is over."

My lips parted as I held her close, a new thought gripping my heart. "Are you . . . in trouble? In a family way?"

"No." She shook her head and pulled back as she sank to her bed. "I wish it was that simple."

I sat beside her and took her clammy hand, my worry increasing. Mary was a beautiful, accomplished, and popular young woman. Her bright and cheerful disposition banished the darkest clouds and brought comfort to those who knew her. I couldn't think of a single person or situation that might bring her this much distress. "What in the world could be wrong?"

"I wish I could tell you, but if I did, you'd be in the same trouble, and I don't want you to get hurt. I must leave. If I stay—" She paused and shook her head. "There is no other option."

"I'm so confused," I said, softly moving aside a tendril of hair that had stuck to her wet cheek, suspecting that she was only being dramatic. Surely, whatever was wrong could easily be mended. "Let's wake Father and Mother—"

Her entire body stiffened. "I can't waste another moment." She rose and wiped her cheeks again, her hands trembling.

As I stared, she closed her satchel and reached for a dark shawl before opening her bedroom door and slipping into the hallway.

Alarm filled me as I realized she was being serious. I followed her and reached for her hand. "Stop this nonsense, Mary. It's not safe out there for a single woman, especially at night." The memory of Dr. Jekyll and Mr. Hyde was still fresh in my mind, though a fictional book was nothing compared to the realities of life on the streets of London. The Wilton Crescent neighborhood was safe enough, but we weren't far from Hyde Park, and we'd been warned since we were young not to wander there, especially toward dark.

Mary looked small and frightened yet determined as she pulled free of my hand and walked down the steps. She didn't hesitate on the second floor near our parents' bedroom doors, nor did she try to be quiet. I paused, hoping Father or Mother would hear and come out to stop her.

But they didn't, and Mary was soon at the front door.

I ran down the steps. "This is madness, Mary. You must tell me what's happening."

She paused only long enough to give me another hug, and then she said, "Good-bye, Kathryn. Don't forget that I love you."

I reached for her hand again, but she pulled away, and then I watched helplessly as she walked out the front door. Alone.

My heart hammered as I tried to decide whether to follow her or go to my parents.

It didn't take long to choose. I ran up the steps to my father's bedroom door and pounded hard, doing something I would not have done under any other circumstance.

I entered his room unbidden.

He stood near the front window, still dressed in his evening clothes, looking down at the street.

"Father," I said as I joined him at the window. "Mary has just—"

"She is dead to us." He turned away from the window, his shoulders stiff with resolve. "I never want to hear her name mentioned again."

I stepped back, as if I'd been struck. What in the world was happening? "But—"

"Never again, Kathryn," he said in a loud voice, slicing his hand in the air with finality. I couldn't tell if he was angry or afraid, but his face had a fierce expression. "If you don't want to end up like her, I advise you to forget all about her. I do not want her name uttered in this house ever again."

"Forget?" Tears stung my eyes as I reached for his arm. "How can I forget my little sister? She's on the street, Father. You must call her back, or she could get hurt."

He pulled his arm away from my grasp and went to his door to open it. His gaze was hard as he said, "This is my last warning, Kathryn. Do not ask any more questions."

My legs were weak, and my stomach turned with dread as I left his room. I raced down the stairs and returned to the foyer, desperate to catch up to Mary and talk some sense into her.

But when I opened the door and stepped onto the street, I was met with nothing but darkness and the swirling mist.

Mary was already gone.

2

LONDON, ENGLAND
AUGUST 30, 1938

It felt strange to stand outside 44 Berkeley Square on that hot August day in 1938. Months of planning and correspondence and worry—at least on Mama's part—had finally brought me to the place I loved dearest of all. And not even the threat of war could dim my excitement.

"Is it much changed from 1888, Kathryn?" Mama asked me as Papa slipped a key into the front door of our rented townhouse.

I took a deep breath, conscious of the exhaust from motorcars and the tense atmosphere that had greeted our arrival at Southampton. Hitler's invasion of Austria earlier that year, and the knowledge of his increasing military strength, had the entire world on edge—but especially those in England who were still recovering from the Great War and depression.

"Things have changed," I acknowledged, "but it's not as different as you might think."

"Are you familiar with Berkeley Square?"

"Somewhat," I said evasively. I didn't tell her that I'd been to tea at a home across the square just the day before in 1888. She was already nervous that I might run into someone I would know from my other path. It was one of the many promises I'd made to convince her that this trip was a good idea. I had to avoid anyone I might know from 1888—though they'd hardly believe it was me anyway.

I had inherited the time-crossing gift from my mother in 1938, Grace Voland. She had given up her life in 1692 to marry my papa, Brigadier General Lucas Voland. I loved her dearly for understanding what it felt like to be a time-crosser—yet her two paths were separated by centuries. Mine were only separated by fifty years. Perhaps the very woman I'd had tea with yesterday in 1888, Lady Woodsmith, was still living in the house across the square.

But that was precisely why I had agreed to come. For months, I had been looking for Mary in 1888 and had not succeeded in finding her. Was she still living in London in 1938? It was one of the questions that plagued me night and day, and because I had more freedom and resources to look for her here, I planned to do just that.

Papa opened the door at 44 Berkeley Square and allowed us to pass inside.

As we entered the front hall, I was duly impressed with the décor. Black and white checkered marble floors were polished to a high gleam, and a sparkling chandelier hung overhead. Down the length of the central hall was a spectacular staircase, and flanking the hall on either side were doors.

"I'm still in awe that Lady Astor offered us her home," Mama said as she set her bag on the floor and looked up at the chandelier. "It's so grand."

Lord and Lady Astor were American expatriates who had acclimated to English society. Lady Astor had become the first female to sit in the House of Commons almost twenty years ago. She was a devoted fan of aviation and had befriended my parents. When the Astors heard we were coming, they had offered to rent one of their many properties to us, and both the Astors and my parents looked forward to a reunion.

As Mama and I inspected the rooms on the main floor, Papa brought the luggage into the foyer.

I took one of my bags and climbed the curving staircase to the second floor. There was a parlor and a study, but the bedrooms were on the third floor. After taking the smaller of the two bedrooms, I set my suitcase on my bed and then poked my head into my parents' room a moment later.

"I'm off," I said, eager to get on with the reason I'd come.

Mama was just kicking off her heels, her eyes creased with exhaustion and concern. She looked up at me with a frown. "So soon, Kathryn?"

My first name was Kathryn in both paths, though my last names were different. In 1938, I was Kathryn Voland, but in 1888, I was Kathryn Kelly. Mama said that her first names had been the same in both of her paths, as well, and that God had ordained our names. She had guided me and taught me the rules of my time-crossing gift—but my parents in 1888 had no idea I lived two lives. Neither of them was a time-crosser, so Mama had cautioned me not to tell them. They didn't know that the birthmark on the back of my head, shaped like a sunburst, was the mark that distinguished me as a time-crosser and indicated that I had twenty-five years to choose which path to keep and which to forfeit. But it was ever-present in my mind.

"I have no time to spare," I told Mama, fighting the urge to use the English accent I was accustomed to in 1888. I didn't use it 1938 in Washington, DC, where I had grown up with Mama and Papa and my older sister, Lydia. She was in California now, living with our grandmother Tacy. "I only have two months to pull the exhibit together, and that's hardly enough time as it is."

"You'll take a cab?" Mama asked.

"I plan to walk since it is only half a mile to Lancaster House. It will be good to stretch my legs after all the travel."

"You'll need to let her go eventually," Papa said to Mama in his French accent as he stood behind her and rubbed her shoulders. "She'll be fine, Grace. She knows this city better than us."

"I'm not afraid she'll get lost," Mama countered. "I'm just—with the war looming—" She paused and shook her head. "When can we expect you home?"

"I'm only going to meet Sir Rothschild and become familiar with the museum," I said. "I'll be home for supper by seven. You can phone me at the museum if you need me."

Mama's shoulders lowered, and she nodded. "Be careful, Kathryn."

I smiled and winked at Papa. "See you soon."

My excitement could hardly be contained as I followed the circular staircase back to the ground level and out into the sunshine, toward my destination.

The London Museum occupied Lancaster House, not far from St. James Palace on The Mall. I'd been invited by the Keeper of the museum, Sir Bryant Rothschild, to be a guest exhibit curator to help him establish a new exhibit. I'd met him the year before in Washington when he'd visited the Smithsonian Arts and Industries building as part of a museum exchange delegation. Because I was an assistant exhibit curator, I had been his guide for much of his visit. I'd told him about my fondness for British history, though he had no idea I was a time-crosser and had a special connection to Victorian England. When I'd received his surprise invitation to come to London a few months later as part of the exchange, I couldn't resist.

I was still shocked that I had been invited. There were so many other people more qualified than me. Perhaps Sir Rothschild had asked me because we had gotten along so well, and my knowledge of British history had impressed him.

It didn't matter to me, even though it put me in a precarious position. At any moment, I might run into someone I knew from my other path—though they'd be fifty years older, and I was still twenty-three. But even if they saw me, they would just assume I looked like someone they used to know. At least, that's what I'd told Mama. And when she'd asked me what would happen if I ran into myself, I told her the simple answer: I didn't plan to stay in my 1888 path after my twenty-fifth birthday, so there was no chance that I'd see myself as a seventy-three-year-old woman.

Mama had only shaken her head and sighed. I'd decided I would accept Sir Rothschild's invitation, and nothing could stop me. Not even the threat of Adolf Hitler.

And perhaps there was a chance I might find my sister Mary. It had been ten months since she'd disappeared on that cold, autumn night in 1887. She had sent me a brief and cryptic letter a couple weeks later, telling me she was living in the Whitechapel district. She had found work as a charwoman, doing daily domestic chores for Jewish families who could afford a little extra help. The thought of my sweet, delicate sister doing such demanding physical labor was hard to imagine. Worse, though, was the memory of how frightened and alone she was the night she left, and how scared she must still be.

I would never give up looking for her, in 1888 or 1938.

Lancaster House sat on the edge of Green Park, not far from Buckingham Palace. Before she left, Mary and I had attended a ball there in 1887, when it was known as the Stafford House. The mansion now contained the London Museum, and I was eager to step inside and see how they had transformed the ornate building to house their collections.

The hot August sun bore down on my shoulders as I approached the Corinthian style mansion. Its plain exterior was no match for the splendor within. Large trees on the perimeter of the property offered a bit of shade and privacy, but the passing pedestrians and motorcars reminded me we were in the heart of the metropolis.

I opened the heavy door and entered the central hall of Lancaster House. The air was cool as my heels tapped on the diamond-shaped marble floor, and my gaze lifted to the ceiling, which was three stories above with a glass dome and a view of the blue sky. Red-carpeted stairs rose ahead and split in the middle to the upper galleries. Ornate gilded trim, blue marble columns, red cloth coverings, and massive murals dominated the room.

There were several people in the main hall, some admiring the murals, others purchasing tickets at the front desk, and still others moving around the upper galleries, from one room to the other.

"Are you here to see the exhibits?" a woman asked as she approached, wearing white cotton gloves and a blue dress suit.

"I'm here to meet with Sir Rothschild," I said. "I'm Kathryn Voland, from the Smithsonian Institute."

Her eyes lit with recognition, and she said, "Sir Rothschild has been expecting you. He's in his office. Won't you follow me?"

She led me across the echoing hall to the stairwell, and we began to climb. When we arrived on the second floor, we crossed a gallery and then took another set of stairs to the third floor.

"The exhibits are housed in the basement, on the ground level, and on the second floor," the docent said as she led me up a staircase with a sign that said Staff Only. "The top floor houses the staff lounge and Sir Rothschild's office."

The docent guided me through a maze of rooms until we arrived at a closed door. She knocked, and when a male voice called for us to enter, she opened the door and let me walk in before her.

Sir Bryant Rothschild was seated at a massive desk. A cold fireplace flanked one wall of his office, and tall windows on the other offered a magnificent view of Buckingham Palace. The room had probably been a bedchamber at one point but was now the office of the Keeper of the museum.

"Miss Voland," he said with a wide smile as he stood to greet me. "How wonderful to see you again. We've been expecting you."

"I'm sorry for the delay."

"Nothing to worry yourself about," he said in his cultured accent. "Our other guest curator hasn't arrived from Scotland yet, so you haven't missed anything." He nodded at the docent and said, "Thank you, Mrs. Turner."

The woman excused herself as Sir Rothschild motioned for me to have a seat.

He was a well-built man, in his mid-thirties, if I had to guess, with straw-colored hair and blue eyes. He'd been charming and intelligent when we'd spent time together in Washington, DC, eager to share his knowledge and glean from those at the Smithsonian. I was excited, though a little nervous, to finally work with him. What if I didn't have the skills needed to do a good job? I would hate to embarrass myself or disappoint him.

"Now," he said as he took his seat again. "We have much to discuss, but I have a feeling you're curious about the project you'll be helping with over the next two months."

I sat on the edge of my seat and nodded. I would be assisting the other guest curator, a man named Calan McCaffrey from the Royal Museum of Scotland, though I hadn't met him yet. "I can't wait any longer."

He smiled, revealing a straight row of teeth, slightly yellowed, probably from the coffee sitting on his desk. "That's why I asked you to come, Miss Voland. Your energy and passion for history is matchless—though, perhaps Mr. McCaffrey and I come in a close second and third." Sir Rothschild leaned forward and placed his clasped hands on his desk, excitement shining in his eyes. "The London Museum has been given unprecedented access to the Metropolitan Police Crime Museum. It's a private collection of evidence that the police have accumulated for over a century, and every so often, they release parts of their collection for public viewing." He paused, as if he couldn't contain his glee. "As of tomorrow, the evidence for the Jack the Ripper case will turn fifty years old, and they are allowing us access for the first time. We will be allowed to look over everything they have on file and create an exhibit for the museum."

My mouth parted at his announcement. I had heard of Jack the Ripper many times. The murders he committed in Victorian England were part of the collective history of the world by 1938—yet I hadn't paid much attention to the dates before now.

"When did the murders take place?" I asked Sir Rothschild.

"I've only done a little preliminary study myself," he said, "so

I'm not as familiar with the case as I'd like. However, I do know that the first murder accredited to Jack the Ripper occurred on August 31, 1888, and the last happened on November 9, 1888."

"August 31st?"

"Yes—fifty years ago tomorrow."

A shiver ran up my spine. That meant that tomorrow, when I woke up in 1888, the first murder would happen in my other path.

"And where did the murders take place?" I asked, my pulse starting to pick up a notch.

"All five murders accredited to Jack took place within a mile radius in the Whitechapel district."

I felt the blood drain from my face as I whispered, "Whitechapel?"

"Yes." He frowned, clearly confused by my response. "At the time, Whitechapel was the most impoverished area of the city, filled with thousands of working-class individuals, most of them down on their luck. All five victims were women, and known to be—" He paused, as if he couldn't say the word, but then he spit it out. "Prostitutes."

"In Whitechapel," I said again, though it wasn't a question.

"Yes. In Whitechapel." He leaned back, clearly concerned with my response. "Do you have a problem working on this exhibit, Miss Voland?"

I swallowed my trepidation and shook my head as I tried to compose myself. One of the rules of my time-crossing gift was that I couldn't knowingly change history. If I did, I would forfeit the path I tried to change. So even if I wanted to stop the horrific murders committed by Jack the Ripper in 1888, I couldn't. I would forfeit my time there—and I wasn't ready.

Yet, that didn't give my heart any comfort. Not now.

"Do you know the names of the victims?" I asked him, almost too afraid to learn the truth.

He seemed to think for a moment and then shook his head. "I'm sorry. I haven't done enough research to be familiar with the details. Tomorrow when we visit the Metropolitan Police Crime

Museum, we'll learn more and then we can start to discuss how we want to proceed with the exhibit as we wait for Mr. McCaffrey's arrival." He rose from his desk. "I'll show you to your office and then I'll give you a tour."

I followed Sir Rothschild through one room and into another with an even better view of Buckingham Palace. This room had also previously been a bedchamber, no doubt, but it now housed another massive desk, a table, some ornate chairs, and a filing cabinet. The walls were painted in a soft green with platinum gilded trim and crystal wall sconces.

"This will be yours and Mr. McCaffrey's office for the next two months," Sir Rothschild said. "I hope it will do."

"Of course," I said absentmindedly, my mind still on the news he'd just shared. "It's lovely."

He motioned toward the door. "Shall we start the tour?"

I tried to smile and nod as I followed him out of my office to see the rest of the museum. Yet, I couldn't shake the foreboding feeling I had or the pressing question that made my heart ache.

I needed to know the names of the victims from Whitechapel, because in 1888, one of the people I loved most in the world lived somewhere in that neglected district.

Mary.

3

AUGUST 31, 1888
LONDON, ENGLAND

The next morning, I woke up in my bedchamber at 11 Wilton Crescent, near the opposite end of Green Park and Lancaster House. It was the only home I'd known in this path, though it was much changed since Mary had left.

"Good morning, Miss Kathryn." My lady's maid, Lucy Duffy, moved aside the heavy drapes to allow the sun to fill my room with light. "I've laid out your dark blue taffeta dress for today's activities. Your mother says you're to be home early to change for the ball tonight."

I groaned, already exhausted at the prospect of another ball.

At the age of twenty-three, I was well-past my debut and quickly approaching spinsterhood—but my mother in 1888 was as fiercely determined to see me married as I was to stay single. I couldn't and wouldn't jeopardize my life by getting married in this path because I didn't plan to stay. My career at the Smithsonian in 1938 had been my greatest dream since I was a child, and I loved my work. And, even though I was passionate about history, I couldn't deny that I enjoyed the modern conveniences of the twentieth century even more. Not to mention all the freedoms I had and my connection to my time-crossing mama, Grace. I didn't want any complications, like a husband in 1888, to hinder my plans.

"Your father is at breakfast," Duffy continued, apparently given a list to share with me this morning, "but he's due at the hospital soon and will have the carriage returned to take you to Toynbee Hall."

I had no intention of joining Father for breakfast. Even though ten months had passed since the night Mary left, I still struggled to be in the same room as him without feeling angry. I never brought up Mary's name again, though she was often on my mind. I couldn't understand how a father could turn his back on his daughter. And it was the fear that he would do the same to me that kept me silent.

"Thank you," I said as I hugged my pillow under my head, not ready to face the day. I'd been going to Toynbee Hall for months, and I hadn't found my sister, but I wasn't going to give up. Especially now, with the news of Jack the Ripper at work. The thought that he was alive and starting his reign of terror in the very city where I lived made a shiver run up my spine.

"There was a terrible murder in Whitechapel last night," Duffy said as she finished opening the drapes, as if she'd read my mind. Her Yorkshire accent deepened as her voice filled with concern. "A dreadful business. They say a woman was killed in a most gruesome manner."

"Do they know her name?" I asked, sitting up, my heart pounding.

"It hasn't been released yet. The murder happened in the wee hours of the morning near a place called Buck's Row. They say she was in her mid-forties."

Relief washed over me at the age of the victim, though my heart still hurt for her. Mary's twentieth birthday would be next month.

As I stepped out of bed, all I could think about was learning the names of the victims. Murders happened in Whitechapel all the time, but yesterday I had discovered by talking to Sir Rothschild that the Ripper victims would draw attention because of the disturbing manner in which the murderer mutilated the bodies.

And the fact that he committed the crimes moments before the bodies were found, yet no one ever caught him.

I'd asked Mama and Papa if they knew anything about the case last night at supper in 1938, but neither one knew any more than I did. I'd have to wait until I went to the Metropolitan Police Crime Museum with Sir Rothschild to see the names. I told myself I had nothing to worry about, since thousands of people lived in Whitechapel and the odds of my sister being in danger were slim. But I wouldn't be at peace until I knew for certain.

"There's a rumor going around downstairs." Duffy interrupted my thoughts as she went to my dressing table to set out the items I would need for my morning toilette.

"You know I don't like gossip."

"You'll like this bit o' news." She grinned. "The stableboy is sparking with the scullery maid next door."

"You've mentioned that before."

"That's not the news," Duffy said, her green eyes wide with excitement. "The scullery maid told the stableboy that Mr. Baird has finally come home."

I paused as I stretched my arms above my head. "Austen is home?"

"Aye, he came home late last night."

Austen was home—was probably just waking up on the other side of the very wall that connected our townhomes. When we were young and had discovered that our bedrooms shared a wall, it was the happiest day of my life. Yet that wall had come to represent a vast divide fourteen years ago—one that I hadn't been able to cross no matter how much I had tried or willed it to happen.

"Some say he was in India," Duffy continued as she pulled items out of my dressing table drawers. "Others say Russia or Japan. But I think he went to America to find a wealthy wife."

"Austen?" I scoffed. "He doesn't need a wealthy wife—and least of all an American."

"He's a fine catch, if I do say so myself." Her cheeks colored, and she looked down at my dressing table with embarrassment.

My own cheeks felt warm as I thought about Austen, not surprised that my maid was attracted to him. "I'd like to get dressed as quickly as possible. I'm expected at Toynbee Hall by ten."

"Yes, miss."

And if I wanted to pay a call to my enigmatic neighbor before I left, I needed to hurry. He'd probably turn me away, as he'd done so many times before, but I had to try, one more time.

Duffy helped me into the beautiful taffeta gown with the generous bustle and tight bodice, which accentuated all my curves. The corset was uncomfortable, but it was more flattering than the dresses I wore in 1938. She styled my dark red hair into a becoming updo and handed me a pair of gold teardrop earrings, which dangled just below my earlobes.

"What do you think?" she asked.

I admired my reflection, pleased with my appearance. I had inherited my mama's brown eyes from 1938 and my thick, red hair from my mother in 1888. Mama said my dimples were from her mother, Maggie. My fierce determination was from my father, Sir Bernard Kelly. And from my papa, Lucas Voland, I'd inherited my fearlessness. I was a combination of both sets of parents, creating a unique me. It was a strange existence, but Mama had made it feel normal. Stranger still, my two bodies were identical, but they didn't affect each other. If I became sick or injured in 1888, I didn't suffer the same maladies in 1938. I'd accepted that I was different a long time ago and didn't waste a minute worrying about it. There were more important things to do than fret about something I couldn't change.

I left Duffy and went down the back stairs and into the courtyard where a secret passageway between the hedges connected our backyard to Austen's. We'd used the passageway countless times as children, and I suspected that our stableboy used it now to court Austen's scullery maid.

It was already stiflingly hot as I passed through our courtyard, while memories of Austen filled my mind and heart. He was two years older than me, but he and I had been the best of friends for as long as I could remember. That was, until the day we'd heard the news that had changed our lives forever—the day Austen learned his parents had died while on holiday with my parents.

It had been a crushing blow to Austen, who had lost his grandparents and his little brother in the years leading up to his parents' death.

After that day, I had only seen Austen at the funeral, and then he'd been sent to Eton, where he'd lived as he attended school. His aunt had moved into his house, coming all the way from America, and when Austen visited home for holidays, he was cold. Distant. Aloof.

As I stepped through the passageway and entered his garden, I wasn't sure why I thought things would be different this time, but my perpetual hope wouldn't die. Papa often told me I was the most optimistic person he knew—but it wasn't always optimism that made me push ahead. It was my unwavering belief that I could fix whatever had been broken. And, in this case, it was Austen's heart. I wanted his happiness—craved it—because there was an ache, deep within me, since I'd lost it.

I didn't care that the staff would whisper about me sneaking through the Bairds' garden early in the morning as I approached the back door. Many of them had known me my whole life, and I had ceased to surprise them.

Though I somehow continued to shock my mother.

After I knocked, the door was opened and one of the maids allowed me to enter the house.

"Is Mr. Baird at home?" I asked her.

"Aye, miss, he's in the morning room, eating his breakfast."

"Thank you," I said as I bypassed her in the back hall and made my way through the house.

It was identical to ours, only in reverse. All the townhouses on Wilton Crescent had the same floor plans, creating a curved row of simple white façades and ornate interiors.

I hadn't seen Austen in over a year and had been waiting eagerly for this day. I didn't give myself time to have second thoughts. Instead, I entered the morning room as if I lived in his home and was simply coming down for breakfast.

"Good morning," I said as I went to the sideboard and lifted a lid to inspect the dishes that had been laid by the staff. "The sausage smells divine."

Austen sighed, and I smiled to myself. He pretended I annoyed him, but I knew the truth. I was still one of his favorite people. I lowered the lid and turned around to greet my old friend.

He sat at the head of the table, a newspaper in hand as his plate of food sat untouched before him. His blue-eyed gaze met mine over the top of the newspaper. I was both elated and sad to see his dear face. Elated because for a moment, I saw his pleasure at my arrival—and then sad because it was quickly replaced with the grief he'd carried for the past fourteen years—a grief that seemed tied to me.

"Hello, Austen."

He studied me as if looking for an ulterior motive for my visit. "Good morning."

I briefly glanced at his butler, Brinley, before saying, "May we have a moment of privacy?"

"And risk your reputation?" Austen asked with a raised eyebrow.

I lowered my chin and gave him a look. "When have I ever been worried about my reputation?"

Brinley's smile was quick, but I saw it nonetheless. He'd always been one of my favorites.

Austen motioned for him to leave.

I took a seat at the table, offering Austen another smile, knowing that—at one point—he'd found my dimples charming. "I've missed you," I said as I laid my hand on his arm.

His muscles tensed beneath my touch, and he pulled away, frowning. "What do you want, Kathryn?"

Disappointment warmed my cheeks as I laid my hands in my lap, wishing that whatever had come between us would have been gone by now. One thing I'd always loved about our relationship was that there were no pretenses. But sometimes, when he was blunt, I would prefer some formality. "You've been away a year." I tried not to sound hurt. "I came to see how you've been. Aren't you curious about me?"

He studied me, and for a heartbeat, there was vulnerability behind his eyes. He was wearing his dark hair a bit long, the ends curling slightly as they brushed against his collar. And he had a beard, which made him look much older than his twenty-five years. Gone was the joyful little boy who used to entertain me with stories about gallant knights, fair maidens, and sprawling castles.

"I have been curious about your other path," he said. "Are you still planning to choose it in two years?"

The question surprised me, and it was my turn to frown. I'd told Austen about my other life when we were children. He hadn't believed me at first, so I had researched and discovered that there would be a mining accident in Cheshire on April 14, 1874, and fifty-four people would be killed. After it happened, he was astonished—and then he had believed me. He was the only person in this path that I had told, and the only person I could talk to about it.

But then his parents had died, and I'd lost my confidant and best friend.

I could see that my answer was important to him. "That's what you want to know?"

"It's a simple question, Kathryn."

It *was* a simple question, and I knew the answer, but part of me didn't want to tell him, and I wasn't sure why.

"You are leaving," he said with little emotion.

"Why do you care?" I asked, the pain of his rejection for the past fourteen years building up inside me. "You disappear for months on end, and I have no idea where you've gone. I don't demand that you explain yourself. Why must I?"

He didn't respond.

"Why does it matter if I leave this path?" I asked, not ready to back down.

He lifted his gaze, and I saw the pain he tried so hard to hide. "I guess it doesn't matter."

All my bluster faded at the look in his eyes.

We were both silent for a moment, and then he asked, "Why have you really come?"

I was trembling, but I needed to pull myself together to tell him about my sister. All that I cared about right now was Mary's safety. "Father turned Mary out of our home ten months ago, and the last I heard she was living in Whitechapel."

Austen's reaction was as I expected. Confusion and shock filled his face. "What? Why?"

"I don't know. Father refuses to speak her name, and I wouldn't even know that she was in Whitechapel if she hadn't sent me a brief letter."

"Did she tell you anything helpful?"

"Just that I wasn't to worry. She was renting a room and had work as a charwoman. That was all. But of course I'm worried."

"Your sister—" He paused, at a loss for words. "She's educated and from one of the best families in London. At the very least, she could have taken a job as a governess or companion. What would possess your father to turn her out on the street?"

"I don't know," I said, feeling as confused as him. Mary had been enjoying her second season and my mother had been close to making a match for her. A match that Mary had desired. She'd had a brilliant future ahead of her.

"What are other people saying?" he asked. "Surely, people are concerned about her."

I pressed my lips together as my anger continued to rise. "People assume Mary got into trouble—with a man—and that she left with him. And my parents haven't corrected the rumors. Mary's life is over, as she knew it, and people are taking pity on my poor parents, as if they are suffering in some way. Even if she wanted to come home, she couldn't. No one would accept her."

"Then perhaps it's best if she doesn't."

"She can't stay in Whitechapel. I've been volunteering at Toynbee

Hall for the past few months, asking everyone who visits if they know her, but no one has heard of her. I would go into the streets to look, but it's far too dangerous and there are tens of thousands of people who live there. It feels impossible."

"What does this have to do with me?" he asked.

"I don't know how to find Mary."

"And you think I do?"

"I can't walk the streets of Whitechapel alone. If I had your help—"

"No." He lifted his newspaper, indicating that our conversation was over.

"Austen, she's my sister—your friend."

"I don't have friends."

I stood, wanting to shake him. Instead I growled, "Why do you have to be so difficult?"

"It's the one pleasure I have in life."

I clenched my hands. "You are maddening."

He looked back at me, his gaze earnest. "Then why do you come here?"

"Because—" I released my fists and forced myself to calm down. I took a deep breath and leveled him with a look that I hoped would convey the depth of my worry. "I learned that there will be several horrific murders in Whitechapel over the next two months, and I'm afraid Mary might be in danger."

He lowered his newspaper. "You heard this in your other life?"

I nodded, speaking quietly in case Brinley was listening. "I was asked to be a guest curator for the London Museum in 1938, and I will be given access to the records at the Crime Museum. It's a case that hasn't been solved by 1938—and the first murder just occurred this morning."

"What could I possibly do to help?"

"Come with me to Whitechap—"

"No."

"Austen, please. Mary needs me."

"It's none of my business." This time when he lifted the newspaper, he blocked me from his vision. "Brinley," Austen called to his butler, "Miss Kelly is leaving."

"I'll be back," I told him.

"I'm sure you will."

Brinley appeared from the servant's entrance and walked across the room to the main door. He opened it and stood back, waiting for me.

I didn't bother to say good-bye as I strode toward the door.

"And see that the staff are instructed to refuse entrance to Miss Kelly," Austen said, "so this doesn't happen again. Put a guard at the door, if you must."

I huffed and held my head high but turned just in time to see Austen watching me leave over the top of his newspaper.

Two hours later, I found myself at Toynbee Hall, still shaken from my encounter with Austen. But I wasn't deterred. I would do whatever I could to convince him to help me find Mary.

Toynbee Hall was the first settlement house in the world, and it was only four years old. It was an ambitious experiment led by reformers and educators. The three-story, red-brick building was as out of place in Whitechapel as the Oxford and Cambridge students who lived and worked there. They came to lecture and teach the impoverished inhabitants about literature, philosophy, art, science, and more. They also taught practical skills like cooking, sewing, and blacksmithing. I had started a history club soon after Mary left so I could visit Toynbee Hall to ask about her.

Mother allowed it because she was a patron of the arts and saw my work as charity.

"Good morning, Miss Kelly," Mrs. Barnett, one of the founders of Toynbee Hall said as I entered the drawing room where I held my weekly history club meetings. The group size shifted each week, with people coming and going as they were able. There were children as young as ten and adults as old as eighty who came to hear my lectures and discuss what they learned. We'd been focusing on the Elizabethan era for the past month, and I'd been teaching them about Queen Elizabeth's accession to the throne—the very history that Austen had taught me when we were children. The stories that had awakened my love for history.

"Good morning," I said as I set my satchel on the closest table. I'd brought books with colorful pictures to show the group.

Mrs. Barnett taught a sewing class before mine, and she was gathering her supplies as her students trickled out of the room and mine came in. The drawing room was spacious with large windows, allowing in plenty of light. "There's been quite a ruckus around here this morning," she said, shaking her head with sadness. "All anyone can talk about is the murder on Buck's Row. 'Tis the second murder this month."

My senses were immediately heightened. The first murder she spoke of was that of Martha Tabram on August 7th. She had been found in the stairwell at George Yard, a building just behind Toynbee Hall. But was her murder linked to the others? If it was, wouldn't Sir Rothschild have told me? "I heard the news about Buck's Row. Does anyone know the name of the victim?"

"There have been whispers about her identity, though the police are waiting on an official identification from those who knew her. It was Mary Ann Nichols, but her friends called her Polly."

I recognized the name. "She's been here before."

"Aye, she has. I saw her just last week when we were handing out clothing to the poor," Mrs. Barnett said. "She took a liking to a secondhand black bonnet, and I saw that she got it. She was so proud to wear it."

"Are you talking about Polly?" a woman asked as she entered the drawing room. She was a middle-aged woman with a missing bottom tooth and a careworn face. She had told me her name was Mrs. Shaw, and though she was impoverished, she was married and living in a respectable home. She came to our meetings to "better" herself, she'd told me.

Though she was probably there to learn the latest gossip, too.

"Yes," I said. "Did you know her?"

"*I* didn't know her." Mrs. Shaw spat her words. "She was a prostitute. I don't associate with *those* women."

Mrs. Barnett lowered her gaze, clearly uncomfortable with the conversation.

"They say she was last seen around 2:30 in the morning, heading toward Whitechapel Road," Mrs. Shaw continued, "wearing a jolly new bonnet."

Mrs. Barnett's face turned pale, and she took a seat on the closest chair. "Oh, good heavens."

I went to her and put my hand on her shoulder.

"The bonnet," Mrs. Barnett said, looking up at me.

"She was found around 3:30," Mrs. Shaw continued, apparently unaware of Mrs. Barnett's unease. "Her throat was cut, which accounts for the lack of a scream to alert those nearby." The woman nodded as if she knew about such things. "But no one saw or heard a thing—isn't that peculiar? They're questioning everyone in the vicinity. There are crowds around Buck's Row even now. It's all anyone can talk about. I went there to have a look-see myself."

"I'd prefer if we didn't discuss it here," Mrs. Barnett said. "We'll let the police do their work, shall we?" She rose from her chair and smoothed her skirt. "Please refrain from discussing the situation with your club members, Miss Kelly, at least while in Toynbee Hall. It's too distressing."

"Of course." I nodded as Mrs. Barnett gathered the rest of her things and left the drawing room.

Three other ladies had entered, all similar to Mrs. Shaw in age and living arrangements.

"She was married," whispered one of the other ladies, "but she'd left her husband and five children several years ago and ended up in Whitechapel."

"She was arrested for drunkenness, prostitution, and disorderly conduct many times," added another with disdain, "and was in and out of the workhouse. She couldn't hold a job because of her need for the drink."

"That's why she sold herself," said the third with pity. "Such a sad state of affairs, that."

"Ladies," I said as I lightly clapped my hands, mindful of Mrs. Barnett's wishes. "Let us leave the unpleasant conversation outside and gather around for our discussion of Queen Elizabeth and the plague of 1563."

"And that's not unpleasant?" Mrs. Shaw asked with a cackle.

The other ladies joined in the laughter, and for a moment, the mood lightened.

It wasn't easy to focus on our history lesson that day. All I could do was wait for tomorrow to learn the names of the victims at the Metropolitan Police Crime Museum and pray that Mary was not one of them.

4

AUGUST 31, 1938
LONDON, ENGLAND

Rain fell from a heavy gray sky as Sir Rothschild and I took a cab from Lancaster House to New Scotland Yard the next morning, not far from Big Ben on the River Thames. I was most familiar with the London of 1888 and marveled at all the improvements and technology I saw fifty years later, though some things, like the Palace of Westminster and the clock tower, were timeless.

"How do you like London?" Sir Rothschild asked as he sat back on the seat and watched me take it all in. "This is your first visit here, is it not?"

I couldn't tell him I lived here in 1888, so I nodded. "It is my first visit—and I love it. American history feels juvenile compared to English history."

He grinned, his blond mustache tilting to the side. "Most Yanks think the Liberty Bell is old."

I lifted a shoulder, smiling. "It's ninety years older than your Big Ben."

He chuckled. "Touché."

Sir Rothschild was an amiable companion as he pointed out landmarks on our short ten-minute ride from the London Museum to the Crime Museum. I was familiar with many of the buildings, but I didn't let on, enjoying his passion for London history, which rivaled my own.

When we arrived at the New Scotland Yard, I was duly impressed. In 1888, it was still under construction, but here in 1938, I could see the full glory of the building on the Victoria Embankment. Red brick and white stone created a series of stripes, which were built upon a gray granite base. The building was several stories tall with a steep black roof, rows of dormer windows, and turrets at each corner. The whole structure overlooked the Thames and, according to Sir Rothschild, housed over ten thousand police officers.

The cab dropped us off near the front entrance, and Sir Rothschild held his black umbrella over my head as we made our way into the building.

Within minutes, we were sent to the lowest level of the police headquarters where the Crime Museum was housed in several connecting rooms.

"You must be Sir Rothschild," a man in uniform said as he rose from a desk in the first room we entered. "I'm Police Constable Harrington, at your service."

"Good morning," Sir Rothschild said as the two men shook hands. "This is Miss Kathryn Voland from the Smithsonian."

"How do you do," PC Harrington said as he shook my hand. "Straightaway from America?"

I smiled at the young, energetic man. "Yes. I arrived just yesterday."

He grinned, though he looked a little nervous as he put his hands on his hips and nodded. "I'm excited to show you around today. The Black Museum is—"

"Black Museum?" I asked.

He dipped his head. "That's what it's been called for the past sixty years since a reporter wasn't allowed access and he dubbed it the Black Museum in *The Observer*."

"We're anxious to see the Ripper archives," Sir Rothschild said, not wasting any time.

PC Harrington nodded. "Of course. Follow me."

He led us out of the first room and down the hall to another door. "The Black Museum was created in 1874, fourteen years before Jack the Ripper was on the loose," PC Harrington said. "And it was moved to this building in 1890 when it was completed."

I loved PC Harrington's enthusiasm, and since most museum curators lived to share their knowledge, I encouraged him. "Why was the museum started?"

He grinned as he turned on a light in the room. "By 1874, Inspector Percy Neame had collected several items to train police officers on how to detect and prevent crimes, so a museum was created. The first exhibit had clothing and items that had belonged to a woman who was murdered when she was only seventeen. Since then, items belonging to criminals and collected from crime scenes have been added—including those from the famous Jack the Ripper crimes."

Sir Rothschild didn't seem as indulgent as me, and he said to PC Harrington, "The Commissioner has given Miss Voland and me full access to the files on Jack the Ripper. After we've gone through the artifacts, we will write formal requests for the items we'd like to borrow for exhibition at the London Museum."

"Correct," PC Harrington said. "Those are the orders I've been given, as well."

PC Harrington showed us into the room. There were two tall filing cabinets and several shelves containing boxes. A long table in the middle was surrounded by four chairs. With one small window near the top of the wall, it was dark, damp, and cool. The darkness and cool temperatures were ideal for artifacts, but not the dampness.

"Most of our high-profile cases are stored in this room," PC Harrington said, "But you'll find the Ripper evidence in this cabinet and these boxes." He pointed them out to us and then added, "If you have any questions, I'm on duty Monday through Friday, nine to five o'clock."

"Thank you," I said with a smile. "We appreciate your help."

The young man left the room, and I took a deep breath. A new research project was invigorating, but at the same time daunting. Although I was especially eager to learn the details about this case.

"Shall we?" Sir Rothschild asked.

I nodded and took off my hat, which I placed on the table with my satchel containing notebooks, pencils, and a small camera. As I walked to the filing cabinet, he went to the shelves and scanned the labels on the boxes.

I held my breath as I opened the top drawer. My heart was pounding as I looked over the tabs.

Each victim had their own file with their name and date of death listed.

Polly Nichols, August 31, 1888.

Annie Chapman, September 8, 1888.

Elizabeth Stride, September 30, 1888.

Catherine Eddowes, September 30, 1888.

Mary Jane Kelly, November 9, 1888.

My heart felt like it stopped beating, and I couldn't breathe.

Mary Jane Kelly was my sister's full name.

I gripped the drawer as Sir Rothschild approached. "Are you alright?" He put his hand on my back, concern in his blue eyes. "Miss Voland?"

"I'm sorry," I said, trying to make sense of what I was looking at while maintaining professionalism and sanity.

"Have a seat." He pulled a chair across the cement floor.

I sat, knowing that I could never explain my behavior. "I'm fine."

"I'll get you some water," he said. "Perhaps the strain of traveling has been too much for you."

I detested weakness—especially in myself. And especially here, when I'd been invited by a preeminent historian to be part of an exhibition research team, looking at primary resources from the Metropolitan Police Crime Museum. I didn't want him to think I wasn't up to the task.

"I'm fine," I said with a smile. "I don't need water."

He studied me with uncertainty.

"I'm just a little overcome," I continued. "It isn't every day that you have access to such important history."

Sir Rothschild smiled at that and then nodded. "If you're certain . . . "

"Quite."

He returned to his perusal of the boxes, and I took a fortifying breath before I rose and went back to the filing cabinet.

Perhaps there was more than one Mary Jane Kelly in Whitechapel. There had to be. And, even if there wasn't, there must be a mistake. It couldn't be my sister.

With shaking hands, I pulled each file out of the drawer and laid them on top of the cabinet. The first four murders were within a month of each other. The women were in their mid-forties and were all murdered in public places. Each victim was known for drunkenness, prostitution, and homelessness. Each was married and subsequently separated from their husbands and children. They followed a pattern.

But as I opened the fifth folder—praying the same would be true for Mary Jane Kelly—my heart fell as I read the words that I didn't want to see. This victim had been in her early twenties, had been killed inside her rented room, and her life before the murder was undocumented, though some believed she had come from a well-to-do family. According to a testimony by a man named Joseph Barnett, who had claimed to be Mary Jane Kelly's sweetheart, she had been disowned by her family, but was still close to her sister.

My knees almost buckled as I read the report. It was clear Mary Jane Kelly had not shared much about her life with the people in Whitechapel, and her family had not come forward to claim a connection to her after her death.

I felt Sir Rothschild's gaze, but I couldn't show him how much the file meant to me.

Was this my sister? Her middle name was Jane, and she would be twenty years old by November 9, 1888. She'd been disowned by our parents and was living in Whitechapel. The coincidences were uncanny.

As my eyes lowered to the coroner's report, I felt like I might vomit. The pictures of her mutilation were unfathomable. Unrecognizable. I closed the files and took several deep breaths. Mary Jane Kelly's murder, perpetrated indoors, with no one to disturb the Ripper, was the most gruesome of them all.

I refused to read the details—refused to believe that this was my sister's fate. Mary was a beautiful, talented young woman. She was funny and intelligent and kind. Though I was three years older than her, she'd always tried to keep up with me and had been a sweet, though sometimes annoying, companion. Her life couldn't come to this, especially when I didn't understand why Father had forced her to leave our home.

I had to find her. Even if my sister wasn't the Ripper's victim, I needed to find *my* Mary and facilitate a reconciliation with my father. Mother had been heartbroken at her departure—though she had stood firm with Father, making me assume they knew something about my sister that I didn't. But could it be that bad?

With a quick glance inside the file one more time, I saw that the address given for Mary Jane Kelly was 13 Miller's Court in Whitechapel. It was the only clue I had to my sister's possible residence.

Tomorrow in 1888, no matter what, I would visit 13 Miller's Court. And I prayed that when I went there, I'd meet the real Mary Jane Kelly—the one documented in this file—and that it wouldn't be my sister.

It was still raining that evening as I stepped out of the cab at 44 Berkeley Square and dashed into the rented townhouse. I climbed the stairs to the second floor, where my parents were waiting. Papa leaned back in his chair, and Mama was sitting on the edge of hers, eagerly listening to his story.

My parents were both in their fifties, active, healthy, and energetic.

Papa had been a daring French aviator when he'd met my mother, who was an investigative journalist living in New York City. Her twin sister, Hope, had been one of Papa's aviation students. Hope had been in love with him, and my mother had not liked him when they first met. But Papa had quickly fallen for Mama, and when Hope died in a flying accident in 1912, Mama had been asked to complete her cross-country flight. Papa taught Mama to fly, and they soon fell in love. When it was time to choose between 1692 and 1912, Mama chose 1912. Hope stayed in 1692 with the man she loved, Isaac.

Mama had told me the tale many times, and I never tired of hearing about my parents' love story. I wanted a romance like theirs—someday—but I'd been so busy in 1938 building my career that I hadn't had time.

"Kathryn," Mama said with a smile. "We were worried that we'd have to leave without you."

Papa sat up in his tuxedo, a frown on his handsome face as he looked at me. "What is troubling you, *ma chérie*?"

I entered the beautiful drawing room, my legs feeling heavy and my heart weak with fear. "I saw the names of the victims today. I had a feeling—I can't explain it—but I'm hoping I'm wrong."

"What are you talking about?" Mama asked as she reached for my cold hand.

"The last victim—her name is Mary Jane Kelly." I choked on the last word, trying not to cry.

"Are you certain it's her?" Papa asked.

"No—but there are several similarities. I'm going to Whitechapel tomorrow, to 13 Miller's Court, to see if I can find her. That's the address of the last murder, where Mary Jane Kelly lives."

"If it's her, what will you do?" Mama asked, patting the spot on the sofa next to her.

I took the seat, happy to be off my feet, and shrugged. I was cold from my wet dress, but I didn't care. I had gone to the General Register Office that afternoon to look for my sister, hoping she was still alive in 1938. But I could find no records to match her, other than those that belonged to the Ripper's victim named Mary Jane Kelly. I didn't want to believe it was her.

"What *can* you do?" Papa asked. He was aware of mine and Mama's time-crossing gift. He knew the rules as well as I did, and I knew what he was asking.

"I can't change history," I told him, feeling helpless. "But I must do something. Why would God allow me to know this history if I wasn't meant to help her? I didn't go searching for it."

"It doesn't matter," Mama said. "If you knowingly change something, then you'll forfeit that timeline."

I sat up, a thought giving me hope. "But I'm going to forfeit it anyway," I told her. "When I turn twenty-five in 1890, I plan to give up that path." Even as I said the words, I thought of my conversation with Austen yesterday. I was still mulling over why he seemed so upset about me leaving when he clearly had no interest in being part of my life. But I had to push those thoughts aside for now. "I can take Mary away from Miller's Court, if she *is* the victim, and all I will do is give up 1888 a little earlier than expected."

Mama's eyes softened with sadness. "I've been told that some of history's greatest tragedies and catastrophes happened when a time-crosser knowingly changed history. One alteration could create a cascade of problems that might hurt countless others, Kathryn."

"But I can't let that possibility stop me—how could one little change make so much difference? If I knowingly allow my sister to be murdered, am I not guilty, as well?"

Mama looked to Papa, helpless.

"God is sovereign," Papa said. "Even when we don't understand, He allows certain things to happen for His purposes. When we say we know better, then it means we don't believe He is sovereign or just. That His will is not as perfect as our own—and that's a dangerous game to play."

I shook my head, struggling to understand. "God is sovereign," I agreed. "But He also gave us a mind, didn't He? And He intends for us to use it. He has given me this information and time to make a difference in Mary's life. I can't sit back and do nothing."

Mama took my cold hands. "This is what I was afraid might happen when we came here. You're too close to this situation, Kathryn. This is a very precarious position you're in. My mother always told me it was best not to study the history we would live through. I didn't listen, and I tried to find answers about the witch trials, but it only brought me grief and heartache. I think it would be best if you stopped digging for answers. Perhaps you should step away from this proje—"

"I can't leave. This is the opportunity of a lifetime." I was beginning to feel desperate. "How could I walk away now?" I took a deep breath. "I don't even know if my Mary is the victim. I must find her—and I'm going to ask Austen to help me."

Again, Mama looked at Papa. I knew that look.

"Austen hasn't been part of your life for fourteen years," Papa said. "You'll only make yourself upset if you ask for his help and he doesn't give it. You need to temper your expectations, Kathryn."

"He'll help me if he knows that Mary's life is at stake," I said.

"Will he?" Mama rubbed my hand, and I realized she was still holding it. "We don't want you to get hurt."

"If Mary is killed by Jack the Ripper and I don't do something to save her, the hurt I'll carry could not compare to the hurt Austen might inflict by rejecting me. But if he'll help me, and I can do something to protect Mary, I will take that chance."

Papa sighed. "If Mary is the Ripper's last victim and you choose to save her—" He shook his head. "Then you'll need to wait until the very last moment, Kathryn. If you try to change things too soon, you could jeopardize the entire history of England. You don't know how deep this thing goes. There have always been rumors that Prince Albert Victor himself was involved."

"I remember my mother telling me that they didn't know Jack's real identity, even in 2001," Mama added. "For some reason, history has chosen to keep him hidden. Whether it's because there are powerful people keeping the truth locked away—or because his real identity could change the course of human history—there's no way to know. Changing even the smallest thing could end up creating more pain and heartache than you bargain for."

My breath stilled as I let their words sink into my mind and heart.

Next to my family, my love for history and for England was second to none. My life's work was to protect and preserve the past so a future generation could know and appreciate the people and events that came before them. How could I knowingly change even the slightest detail?

"You have a lot to ponder," Papa said as he rose from his chair. "We've been invited to dinner with the Kennedys at the Ambassador's Residence. If you don't feel like going, we can give your apologies."

As a brigadier general in the Army Air Corps, and as popular figures from their days as aviators, Papa and Mama had been invited to several events and dinner parties during our stay. I wouldn't be able to attend them all, but I could go to this one.

I took a deep breath and shook my head. "Mama has always told me to not let one life affect the other—and in 1938, all is well. I want to go."

"All is well for now," Mama said as she, too, rose. "Germany is an ever-present threat, and the Soviet Union isn't too far behind."

"But those are not worries for today," Papa reminded her. "You lived through the Salem Witch Trials, and God never left your side, Grace. He'll give us strength to endure whatever comes our way."

Mama took his hand. "What would I do without you?"

He kissed her. "Thankfully, you don't need to find out."

I sat on the sofa, painfully aware of the troubles I faced in both paths. Mama and Papa would keep me grounded in 1938, but in 1888, I was alone.

Though I did have one ally—if he'd only agree to help.

5

LONDON, ENGLAND
SEPTEMBER 1, 1888

It was past ten when I woke up the next morning in my room at 11 Wilton Crescent. My physical body slept while my consciousness was away. If I fell asleep and then woke again before midnight, I would wake up in the same time and space, but if I slept until after midnight, I woke up in my other path. If I stayed awake past midnight, I would remain in this timeline until I fell asleep. On my twenty-fifth birthday, I would stay awake past midnight in whatever time I wanted to keep, and I would forfeit the other path.

That is, unless I knowingly changed history here in 1888. Then I would stay in my other path forever.

I climbed out of bed and rang for Duffy. I had no time to lose today. I needed to get to 13 Miller's Court as soon as possible. I couldn't ask for the family carriage, since the driver would tell my parents. Mother didn't like it when I left home without a chaperone, though she usually spent most of the day in bed. The only way she'd know was if one of the staff told her.

Duffy soon arrived and helped me into a simple green skirt and matching green jacket with a white blouse. It was one of the plainest outfits I owned, but it complimented my hair beautifully.

Austen had once told me he liked a green dress I wore when I was younger, and the praise had stayed with me ever since. I thought about it every time I wore a similar color.

Within the hour, I passed through the hedge again, this time armed with more knowledge.

"Good morning," I said to the same maid who had greeted me the day before. "Is Mr. Baird at home?"

"Yes, miss." She quickly glanced behind her, and then said, "but Brinley has told us to alert him if you come again."

"She's welcome to come in." Mrs. Leslie, the housekeeper, appeared from the back stairs. I'd known her most of my life, and like Brinley, she had always been very kind to me. She longed for Austen's happiness as much as I did.

"Thank you," I said as the maid stepped back and held the door open for me.

"How are you, Miss Kathryn?" Mrs. Leslie asked as she smiled.

"I'm doing well," I told her, though it wasn't quite the truth. I was anxious about Mary. "Can you tell me where to find Mr. Baird?"

"He's in his study," she said, "but I'd knock before entering. He's been working all morning."

I nodded at her instruction and then made my way up the back stairway and toward the study on the second floor. I hadn't been in the study since Austen's parents had died. It had once belonged to Austen's father, and I'd spent many happy hours in there with Austen as a child, looking over the history books that he knew were my favorites. For years, I'd been trying to find a copy of the book about Queen Elizabeth that had so enthralled me, but I had to settle for the one I brought to Toynbee Hall yesterday.

When I reached the door, I took a deep breath and then knocked.

"Give me a moment," Austen said, though the sound was muffled.

He had inherited his family's properties and had been educated at Eton and then Oxford, but I wasn't sure what occupied his time now. He had traveled quite a bit since graduating from university, often leaving for months—or a year—at a time. But when he was in London, he stayed at home and didn't move about in society. I never saw him at balls or other social events and wasn't even sure if he had a club.

What did he do with himself all day?

The door opened, and Austen stood before me in his shirtsleeves and waistcoat, his jacket discarded. His hair was disheveled, and his beard needed a trim.

And he was surprised to see me. I glimpsed pleasure in his eyes, but then he frowned and said, "I thought I told you not to return."

"And I told you I'd be back."

He closed the door again, murmuring, "Give me a second."

I waited, and when he returned, he had on his jacket and his hair looked as if he'd run his hands through it. I tried to peek into the room, but he closed the door firmly.

"What do you do with all your time?"

He frowned. "Is that what you came to ask me?"

"No. But I'm curious. Do you work?"

"It really doesn't concern you."

I sighed, not wanting to fight with him when I had a more important topic to discuss. "I learned something yesterday, when I was in 1938, and I was hoping to discuss it privately with you."

"Does this have to do with your sister?"

"Yes."

"I told you that I can't get involved."

"Austen." I laid my hand on his forearm. He tensed, trying to pull away from me again, but I wouldn't let him. "Her name is listed as the last victim of the Whitechapel murders. She'll be murdered on November 9th—that is, if she is the same Mary Jane Kelly listed in the files."

He studied me for a moment and then withdrew his arm, motioning to the drawing room across the hallway.

"Can't we go into the study?" I asked him. "The drawing room isn't as private."

He strode across the hall and entered the drawing room without answering.

I stood for a moment, wondering what he had in the study that he didn't want me to see.

But I wouldn't quarrel with him. He was willing to hear me out, and that was more than he'd offered yesterday.

When I entered the drawing room, I found him standing near the cold fireplace, his arms crossed, waiting.

I missed Austen's smile. I missed the way he used to playfully tease me and bring me gifts and sit with me for hours, talking about nothing and everything.

Now, he scowled and acted like I was an inconvenience.

The drawing room was decorated much differently than my own. Mother kept the furnishings in ours up-to-date and changed the wall color whenever she felt the need. Austen's drawing room looked exactly as it had fourteen years ago when his parents died. The entire house was like a time capsule.

"Should we take a seat?" I asked him.

"Just tell me what you want so I can refuse you and then get on with my day."

"Hiding in your study? Pretending the rest of the world doesn't exist?"

"Did you come here to badger me in my own home?"

"Where else can I badger you?"

"Tell me what you want."

"It's not what I want—it's what I need. I *need* to know if my sister is the woman who will be killed on November 9th. And the only way I can do that is if I go to 13 Miller's Court to see if she's living there."

"And if she is?"

"I'll find a way to get her out of there."

"You'll change history and forfeit your time here even sooner." There was something in the tone of his voice that I hadn't heard before, or perhaps I hadn't wanted to hear.

I stared at him, surprised. "Are you angry with me for choosing my other path?"

"What?"

It all returned to me, like a movie playing across a flickering screen in my mind's eye. The day before we'd learned about his parents' death was the day I had told Austen that I had to make a choice when I turned twenty-five—and I'd told him I was choosing my other path. Even then, I'd recognized that all my hopes and dreams were centered on that life. I suddenly recalled how he'd left me in the garden, confused and angry at my words. I planned to go to him, to try to make him understand. But then, we'd heard about his parents the next day and that had overshadowed our previous conversation.

I'd always assumed his anger had to do with his parents' death.

Now I wasn't so sure.

"The day before we learned about your parents," I said, slowly, trying to remember all the details as I studied him. "I told you that I wasn't staying here, and you got upset."

He stared at me but didn't respond.

"Is that why you've been pushing me away all these years, Austen? I thought it was simply because of your grief. Now I'm not so sure."

"You didn't even give me a chance."

My lips parted. "What?"

He ran his hand through his hair and walked to the window. "You made up your mind that you were choosing the other path, and you rejected me and everything about this life."

"Rejected *you*?" I was at a loss for words. "*You've* been rejecting me!"

"It doesn't matter anymore," he said, not looking at me. "I was a foolish child who thought the world was a better place. I quickly learned that anything I loved would be taken from me, so it was easier not to care."

I walked to him, uncertain. "Fourteen years ago, I knew it mattered to you. But since then, you've done a good job showing me it didn't."

He turned to me then, and I saw the truth in his eyes. It mattered far more than I'd ever realized—far more than maybe he even wanted to acknowledge.

I took a step back, shocked that I'd never noticed it before.

"Of course it matters, Kathryn." He looked out the window again. "Why do you think I spend so much time away from here? I can't stand to be this close to you and not—" He took a deep breath. "I thought that this time, things might be different. But you're still set on leaving and I don't want to play the fool anymore."

"The fool?" I shook my head. "What do you mean?"

He finally looked at me. "You really can't see it, can you?"

I wanted desperately to understand what he meant. Austen was my friend. Had always been my friend.

Had he wanted more?

"I'll call for my carriage," he growled as he walked past me to the door. "Meet me downstairs."

I blinked several times—trying to process his shifting moods and what he was trying to tell me. "You'll take me to Miller's Court?"

"Against my better judgment."

And then he was gone.

I sat next to Austen twenty minutes later in his carriage. I'd gone home to grab my bonnet and reticule, and then I'd met him outside when the carriage had been pulled around to the front of his townhouse.

The coachman had helped me into the small conveyance and then Austen had stepped inside, without saying a word to me. He wore a top hat and a pair of gloves, but his clothing was worn and outdated as he sat stiff beside me.

I was still trying to understand what had happened between us. I'd never suspected that he wanted more from me, especially because he had spent the past fourteen years avoiding me. Was that what he'd meant? That his feelings ran deeper than friendship?

It was ridiculous to even think about. We were friends and nothing more.

"I hate when you stare at me," he said as he looked out the window.

"How do you know I'm staring at you?" I asked as the carriage passed Green Park and took a left onto Victoria Street.

"I can feel it."

"I'm trying to understand what you meant—"

"I don't want to talk about it."

The truth was that I didn't really want to talk about it, either. I'd never thought of Austen as anything other than a friend. It would be better to return to safer topics. "Where have you been for the past year?"

"Italy."

"What were you doing there?"

"Are you going to drill me with questions the whole way?"

"If that's what it takes to find the answer."

This was safer. The bantering side of our relationship.

I played with the fastener of my reticule, clasping and unclasping it. "I have been waiting for a long time to have your undivided attention."

He put his hand on mine to stop me from fidgeting and met my gaze. "If you stop this infernal clicking noise, I'll answer you."

A different sort of tension started to coil inside me at the feel of his hand.

I nodded as I set the reticule aside, forcing him to remove his hand. It took me a moment to remember what we'd been saying. "Why were you in Italy for a year?"

"Studying."

"Studying?" I frowned. "What?"

"I'd rather not say."

"Why not?"

"Kate—" He paused. "There are some things that even you don't need to know."

He hadn't called me Kate in years. It reminded me of our childhood. Of a time and place that made more sense.

"Does it have something to do with your work?" I asked.

"Yes."

"And what is your work?"

"Let's talk about something else."

I wasn't sure why his work was so secretive, but I'd get it out of him eventually.

As we made our way to Dorset Street, where Miller's Court was located, things began to return to their normal cadence between us and I breathed a sigh of relief.

The city seemed to decay the farther we drove into the Whitechapel District. The sanitation and health conditions were abysmal. The stench of dead animals and waste was overpowering on the hot September day, and crime was an ever-present danger. Even in broad daylight.

Commercial Street was clogged with carriages, wagons, carts, and pedestrians. Dirty children darted between the vehicles, and stray animals wandered from one trash pile to the next.

"We do not belong here," Austen said as we drove toward Dorset Street. "Don't do anything to draw more attention than necessary."

I moved a little closer to Austen on instinct, and he glanced down at me.

"It's strange and scary to think that Jack the Ripper could be walking this very street right now, looking for his next victim, and we wouldn't even know him," I said.

"Jack the Ripper?"

"That's what they'll call him after the second murder when he sends a letter to the *Central News Agency* and signs it that way."

"And they never learn his identity?"

"There are theories—but nothing concrete, though everyone agrees that he was a madman."

"How many murders will he commit?"

"Experts link only five together—the canonical five—though there are other murders in Whitechapel around the time of his killing spree. Do you remember hearing about Martha Tabram? Some people think he murdered her, but most experts think she had a different killer because her death didn't fit the same modus operandi."

"He commits five murders and then what happens to him?"

"I don't know. No one does for sure."

"He just quit suddenly?"

"Yes. Some say he was forced into an insane asylum or committed suicide and that's why the murders stop."

"What do you think?"

"I don't know—I've only just begun to research the case. I didn't know much about it until two days ago. But all I can focus on right now is knowing if my sister is the last victim."

"And when does that murder take place?"

"November 9th."

"So we have time."

The way he said it made me pause. Had he meant we still had time to save Mary? Or that we still had time together?

When the carriage finally came to a stop, the coachman got out and opened the door for us.

"Stay close," Austen said to me.

I nodded and then accepted his hand to step out of the carriage.

The smell was worse outside. I wanted to put my handkerchief up to my nose, but I refrained.

Instead, I walked close to Austen as we approached a brick building that said Miller's Court on a weathered sign. There was a narrow passage with several doors on either side. We walked along the passage and found the number thirteen on a door at the back. Next to the door was a small window, which was broken and had a piece of clothing pushed through it.

"This must be it," I said to Austen.

Austen knocked on the door, and we stepped back to wait.

My hands were sweating, and my pulse was thumping hard. There were so many things I wanted to say to my sister, so many questions I wanted to ask. But if this was her, I would have to be very careful. I couldn't change history before just the right time, or I could mess it all up—and lose my place here sooner than necessary, while putting other people's lives in danger.

More than anything, though, I wanted to know why our father had not stopped her from leaving.

Austen knocked again, but there was no answer.

"Perhaps she's working," he said.

"Can I help you?" asked a man as he walked down the passageway toward us. He was in his mid-thirties. His worn clothes and thick accent suggested he lived in Whitechapel.

"We're looking for Mary Jane Kelly," Austen said. "We were told she lives at this address."

He frowned. "I'm the landlord of this place, and there ain't no Mary Jane Kelly what lives here."

"Do you know who rents number thirteen?" I asked him.

"What's it to you?"

Austen reached into his pocket and removed a coin. He discreetly handed it to the man and said, "Please answer the lady's question."

The man pocketed the coin and nodded, his gaze trailing up the length of my body. I was thankful for the simple, modest gown, though it still looked out of place in this neighborhood. "The room is currently empty. Are you looking for a place to stay?" He glanced at Austen and then back at me. "Or only a room to rent for the hour?"

My lips parted at his insinuation, and Austen took a menacing step forward.

The man backed up, his eyes widening.

"Do you know a woman named Mary Jane Kelly or not?" Austen demanded.

"Never heard of her before," he said quickly.

"And this room is empty?" I asked. "No one is currently living here?"

"Bertha Parker was the last tenant, and she moved out this morning. Found herself a man to live with, she did. I say good riddance. She was always late with her rent."

"Mary Jane must not live here yet," I said to Austen, disappointed that we hadn't found who we were looking for but still praying it wasn't my sister.

"Thank you for your time," Austen said to the landlord as he put his hand on the small of my back and led me through the passageway, back to Dorset Street, where the carriage was waiting.

When we arrived at the carriage, Austen helped me inside and then tapped on the roof to let the driver know we were ready to pull away.

"I'm sorry, Kate," he said to me.

I nodded as I looked out the window, not wanting him to see how disappointed I was.

"We'll find your sister." His face was serious. "I promise."

I wasn't sure what was happening between Austen and me, but I knew one thing for certain. My friend had returned, just in time.

6

SEPTEMBER 1, 1938
LONDON, ENGLAND

The following day, I found myself walking down the stone steps and into the basement of New Scotland Yard. This time, I was alone. Mr. McCaffrey had not arrived from Scotland, and Sir Rothschild had other matters to attend to. I'd been told a team was being assembled to put the exhibit together after Mr. McCaffrey and I laid out the design—but for now, I wanted to dive deep into the case and get familiar with the events that had taken place in 1888. It helped that I would experience it firsthand in my other path, but I also had the advantage of hindsight looking at it from 1938's perspective.

"Good morning, Miss Voland," PC Harrington said as I entered the first room. He was a handsome young man, about my age, with dark hair and brown eyes. His blue uniform was spotless, and based on the cleanliness and order of the Crime Museum, he took great pride in his work.

"Good morning," I said. "I'm here to continue my research."

"I've been expecting you." He rose from his desk and motioned for me to follow him. "I hope you've found everything you need."

We entered the room where I'd been working the previous day

in this path, and PC Harrington turned on the lights. The room was exactly as we'd left it.

"It must get lonesome down here," I said as I took off my hat and set it on the table with my satchel.

"There are more visitors than you might imagine." He smiled at me. "And there is a lot of work to be done, cataloging and accessioning items. With ten thousand police officers on the force and more crime than we can handle, there are new items coming in every day—not to mention those that are used as evidence in current cases. I manage it all."

"That's quite a job."

He nodded. "But it's the old cases, like the Ripper, that keep my interest. I like to study them in my spare time."

"Have you done a lot of research on the Ripper case?" I asked, eager to speak to someone who knew more about the case than me.

"I have, but I didn't think Sir Rothschild was interested in my opinions yesterday."

I laid my hands on the back of a chair and shook my head. "I'm sorry about that. I'd love to hear your opinions, PC Harrington."

"Please, call me Simon. At least when no one else is around."

I smiled. "And I'm Kathryn."

He motioned to one of the chairs at the table and said, "Mind if I sit?"

"Go ahead." I opened my satchel and took out a notebook and a pencil and then sat on the chair across from him. "I have a feeling I'll need to take notes."

"I don't claim to be an expert, mind you, but I've had enough time to examine a lot of theories." Simon leaned forward, his brown eyes sparkling with excitement. "I think it's safe to say that someone—or several people—spent a lot of time covering up after Jack the Ripper. Whoever he was, he had some powerful friends trying to keep his identity a secret. I've read many eyewitness accounts of the murder scenes, and dozens of people claimed to have seen the killer. Yet none of those people were ever brought in as witnesses during the inquests. Clues and evidence were destroyed, and other clues were brushed off. None of it makes sense. The killer should have been caught."

I also leaned forward. "What are the theories?"

"The more popular theory is that it was a coverup concerning the royal family. That perhaps it was the lunatic grandson of the Queen or that Prince Albert Victor had sired a child with a Whitechapel prostitute and the victims were all witnesses."

"But you don't think those are true?"

"No. The murders were all done within a mile of each other, and whoever did it had to have good knowledge of the streets and alleyways. Since over thirty thousand people lived there at the time, it could literally be anyone."

He went on to tell me about some of the more common suspects, and I took notes as he spoke.

When he told me all that he knew, I had more questions about the victims and tried not to seem unusually interested in Mary Jane Kelly. "The first four women have a lot of similarities," I said. "Their age, living conditions, and even the way they were murdered. Why was the fifth victim different?"

"I think it was all about opportunity," he said. "The first four women were basically homeless, trying to make their doss money each day to have a place to stay. They worked on the street, and that's where Jack found them. His murders had to be quick because there was no privacy in Whitechapel. Mary Jane Kelly was the only one who had her own room, so Jack took the opportunity to murder her in the privacy of her home, where he wouldn't be interrupted."

"Do you think they were random murders?"

Simon dipped his head. "Well, I can't say that for sure. There are theories that the women were connected some way, but whoever hid Jack's identity hid the victims' connections, too."

The phone rang in the other room. Simon's face fell in disappointment. "Sorry about that, but I should answer the call."

"Of course."

I sat for a moment, looking over the notes I'd taken, thinking about what he'd told me. I wasn't anywhere closer to knowing Jack's identity or if Mary Jane Kelly was my sister. Even the theories he'd shared with me didn't seem to add up.

I stood and pulled the victims' files out of the cabinet again. As I studied the information available, from the coroner's reports to family and friends' depositions, I couldn't find anything connecting their lives. Polly, Annie, and Catherine were all English born, while Elizabeth was originally from Sweden, and Mary Jane's origins were unknown, though it was believed she was also English. Were they random victims that happened to have similar backstories, or had Jack hunted them?

The next victim would be Annie Chapman, who would be killed on September 8th. Her body would be found in a courtyard at 29 Hanbury Street, not far from Commercial Street, and only half a mile from where Polly Nichols had been murdered. It was a week away. Perhaps Austen would take me there to inspect the area and see if there were any clues that might help us. Maybe I could even look for Annie and ask her a few questions, though the prospect of meeting one of Jack's victims, and knowing her fate, would be horrifying. Maybe she knew Mary Jane Kelly and there were connections between them. Any bit of information would help.

As I looked through Annie Chapman's file and learned the name of the boardinghouse where she lived, I couldn't help but wonder if Jack was also searching for her in 1888.

But if he was watching her, might he also start to watch me? I had to be careful that I wasn't putting myself in his path—a prospect I had not considered until now.

I was ready to forget about my work that evening as our cab pulled up to the luxurious home of 4 St. James Square, the residence of Lord and Lady Astor.

"I am eager to see the Astors again," Mama said as Papa opened the cab door and stepped out. She was wearing a beautiful evening gown that shimmered in the streetlamps. I loved to think of all the life she had lived as an early aviator and a Puritan in Massachusetts. It was a shame that she couldn't share her stories beyond the small circle of family who knew of her time-crossing. It was one of the many reasons I wanted history to come alive for others, so that people like us, who lived such a strange and wonderful existence, could let others experience the beauty of time.

I stepped out of the cab behind Mama, wearing a long black gown with short sleeves and delicate embroidered silk flowers and leaves crisscrossing over the bodice. I kept my dark red hair shorter in my 1938 path, since it was easier to manage, and the current style lent itself to a shoulder-length bob. One side was clipped up with a jewel-studded barrette, and the ends were curled under.

Before we arrived at the door of the three-story townhouse, a butler opened it and bowed. "Welcome. Lord and Lady Astor have been expecting you."

As we entered the front hall, a middle-aged woman blew into the room with a wide smile. She, too, was wearing a long evening gown and had diamonds on her rings, earrings, and bracelets. "Good evening, my American friends. It's wonderful to see you again."

There was no need for pretense or guile in Nancy Astor's home. Though she was a viscountess and a member of Parliament, she was first and foremost a Virginian who had married into a wealthy family and earned a place in the hearts of the British people through her outgoing and charming personality. She never met a stranger and made friends with people from all walks of life. Her interest in aviation had bonded her to my parents years ago.

She kissed my parents' cheeks and then linked arms with me as she led us into the main parlor off the front hall. "I hope you remember," she said, "in this house, there are no formalities or hierarchies. I insist that we call everyone by their first name."

"Of course I do," I said with a smile.

Waldorf Astor, Nancy's husband, approached in an evening

coat and extended his hands to greet Papa, then Mama, and finally me.

"It's a pleasure to see you all again," Waldorf said to each of us. "How are you finding jolly old England?"

Waldorf and Nancy Astor's story had always enthralled me. Waldorf's great-aunt, Mrs. Caroline Astor, had been the head of New York Society for decades. Because of it, she had been in a feud with Waldorf's father, William Astor. William had left America at the height of the feud and quickly acclimated to British Society. William eventually became the first Viscount Astor. His son, Waldorf, had married Nancy, and together they had continued the Astor legacy in England. 4 St. John's Square was their townhouse, but Cliveden, the country mansion that William had given to Waldorf and Nancy as a wedding gift, was their home.

"We hope you're enjoying your stay at Berkeley Square," Waldorf said.

"It's been very nice." Papa nodded. "Thank you for the generous offer."

"There are so many people for you to meet," Nancy said as she led us further into the parlor, where at least a dozen people were already mingling over drinks. She paused, as if an idea had just come to her. "Do you have any plans for the weekend? We're all heading to Cliveden tomorrow for a Friday through Monday. It would be lovely to have you join us. Charles and Anne Lindbergh will be there—I believe you know them."

"I've met Colonel Lindbergh on a few occasions," Papa said. "Grace and the girls and I were on the stage when he was given the Distinguished Flying Cross medal right after his transatlantic flight in 1927."

"Oh, do say you'll come," Nancy persisted. "We'd love to have you."

Mama and Papa glanced at each other, and then Mama looked at me. "Can you get away for the weekend, Kathryn?"

"I had planned to research, but I could take my work with me."

"I'm so eager to hear all about your project at the London

Museum," Nancy said with a smile, her eyes filling with youthful eagerness. She turned, as if searching the room. "I do believe there is someone here that you haven't met. He'll be joining us at Cliveden."

She didn't let go of my arm as she led me through the group of people while her husband took my parents in a different direction.

"There you are," she finally said as she interrupted two gentlemen who were talking near a large, beautiful painting of a gorgeous manor house—which I immediately assumed to be Cliveden.

Both men turned, but it was clear that Nancy was speaking to the younger of the two.

"Calan," she said, putting her free hand on the gentleman's arm, "this is Miss Kathryn Voland. I believe you two will be working together at the London Museum."

"Mr. McCaffrey?" I asked, surprised.

He smiled. "How do you do, Miss Voland?" His Scottish accent was thick and deep. "I had hoped to get to the museum before it closed today so we could meet properly, but I just got into town."

"Just in time for my dinner party," Nancy added.

I shook Mr. McCaffrey's hand, charmed with his accent and his handsome blue eyes.

"This is Lord Trevaun," Calan said as he indicated the other gentleman, "a member of Parliament."

"How do you do, Lord Trevaun?" I asked as I shook his hand.

"Call me George," he said with a dry, cultured British accent. "Nancy insists."

Nancy's head tilted back as she laughed. "I do, indeed." She let go of my arm and linked hers with George's. "Let's leave the young people with their energy and optimism and go find somewhere to complain about our aching bodies and the state of affairs in the world, shall we?" As they walked away, she turned and said, "Supper will be served in a few minutes. Perhaps you'd like to sit together."

Mr. McCaffrey smiled at me. "It's a pleasure to finally meet you, Miss Voland."

"I think you're supposed to call me Kathryn," I said in a conspiratorial tone, "or Nancy might kick us out."

His grin was infectious as he laughed. "We don't want to test her, do we?"

"I've heard she's a force to be reckoned with—both in and out of Parliament."

"That she is."

We were both quiet for a moment, so I said, "I hope you don't mind, but I'm curious as to why you've come from Scotland to work on an exhibit at the London Museum."

"I've known and worked with Sir Rothschild for years. He said he was assembling a team to help build a very special exhibit and only wanted the best to work on it." His blue eyes sparkled. "I assume that means you're the best America has to offer."

His laid-back personality put me at ease, yet I sensed he was used to women being fascinated by him.

"I'm not sure I'm the best," I said, "but I do have a passion for history and a special place in my heart for England."

"This secret project of Bryant's just got a lot more interesting," he said with a laugh. "Perhaps you could give me a hint as to what we'll be working on."

"You don't know?"

He shrugged.

I wasn't sure why Sir Rothschild had kept the exhibit so secretive, but surely Calan could be trusted if Sir Rothschild had asked him to lead the team.

"Dinner is served," the butler said as he entered the room, interrupting several conversations.

Calan offered me his arm. "Shall we? I can't wait to hear more about this top-secret project of ours."

I took his arm and smiled at several other guests as we made our way across the hall and into the formal dining room. The rounded ceiling was painted with cherubs and clouds, while a heavy chandelier illuminated the large paintings on the walls. In between each painting was an enormous mirror, making the massive room feel even bigger.

Down the center of the room was a long table, laden with fine linen, china, and crystal. Calan led me to two chairs close to the end and pulled one out for me.

"Thank you." I took the seat, smiling at the gentleman to my left, who I had not yet met.

Introductions were soon made, and the first course, a tomato bisque, was brought to the table by footmen.

"There are so many things I want to know about you," Calan said as he took up his spoon to sample his soup. "I don't even know where to begin."

I laughed. "You're very charming."

He grinned. "I'm looking forward to spending time with you on the project. I'm excited to know more about it."

The exhibit would be opening in November, and Sir Rothschild hadn't told me to keep it to myself, so I saw no reason Calan couldn't know. "We've been given access to the Jack the Ripper files at New Scotland Yard. Sir Rothschild wants us to create an exhibit, the first of its kind, for the London Museum."

Calan's eyebrows rose, his soup spoon midway to his mouth. Slowly, he lowered the spoon. "So, the funny little game is going to be made public."

"Funny little game?" I shook my head, frowning.

"Haven't you read the *Dear Boss* letter yet?" he asked.

Again, I shook my head. "Not yet. Isn't that the letter that he signed Jack the Ripper for the first time?"

"The very one. Jack sent it to the Central News Agency of London. In it, he called the murders his 'funny little games.'"

I turned to look at him more fully. "So, you're familiar with the case?"

"Very familiar. My uncle was John Chapman, Annie Chapman's husband. I have a feeling that's why Bryant asked me to be part of this project. I've done quite a lot of research on the case already."

"You're related to one of the victims?"

"Through Annie's husband, yes, but he died from liver disease two years before her murder." He lifted the spoon to his mouth, becoming serious as he stared into his soup bowl. "I've always felt a strange connection to the case because of Annie."

"I'm sorry for your loss."

He seemed to pull himself from wherever his thoughts had drifted and lifted a shoulder. "It happened a long time before I was born, but it's been a part of our family's story. I've spent years trying to unravel the funny little game myself."

"I'm finding that there are not a lot of clues, and the ones that were preserved don't tell us much."

"You need to know who you can trust, and who you can't trust," Calan said, for my ears only. "As a historian, and in life, I've learned to not accept things or people on the surface. Take, for instance, this room."

I glanced at the people around the table, all of them smiling and having a good time. The conversation in the Astors' dining room was glittery, full of laughter and joy. Nancy Astor clearly reigned over her table and enjoyed every moment.

"Lady Astor is a controversial figure," Calan said quietly. "She loves good banter, and sometimes her conversation is raw, but she's known as a prude where her behaviors are concerned. It has confused people for decades. But," he paused, and I turned back to look at him, "she's an enigma for other reasons."

"What do you mean?"

"She is so against Communism that she has publicly praised Hitler and Fascism as a buffer between the Communist Soviet Union and the western world. She vehemently opposes Catholicism, but is a good friend of Ambassador Kennedy, who is a staunch Catholic. She has strong views about Judaism while maintaining friendships with many Jewish people. She takes pride in her wide range of friendships and is truly kind to everyone—yet she is a force to be reckoned with when she is in Parliament, fighting some of the people who are sitting here at this very table." He smiled and shook his head. "So you see, Kathryn, not everyone and everything are as they appear. We're living in very dangerous times, with Nazi and Communist spies working in our very midst. The British Union of Fascists has over fifty thousand members here in England." He paused and then said, "Perhaps there are Nazis and Communists at this table. And, as I've said, it's important to know who you can trust and who you can't trust."

I smiled at him. "Can I trust you?"

His laughter was melodic as he dipped his spoon into his soup. "I wouldn't."

Several guests looked in our direction, including my parents, and smiled.

"What about you?" Calan asked me. "Can I trust you?"

"Of course," I said, though I carried a secret about my time-crossing that I could never tell him. But that didn't make me untrustworthy—did it?

"Good." He nodded. "That's what I hoped you'd say." He touched my arm and said, "And I was only teasing you, lass. You can trust me, too."

As the meal progressed, I thought about the things I'd learned that day, and I realized how naïve I'd been. There was a web of secrets, power, and illusions casting its shadow on 1888 and 1938.

Tomorrow, I would seek Austen's help again. I wanted to find Annie Chapman to see if she knew anything about my sister and if I could discover clues about why Jack would murder her.

Yet, as I considered all the obstacles before me, I had to remind myself that even if I unlocked the secret to Jack the Ripper's identity, there was little I could do about it.

My only concern was saving my sister, though I was starting to fear that I might get entangled in Jack's funny little game after all.

7

LONDON, ENGLAND
SEPTEMBER 2, 1888

The next morning, I was up and dressed earlier than usual. It was one thing to investigate the Jack the Ripper case from a vantage point fifty years in the future, with all the evidence and depositions obtained, but another thing entirely to investigate it as it unfolded. I was fighting time and history, and I needed to work fast.

I entered the breakfast room on the main floor of our townhouse, where my father was already seated. Mother took her first meal of the day in bed, as was common for married women, though her first meal was often at noon.

I had been avoiding Father for the past ten months, as much as I could, and usually came down after he left for King's College Hospital, where he was a surgeon and a lecturer, serving as the chair of systemic surgery. He had warned me not to mention Mary's name again, but that was before I knew she might be the last victim of Jack the Ripper.

I had to take a risk.

"Good morning," I said, trying not to let my anger and frustration at his treatment of Mary color my words.

Father was seated at the head of the table, eating his breakfast with the same determination he did everything. With single-minded focus. He was a tall man, with thick, gray side whiskers and a spreading middle, a testament to his love for food.

"Kathryn." He looked up from the sausage he was cutting. "I haven't seen you at breakfast for some time."

I went to the sideboard and helped myself to a plate of eggs and a muffin, though I had no appetite. Our butler, Jenkins, stood at attention but didn't acknowledge me. He had not been with us for long. Mother's penchant for change, if it could not be met with new drapes or wallcoverings, came at the expense of new staff.

"I've been a little busy," I said as I took a seat next to Father.

"Your mother's social calendar is daunting," he agreed as he continued to cut his sausage. "She only wants the best for you."

"And now that Mary is gone, I'm her sole focus."

His fork paused on its way to his mouth. He glanced at Jenkins quickly before he said to me, "I've warned you not to say her name."

I leaned forward, desperate. "I need to find her—"

"She is dead."

"You mean dead to us? *Why*? What did she do? I don't under—"

Father speared me with a look that made me close my mouth. "If you don't want to end up like her, I'd suggest you heed my words, Kathryn. Your sister is dead and nothing you say or do will bring her back. Do I make myself clear? I will not say it again."

My heart was pounding hard as I stared at him. I wanted to ask him how he could turn out his own flesh and blood to the horrors of Whitechapel, but I believed he could—and would—send me to the same fate if I persisted. He'd always been a kind and generous father, but he was also demanding and disciplined.

With a scowl, Father wiped his lips and tossed his napkin onto his half-eaten plate of food, proof that he was livid, and then he rose from the table and left the breakfast room.

I sat at the table until I heard him leave the house, staring at the empty seat across from me where my sister used to sit, filling each new day with her happy chatter. My chest rose and fell with memories of her excitement over a new dress, or her colorful description of a ball or event she'd attended without me. She had been all that was good and happy in our home.

Jenkins didn't move behind me, but I knew he was there, and I didn't want to show him the depth of my pain.

I rose, leaving my food uneaten, and left the breakfast room. If Father wouldn't help me, then perhaps Austen would. I needed to get back to Whitechapel and find Annie Chapman, or one of the other women who would be murdered. If there was a connection between the victims, it might point me to Mary.

The hem of my day dress brushed the floor as I walked toward the back door. My corset felt too tight, and my collar choked me as I stepped out into the courtyard. Clouds marred the sky, and the lack of wind made the hot air feel thick with smog.

When I was a child, I often came into the garden to pray. I hadn't understood my time-crossing gift, and it had scared me, though Mama had done a good job explaining it to me. I had spent hours asking God why I had to endure such a strange existence. I hadn't started to appreciate it until Austen had brought me history books, and his excitement about the past had filled me with a newfound appreciation for what I experienced. I had started to wish that I could live even further back in time, during the days of knights and fair maidens. And I wanted to take him with me.

But that wasn't the way my gift worked, so instead we'd traveled there together through books.

I stepped onto the green grass and walked toward the hedge, realizing that the more confident I grew in my time-crossing gift, the less I had come to God with my concerns. Mama had always said I was headstrong and determined, often taking matters into my own hands, which hadn't left much need for God.

For the first time in a long time, I realized I was facing something that felt bigger than me. I had a plan to save Mary, if she was the last victim, and I would not waver in seeing it through, but what if it didn't go as I hoped? I glanced up at the cloudy sky, feeling guilty that I'd grown so distant from God. I didn't want to go to

Him only when I needed something or when I was desperate. I often attended church in both paths, and I knew He was there, but I usually felt confident to proceed without consulting Him. And things had generally worked out as I hoped.

But this time, I was thinking about changing history, and that didn't sit right within my spirit—no matter how confident I appeared to Mama and Papa. Yet, God had revealed this piece of history to me, and I didn't think He wanted me to sit back and do nothing.

"I'm sorry," I whispered in prayer as I passed through the hedge, my heart heavy. "Please help me find Mary, and please direct my steps. I don't want to do anything that might hurt Your plans, but I also don't want my sister to die. Please help me find a way to keep her safe."

If the victim Mary Jane Kelly *wasn't* my sister, I had nothing to worry about. But if she was, then I would need to save her. Changing history wasn't a *sin*, I had to remind myself, just something that wasn't advised. The cost would be forfeiting this path earlier than I had planned, but I would make that sacrifice, if necessary.

I knocked on the back door of Austen's home, and a maid answered. "Is Mr. Baird in?"

"He's in the front hall, miss," the maid said.

I moved past her through the back hall and entered the front.

There were two large wooden crates in the hall, tall and thin. Three men were hauling them out the front door.

Austen stood nearby, looking anxious as the boxes were transported. "Be careful," he cautioned them.

"Are you selling some of your parents' artwork?" I asked.

He didn't even bother to turn at the sound of my voice. "Something like that," he said.

It surprised me that he would sell items that had belonged to his parents. Nothing had changed since they'd died. Not a single piece of furniture had been moved. Even when his aunt had lived with him, he hadn't let her change a thing.

"What paintings are you selling?" I asked.

"You don't know them."

I frowned. "I know all the paintings in this house."

"Not these."

A fourth mover entered the house and handed Austen a piece of paper, which he signed, and then the mover doffed his cap and helped remove the last crate, allowing Brinley to close the door behind them.

"Has it gotten that bad?" I asked Austen, taking a step closer to him, conscious of his worn clothing. "If you need financial help—"

He gave me a look that silenced my offer.

Brinley left us alone in the hall.

"Are you back to fight with me again?" Austen asked me, crossing his arms.

"I need to return to Whitechapel and look for a woman named Annie Chapman."

He sighed.

"Do you not have time to take me?" I asked him.

"I have the time, but it's not safe, Kate."

"You promised you'd help me find Mary, and I can't find her unless we go there."

"Perhaps we should hire a private detective."

"I can't afford one, and you . . ." I trailed off, not wanting to remind him of his financial troubles.

"I can afford to hire a private detective. I'm not destitute."

"I don't see the need, if we have foreknowledge to help us."

"Who is Annie Chapman? Does she know your sister?"

I pressed my lips together, not wanting to admit the truth.

He narrowed his eyes. "Who is she, Kate?"

At least he was still using his pet name for me. I glanced behind me to make sure we were alone, and then I leaned toward him. "She's the Ripper's next victim."

He briefly closed his eyes as he shook his head.

"I know the boardinghouse that she frequents and where she'll be murdered," I whispered. "It shouldn't be hard to find her."

"And what happens when she's killed and the police start asking questions, and someone mentions that a well-to-do couple was seen with her just days before her murder? Guess who comes knocking on our doors?"

I bit my bottom lip. "I hadn't thought of that."

"We can't talk to her."

"I need to try. We can be discreet."

"It's out of the question."

I let out a frustrated breath. "Can we at least go to the murder site?"

"What do you think you'll learn?"

"I don't know. That's why this is called an investigation." I put my hands on my hips. "I learned some things yesterday in 1938, and I need to get my questions answered."

"What things?"

"Will you take me to Whitechapel? I'll explain it on the way."

He shook his head. "I don't think I'm going to like this."

"Probably not."

He let out an exasperated breath. "Meet me outside in twenty minutes. I'll have Miles pull the carriage around."

I smiled and stood on tiptoe to place a kiss on his whiskered cheek, but the simple act—one I'd done several times as children—felt much different this time.

Austen grasped my upper arms—more out of surprise than affection—and I paused, my lips on his cheek. He wore a foreign cologne I'd never smelled before, so subtle I hadn't noticed it until I was this close.

My breath caught as he slowly pulled back, and I lowered off my tiptoes.

His eyes were dark with emotions. "Don't do that again, Kathryn." He let me go. "I'll be ready in twenty minutes."

And with that, he strode up the stairs and disappeared.

Neither Austen nor I spoke as we walked down Hanbury Street on our way to number 29, where Annie Chapman would be murdered on September 8th. The stench of Whitechapel was heightened by the rain, and the addition of mud had ruined the hem of my gown.

A light drizzle pattered against the black umbrella he held over our heads, both for protection from the weather and from prying eyes. We were wearing plain clothing so we wouldn't draw unwanted attention. Austen's coat and hat were worn and dated, which helped us to blend in. I didn't want anyone to remember us after Annie's death, which was six days away.

We'd left Miles with the carriage several streets over, hoping to stay as inconspicuous as possible. I kept an eye out for anyone who might look like Annie. She was the only victim of Jack the Ripper with a photograph before her murder. It was taken on the day she married John Chapman, and though she had aged, I had also seen her postmortem picture and had a good idea of her likeness.

Hanbury Street was mostly commercial, with storefronts on the main level and rooms above for tenants. Austen and I were stopped by various peddlers, but we shook our heads at most of them and continued down the dirty street.

We hadn't said much since we left Austen's home. My cheeks were still warm from the kiss as I tried to understand both his feelings and mine. But I couldn't remain silent any longer.

"I'm sorry," I said as I looked down at my gloved hands. "I didn't mean to make you feel uncomfortable before."

He was quiet for a moment, and I was afraid he wouldn't respond, but he finally said, "I wasn't uncomfortable."

I glanced up and found him watching me. His eyes were so clear and perceptive.

"Then why did you tell me I must not kiss you again?"

He shook his head and turned his gaze away from me. "If you don't know, then there's no point in explaining."

I frowned. "That doesn't make any sense."

"What else can you tell me about Annie Chapman?"

I blinked several times, trying to grasp what he'd meant, even though he had tried to change the subject. "What don't I know, Austen?"

When his blue eyes returned to mine, there was a question in their depths. "Do you really not know, Kate?"

My pulse sped at the intensity in his gaze, but the answer was just out of my reach—not because I was an idiot, but because I wouldn't allow myself to search for the truth.

Instead, I answered his earlier question.

"I don't know a lot about Annie Chapman. That's why I want to speak to her."

Austen's mood shifted from vulnerability to indifference in a heartbeat.

"I'm afraid that there is something connecting the five victims," I continued, needing to talk about something other than us. "But I don't know what it might be. The first four victims are similar in age, marital status, and living conditions, but they all came from very different places. Annie's husband, John, was a coachman in Windsor for a man named Francis Tress Barry."

"I've heard of him. He is a good friend of Prince Albert Victor and often hosts the prince in Windsor."

I nodded, thankful that he would change the subject with me. "From the records I have in 1938, Annie was arrested for drunkenness so often her husband's employer, Barry, said that if she didn't leave his property, John would lose his job. So, Annie and John separated, and Annie has been in the Whitechapel District for the past three years."

"And what of the other one? Polly Nichols? Have you found a connection between her and Annie?"

"Not yet. Polly's husband was a printer on Fleet Street. They lived a very respectable life until her last child was born. She claimed that her husband was having an affair with the neighbor who helped her deliver the baby. Polly eventually left him and the children and spent years on the streets, and in and out of workhouses."

We came to a stop at number 29, which was a dilapidated building with broken windows, rotting doorframes, and cracked brick. An old storefront window was covered with advertisements and years of smog and dust.

"Does Annie live here?" Austen asked me quietly.

"No. She stays in a boardinghouse on Dorset Street when she has her doss money. This is simply a dark corner for her to take—" I paused, my cheeks growing warm.

"Her customers?" Austen asked with a raised eyebrow.

I didn't respond but motioned to a door that led into a passageway. "It happens in the courtyard behind the building. Sometime between five and six in the morning. Around 5:15, a neighbor in the next yard at 27 Hanbury Street will come down to use the lavatory, and he'll claim to hear a woman say no twice before something or someone falls against the adjoining fence."

"Can you spare a sixpence?" a woman asked from behind us.

Austen and I turned and found a middle-aged woman standing on the street with no umbrella to protect her from the rain. Her dress was worn and tattered, and her dark, curly hair was streaked with strands of gray. She extended a dirty hand to us as she turned and coughed into her shoulder.

My hand tightened on Austen's arm.

It was Annie Chapman.

Her eyes were glossed over as she stared back at me.

"Annie?" I asked.

Slowly, her hand came down and she frowned, squinting at me. "Who are you?"

I couldn't tell her my name in case she repeated it to someone who would tell the police after her death.

Her death.

Gooseflesh covered my skin as I realized this woman would be murdered by Jack the Ripper in less than a week.

"I'm . . ." I smiled, trying to calm my nerves. "I heard that you might know someone I'm looking for."

Annie continued to frown as suspicion darkened her gaze. "Who are you looking for?"

"Mary Jane Kelly."

Annie's eyes cleared for a moment as she took a step back, looking between me and Austen. "Why do you want to know about her?"

"You do know her," I said quickly.

"I know *of* the girl," she said, her voice and gaze drifting off, "but that was a long time ago. In a world that doesn't seem to exist any longer."

I frowned, confused by her words, but pressed on. "Do you know where she lives?"

"The less I know, the better, that's what John always said. Take a drink, Annie, and forget. Forget about all of it." Her gaze clouded over again, and she lifted her hand. "Spare a sixpence, love?"

Austen reached into his pocket and pulled out a shilling. Annie's face filled with wonder as she looked up at him quickly and nodded. "God bless you, sir."

She started to leave, but I put my hand on her shoulder to stop her.

"Do you know Polly Nichols?"

Annie's muscles were stiff as she turned back to me. "Do *you* know Polly?"

I shook my head. Though I had seen her at Toynbee Hall, I didn't know her.

Annie swallowed hard and looked over her shoulder, then leaned forward and said, "I don't know anything. Drink to forget, Annie. Drink to forget." Her gaze wandered, as if she was looking for somewhere to get the drink she needed.

She slowly pulled back from me and simply walked away, dazed and troubled.

I started to go after her, but Austen captured my hand and shook his head. "Let her go, Kate. Even if she does tell you something, it would be hard to believe her. She's clearly troubled and unwell, and if we make a scene, someone will notice."

"What if she knows Mary or Polly?"

"We'll find Mary a different way." Austen lifted his gaze to look at the street. "Besides, if a madman is on the loose and he has a target on Annie, he could be watching us right now. We shouldn't stay." He gently brought my hand into the crook of his elbow and motioned with his head the way we had come. "Let's get you out of this rain."

We didn't speak as we walked back to the waiting carriage.

After we got inside, Austen tapped on the carriage roof and it began to move.

"What do you think she meant?" I finally asked Austen. "Did she really know of Mary from a long time ago?"

"I'm not sure. She seemed certain at first, but it was hard to tell. How could she have known of Mary from a long time ago? Mary is only twenty, and Annie is in her forties. Did she know her as a child? I wouldn't put too much stock into her responses."

"But her recognition when I said Mary's name—it has to mean something."

The carriage bounced through the rutted street, pressing me closer to Austen.

At first he was stiff beside me, but he eventually softened and allowed me to lean into him.

"Kate."

I looked up at him, waiting. His hair was combed, but it was still long, and his beard was unkempt. If it wasn't for his clothing, though worn, or the way he carried himself, he might be mistaken for a commoner and not a gentleman.

"What is it?" I asked him.

He started to speak, but then he shook his head and looked out the window. "Nothing."

I sat up straighter. "You must tell me."

"I shouldn't. It's nothing." He turned back to me, and I saw in his eyes that something was troubling him.

"Whatever it is," I said as I laid my hand on his arm, "you can tell me."

He looked down at my hand and slowly took it in his own. With a sigh, he said, "I admire your tenacity."

I could tell it wasn't what he had intended to say, but I didn't want to press him. I had loved spending time with Austen over the past few days, and I wanted more of it. I didn't want to complicate things.

So instead of convincing him to tell me what he had been thinking, I made a proposition. "Perhaps I can persuade you to attend the ball Mother is planning this Saturday night."

He let go of my hand, and whatever gentleness had come over him, it was suddenly gone. "No."

"Please," I said. "Mother's parties are so boring."

He frowned. "If you're trying to convince me to attend, you're going about it the wrong way."

"What I mean," I said, "is that you would make it fun."

He gave me a side eye, his voice dry. "Because I bring so much life to a party."

"You could, if you wanted to. Mother has a performer coming, and she will no doubt have a handful of eligible bachelors there to meet me. Please save me from the boredom."

Something flickered in his gaze, but it was gone before it fully formed.

It almost looked like jealousy.

8

BUCKINGHAMSHIRE, ENGLAND
SEPTEMBER 2, 1938

Sunshine warmed the car as Mama, Papa, and I made our way to Cliveden House in Buckinghamshire, just outside London. It was refreshing to be back in 1938, away from Whitechapel and Jack the Ripper—and Austen, whose behavior had started to puzzle me.

Austen usually said exactly what he thought, without care as to how I would perceive it. But the conversation in the carriage the day before, after meeting Annie, was strange. He had wanted to say something but had chosen not to. It wasn't like him, but then again, Austen wasn't acting like his old self since returning from Italy.

Something was different, and it was all I could think about.

"You're quieter than usual," Mama said as we turned down a long drive with trees on either side. Ahead was Cliveden House, the Astors' country home.

"I met Annie Chapman," I said, though it wasn't the reason I was being quiet.

"Who is she?" Papa asked.

"One of the victims—the next victim."

Mama's eyebrows rose high. "Do you think it's wise to be in contact with the victims? What if you change history?"

"Or are seen by Jack?" Papa added.

"I just wanted to ask her if she knew Mary or Polly Nichols." I felt defensive, probably because I knew they were right. "I wasn't going to change anything."

"You need to be more careful," Mama said. "I hope you didn't go alone."

"Austen took me to Whitechapel both times I've gone."

"You've been there before?" Papa shook his head and sighed. "One of the most dangerous places in history."

"Austen will take care of me." Even as I said the words, I realized I meant them wholeheartedly. I trusted Austen with my life.

So why did I hesitate to trust him with my heart?

The thought made me pause. His response to my kiss, and his strange words about not giving him a chance, swirled within my mind.

"Isn't it magnificent?" Mama asked as she stared at Cliveden House.

I was thankful she tore my thoughts away from Austen—though it would be impossible to forget about him completely.

The central part of the mansion was a three-story rectangular structure with dozens of windows, and along the sides were corridors leading to two-story buildings flanking either side. The River Thames hugged the edge of the beautifully landscaped property, and the first yellow tinges of autumnal color were starting to appear, though the weather felt like July.

"It's remarkable that this home was a wedding present," Mama said. "I can't imagine such wealth."

My parents lived a very comfortable lifestyle, but it wasn't grand. They'd purchased Mama's childhood home on Lafayette Square in Washington, DC, and had taken care of my grandparents Maggie and Graydon in their old age. My older sister, Lydia, and I had been raised with them. Losing Grams and Gramps within months of each other just two years ago had been a difficult loss, but I had taken comfort in knowing they'd led good, fulfilling lives. They hadn't left much of a financial legacy since they'd spent most of their money caring for orphans, but the legacy of faith and love was priceless.

The cab took us to the front entrance. A butler was waiting for our arrival, and he ordered two footmen to take our bags to our rooms, but Nancy Astor had requested that we be brought to the terrace as soon as we arrived.

The back terrace of Cliveden House was even more impressive than the front entrance, looking out at a pristine lawn with hedges and flowerbeds. It also afforded a better view of the river.

There were several people already gathered on the terrace, laughing, enjoying hors d'oeuvres and drinks. Some were sitting at tables, others were standing in small groups, and still others were on lounge chairs. The ladies wore large hats and light-colored dresses, while the men were in summer suits and brimmed hats. It was a festive, happy crowd. I recognized a few from the Astors' dinner the night before, but there were others I didn't know.

"Finally," Nancy said as she left a group of people and joined us. "Now the weekend can start."

We greeted our hostess and allowed her to introduce us to several of her guests. I was surprised to see Sir Bryant Rothschild and his Italian wife, Bianca, among the group. I wasn't aware that the Rothschilds were friends with the Astors.

But it was Charles and Anne Lindbergh whom I was most eager to see. The famous aviator and his wife had been living in England for the past three years, having left America after their first-born son, Charles Jr., was kidnapped out of their home and found dead in a wooded area less than five miles away a couple months later. The press had been unbearable, forcing the Lindberghs to flee for the safety of their second child.

"Colonel Lindbergh," Papa said as the Lindberghs rose from their place at a wrought iron table to greet my parents. "It's good to see you again."

I'd seen Charles Lindbergh the day he received the Distinguished

Flying Cross medal from President Calvin Coolidge eleven years ago. I had only been twelve years old as Mama, Papa, Lydia, and I had stood on the makeshift stage under the Washington Memorial with hundreds of thousands of people watching. Charles Lindbergh had been the first person to fly solo nonstop across the Atlantic Ocean in 1927, and the world had not been the same since. He'd gone on to promote aviation and had married Anne Morrow, an American ambassador's daughter, two years later.

His famous airplane, *The Spirit of St. Louis*, hung in the North Hall of the Arts and Industries Building at the Smithsonian. I walked under it every day.

"It's good to see you, too, General Voland," Lindbergh said. He was a tall, thin man, known for his good looks and private demeanor. "I was surprised when we learned that you and your family would be in London." He motioned to the woman standing beside him. "This is my wife, Anne."

Anne was just as quiet and reserved as Charles, though she was dwarfed in comparison to his height. She shook my hand and then Mama's before smiling at Papa. It was hard to imagine what her life had been like since the kidnapping of her son. But one of the reasons they'd come to England was to stay out of the limelight and not talk about it—so I wouldn't. But she was an author, with two books about the famous flights she and her husband had taken, and I hoped to talk to her about them.

"Ever since I heard you'd be here, I've been eager to discuss an opportunity with you," Lindbergh said to Papa. "I've recently made two trips to Germany at the invitation of the American military attaché in Berlin to inspect the Luftwaffe."

The Luftwaffe was the aerial warfare branch of the German military—something Papa had spoken about often since it became known that Germany was rearming themselves despite their agreement not to do so after the Great War.

"It's been fascinating to see their aircraft and factories," Lindbergh continued. "I've sent reports back to Washington, but I'd like to return to Berlin to see more of their aircraft factories and get a better understanding of their capabilities. I would appreciate your perspective, if you'd like to join me."

I looked to Papa, expecting him to decline the invitation. If Mama thought England was a dangerous place right now, Germany was far worse.

But I didn't see fear or even concern in Papa's face. What I saw was excitement. "You'd like me to join you in Berlin?"

"I think we could both help the US by offering our opinions on Germany's airpower. My report didn't seem to alarm President Roosevelt, but if he had another respected member of the US Army Air Corps take a look, perhaps we could persuade him that we're not in a place to fight Hitler at this time."

Mama's eyes widened as she looked at Papa. I knew what she was thinking—what she would say to him later. She would not be pleased with the invitation, or the fact that he seemed to consider it.

"Take your time in deciding," Lindbergh said. "I won't be going for several weeks. But it would be good to have you."

"I've gone with him," Anne said to Mama, her voice just as quiet and unassuming as her gentle appearance. "It's a marvelous city, and I plan to return with Charles on his next trip. Perhaps you'd like to join us, as well, Mrs. Voland."

Mama offered a tight smile, though I could tell she had no intention of accepting the invitation, even if it had come from the Lindberghs.

My gaze shifted to Sir Rothschild and Calan, who were speaking with Sir Rothschild's wife, Bianca. When Calan caught my eye, he motioned for me to join them.

"You've met?" Sir Rothschild asked as I entered their small group.

"At the Astors' townhome, last night," Calan said.

"Do you mind working with an American woman?" Bianca Rothschild asked in an Italian accent.

Calan grinned. "Not when she's such an attractive and intelligent one."

"Now, none of that." Sir Rothschild's voice was serious. "You two need to remain professional at all times."

"But we're not at work right now," Calan protested. "And what happens at Cliveden stays at Cliveden. Isn't that right, Nancy?"

Nancy was just passing by, but she stopped and said, "Quite."

My cheeks warmed as Calan met my gaze again, though I suspected he was a rake and only trying to make me blush. I'd had my head turned a few times before, but I wasn't planning to have it happen now. The next few months would be too complicated as it was—and for some reason, each time my mind wandered, it landed on an entirely different man. One who was living next door to me in 1888. A man who had frustrated me endlessly for the past fourteen years, but one who was starting to intrigue me instead.

A man who called me Kate.

The conversation shifted from one topic to another, inevitably landing on one of the more popular subjects that had most of England—and the world—talking.

"Do you think Hitler is dangerous?" Calan asked the group at large.

"I think Hitler is necessary," Nancy said with a decisive nod. "He stands between us and the Communist Soviet Union. Joseph Stalin is the real danger."

"I can't imagine that's a popular opinion," Calan said, though he didn't seem surprised that she'd said it.

"It's the truth." Nancy set her empty glass on the tray of a passing footman and took another.

"There are things to be admired about Hitler," Sir Rothschild said, surprising me. "He's organized, focused, and has the German people's best interest in mind."

I had not heard anyone praise Hitler. On the contrary, I'd heard nothing but concern and dismay among my friends back home.

"I've heard Lindbergh speak of Germany's strength," Sir Rothschild continued. "I agree with Lindbergh. We shouldn't try to anger Hitler. It would be like stirring up a bee's nest."

"Then you favor appeasing him," Calan said. "Giving him what he wants? You had no problem with him taking control of Austria, or wanting the Sudetenland in Czechoslovakia?"

"I say, let the Czechs decide."

"But they don't want to be annexed by Germany," Calan said.

Sir Rothschild shrugged as he offered his arm to Bianca, apparently ready to leave the conversation. "It is not our concern. Let the Czechs worry about Hitler."

Calan met my gaze, and I feared he'd ask me my opinion, but I wasn't in a place to give one. I didn't know enough about European politics to share my thoughts.

It was concerning enough to learn that Sir Rothschild and Nancy Astor were in favor of Hitler.

After supper, the party gathered in the north drawing room, which was decorated with dark-paneled walls, deep red upholstery, and a beautiful stone fireplace that dominated one wall. The room was large enough to easily accommodate the eighteen guests the Astors had invited for the weekend. Though it was an informal gathering and Nancy insisted upon everyone using their first names, we'd all dressed for supper, and the wealth in the room was apparent with all the fine clothing and jewelry.

It was as far removed from Whitechapel in 1888 as one could get.

There were several tables set up to play cards or games, and I found myself at a table with Calan to play mah-jongg. The Chinese tile game had become popular in the United States in the 1920s and was still all the rage in England.

"I really shouldn't be playing games," I said to Calan, who had been a charming dinner partner again that evening. "I have so much work to do."

"You Americans," he said in his Scottish brogue. "You work too much."

"We only have two months to pull the exhibit together."

"Two months is plenty of time."

"I don't usually go into a project without knowing something about the subject, and until I came here, I knew very little about Jack the Ripper."

"What would you like to know?" he asked as he began to stack his tiles.

"Do you know who did it?"

Calan shook his head. "I don't know who did it, but I think I know who covered it up."

"Really? Who?"

He finally looked up and leaned forward, lowering his voice. "Tell me what the police commissioner, police surgeons, chief inspector, coroner, several journalists, the city solicitor, several members of Parliament, and the prince of England all had in common in 1888?"

I lifted my eyebrows, waiting.

"They were all Freemasons."

My mouth slowly parted as I absorbed the information. "The chief of police—"

"Almost everyone who was in a position of power or authority during the investigation of Jack the Ripper was a high-ranking member of Freemasonry," Calan said quietly, glancing at the next table to see if anyone was listening. When he looked back at me, he said, "Even Prince Albert Victor himself was a Grand Master of the Freemasons. In the 1870s, Prime Minister Benjamin Disraeli said, 'Royalty cannot survive without Freemasonry, and Freemasonry cannot survive without Royalty.'"

"Who were the Freemasons?"

"You mean, who *are* they. The Freemasons are a secret fraternal society that started to become powerful in England in the 1700s. Different histories link them to the original stonemason of King Solmon's Temple in Jerusalem, Hiram Abiff. Their membership is not secret, but their rituals are, though I've done enough research to have an idea as to their activities."

My curiosity was piqued. "And you think the Freemasons covered up the identity of Jack the Ripper? Why?"

"Because if Jack was one of them, they were honor bound to protect him."

"Why?"

"If the killings were linked to a Freemason, or it became obvious that the other Masons were destroying evidence to keep his identity a secret, the entire society would crack open—and no one was more worried about that than the prince of England, who needed Freemasonry to survive. The Freemasons have unthinkable power in unity, and the prince couldn't lose that power."

"But who was Jack?" I asked.

"I don't know. They've buried the truth too deeply." He continued to lay out his tiles. "Anything that could point to the truth was destroyed or hidden."

It was an intriguing theory. "Do you really think Freemasonry has so much power?"

"I know it does. The world headquarters are in London, but there are over a million Freemasons still active around the world, and they have a secret network of power, for good and for evil." His face was so serious, I couldn't look away. "The Freemasons have always fascinated me, especially because of their connection to Jack the Ripper, so I have visited the headquarters myself, which are open to the public. I discovered a book called *England's Masonic Pioneers*, written by a man named Dudley Wright. He claims that one of the oaths a Freemason makes upon his entry into the secret society is, I quote, to 'hide and conceal and cover all the sins, frailties, and errors of every Brother to the upmost of my power.'"

I looked down at the mah-jongg tiles, trying to wrap my mind around what Calan was saying. Could his theory be correct? Had the Freemasons covered up the identity of Jack the Ripper? If the prince of England was involved, and the police commissioner, and even members of Parliament, then there wouldn't have been any trouble keeping the truth hidden.

"There are still powerful people in Freemasonry," Calan said quietly, "perhaps even men in this room, so tread lightly."

I nodded, glancing around the room. I'd never spoken to anyone about Freemasonry before, though I had heard it mentioned a time or two.

"The police commissioner, Sir Charles Warren, was responsible for leading a group to the Temple Mount in Jerusalem in 1874," Calan said as he crossed his arms.

My head came up quickly. "Jerusalem in 1874?"

Calan nodded.

Mine and Austen's parents had gone to Jerusalem in 1874. It was there that Austen's parents had been killed. Had they gone with Sir Charles Warren?

"The Temple Mount is the center of all Masonic legends," Calan continued. "It's there that Solomon's Temple was built. And the builder of the temple was a master artisan and mason, Hiram Abiff, the first Grand Master of the Freemason."

Had my parents gone to Jerusalem because of the Temple Mount? And, if they had, could my father be a Freemason?

"Ah, there you are," Nancy said as she approached our table, a bright smile on her face. "Mah-jongg. How marvelous. I'll find another player, and we can make it a foursome."

Our conversation came to an end, but I couldn't stop thinking about what Calan had said—or the fact that Father and Mother had gone to Jerusalem in 1874. It might be a coincidence, or it might not. But I would need to find out.

Later that evening, I left the drawing room with my parents. Their room was next to mine, so we climbed the grand staircase together. I wanted to talk to them about Freemasonry, but Mama had something else in mind.

"You're not really considering Colonel Lindbergh's invitation, are you?" she asked Papa.

"I'm not going to lie, Grace," Papa said. "The thought interests me. And Lindbergh assures me it's safe. He wouldn't ask Anne to go if it wasn't. The American military attaché wouldn't invite Lindbergh, or any other military personnel, if it was dangerous."

We walked down the long hall toward our rooms, and Papa took

Mama's hand in his. "I won't go if you don't want me to, but I don't want to miss this opportunity. If I can help America prepare for whatever lies ahead, then I want to do my part."

I stopped at my door and said goodnight, but I knew their conversation would continue as they went to their own room.

My room was cool as I entered and flipped on the light. A window was open, allowing in a soft breeze.

I went to the window and looked at the River Thames, glistening under the bright moon. My thoughts were so full tonight, but I couldn't wait to get back to 1888 and find out if my father was a Freemason. I wasn't sure how that might help me find my sister, but if all the people in power surrounding Jack the Ripper were Freemasons, then perhaps there was something to it. And if all the victims were somehow linked, could they be involved with the Freemasons, too?

It was an interesting theory to consider.

9

LONDON, ENGLAND SEPTEMBER 8, 1888

Our townhouse was warm and crowded that Saturday evening as I stood near Father and Mother by the front door, greeting guests. Mother's laughter was only reserved for nights such as this, and it was so unnatural to my ears that it made me tense each time I heard it. She was a lovely woman with dark red hair like mine, and clear, beautiful skin, especially for her age. She stood next to Father with pride and thrived on hosting events like this one. They filled her days with purpose, especially when she could highlight a favorite performer or artist.

"Ah, there you are!" Mother said with a cry of delight when a tall, handsome man entered the front door of our townhome. He looked to be in his early thirties and carried himself with the suave confidence of a performer. "Mr. Maybrick, how good of you to come."

Michael Maybrick was one of the most renowned composers and performers in Europe. We had seen him on stage at the London Opera House the year before. Mother had been trying to get him to come to her dinner parties ever since.

Mr. Maybrick bowed deeply before Mother as many of her guests turned to see the famous musician. "It is a pleasure to be in your home, Mrs. Kelly."

Mother's cheeks filled with color as she allowed him to kiss her hand. Then she turned to me, her eager expression telling me all I needed to know. Mr. Maybrick was single, and Mother would use any excuse she could to push me in front of an eligible bachelor. "Mr. Maybrick, may I present my daughter *Miss* Kathryn Kelly?"

He took my hand and bowed over it. "It is an honor to meet you, Miss Kelly."

I curtseyed and smiled. "And you, Mr. Maybrick."

When he straightened, he offered a dashing smile and his gaze lingered on me for a moment before he tore it away to be introduced to some of Mother's friends.

I stepped back, happy to be out of the spotlight for a moment. My corset had been pulled especially tight tonight, and I struggled to catch my breath. Pungent perfume cloyed the air, and the extravagant jewelry and clothing in the room made me feel uncomfortable. I was wearing one of the most expensive—and exquisite—gowns I'd ever owned. It was a House of Worth creation, sent from Paris for this event and made of the finest gold silk I'd ever seen, with dark purple silk embroidery along the bodice and the skirt.

But all the finery only made me think about Mary even more. She'd been raised with the same wealth and privilege, the same set of skills. How was she surviving on her own? Was working as a charwoman enough? Or had she resorted to taking a male companion to help pay for her room and board? Was she a night worker, as Mrs. Barnett called prostitutes?

The very thought made a shiver run up my spine. I couldn't imagine such a life for Mary.

At the appointed hour, Mother allowed Mr. Maybrick to escort her up the stairs and into the drawing room. It was the largest of the rooms in our home, and all the furniture had been moved to the attic to allow everyone to fit inside.

Father offered me his arm to escort me upstairs. It was the first time we had been within speaking distance since I'd woken up that morning, and it might be the only chance I would get.

"Do you know anything about the Freemasons?" I asked him.

His footsteps faltered, and he almost tripped as he turned his face toward me. "What do you know of the Freemasons?"

"Very little."

"Why would you think I know something about them?"

How was I supposed to answer that? He would never believe me if I told him the truth. "I'm just curious. I have heard it whispered that most of the powerful and influential men in London are Freemasons, so that made me think you might be."

His chest puffed out just a bit with pride, but he frowned at me. "It's no secret that I'm a Freemason, though I rarely talk about it outside of my meetings."

It was my turn to miss a step, but I held tight to him as we continued up the stairs. "Is that why you went to Jerusalem? To the Temple Mount?"

I'm certain he would have stopped on the stairs had there not been people behind us. "This isn't the time or place for that conversation, Kathryn. And it really doesn't concern you."

Every time I was told that something didn't concern me, it meant I had hit on something important.

Father left my side the moment we entered the drawing room, and I was certain it was because he didn't want me to ask him any more questions.

After everyone quieted, Mother went to the front of the room and introduced Mr. Maybrick.

The audience clapped politely as Mr. Maybrick took his place. He wore a thick mustache and had combed his hair back into a shine. He caught my eye and dipped his head in my direction, causing several people to look at me and smile.

Soon, Mr. Maybrick was entrancing the audience with "Nancy

Lee," "Midshipmite," and "They All Love Jack," one of his more recent compositions—and one that hit too close to home. That morning, Annie Chapman's body had been found in the small, enclosed yard at 29 Hanbury Street, and the reporters had gone wild with the news. The police surgeon had immediately linked it to Polly Nichols's murder because both women had died in the same manner, their throats slit from ear to ear and their bodies mutilated. However, Annie's had been even worse than Polly's. She'd been disemboweled, and portions of her intestines had been placed over her right shoulder. I'd heard some people whispering about it tonight, but polite society wasn't discussing it like they would in Whitechapel.

Mr. Maybrick's performance came to an end, and everyone clapped, then it was time to begin the dance. Mother whispered into his ear, and he nodded and smiled, then came to me and offered his hand.

"May I have this dance?" he asked.

"Of course." I couldn't say no, not with everyone watching. "Your performance was wonderful," I said with a genuine smile. "My mother seems very pleased."

He took me into his arms for the dance and returned my smile, pulling me a little too close. "I hope my singing pleased you, as well."

His behavior and tone made me uncomfortable, but I said, "Of course."

The three-string orchestra began to play a waltz, and Mr. Maybrick twirled me around the room with confidence. As we passed the entrance to the drawing room, a new arrival caught my attention. He was handsome and stylish, but there were so many people and we moved so fast, I didn't have a chance to catch his eye. He was probably another of Mother's bachelors, invited to try to convince me to get married. Others were taking notice of him, too, as people turned their heads to look in his direction.

Mr. Maybrick was entertaining as we danced, complimenting

my abilities, though I wasn't under any illusion that I was especially talented.

As the night progressed, I danced with each of the men on my dance card, making small talk, trying not to yawn or show my boredom. I looked for the stranger who had caught my eye before, but he remained elusive. No doubt he would appear at the appointed time, if my mother had anything to do with it.

When it was time for me to take a break, I slipped out of the drawing room and made my way to the back stairway, needing some time alone. The courtyard beckoned, and I wanted to escape before someone stopped me.

The night was cool, and the air was crisp as I stepped outside. Several of the windows were open on the second floor, allowing the faint strains of the orchestra to drift outside. A clear sky offered a brilliant view of the stars, and there were torches lit around the courtyard, though they offered scant light.

"I was hoping you'd come out here," a deep male voice said from a corner of the courtyard, drawing my gaze down to earth again. "I hate crowds."

The man I'd glimpsed earlier was sitting on a stone bench, and the soft glow of torchlight illuminated his handsome features. His voice was Austen's, but his appearance was unfamiliar.

"Austen?" I asked as he rose and walked across the courtyard.

His transformation was remarkable. With no beard, he looked ten years younger—more like the boy I'd once known—though there was nothing boyish about Austen Baird.

He'd had a haircut, as well, and his evening clothes were fashionable and new.

My lips parted as he walked toward me, and my pulse began to pound in a way it had never pounded before.

I was suddenly aware of everything about Austen—the way he moved, the way he looked at me, the way my entire body responded to his presence. I was reminded of how he'd reacted when I kissed his cheek and the strange words he'd said to me in Whitechapel afterward. That if I didn't know why I shouldn't have kissed him, then he wouldn't bother explaining.

I was suddenly very aware of why I shouldn't have kissed Austen Baird.

We were no longer children.

The innocence that had once cocooned our relationship had fallen away, creating a sense of vulnerability that overwhelmed me. Our previous intimacy was meant for children, not grown adults.

How had I been so naïve?

This was a man—a handsome, mysterious, intriguing man.

The closer he came, the more aware I was of this truth, and I began to back up on instinct. It was as if a veil was lifted, and I could see clearly for the first time.

I didn't know him anymore, not really, and that made me feel breathless. Excited.

Terrified.

When he stopped in front of me, I could only stare.

"Don't look at me that way," he said, his voice low, almost pleading.

I swallowed. "How am I looking at you?"

"As if you don't know me."

"I'm afraid I don't."

When he reached for my hand, it sent a shock up my arm and my gaze locked on his.

We stared at each other for a moment before he led me to the bench he'd just occupied and we took a seat. I was conscious of his leg pressed against mine, the smell of his cologne, and the way my hand still tingled from his touch.

We were both quiet for a moment, and my breath began to return to its normal rhythm, though my heart was still hammering.

"You came," I finally whispered, clasping my gloved hands in my lap.

"I couldn't stay away," he said just as quietly.

He didn't need to explain what he meant. Something had drawn Austen and me together since we were children. An invisible force that neither of us could deny, though he had tried for years. Even when we were not together, I was always conscious of him, wanting to see him, be near him, hear his voice.

It was almost as if . . .

He turned to me as the truth pressed against my heart, and my mouth parted in surprise again.

The thing that he couldn't tell me, and I had never allowed myself to acknowledge, was now as obvious as the rising sun, shedding light on every part of my life.

I was in love with Austen Baird.

"Kate—"

I stood, my breath shallow as panic overwhelmed me. I couldn't love Austen. I wasn't staying in 1888. And, even if I wanted to, I couldn't. Not if I was going to save my sister.

He also stood, and the anguish in his eyes finally made sense. His behavior toward me these past fourteen years wasn't because he was mourning his parents' loss. He'd been pushing me away because he was heartbroken. He was in love with me, and I had not returned his affection.

Had not given him a chance.

"Why?" I asked, almost angry.

"Why what?"

"Why didn't you tell me?"

Austen stared at me, his emotions raw and intense as they crossed his handsome face. "What did you want me to say? That the day you told me you were leaving this path was the worst day of my life?" He took a step closer to me, years of disappointment tightening his voice. "That I've tried to push you away every day since then, and I hate myself because I still yearn for you? That even when I'm in Italy, or India, or France burying myself in work, I can't forget you?" He put his hands on my cheeks as he lowered his voice. "That my pulse beats faster every time you're near and my heart longs for a glimpse of you, a touch of your hand, or a whisper of your voice?"

I couldn't breathe. I couldn't think.

He stepped closer to me, and my senses were overwhelmed.

"That when you kissed my cheek the other day," he said as his face lowered to mine, "it took all my willpower not to pull you into my arms and kiss you until this madness inside of me subsided and I could think clearly for the first time in fourteen years?" He stared deeply into my eyes. "Is that what you wanted me to tell you, Kate? That the only reason I returned to London was to try to convince you to love me, too?"

I was trembling, and tears filled my eyes. I was in love with Austen, but knowing he loved me—accepting the truth after years of denial—brought such profound grief, I felt like I might suffocate.

He was breathing hard, but when I didn't answer him, he pulled back, his emotions retreating behind the wall of anger and indifference he hid behind. His hands fell to his sides in defeat. "That's what I thought. Those weren't the things you wanted me to tell you."

"Pardon me," said a male voice behind us. "Am I interrupting a tryst?"

My heart was pounding so hard, I was afraid I might pass out as I turned and found Mr. Maybrick standing behind us.

There was a light of humor in his eyes until his gaze caught Austen's, and then all humor fled.

Austen stiffened, and his jaw tightened.

I didn't know what to say or do, so I motioned to Austen and said to Mr. Maybrick, "This is my—my neighbor, Mr. Austen—"

"Baird," Mr. Maybrick finished as he advanced toward us. "How are you, Austen?"

"You two know each other?" I asked as I looked at Austen.

"We belong to the same club, don't we, old chum?" Mr. Maybrick asked Austen.

Austen didn't smile, nor acknowledge that he knew Mr. Maybrick.

I was again at a loss, my mind swirling with Austen's declaration and Mr. Maybrick's presence, so I said the first thing that came to mind. "I didn't know you had a club, Austen."

"I don't," he said, his breathing still erratic as he looked at Mr. Maybrick.

"He could, if he wanted one." Mr. Maybrick smiled, though it didn't quite reach his eyes. "It's not really a club, but a secret society, a brotherhood. I'm a proud member, and Austen should be, too. His family has a long history of membership. It's a shame he doesn't want to join in the fun."

My eyes widened as I stared at Austen. "Is he speaking of the Freemasons?"

Without even looking at me, Austen nodded.

"Your family were Freemasons?" I asked, shocked.

"Not only were they Freemasons," Mr. Maybrick said, "but his father was a Grand Master, of the highest order. He died defending the Brotherhood in Jerusalem at the Temple Mount."

My heart thudded as all the pieces started to fall together. I couldn't be more surprised—though Austen's face was devoid of emotion, suggesting that he knew all this information. I'd always thought his parents were accosted by robbers, but had his father truly been defending the Freemasons? How?

"You look surprised, Miss Kelly," Mr. Maybrick said. "I thought perhaps you knew, since your parents were on the same trip, excavating Solomon's Temple in search of the great secrets of the Knights Templar."

"That's why they went?" I asked and turned to Austen. "Did you know?"

Austen's cheek muscles twitched as he continued to stare at Mr. Maybrick, but he offered a slight nod, acknowledging my question.

"I hate to be the one to tell you," Mr. Maybrick said, though he didn't seem contrite. "But, perhaps now that you know, you might convince Mr. Baird to join his rightful place with us." He looked from Austen to me, his lips curling up in a half smile. "Since it seems you two are close."

Austen lifted his chin but didn't respond.

"Your mother sent me out to retrieve you, Miss Kelly," Mr. Maybrick said as he offered me his arm. "Shall we?"

I stood between Austen and Mr. Maybrick, unsure what to do. There were so many things Austen and I needed to discuss.

But he made the choice for me.

"Goodnight, Miss Kelly." Austen gave a stiff bow and then turned and walked toward the hedge, disappearing into the night.

10

LONDON, ENGLAND
SEPTEMBER 15, 1938

It had been a week since I'd seen Austen, but whether I was in 1888 or 1938, thoughts of him and our night in the garden shadowed everything. Duffy told me that he had left London the morning after the ball, but no one knew where he had gone, or when he might be back. My heart ached not knowing. I wanted to talk to him, ask him if he had truly returned to London to convince me to love him, because his behavior up until the night in the garden suggested otherwise.

The day was bright and warm as I walked from Lancaster House toward the Café Royal on Regent Street, where I would meet Mama and Papa for lunch. The air was thick with tension as people mobilized for potential war. Hitler had given a speech during the final hours of the Nuremburg Rally three days before, indicating his intention to annex the Sudetenland, a part of Czechoslovakia that was home to three and a half million Germans, regardless of whether they wanted to be annexed to Germany or not. England held no obligation to help Czechoslovakia, but France did, and England was obligated to help France should she go to war. No one wanted another war, and least of all the English prime minister,

Neville Chamberlain. He'd boarded an airplane that morning to fly to Germany to negotiate with Hitler.

The entire country—the world—held their breath.

Men calling out instructions as they dug trenches in St. James's Park was disconcerting, but even more so were the lines of people waiting outside the London Library in St. James Square waiting to get fitted for their gas masks. Everyone over the age of four would receive one, and they were urged to carry it with them both day and night, no matter where they went. I carried mine like a purse, inside a box with a strap to wear over my shoulder. I'd been fitted for it just yesterday.

I knew war was coming from my grandmother, Maggie, who had told us about the Second World War, but I didn't know details. She'd spoken of being in Pearl Harbor in December of 1941, when she was a nurse on a hospital ship. She had said America entered the fight after that. I had assumed the war wouldn't start until then, and that Mama and Papa and I would be safe in London for a couple of months.

Now I wasn't so sure.

It took me about fifteen minutes to walk to the Café Royal. Mama and Papa were waiting for me inside the opulent restaurant, sitting at a little table in the corner, their faces serious as they conversed.

"There you are," Mama said, offering me a smile as Papa stood and pulled a chair out for me.

"I'm sorry I'm late." I smiled, trying to ease her worries. "I got caught up in my work."

Calan and I had been busy discussing the items we wanted to display at the London Museum and how we wanted the exhibit to look. I hadn't even begun to sift through the hundreds of letters that had been sent to the Metropolitan Police in 1888, many purporting to be written by the killer.

"This was a wonderful suggestion," Papa said as he motioned to the room. It was decorated with a heavy Victorian influence, thick gilded trim, mirrors, and plush furniture. The tables were covered in white cloths, with dripping candles in the center.

"I've eaten here many times in 1888," I told them. "It's a popular restaurant for society."

We looked over the menu and placed our orders with the waiter, and then my parents looked at each other before turning to me. Mama wore a pretty, brick-red dress with a matching hat which partially covered her face, though I could still see her concern.

"You want to go home," I said, not even asking. I could see it written all over their faces.

Mama sighed and spoke quietly. "I don't know enough about what will happen here, Kathryn. We thought we had time. But the war could start any day and then we might be stuck here until it's over."

"The safest place will be in America," Papa added, his French accent thickening with his concern.

"I can't leave, not yet. I need firsthand access to the Ripper case to help Mary. And we're just starting to lay out the design for the exhibit. I still have weeks left of work."

"We might not have weeks left to get out of England," Mama said. "Nothing is more important than your safety."

My heart was already heavy with disappointment and sadness in 1888. I couldn't face it here, too.

"You two should go," I told them. "I'll stay."

"Kathryn." Papa shook his head. "We won't leave you with the threat of war hanging over Europe."

"I can't go. I have an obligation to the museum. Besides, we don't know if the war will start now or later. And if Hitler invades the Sudetenland, we'd still have time to get out of England before anything happened here. Please. Let me have more time."

They looked at each other again, and Mama lifted a shoulder.

"Fine," Papa said, "but if there's even a hint of danger, we will be on a ship heading home within hours. Do you understand?"

I nodded, wishing I felt relieved. But the threat of war, and of going home sooner than we planned, was daunting. I wanted to finish what I started, but more importantly, if I left, I wouldn't have access to the evidence from the Jack the Ripper case. There were still so many unanswered questions. I had been to the Crime Museum several times, but I hadn't scratched the surface of records, letters, and transcripts from the inquests into each murder.

I played with my water glass, lost in thought, when I felt Mama's hand over mine.

"Have you heard from Austen?"

I shook my head as I nibbled my bottom lip, not wanting to look at her. I had told my parents that Austen left, but I hadn't told them about our conversation in the garden or learning about how his parents had died. I was still trying to understand it all myself. "Duffy inquired, but not even Brinley knows where he went."

"I'm sorry," she said, and then she put her hand on my shoulder, drawing my gaze to hers. "I know something happened, Kathryn. You've never been this upset when he's left in the past."

I usually shared everything with my parents, and I trusted their wisdom, but I wasn't sure what they would say about this. I took a deep breath and said, "I—I think I'm in love with Austen." I swallowed the emotions that came with the confession. "And I know he's in love with me."

My parents didn't speak for a moment, so I finally lifted my gaze.

There was a sad smile on Mama's face. "You're just now realizing what we've suspected for years."

I blinked and frowned. "What? You knew?"

"I *suspected*," Mama corrected. "At least on his part, based on what you've told me. It was your feelings for him that I wasn't sure about. You've always spoken of him as more of a brother, but I noticed a shift in the past year, the longer he stayed away."

I leaned back in my chair and crossed my arms, trying not to cry. "He was so upset when he left the other night—and now I don't know where he is or if he'll come back."

"He'll be back," Papa said. "*C'est l'amour*. It's love, Kathryn."

"But he knows we can't be together."

"Why not?" Mama asked.

I stared at her, frowning. "What do you mean?"

"Why can't you be together?"

"Because." I was at a loss for words. "Because I'm staying here."

"Plans can change."

Frustration and sadness and anger bubbled up inside of me. "I fought hard to get my job at the Smithsonian, and I love my work there. My life in 1888 is full of restrictions and expectations and—and—" I was at a loss, because suddenly all the reasons for choosing 1938 seemed to pale in comparison to the love I felt for Austen. I could still follow my passion for history in 1888, and I had my teaching at Toynbee Hall. It wasn't the same as the prestige I felt at the Smithsonian, but what was the praise of several men compared to the true love of one?

Mama took my hand. "We might make plans, but God is the one who determines our steps. His plans are far better than ours."

"You've always liked to make plans, so your mind was made up," Papa said. "Sometimes, plans need to be flexible to see what God wants for us."

He was right. I hated indecision and uncertainty. Sometimes I made decisions and plans far too soon simply because I didn't like not knowing. Even if I later regretted my choices, I stuck to them with stubborn determination.

But this was different—except that it wasn't. "I'm planning to save Mary, if need be, so none of this matters. I will have to forfeit 1888."

"What if the Mary Jane Kelly you're looking for isn't your sister?" Papa asked. "What then? Will you still give up 1888 and Austen?"

Sweat began to form down the crevice of my back as my pulse increased. Uncertainty made me feel panicked. I wanted to get up and pace away from the table, but I forced myself to stay seated. Every choice I made, in both of my lives, was because I knew I was staying in 1938. If I changed my plans now, I would have to rethink everything.

"You have time," Papa said as he put his hand on my arm. "Pray about it, Kathryn. Ask God what He wants you to do. And talk to Austen. Tell him how you feel."

"I don't think he'll ever talk to me again."

"Don't be so dramatic," Mama said. "He'll want to talk to you. But you need to be ready to open your heart to a new possibility."

"I thought you wanted me to stay here."

Mama dipped her chin to meet my gaze. "My greatest hope and prayer has always been that you would stay with us forever. Losing my sister in 1692 was one of the most devastating experiences of my life—but I've never regretted my choice. I know I'm where I belong, even though it wasn't what I had planned. Don't miss out on being in the middle of God's will just because you've set your mind and won't be open to other possibilities."

"If you love Austen," Papa said, "and you want to spend your life with him, then don't be afraid to choose 1888. But it's okay to choose 1938 and all the things you love here, too. Either way, Mama and I will understand. Don't let worries about us affect your choice."

Setting my mind had made so many things easier.

"This conversation might be pointless if the last Ripper victim is my sister," I said. "If it's Mary, then I'm sacrificing everything to save her. I couldn't live with myself if I didn't."

"You have time," Mama echoed Papa. "Mary Jane Kelly won't die for almost two more months. There's no need to rush toward a decision."

"I just wish I knew where my sister was," I said, trying not to let tears of frustration fill my eyes. "I can't take my parents' carriage to Miller's Court alone, and it wouldn't be wise to take a hired carriage there, either."

"Then use the time until Austen returns to do more investigating," Papa advised. "Find out if the Freemasons were involved, like you suspect. There are other things you can do outside of Whitechapel."

I nodded. "Perhaps then I can learn the Ripper's identity."

"Why? What would that accomplish?" Mama asked. "You can't reveal his name."

"No, but there's a part of me that *needs* to know. Are the

Freemasons connected? And is Father part of the coverup? If he tossed Mary onto the street and she becomes one of the victims, doesn't that seem suspect? I can't rest until I know the truth."

My parents shared a glance, and Mama said, "Be careful, Kathryn. That's all I'm asking."

"I will." I smiled, trying to reassure her.

I just wished I could reassure myself.

When I returned to the London Museum at Lancaster House after lunch, I had a newfound purpose. I needed to learn as much as I could about the next two murders—the Double Event—and see if there was a way I could get a glimpse of Jack the Ripper in person. Was he a prominent member of society? One I might recognize? And was he a Freemason? If so, then perhaps I could find out what his connection was to Mary Jane Kelly and the other women.

It was the opposite of promising to be careful.

Lancaster House was quiet. Most people were too occupied with the threat of war to spend their free time at a museum. They were busy building makeshift bomb shelters in their backyards and canning vegetables from their gardens and trying to decide if they should stay in London or leave for their country homes—if they were fortunate enough to have a country house.

"How was lunch?" Calan asked as I entered the office we were sharing.

"It was nice," I said, trying not to reveal the depth of my emotions. As I took off my hat and laid it on my desk, I asked, "What do you know about the Double Event?"

His eyebrows came up as he leaned back in his chair, a file in hand. "Hi, how are you? I'm fine."

"I'm sorry for being so abrupt." I took a seat, suddenly feeling weak and exhausted. "My parents are threatening to take me back to the States because of Hitler. I'm desperate to get this exhibit put together, but I haven't even completed all the research I need." It was only part of the reason I'd asked him about the Double Event, but it was the part he might understand.

He sat up in his chair, a frown marring his handsome face. "You're leaving?"

"Not yet, not if I can help it, but they're nervous."

"And rightly so." He had been looking over a file of letters that we borrowed from the Crime Museum, but he put them on the desk and gave me his full attention. "I don't want you to leave yet."

"I don't either."

"I was just getting up the nerve to ask you out." His mouth came up in a grin, and I knew he was teasing. Calan was a flirt with all the female staff at the museum, even Gloria, the seventy-year-old volunteer docent who gave tours of the Costume Gallery.

"Even if that were true," I told him, "my answer would be no."

"Which would only encourage me to keep trying," he said with a wink. "I love a good challenge."

I took a deep breath and said, "Do you know anything about the Double Event?"

He grew serious as he nodded. "I do."

"What can you tell me?"

He leaned his forearms against the top of the desk as he spoke. "The name of the first victim of the Double Event was Elizabeth Stride. She was born in Sweden and went to work as a domestic servant in Gothenburg, where she was arrested for prostitution and treated twice for, ah, diseases related to her profession. She also gave birth to a stillborn daughter, probably due to her health. She then came to London and tried to get a fresh start. She met and married a man named John Stride. He was from a wealthy family in Sheerness. His father—a Freemason, I might add—was a property owner, but he left nothing in his will to Elizabeth's husband. It was the final blow after several years of difficulty, and John and Elizabeth separated. Eventually, Elizabeth returned to her old trade and became the Ripper's third victim."

"John Stride's father was a Freemason?" I asked. "Was everyone a Freemason in 1888?"

Calan shook his head. "No, but usually the wealthy and powerful were part of the Brotherhood."

"Do you know anything about Elizabeth's murder?" I asked him.

"Around one in the morning on September 30th, her body was discovered in Dutfield's Yard by the steward of the International Working Men's Education Club, the building adjacent to the yard. It's believed that Jack had just slit Elizabeth's throat in the dark courtyard and was interrupted by the steward's arrival, because there were no other mutilations to her body.

"Less than an hour later, at 1:44 in the morning, Catherine Eddowes's body was discovered in Mitre Square, less than a mile away from Elizabeth Stride's body. But Jack wasn't interrupted during the second murder. He slit Catherine's throat and then mutilated her body, placing her intestines over her right shoulder. The lobe and part of her right ear were cut off and were not with the body, and her left kidney had been removed." He paused and let out a breath. "Also, her apron had been cut off and was no longer with the body. But it was found an hour later, bloodstained and resting at the bottom of the steps of a tenement building on Goulston Street, a ten-minute walk from Mitre Square. The officer who found it said it had not been there thirty minutes before when he'd been by on his beat. Above the apron, on the side of the building, was a message written in chalk that said, 'The Juwes are the men that will not be blamed for nothing.'"

I had heard about all of this, but it was all starting to take shape in a different way. "The Juwes?" I asked.

"J-U-W-E-S. Some think it was a misspelling of Jews and referenced the Jewish immigrants in the area who had been flooding into Whitechapel since 1880, fleeing persecution in eastern Europe and Russia. There was a lot of antisemitism, and many believed Jack the Ripper was a Jewish immigrant, not accepting that he could be English."

"What do you think?" I asked him.

"I think it had something to do with the Freemasons. You see, in Freemason legend, Hiram Abiff, the first stone mason who built King Solomon's temple, was assassinated by three jealous craftsmen. Their names were Jubela, Jubelo, and Jubelum. The first assassin, Jubela, was not able to learn Hiram's masonry secrets, so he struck Hiram across the throat. Hiram got away, but he was accosted by Jubelo next, who struck him across the breast when Hiram refused to answer his questions. Again, Hiram got away, but was confronted by the third assassin, Jubelum, who struck him on the head, giving Hiram the fatal blow. Not long after, King Solomon realized that Hiram was dead and had his assassins brought to justice. Jubela's throat was cut from ear to ear, like all the Ripper's victims. Jubelo's breast was torn open, like the Ripper's victims, and his heart and vitals taken out and thrown over his left shoulder. Jubelum's body was severed in two and his bowels burnt to ashes, which is what the Ripper did to Mary Jane Kelly's organs in her room at Miller's Court."

A shiver ran up my spine at that last comment.

"All I know is that until then," Calan continued, "the police commissioner, Sir Charles Warren, had not gone to Whitechapel to investigate any of the murder sites. But that night, he made his way to Whitechapel to inspect the chalk graffito on the wall—and he promptly had it washed clean before it could be photographed and used for evidence."

"Wasn't there an uproar when he erased the message?" I asked.

"Yes. But Warren claimed he was trying to prevent retaliation against the Jews living in Whitechapel. Though, why the police couldn't keep the alley clear while they waited for a photograph is the biggest mystery. When his claim to prevent a riot wasn't accepted, the police tried to say that the chalk graffito had nothing to do with the killings and that the apron, which proved to belong to Catherine Eddowes, was thrown there casually by the killer. Though the copper who found it said neither piece of evidence had been there half an hour before it was discovered."

"The first murder in the Double Event was undertaken in a more public location," I said, almost to myself, "but it was interrupted. So the killer went to a different location and found his second victim."

"Exactly."

"And do we know what Elizabeth Stride was doing before she was murdered in Dutfield's Yard?"

"According to witnesses, a man and woman were seen standing together for almost half an hour in the rain across the road from Dutfield's Yard around twelve-thirty. Some say they had been at a grocer's just a few doors down from Dutfield's purchasing grapes. Original reports, given to the newspapers from those who were there, said that pits from the grapes were found in Dutfield's Yard and there were grapes clutched in Elizabeth's hands, but the official witnesses that were chosen to give testimony said nothing about the grapes. The man who owned the grocery story said that he had seen the couple, even talked to the man, but he was never brought in to give testimony."

"Why not?" I asked.

Calan gave me a look. "Because then Jack might have been identified—and that wouldn't look good for the Freemasons if the killer was linked to them."

"Do you believe the Freemason theory, then?"

"Given the information I've gathered over the years, I wouldn't be surprised."

I nibbled my bottom lip as I thought through the things Calan had said. If it was true that Jack and Elizabeth stood in the rain across from Dutfield's Yard for half an hour—and that it was a public space—I could easily position myself to get a good look at Jack on the 30th of September without being noticed.

But it wouldn't be safe to go alone, especially so late at night. And it might be almost impossible to get away from my parents without raising suspicion.

There had to be a way, though, and I was going to find it.

11

LONDON, ENGLAND
SEPTEMBER 22, 1888

The carriage was dark and cold as I rode to the West End with Father and Mother a week after my conversation with Papa and Mama at Café Royal, and two weeks since I'd seen Austen in the garden. We drove through Green Park, near Buckingham Palace, and onto the Strand toward our destination.

"Do you think this is wise?" Mother asked Father as she looked out the window at the dark street.

"You've had these tickets for an age," Father said in a dry tone.

"But I purchased them before—before—" She floundered. "Before all this madness. You know what they're saying, don't you?"

My parents sat stiff on their seats across from one another, both dressed in their fine evening clothes. Mother wore glittering diamonds at her ears and throat. She swallowed several times as she looked out the window, while Father sat stoic and undeterred.

"I've heard all the rumors," Father said. "And it's nonsense."

"But they've said that Mr. Mansfield's transformation from a doctor to a monster is uncanny."

"Mansfield is an actor, hired to portray both Dr. Jekyll and Mr. Hyde," Father said with little emotion. "If he wasn't good at transforming from one character to another, he wouldn't have been hired."

I sat quietly beside Mother in a Worth gown, watching the street pass, my own trepidation about seeing the play and being out at night making me silent. The story of Dr. Jekyll and Mr. Hyde had taken the world by storm and the play had been a smash hit on Broadway and the West End. But many people were starting to worry that perhaps the story had inspired Jack the Ripper—or worse, that Mr. Mansfield, the actor in the show, was Jack himself.

The Strand was brighter as we passed Trafalgar Square and made our way to the Lyceum Theatre. Everywhere we went all anyone could talk about were the murders that had taken place in Whitechapel. Several suspects had been questioned and let go, including a man referred to as Leather Apron because of the garment he wore. Many of the prostitutes had claimed that he'd been extorting money out of them. And because he was a Jewish man, who some thought was a butcher, he would have access to knives. It turned out that his name was John Pizer and he was a bootmaker. After giving his alibis for the two murders, he was released in mid-September. But that only fueled more fear in the general population. Why couldn't the police find the murderer?

"What if the killer is one of us?" Mother asked in a choked voice. "What if he *is* a physician, like Dr. Jekyll? Might we know him, Bernard? Might we be seated next to him at the theatre tonight?"

"Good gracious, Agatha," Father said, clearly having enough of her fear as he glanced at me and then back at her. "The killer is a madman in Whitechapel, like I've told you. Probably a poor immigrant chap, as they all suspect. If he came to this end of town, we'd all recognize him in a moment. He'd stand out like a sore thumb. You have nothing to worry about."

"I hope you're right, but don't you think it's odd that Polly Nichols *and* Ann—"

"That's enough." Father's voice was thunderous, making both Mother and me jump.

The carriage ride was silent the remainder of the way, and I wished I could be anywhere but there. I'd done as much research in 1888 as I could without drawing attention from my parents. I'd even had our driver take me to Fleet Street on the pretense of getting new stationery printed so I could inquire after William Nichols, Polly's ex-husband. I had discovered that he was no longer working at his former place of employment, and his employer was unwilling to give out his new address because he'd been bombarded by the press since Polly's murder. I continued to volunteer at Toynbee Hall, asking anyone and everyone I met if they knew Mary Jane Kelly, but no one knew her. And I discreetly asked around about the Freemasons, but no one seemed to have any new information for me. And, if they did, they kept it to themselves.

The carriage came to a stop outside the Lyceum, but it was oddly quiet on the street.

Father sat forward and looked through the window at the closed doors of the popular theatre. He pounded on the ceiling of the carriage with his walking stick, and our footman jumped off the vehicle to come to the window.

"See why everything is so quiet," Father said to the young man. "And be quick about it."

"Yes, sir."

"Oh, what could be the matter?" Mother asked as she, too, looked out at the empty street. "There should be dozens and dozens of people going into the theatre tonight. Where is everyone?"

When the footman returned, he had stunning news. "The play has been closed due to the Whitechapel murders, sir. Attendance was down, and the police have been receiving so many letters of concern that Mr. Mansfield has postponed the show until further notice."

Relief washed over me. The book had terrified me enough as it was, and it was so intricately linked to the night Mary had disappeared that I hadn't finished it, nor had I relished the thought of seeing the show.

"Where would you like to go, sir?" the coachman asked as he, too, came to the window.

Father glanced at Mother and asked, "Would you like to go to Café Royal for a late supper?"

"I just want to go home," Mother said, putting her forehead into her hand. "I don't feel safe out here, and I'm starting to get a headache."

Father sighed and said to the coachman, "Take us home."

"Very good, sir."

Soon, we were on our way back to 11 Wilton Crescent, though I wasn't sad to return to the safety of our home. Even though I knew that the next murder wouldn't happen until the 30th of this month, I still didn't like feeling exposed. Perhaps Jack the Ripper *was* someone close to our family. Someone my father knew as a Freemason.

Someone who I might interact with frequently.

As soon as we entered the house, Mother went to her room and Father went to his study. I wouldn't see them for the rest of the evening.

Duffy was in my room tidying up after helping me prepare for the theatre. But the moment I entered, she looked relieved.

"It's happy I am to see you," she said without even asking why I had come home so early. "Mr. Baird was here looking for you right after you left."

My heart skipped a beat with relief and joy. "Mr. Baird has returned?"

"Aye. The scullery maid, Bessy, said that he was so fine and dandy when he left, they thought he was going to woo a bride. But the prospective bride must had spurned him, because he hasn't shaved in weeks and he's back to his old ornery ways."

"Did Bessy say where he'd gone?"

"No one knows."

I didn't care. All I wanted was to see Austen again, to ask him what had happened in the garden. I'd replayed his passionate speech a hundred times over in my head since that night, and every time I thought about it, my heart yearned for more. Yet what good could come from giving in to my desire?

The uncertainty in my heart was crippling. My conversation with Mama and Papa at Café Royal had replayed in my head as often as Austen's speech in the garden. What if God's plans were different than mine? I never took the time to stop and ask Him what He wanted. I just assumed that if I wanted something, then God did, too. But I was starting to see that this type of thinking could be dangerous. I had free will, but that didn't mean that I wanted to be out of God's will.

I left my room without another word and raced down the steps, the thick petticoats of my heavy skirts feeling cumbersome. I might not be sure about which path I would choose, but there was one thing I knew for certain. I needed to see Austen. I could not pretend like nothing happened and leave things as they were. We were drawing closer to November 9th, and one way or the other, I would have to face the possibility of leaving 1888. I couldn't do it without fixing the rift between us—or exploring the option of staying.

And I would do it properly this time. I would treat Austen as the man he had become and no longer the child that he had been. I would go to his front door.

Taking a deep breath, I left our house and walked down the three short steps and turned left to get to his. I stopped in front of number 12 Wilton Crescent and knocked, waiting for Brinley to answer the door. Thankfully, it didn't take long.

"Miss Kathryn," he said, his eyebrows raised.

"Is Mr. Baird at home?"

"Yes, of course. Please come in."

I entered the house, and Brinley led me to the parlor before he left to tell Austen I was there. It felt like an eternity before there was a noise at the door.

I turned, and my breath stilled as my gaze met Austen's. His hair was disheveled, and he had a shadow of a beard on his cheeks, but I'd never seen him look so handsome or attractive—or so desperately in love. Now that I recognized that look in his eyes, I realized I'd seen it countless times. I wanted to run to him, to throw myself into his arms and give in to the ache that had been building inside me, but there were so many things I still didn't understand.

"Is it true you came from Italy to convince me to love you?" I asked, just above a whisper.

He didn't have to answer because I saw the truth in his eyes.

I rushed across the room and entered his embrace.

He put his arms around me, holding me with a sense of urgency that took my breath away.

"I've been such a fool," he whispered close to my ear.

I held him tighter, needing the reassurance of his love and friendship more than anything else. "So have I," I said, pulling back to look at his dear face.

It would have been so much easier if he was in 1938 so that my choice could be simple. I didn't want to lose Austen—not now and not in the future.

The longing in his eyes soon changed, and he pulled away, his face growing serious. "I went to your house earlier tonight to tell you that I hired a private investigator to find Mary. And I just received word that he found her, Kate."

I blinked several times, hope filling my heart. "You found Mary? Where? Is she safe?"

He was quiet for a moment as he studied me, sadness filling his face. "She is going by the name of Marie Jeanette Kelly, and she lives at 13 Miller's Court."

It felt as if a fist landed in my gut and all the air was knocked out of my lungs. The hope I'd held that she was not Jack's victim bled away, and dread filled its place.

"I'm so sorry, Kate."

"I want to go to her immediately."

"It's too late. I'll take you there tomor—"

"I'm going now, Austen, whether you're with me or not."

He pressed his lips together. "Fine. But you must change. I won't take you there looking so—so elegant."

His compliment would have pleased me if I wasn't reeling with the truth.

History claimed my sister would be Jack the Ripper's last victim.

For the first time in my life, I hated history. And I wouldn't let it win, no matter what it cost me.

It felt as if my entire world had shifted in an instant. I had known it was a possibility that Mary was Jack's last victim, but now that I knew it was true, everything was different.

As the carriage turned onto Commercial Street, the filth and stench of London's East End clawed at my throat. If I had thought being in the glittering West End at night was terrifying, it was nothing compared to entering Whitechapel after dark, especially knowing Jack the Ripper might be stalking the streets.

Austen had been silent since we entered the carriage, but now he asked, "What will you do?"

"I don't know." It was the truth. Plain and simple. "I can't be rash or foolish. Papa warned me not to change history before it's necessary because it could cause so many other problems." I pressed my lips together as I thought about my sister's life. "I still don't know if she'll be a random victim or if she's part of a Freemason plot."

"What Freemason plot?" he asked with a frown.

We still hadn't spoken about his parents' involvement with the Freemasons, or why they had been in Jerusalem with my parents in 1874. But he had made it clear in the garden, speaking to Mr. Maybrick, that he had no interest in joining the brotherhood.

"One of the curators I work with in 1938 believes that the Freemasons are responsible for covering up Jack's murders." I quickly told him Calan's theory as the carriage rolled along Commercial Street. "If Mary's death is supposed to be random, then I could simply force her to leave the morning of the intended murder." I paused, feeling overwhelmed with all that was against me. "But if it's linked to Freemasonry, then things are different. What if Jack has plans to kill her, no matter where I take her? Can I protect her from him?"

"I don't know the answers to those questions. But I do know the Freemasons are dangerous. That's why I've refused to join them. If they're involved, then this thing is much bigger than we can imagine."

"I need to know who Jack the Ripper is, Austen. If I can learn his identity and find out if he's linked to the Freemasons, then maybe I can unearth the connection between the women."

"How would that help Mary?"

"If he's not a Freemason, and just a random madman, I would have the assurance that if I send her somewhere else, she would be safe from him. But if he is a Freemason and I need to reveal his identity to put him behind bars, to keep her safe, I would do that."

"The Freemasons are powerful."

"They don't scare me."

"They should."

The way he said those two words made me turn to him. "What do you know about them, Austen? Mr. Maybrick made it sound like you know more than you let on."

"The less you know, the better. Please believe me when I tell you that. Nothing good would come to you if you knew what I know about the Freemasons."

"But I want to save my sister."

"What I know wouldn't help. If it would, I'd tell you."

I believed him. And even though it was hard to not know, I would trust him.

As we drew closer to Miller's Court, there was something else that was gnawing at my thoughts. "I can understand why the authorities were trying to cover up the identity of Jack, if he was a Freemason, but what compelled him to go on the killing spree? What was his objective? Was it simple insanity, or was he trying to accomplish something?"

"I wish I had answers for you, Kate."

I took a deep breath and then said, "The next two murders will happen on the same night. One will be in a highly public place, and Jack will loiter around the scene of the crime for at least half an hour before he kills Elizabeth Stride. It will happen around one in the morning on September 30th. Lots of people saw him."

Realization dawned in Austen's gaze, and he began to shake his head.

"Please," I said. "We can dress in shabby clothes and find a place to hide. It'll be dark and raining, so we can stay hidden."

"It's a ludicrous idea. What if we run into the killer? What if we change history somehow? Would I forfeit my life if *I* knowingly change history?"

"I—I don't know." I'd never wondered. I had always known that time-crossers forfeited their lives in the path they changed, but what about non-time-crossers? Did the same rule apply to them?

"Not to mention your safety in other regards," he continued. "It's insane to go there now, and the only reason I'm taking you is because we know that Mary lives at Miller's Court and she's someone we can trust. But to just loiter in Whitechapel, knowing Jack the Ripper is somewhere in that area—it's out of the question."

"I will go, Austen. Whether you're with me or not."

His face was grim. "You have always vexed me, Kathryn Kelly, but never more so than now."

"I've never been as desperate as I am now."

We stared at each other for a moment, and then he growled and said, "Fine. I'll take you."

I smiled, though I didn't feel relieved or even happy. Just grateful that I didn't have to go alone.

When we arrived at Miller's Court, Miles opened the door for us and Austen stepped out, then offered me his hand.

It was firm as I exited the carriage. I wanted to cling to it, but I let go as we walked down the passageway to the back of Miller's Court, conscious once again that I didn't fit in here and neither did Mary.

I'd changed into the plainest gown I owned and wore a dark bonnet with a wide brim to cover my face. But I still felt like I was drawing unwanted attention. Even though I didn't see anyone, it felt as if there were eyes everywhere.

I knocked on number thirteen, relieved and anxious and desperate to finally see Mary again.

"Who is it?" came a small, feminine voice on the other side of the door.

My heart squeezed at the sound, and tears stung my eyes. "Mary, my love. It's me. Kathryn."

The door creaked open, and Mary stood before me, a shell of the woman she'd once been. Tears of shock and joy filled her eyes as she fell into my embrace. "Kathryn."

I clung to Mary with desperation, horrified at how thin and careworn she looked. There was a stench about her that was appalling, though she probably didn't notice. The thought of a warm bath and clean clothes was a luxury in Whitechapel. I wanted to take her away with me at that very instant—but a voice of reason spoke from behind me.

"Perhaps we had better go inside before we're seen," Austen said as he touched my lower back.

Mary pulled away from me and glanced at Austen, fear and uncertainty in her gaze.

"Hello, Mary."

She nodded at him and then said, "Come in," as she opened her door wider, allowing me to see her foul living conditions. The fact that she could afford her own room was a miracle. Jack's other victims were all homeless, living on the streets, prostituting themselves for doss money to have a shared bed in a boardinghouse.

Mary glanced behind us toward the courtyard, as if she was looking for something—or someone.

Her home was smaller than I imagined, only about twelve feet square, with a single bed, three small tables, and a chair. A picture of a forlorn woman sitting near the seaside hung above the fireplace, and there were two irregular sized windows looking toward the yard. Three of the walls were made of brick, but a fourth was made of wood and looked like it was a partition that separated this room from the rest of the larger house.

Mary closed the door again and then looked out the window, clearly worried. "I don't know how long you can stay before Joseph returns."

"Joseph?" I frowned. "Who is Joseph?"

Embarrassment and shame colored Mary's cheeks as she went to the small fireplace and moved a tea kettle off the flames. "Joseph is my—my man."

I'd forgotten about Joseph Barnett. He was the man who would give testimony about Mary after the murder. A murder I wouldn't let happen. "Your man?"

She turned to me, her eyes pleading with me to understand. "If you don't have a man to protect you in Whitechapel, then you're forced to have several men."

My stomach turned, but not because of Mary's decisions. She was simply trying to survive the unthinkable. Everything about her current life contradicted the one she used to lead, but she had no choice.

She stood before me, her hands clasped in front of her dirty apron, and she couldn't meet my gaze. She had aged in the past eleven months. She'd always been pretty, but now she looked gaunt and haggard. Her red hair, so much like mine, was thin and dirty. Her dress was worn and hung on her frame. And her green eyes had lost their shine.

"Don't look at me like that, Kathryn," she whispered. "I don't want your pity."

I glanced at Austen, but he wasn't looking at me or Mary. He was looking at his feet, probably to spare Mary from embarrassment and shame.

"How did you find me?" she asked.

I couldn't tell her the truth because Mary didn't know I was a time-crosser.

"I hired someone to look for you," Austen said.

Fear tightened the edges of her eyes. "You cannot tell anyone where I'm at."

"We won't," Austen assured her. "The man who found you is someone I trust with my life."

"If a hired man could find me, then I'm not safe."

"You're safe for now," I said to Mary, taking her hand in mine. "I promise you." I swallowed and looked at the small, uncomfortable room. "What happened? Why did you leave without telling me? Did Father force you out? He and Mother refuse to speak of you or allow me to speak of you."

Mary shook her head and pulled her hand away. "It doesn't matter. This is my life now. I'm getting along as best I can."

"It *does* matter. You left without warning, Mary. And look at where you're living. None of this makes sense. You're from a genteel family. We love you. We want you to come home."

"I know you thought you were coming to help me," Mary said, her voice tightening. "But you're putting me in more danger, Kathryn. You're right. I left without warning, but not because Father forced me to leave."

I stared at her, speechless.

"I chose to leave, to come here—"

"You *chose* this?" I asked, unable to believe such a thing. "Then why can't I say your name? Why hasn't Father searched for you?"

She looked as if she was going to speak, but then she shook her head. "It's best if you leave—right now, before Joseph returns. He doesn't know anything about my past, and I want to keep it that way. It's safer for all of us if he believes I'm Marie Jeanette."

"I'm not going anywhere until I understand why you left home."

"You need to go. Now." She put her small hand on my back and nudged me toward the door. "Don't come back here, Kathryn. Joseph is already upset with me because I've been letting friends stay here at night. It's too dangerous for them to be on the streets with a murderer on the loose."

"About that—" I wanted to tell her to be careful, but Austen reached out and put his hand on my arm to stop me. He shook his head, as if warning me not to say too much.

"Mary, please," I said as I tried to pause.

She opened the door, more tears in her eyes. “If you want to keep me safe, please don’t come back. For your sake and for mine.”

“I’ll send money,” I told her.

“I don’t need—or want—anything from you. No one must know about you. I can’t risk that they’ll find out who you are—or who I am.”

“I don’t understand any of this,” I said. “Please, help me understand.”

She put her hand on my cheek, and I felt like the younger sister for the first time. “Good-bye, Kathryn.”

Austen put his hand on the small of my back. “We should leave. We don’t want to put Mary in a difficult position.”

I wrapped her in another embrace and whispered, “Please be careful.”

She nodded and then pulled back, anxious for me to leave.

When we stepped outside, Mary closed the door behind us, and I leaned into Austen as he led me down the passageway. A curtain moved aside from one of the other rooms, and an old woman peered out at us.

“I don’t understand,” I said again as Austen led me to his carriage. “None of this makes sense.”

“I don’t understand it, either, but we have to honor her wishes.”

“She said that Father didn’t force her to leave. Why would she abandon the comfort and safety of our home? Why would he let her go?”

“Perhaps it was more dangerous for her to live at home than it is for her to live here.” Austen helped me into his carriage and then tapped on the roof to let Miles know we were ready to head back to Wilton Crescent.

“That can’t possibly be true.”

“I’m sorry, Kate,” he said as he put his arm around me and held me close. “I wish you had more answers. But that doesn’t mean that you can’t save her. We must be patient.”

I didn’t want to be patient. I just wanted to save my sister.

12

LONDON, ENGLAND
SEPTEMBER 28, 1938

The basement of Lancaster House was filled with the London Museum's special exhibits. There was a cell from Newgate Prison, items from the Tudor Dynasty—including medical paraphernalia from Queen Elizabeth's physician, Doctor Bromley—models of Old London, and even a Roman boat. Calan and I had been given a large, empty room in the corner to turn into an exhibit for Jack the Ripper. It was a dark, dank area and offered just the right amount of atmosphere to create a sense of foreboding. We'd decided to make the long, narrow room look like Buck's Row, the site of Polly Nichols's murder—the first of the canonical five victims that were attributed to Jack.

"On the left wall," Calan said to the museum's carpenter, who had joined us for a meeting in the basement, "we'll want a façade of the brick buildings along Buck's Row. At the end, we'll re-create the gate that led into the stable where Polly's body was found." He pulled several photographs out of a file taken around the time of the murder. "The architecture was very simple," Calan noted as he pointed to one photo. "Just keep it as true to the photographs as possible."

"Alright, mate," the carpenter said. "And what will we do for the floor?"

"We'll keep the floor natural," he answered.

"The concrete will do quite nicely as a road," I added. "You'll also find a rendering with proper measurements in the file for the brick façade. If you have any questions, feel free to ask either Calan or myself."

The carpenter nodded as he looked over everything we'd given him.

"And when do you think you can get this done?" Calan asked.

The man shrugged as he scratched the stubble on his chin. "Three or four weeks."

"The sooner the better," I told him. "After the façade is finished, we'll still need time to assemble the rest of the exhibit, and we hope to have the grand opening the first week of November." I took a breath. "Around the anniversary of the last murder on November 9th."

"I'll see what I can do."

"Thank you."

Calan and I left the empty room and walked up the stairs toward the main floor.

I tried keeping myself busy with work, but all I could think about was tomorrow in 1888. It would be September 29th, and Austen and I had plans to head to Whitechapel well before midnight to find a place to hide on Berner Street so we could watch for Jack the Ripper. I was so nervous in both paths, I hadn't eaten in days.

But it wasn't only visiting Berner Street that had me worried. Ever since we'd visited Mary at Miller's Court, Austen had been distant. He wasn't as unpleasant as before, but I knew what he was thinking. What we were both thinking.

Mary needed me to save her, and the only way to do that was to sacrifice my path for her.

"You've been quieter than usual," Calan said, interrupting my thoughts. "Worried about Hitler?"

I almost laughed. Yes, I was worried about Hitler—but right

now, I was more concerned about Jack the Ripper. I couldn't tell Calan that, so I said, "Who isn't?"

Neville Chamberlain was in Germany for a third visit because the Czechs and the French didn't like the plan to hand over the Sudetenland to Hitler—and now Hitler was threatening an invasion on October 1st, only three days away. Chamberlain had called for a summit with Germany, France, Italy, and Britain. It was currently happening in Munich. If the prime minister couldn't find a way to get Hitler to compromise, then war was inevitable, and Mama and Papa would insist we leave for home.

"I don't want to go back to the US," I told Calan as we walked across the main gallery of the London Museum toward the stairs that would take us to the second floor. "I could be on a ship heading home in just three days' time. But there's so much more to do here."

"Hopefully Chamberlain can get a compromise," Calan said, "though I'm in agreement with Winston Churchill. I don't think appeasing Hitler is the answer. He's a bully, and nothing is ever good enough for bullies. They take and take until someone stops them. Appeasement will only buy us a few more months. I think war is inevitable."

I couldn't let on that I knew he was right. I just didn't know enough about the timeline to know when war would begin. Would it start in three days? Three months? Or three years?

"Is that all that's bothering you?" Calan asked, his perceptive gaze on my face.

I smiled, despite the uncertainty of both my paths. "I appreciate your concern, but I'm not one to confide in coworkers."

"Ah," he said. "This has something to do with a man, doesn't it?"

"What?" I frowned at him as we climbed the large staircase. Again, the museum was quiet as people continued to prepare for war. Several of the volunteers had even stayed home. "Why would you assume my unwillingness to confide in you is because of a man?"

"If it was about a friend or an elderly aunt, or some such thing, you wouldn't have trouble telling me. But if it's about a man, I could understand your reticence. You might be afraid that I would get jealous."

I laughed. "That is the least of my concerns, Mr. McCaffrey."

He joined in my laughter, and I appreciated a moment of lighthearted banter. It was difficult to come by on days like today, but Calan had become a good friend and had made many hard days bearable.

When we arrived in the office we shared, Calan went to the folder with some of the Jack the Ripper letters, which was lying on the desk. "I plan to go through more of these today." He shook his head. "It's a daunting task to sift through them and determine which ones are real and which ones were written by imposters."

"Sir Rothschild brought another file over from the Crime Museum yesterday. There are hundreds of letters to comb through. I can look over the other file while you're working on this one."

"Would you please?" he asked. "I'd like to put a few of them on display. The *Dear Boss* letter, the *Saucy Jacky* postcard, and the *From Hell* letter are the ones most likely written by Jack." He had kept these aside, and I'd looked over them already. They were all written in similar handwriting, with words intentionally misspelled, and they each addressed information about the murders that wasn't widely known to the public when they were written. The *Saucy Jacky* postcard was postmarked October 1, 1888, and referenced the Double Event, but it appeared to have been written before September 30th, which was the date of the murders. People in 1888 questioned if the Double Event was intentional or accidental. Had Jack targeted Elizabeth Stride and Catherine Eddowes, or were they random victims? If they were both linked to the Freemasons, then I knew they weren't random. It was one of the reasons I wanted to be on Berner Street tomorrow. To see if I could figure it out.

"The others are harder to pinpoint," Calan said. "They were

sent from all over the place, but they all have such similar themes and wording."

"I'll grab the other file from Sir Rothschild's desk," I offered.

I left our office and entered Sir Rothschild's. He left every Wednesday afternoon at the same time and didn't usually return until close to four. He had told me that I could find the file of letters in his locked drawer and that the key to his desk was under volume one of *The Building of Britain and the Empire* on his bookshelf. Once I had the key, I took a seat at his desk to open the lock.

The drawer was full of several files. I set the key aside and began to look through them to find the one I needed.

One of the folders wasn't labeled, so I took it out to glance at the contents and was surprised to see a familiar name on several newspaper clippings. Michael Maybrick.

But what was even more shocking was the contents of the file. From what I could gather, Michael's brother, James Maybrick, a cotton merchant, died of arsenic poisoning on November 10, 1888, and his wife, an American named Florence Maybrick, went on trial for his murder. The case was made even more high-profile because of their connection to Michael, the famous composer. Michael believed Florence was guilty and was one of her biggest adversaries in court and in the newspapers. It was known that Florence had cheated on her husband and that she wished him dead.

"May I help you, Miss Voland?" Sir Rothschild stood at his office door wearing his coat and hat, carrying a walking stick.

I jumped, though I hadn't been doing anything wrong, and glanced at the clock. I'd been looking through the file for over half an hour. "I'm sorry. The time slipped away from me. I was looking for the Ripper letters, and I stumbled upon this, instead."

He took off his hat and set it on the coat-tree in the corner of the room. "Are you familiar with the history of the Maybrick trial?"

"This is the first I've learned of it, though I am familiar with Michael Maybrick."

"Ah, yes, the composer." Sir Rothschild took off his coat and hung that up next. "An exceptionally talented man. Some think that if he wasn't part of the trial, Florence Maybrick would have been acquitted. She spent fourteen years in prison before her sentence was overturned and she was released."

"She didn't do it?"

"Who is to say? The courts decided that she was guilty, and then they overturned their verdict years later."

What would Sir Rothschild think if I told him I knew Michael personally? That I'd heard him perform in my mother's drawing room?

"It was a sad case," Sir Rothschild said. "But nothing you need to concern yourself with. The file you're looking for should be clearly labeled."

"Of course." I tucked all the newspaper clippings back into the Maybrick file and returned it to the drawer before finding the file I'd come for.

"Would you like me to relock the drawer?" I asked him.

"It's not necessary. I have some work to do with the files. Feel free to leave the key on the desk."

I smiled and then stood, trying not to feel awkward. Even though I had been in the drawer before and Sir Rothschild had shown me the key, I still felt like I was trespassing.

When I was just about to leave the room, Sir Rothschild's voice stopped me. "Will you be joining us at Cliveden again this weekend?"

"That is the plan. Though I suppose it will all depend on whether we're at war with Germany by then."

"Ah yes, that. One can only hope that Chamberlain is doing the right thing. It would be a shame to go to war again when Hitler is only trying to take care of the Germans in the Sudetenland."

"You think it's wise to give in to Hitler's demands?" I asked, a little surprised.

"I don't think they are unreasonable. He just wants what is his. Can you fault him for that?"

"The Sudetenland belongs to Czechoslovakia."

"Only since the Great War."

"I suppose I don't know enough to make an informed opinion."

"No, you do not, Miss Voland." He smiled, and his mustache curled up, but there was no warmth in his gaze. "I do not mean to insinuate that you are incompetent, on the contrary. But this is so much bigger than it appears on the surface. Millions of lives will be affected by the decisions made in Munich. We can only hope that things turn out for the best."

I returned his smile, though I sensed condescension in his voice. It was the first time I'd heard it since I'd met him.

I left his office, wondering not for the first time where Sir Rothschild placed his allegiances. He'd spoken highly of Hitler at the Astors' house party a couple weeks ago, and again today. Did he really think the German dictator was a good man? Or that Fascism was a smart move for Europe? He wouldn't be the only one, but it was still alarming. My grandmother Maggie had lived through WWII and watched the fall of Fascism, claiming it had become disgraced after the war. But here in 1938, there were still many who applauded its ideals.

I was not one of them.

"Did you find what you were looking for?" Calan asked as I reentered our office.

"Yes," I said, holding up the file of Ripper letters.

"That should keep you busy for a while."

As I sat at my desk, I was thankful for the letters, hoping they'd distract me from thoughts of tomorrow in 1888.

If all went as planned, I would see Jack the Ripper in person.

13

LONDON, ENGLAND
SEPTEMBER 29, 1888

It had been raining all day, just as I knew it would from reports I'd read in my other path. My feet and hands were so cold, I could do nothing to get them warm, though I suspected it was more from my nerves and less from the weather.

"Are you certain you're ill?" Mother asked as she entered my bedroom one more time before she and Father left for a ball at Devonshire House. "I really hate for you to miss the ball. The duke's son will be there tonight."

"Spencer Cavendish is over fifty years old," I protested.

"And a bachelor. It's rumored that he's looking for a wife, and a young one at that. He needs an heir."

I pulled the covers closer to my chin, truly feeling ill—not only from the fear of going to Whitechapel tonight and seeing Jack the Ripper, but from the thought of marrying a man older than my father.

"I do not feel well enough to attend the ball," I told her. "Please give my regards to the duke and duchess."

Mother was wearing a beautiful blue ball gown with sapphire earrings and a matching necklace. She was lovely. I almost envied her passion for society. I didn't mind a party or two, and I enjoyed things like the house party that the Astors hosted at Cliveden, but balls, especially in 1888, were another thing entirely. They were so exhausting.

"I'll have Duffy bring you some ginger tea and honey." Mother shook her head in disappointment. "If this infernal rain would stop, perhaps you would feel better."

She left the room with the train of her gown sweeping soundlessly across the carpeted floor. I stayed in bed for another half hour, accepted the tea that Duffy brought for me, and then told her she needn't check on me for the rest of the evening.

When the house was quiet, I slipped out from the covers and removed a pile of clothing from under the bed. I'd been collecting them for the past week, asking Duffy if there were any discarded items that the staff might want to donate to Toynbee Hall. She'd asked the servants in the neighboring homes, and they'd brought several things to me. I'd gone through them and created an outfit that I hoped would disguise me in Whitechapel. After I was done with them, I'd see that they were donated to those in need.

Within ten minutes, I was dressed in a worn gown with a tattered jacket and a shabby bonnet. I hoped it would be enough to keep me warm, though I doubted it. Once it was wet, I would be colder than ever. I shivered just thinking about it.

The clock in the hall struck eleven times, which meant that Austen would be waiting in his carriage out front. We would get to Berner Street around eleven thirty and then wait for Jack and Elizabeth to appear.

I turned out the light in my room and then tiptoed through the hall, down the stairs, and into the front entry. Thankfully, the staff were probably in bed and my parents weren't expected back until close to sunrise, so I could leave without notice.

The rain fell at a steady cadence as I left my house. Austen's carriage was waiting just as he promised, and when I appeared, he stepped out of the vehicle and sprinted toward me with an umbrella.

"Thank you," I said quietly as he put his hand on the small of my back and led me to the carriage. Miles offered his hand for me to climb in, and Austen followed.

"I cannot stress enough the foolishness of this errand," Austen said without a proper greeting. "I pray you and I do not live to regret it."

"Good evening, Austen," I said as I sat next to him, pressed close in the tight carriage. "I hope you're well tonight."

"I don't know how you expect to identify this man in the darkness. No doubt he prowls about on nights such as this because he knows it's impossible to see him."

"There will be some light from the businesses and homes nearby."

"Your optimism is unfounded, Miss Kelly."

I sighed. When he used my last name, it was never a good thing.

The sound of the horse's hooves against cobblestone was the only noise that filled the carriage as we traveled across London to the East End. The damp, cold air seeped into my bones, and I longed to press against Austen for warmth, but it would be foolish. The more I touched him, the more I longed for his touch. The more time I spent with him, the more I wanted to be in his company. I still thought of his impassioned speech in the garden the night of my parents' ball, and I often wondered what might have happened if I had encouraged him—if I would encourage him now.

If I didn't need to sacrifice this life for Mary, would Austen and I be planning a wedding even now?

The tension between us suggested that perhaps we would.

"Miles will drop us off several blocks away from Berner Street and return for us later," Austen finally said as we neared Whitechapel. "You must stay close at all times, and do not question me. If I say run, run. If I say hide, hide. Do you understand?"

"Of course."

"We cannot change history in any way. You cannot try to be a hero."

"I'm well aware." I started to feel irritated at his tone, as if I were a child and didn't understand the dire circumstances of our errand.

"We are there to observe," he continued, "and if you don't get the view you want, then you have to accept it."

I finally turned to him. "I'm not foolish, Mr. Baird."

"I've never thought you were foolish." He studied me in the darkness, his voice softening. "I do not wish for you to be disappointed, Kate, that is all."

His words warmed me, and I leaned back in the seat, allowing our shoulders to brush. "Thank you for coming with me."

"This goes against my better judgment, but I know how much it means to you."

He didn't move away from me as we turned onto Commercial Road and then a smaller lane where the carriage came to a stop.

Austen stepped out of the carriage and helped me alight. The street was darker than I anticipated, and the rain was falling faster, but Austen opened his umbrella and held it over my head. My heart pounded hard, and my palms were sweating, despite how cold they were. Thankfully, there was no one within sight to see the two of us leaving a gentleman's carriage.

"I'll return here at 1:30 to collect you," Miles said. "The copper on this beat comes by every thirty-five minutes, and his last round will be at 1:20. If you're not back by 1:50, I will leave and then return."

"We should be here by 1:30," Austen assured him.

Miles nodded and then clicked his tongue as he prodded the horse to move.

"How does Miles know the police officer's schedule?" I asked Austen.

He didn't answer, but wrapped my hand around the crook of his elbow and held the umbrella over us as he directed me toward Commercial Street.

"Is Miles not concerned about what we're doing in Whitechapel at this hour?" I persisted.

"Miles has been with me for many years," Austen said. "He doesn't ask questions."

"That's a bit disconcerting. Do you two often find yourself in situations such as this one? Should I be worried?"

He drew me closer and sighed. "You, on the other hand, ask a lot of questions."

"Because you don't give me enough answers."

"Perhaps that's by design."

"Where were you those two weeks after my mother's party, Austen? Your staff doesn't even know where you go."

He was quiet for so long, I wasn't sure he would answer, but he finally said, "I have a little cottage near Loch Lomond. I go there when I don't want to be disturbed."

"I remember the cottage," I said, though I hadn't thought of his Scottish getaway in a long time. It took almost an entire day of travel to get there. "You used to go there with your parents."

"It's the only place I feel like I can think properly."

I let the discussion go because I knew why he'd gone there after our conversation in the garden. He needed space and time away from me.

Though it was now half past eleven, the activity on Commercial Road was surprisingly busy. Pubs and lodging houses lined the street with grocers' and coffee houses still open. In the glow of the lights from doors and windows, I saw that Austen had also dressed a little shabbier than usual, and he had a shadow of a beard on his face. He wore a flatcap and a wool jacket that looked worn. But regardless of his clothes, he was still handsome, and when his gaze caught mine, it caused my pulse to skitter in a way that was new and unfamiliar.

As we passed rough-looking men on the street, I was thankful for Austen, who had a commanding and possessive presence about him. The other men looked at me, but none approached. Though it didn't stop women from calling out to him or using suggestive language as we passed by.

Soon, we came to the corner of Commercial Road and Berner

Street. Dutfield's Yard would be on the right, about a hundred yards from the corner.

"Elizabeth Stride is supposedly an attractive woman," I whispered to Austen as we turned onto Berner Street and walked slowly. "She was seen with at least three different clients the night she was killed. The first was around eleven o'clock, somewhere here on Berner Street. The second was at quarter to twelve near 58 Berner Street. And the third is supposedly Jack, who was seen with Elizabeth around 12:35 and 12:45 by two separate individuals here on the corner. Then, according to contemporary eyewitness accounts, though the police never took official statements, they were seen by a fruit seller—" I paused as we passed a grocer on the right. The building was dark, but there was a half window on the main level with an oil lamp burning, displaying fruit and sweetmeats. "There, a man named Matthew Packer said that a man and woman, the woman meeting Elizabeth Stride's description, purchased grapes from him at quarter past twelve. Then, they stood across the street for some time in the rain eating them."

"Why didn't the police take his testimony?" Austen asked as we passed the fruit seller, who was standing at his window. He nodded at us as we walked past.

"Because he got a good look at Jack," I whispered, "and the chief of police, Sir Charles Warren, couldn't have an eyewitness to the murderer. If he did, and Jack was caught, then people might connect him to Freemasonry."

"Do you really believe that?"

"It makes sense. Eyewitnesses will claim that Elizabeth had grapes clutched in her hands the night of the murder, and two private detectives later open a grate in Dutfield's Yard and will find grape stalks that were washed into the drain from all this rain. But if the police can deny that there were grapes involved, which they do, then they won't have to call on Matthew Packer or get his testimony."

The hem of my worn skirt was heavy with rain and mud as we walked along Berner Street, passing the gated entrance into

Dutfield's Yard near the International Working Men's Educational Club. Music seeped from the building, and several windows were filled with lights. The gate to the yard was open.

I shivered, thinking that Elizabeth would soon be killed there.

A woman and a man exited the alley coming from the yard. I paused and Austen stopped, looking in the direction I was staring.

"That's her," I whispered. "And one of the men she was seen with that night—this night."

Austen walked me closer to the building on the opposite side of the street from Dutfield's Yard, and we stopped again.

"She must know it's a quiet place to bring her clients," I whispered.

The man and woman parted ways. I knew it was Elizabeth because the reports had said that she was wearing a black skirt, a black jacket, a black crepe bonnet, and a red posy in her lapel. Even in the darkness, the red flower stood out.

She walked to the end of the street and stood on the corner, probably waiting to find another client.

Every muscle in my body was tense. I wanted to call out to her, tell her to find a safe place to sleep for the night. In about an hour, she would be dead. Her life snuffed out by a madman.

Austen's muscles tightened around my hand, and when I looked up at him, he shook his head. "It's not your place to stop this from happening."

"It seems like—like a sin," I whispered, trying to control my emotions. "To know that something horrible is about to happen and not be able to stop it."

"It's the burden that all time-crossers bear," he said. "You told me stories about your mama in Salem. I'm sure it was hard to watch as the accusers and magistrates put innocent people in jail."

I thought of Mama and all she'd endured. I couldn't imagine the horrors. "I don't give her enough credit," I said softly. "Sometimes I feel like I'm the only one who has had to endure this weight, but others have had to face more difficult situations than this one."

"I hope you take comfort in knowing you're not alone, Kate."

He was watching me as he spoke. "God gives us encouragement from those who have gone before us. Sometimes it's the only reason I can find for suffering. That perhaps my experiences with suffering will help someone else down the road."

I placed my free hand on his forearm. "You've suffered more than most, Austen. I hope there have been people in your life to ease your suffering."

"Some who don't even know how much they've eased it. Like you."

"Me?"

"Does it surprise you?"

"Indeed. I thought I made your life more unbearable."

He smiled. "That's what I wanted you to believe." He motioned to a coffee house down the street. "Let's get some hot coffee to warm up. We'll come back in about a half hour to see if we can spot Jack."

I let him guide me toward a coffee shop, pleased that I had brought Austen comfort.

Thirty minutes later, we were back on Berner Street. This time, we stood under the alcove of a door across the street from the gate at Dutfield's Yard. Austen had closed the umbrella and laid it next to the building, not wanting to attract attention.

I was shaking from the cold and from my nerves, despite the warm coffee we'd just drank. Thankfully, the alcove offered a respite from the rain, though the damp air was still uncomfortable.

"Your hands are like ice," Austen said as he took my hands between his and rubbed them gently. "I hope you don't get sick."

I loved the feel of his hands engulfing mine. And I suddenly realized how close we were standing. Berner Street in Whitechapel was the furthest thing from a romantic setting I'd ever experienced, but I was beginning to see that no matter where Austen and I were together, the air felt electrified and tense.

He lifted his penetrating gaze as he rubbed my hands, and though we'd looked into each other's eyes countless times, things were different.

A couple walked down Berner Street, drawing my attention away from Austen, and my body went stiff.

"There," I whispered.

It was Elizabeth again. She was still wearing the black skirt and jacket, and I could see the red posy in her lapel. The man at her side was medium height, wearing a peaked cap and an oversized jacket, and he was carrying some sort of package.

Was I looking at Jack the Ripper? The shiver that ran up my spine this time was from terror and fascination.

We were so far away, it was impossible to make out either of their features in the darkness and rain. I couldn't see the color of his hair or what his face looked like. All I knew was his height and approximate build, but there were thousands of men who shared the same description.

The couple stopped at the grocer's and spoke to the proprietor for a few minutes. They accepted a handful of grapes and then crossed the street—not far from where we were standing, though they would struggle to see us in the alcove.

I held my breath as I tried to listen to their muffled conversation. I couldn't make out their words, but I heard the low hum of their voices and Elizabeth's laugh now and again.

Many people said that Jack had to be charming. It was the only way he could convince women to go into dark alleys with him while a murderer was on the loose. From the sound of Elizabeth's voice, this man was doing a good job convincing her he was safe. He was also dressed well—not as shabby as many of the men in Whitechapel, but not like a dandy, either.

Austen stood just as still and stiff beside me, holding my hand.

The couple began to move in our direction, something I hadn't anticipated. If they walked past us, they would see us standing there, and if they looked close enough, they'd be able to see our faces. The last thing I wanted was for Jack the Ripper to get a good look at either of us. If he was someone prominent or a person that one of us might recognize, then it went without saying that he might know us, too, and we'd be in danger.

As the couple moved closer, I sensed that Austen was thinking the same thing, and without warning, he turned so his back was toward the street and he was standing face to face with me.

My breath caught as I looked up at him. He placed his hands on either side of my face and lowered his lips to mine, hovering for just a moment, as if allowing me to say no.

But I didn't say no. Instead, I grasped his forearms and lifted myself just enough for his mouth to meet mine.

His lips were soft, and his kiss was achingly tender. He seemed on the brink of pulling away, so I slipped my hands up to his face, inviting his unexpected kiss.

He paused for only a heartbeat, and then he wrapped his arms around me, pulling me close as he deepened the kiss. This was no longer a kiss to temporarily distract the passersby.

This was a kiss years in the making.

Everything began to fade. The rain, the smell of the street, the fear of Jack the Ripper. All I could feel was Austen. All I could think about was his lips upon mine, his arms wrapped around me, and my body pressed against his.

And I wanted more of it.

He slipped his hand up to the back of my head and drew me closer, his chest rising and falling against mine. His other hand pressed against my low back as my arms went around his neck. He was warm and gentle, yet I sensed something powerful and raw just beyond my reach.

He was restraining himself.

I recalled the words he'd said in the garden. He wanted to kiss me until the madness inside of him subsided and he could think clearly for the first time in fourteen years.

As I responded to his kiss, I suddenly understood the madness he spoke about. The deep yearning that enveloped me and overpowered all my senses. Yet it wasn't subsiding as we kissed. It was only growing with intensity.

When he finally pulled away, he was breathing heavily, and his body was trembling. Or was it mine?

"Kate," he whispered my name on a ragged breath, half apology, half question.

I slowly lowered my hands and tried to take a step back, but the wall was behind me and there was nowhere to go.

He took a few more breaths and then straightened.

We stood that way for several heartbeats, and then I realized there were no more footsteps nearby. The emergency had passed. The couple was just entering the gate leading to Dutfield's Yard.

"I think we're safe," I whispered.

"Are we?" Austen asked, but he wasn't looking at the gate.

I swallowed the rush of emotions cascading through me, and I shivered again.

Austen moved to my side, his chest rising and falling.

All I could hear was our breath and the tapping of the rain. Elizabeth's laughter had faded and would never be heard again. The sudden and overpowering knowledge that she was being murdered while we stood there and waited pressed upon my chest, chasing away all thoughts of Austen's kiss.

"She's—right now—" I leaned into him, and he put his arm around me as if he might shield me from this horror, as well. He held me in his arms, and this time there was no passion, no urgency—just comfort.

My emotions had swung from wonder to terror in the blink of an eye, and tears threatened to choke me.

A two-wheeled cart approached from Commercial Road with a single horse and driver.

It would be Louis Diemschutz, the steward of the International Working Men's Educational Club. He was also a peddler and would be coming back for the night.

He turned into the gated yard, and I pressed my face into Austen's chest, knowing that there was no way out of the yard but through this one entrance. Elizabeth was now dead, and Jack would soon escape.

Austen placed a kiss on the top of my head as we waited in the terrible silence.

A minute passed, and then the man in the peaked cap emerged.

My heart pounded at the sight of him. The monster that would capture the attention of the world—and get away with murder—was across the street from us.

He was not running, but he moved at a fast pace, slipping something inside his inner jacket. As he hurried past on the opposite side of the road, he suddenly stopped and looked in our direction. His face was shadowed under the brim of his hat.

I was still in Austen's arms, so he simply turned me toward the wall and kissed me again, his heart hammering so hard, I could feel it against my chest.

There was a scream from Dutfield's Yard, and Austen pulled back.

Jack was off again, running in the opposite direction of Commercial Road, where there would be fewer coppers.

My entire body was shaking, and I swallowed, trying to control my breath. "Do you think he saw us?" I whispered.

Austen didn't answer but took my hand and led me toward Commercial Road and onto the side street where Miles would pick us up.

He didn't need to answer. I knew the truth.

Jack had seen us standing there—but had he seen our faces?

14

BUCKINGHAMSHIRE, ENGLAND
SEPTEMBER 30, 1938

There was a festive atmosphere in the Astors' golden ballroom that belied my mood that Friday night. Heavy gilded trim, floor-to-ceiling mirrors, and dark green wallpaper made the long, narrow room feel much bigger. The Munich Agreement had been signed that day by Neville Chamberlain, Adolf Hitler, Benito Mussolini, and Édouard Daladier, the prime minister of France. The Sudetenland, a large portion of Czechoslovakia, was now under German authority—and the Czechs were not given a choice.

Many British citizens thought that a war had been avoided and were celebrating. Others, like Winston Churchill, a prominent and outspoken member of Parliament, knew it was only a matter of time before Adolf Hitler would demand more, and he was vocal about his concerns.

"You've been quieter than usual tonight," Mama said as she approached me on the edge of the dance floor at Cliveden House. She slipped a wayward lock of my red hair behind my ear. "I miss seeing your dimples. Is everything okay?"

The band sounded out of tune, the clomping feet on the wood floor were too loud, and the laughter in the ballroom grated on my headache. I would have rather spent the day buried in research for the exhibit at Lancaster House, trying to find answers about Jack the Ripper, but I'd spent part of it traveling to Buckinghamshire and the other part trying to make small talk with the Astors' guests.

"I'm fine," I said to Mama, trying to put a smile on my face. I hadn't told her about Austen's kiss, or how it had completely upended me. Nothing had made sense since then. I felt like I was in a daze. What made it worse was that Austen and I hadn't said a word to each other all the way home from Whitechapel that night. What was there to say? He'd kissed me to blend in with the other couples lurking on Berner Street and to avoid being seen by Jack the Ripper, but it had been the most exquisite and heart-wrenching thing I'd ever experienced. And in the end, Jack might have seen us, anyway—which was something else I hadn't told Mama. I was still trying to process it myself.

"You don't look fine," she said as she studied me. "You can confide in me, Kathryn. I know what it's like to lead two separate lives. It's confusing and scary and thrilling, all at the same time. But more than that, it can feel lonely."

I took a deep breath, not able to hold it in any longer. "Austen kissed me."

Her eyes betrayed her surprise. "Just like that?"

I swallowed, realizing that I would need to explain the kiss and how it had come to be, but that also meant I would have to tell her about Berner Street.

"Please don't be angry at me."

"Why would I be angry? I've never met Austen, but I feel as if I know him. And he's a wonderful man, Kathryn. Honorable and clearly devoted to—"

"He didn't kiss me out of passion or desire—although—" My face began to burn as a group of three ladies walked toward us on the edge of the dance floor.

I didn't want to be interrupted now that I'd begun to tell her, so I slipped my arm around her and led her to a couch in the corner.

"What is it?" she asked, taking a seat next to me.

Thankfully, there was no one close enough to hear our conversation in the corner. Papa was on the opposite side of the ballroom, speaking to Charles Lindbergh. No doubt they were planning their trip to Berlin again, now that the Munich Agreement had been signed, and it seemed all was peaceful in Germany. For now.

"The kiss started out as a diversion, but it quickly turned to something more," I said. "So quickly, in fact, I'm still reeling."

"A diversion?" She frowned. "From what?"

It wouldn't pay to avoid the truth, so I whispered, "Jack the Ripper."

She stared at me and shook her head. "I don't understand."

I told her we had gone to Berner Street to try to get a look at Jack and how he and Elizabeth had unexpectedly come our way.

"Before we'd arrived in Whitechapel," I explained, "Austen had warned me to do as he said. To run if he said run, to hide if he said hide. Neither of us expected that he might have to kiss me to blend in. I think he was just as surprised as me at first—but then, I realized how much I liked it, and I drew him closer. The worst part is that neither of us said a word to each other on the carriage ride home." The heat in my cheeks intensified just thinking about it. "When we arrived at Wilton Crescent, he walked me to my door and I turned to him, waiting for him to say something—but when he didn't, I stepped inside and had a good cry."

Mama was still staring at me. "You went looking for Jack the Ripper?"

"Is that all you can say?"

"Of course that's all I can say!" She rarely got angry at me, especially in public, but she was upset now. "Austen's kiss pales in comparison, Kathryn. What are you thinking? You're talking about the most notorious killer of all time. What if he saw you?"

I pressed my lips together.

Hers parted. "No." She shook her head. "He didn't see you, did he?"

"I don't know for certain. It was dark, and I couldn't see his features, so I don't think he could see ours, but he looked in our direction and knew we were standing there watching."

She blinked several times, as if she could hardly believe what I was saying. "What if he recognized you? What if he comes for you next?"

"There are over five million people in London in 1888. What are the odds that he knows me? Besides, there were other people who saw him, like the grape seller, and none of them become victims." I was trying to convince myself as much as I wanted to convince her. "I'll be careful. I promise."

"You can't be one of his victims," she said, quietly. "It's not part of the original history, and if you're killed there before your time, then who will save Mary? Not to mention that it would be a deplorable and gruesome way to die."

"I will be fine." I tried to reassure us both. "And if I'm not there to save Mary, at least Austen still can."

"And risk losing his own life?" Her words struck a chord deep within me. It wasn't a risk I wanted him to take.

"You're right," I said. "I will do my best to stay safe in 1888."

"And here," Mama added, clearly trying to rein in her frustration with me. "Don't forget to stay safe here."

I was finally able to muster a smile, though it wasn't big. "Why wouldn't I be safe here?"

"Because you're so headstrong that you charge into battle without a second thought?" she asked. "Or you get so engrossed in your work that you start to neglect the relationships around you?" She put her hand on my cheek. "Or you think that something can't be done unless you're the one to do it? There are a dozen different ways you could get yourself into trouble here. Just be careful, sweetheart."

I laid my hand over hers as my eye caught on Calan McCaffrey and Sir Rothschild, speaking together in the opposite corner of the ballroom. Their faces were grim.

What if something had happened at the museum? By the looks of them, any number of things could have gone wrong.

"Excuse me," I said to Mama as I rose. "I'm going to speak to Calan and Sir Rothschild. It looks like there is trouble."

"Just as I said." Mama lifted her eyebrows at me. "Instead of running away from trouble, you seem to run toward it."

I smiled and left her side to approach my colleagues.

Both men were wearing tuxedos, and I'd seen each of them dance already that evening. Sir Rothschild had brought Bianca to the ball, and they were staying in a room across the hall from me. Bianca was a quiet, unremarkable kind of woman who sat on the edge of the room and observed rather than partook of the festivities. She watched me as I crossed the room to speak to her husband.

"I hope all is well," I said to Calan and Sir Rothschild as I approached them.

They were talking in low tones, and I couldn't make out their conversation, but they paused when I joined them.

"Is something wrong? Is there a problem at the museum?" I asked.

"It's nothing about the Ripper exhibit, if that's what you mean," Calan answered. "I recently acquired a large collection of paintings for the Royal Museum of Scotland. But because the artist is English, Bryant has been working with the Royal Museum to get some of the paintings sent to the London Museum for a special exhibit."

"It's one of the reasons I asked Calan to join our team," Sir Rothschild confessed. "I was hoping he could be a liaison between the two museums."

"The Royal Museum is happy to loan the paintings," Calan continued. "But it seems they have been lost in transit."

Sir Rothschild's face became serious again. "They were supposed to arrive yesterday, but there's been a delay, and we're having a hard time tracking them down."

"Not only is there a huge monetary value involved," Calan said, "but these paintings are one of a kind. Irreplaceable."

"Who is the artist?" I asked.

The men glanced at each other, and then Sir Rothschild said,

"I'd rather not say—just yet. I know you're trustworthy, but if news of this leaks, we would be facing significant backlash. Please don't say anything."

"Of course not." I frowned, curious about their secrecy.

"Shall we take a turn on the dance floor?" Sir Rothschild asked, surprising me with the sudden shift in conversation, as if he was trying to distract me.

"Of course." I smiled as he offered his arm.

We walked onto the dance floor, where dozens of people were dancing a foxtrot.

"This is a pleasant change of pace," Sir Rothschild said as he slipped his arms around me, and we melded onto the dance floor. "I can almost forget all of my other troubles when I'm dancing."

He was a surprisingly good dancer, and it was a challenge to keep up with him, though I didn't mind.

"I'm sorry about the paintings," I said. "Is there anything to be done about it?"

"I sent a man to investigate. If he has not located the shipment by tomorrow afternoon, I will travel to Glasgow and see what I can find." He smiled, and his mustache came up at the corners. "But I really don't want to ruin this evening with worries about the paintings. We have much to celebrate. The Sudetenland is now secure, Germany has her people back where they belong, and not a single drop of bloodshed was required."

"I had forgotten that you were in favor of Hitler's acquisition of the Sudetenland." I couldn't hide the displeasure in my voice.

Sir Rothschild was quiet for a moment, and then he said, "Perhaps history will prove me wrong, but I believe Adolf Hitler is one of the most brilliant men to have walked this planet, and while I'm a Brit through and through and loyal to my king and country, I think we could learn some valuable lessons from the Germans. Is there anything wrong with that?"

It was a sentiment I'd heard from countless people in London, and it didn't surprise me. Not anymore. Yet, I knew that history would prove that Adolf Hitler was a madman—whether he was brilliant or insane, or perhaps both, was up for debate. Grandmother Maggie had told us that she lived long enough in her 1940s path to see Hitler's downfall, but it came at the expense of millions of lives. That didn't seem brilliant to me.

"May I have this dance?" Calan asked as soon as I was finished with Sir Rothschild.

I smiled and nodded. "Of course."

He took me into his arms, a little closer than Sir Rothschild had, as the band played "They Can't Take That Away from Me." Calan began to hum the tune, and I closed my eyes, imagining what it would be like to dance this close with Austen.

Melancholy struck me so quickly, it took my breath away. All I could think about was Austen—his passionate words in the garden. Then, his arms around me on Berner Street and his lips against mine, overwhelming all my senses until I felt as if I might drown in them. I wanted him here, to talk about the kiss, to ask him why it had taken so long for him to confess his feelings and why he continued to keep them locked inside. I wanted to introduce him to Mama and Papa and show him this other world I occupied, one that looked much like 1888 but where I was free to pursue the things I loved.

It suddenly occurred to me that perhaps Austen *did* know this life.

I stumbled, causing Calan to come to a stop.

"Is everything alright?" he asked.

"I'm sorry," I said as I took an unsteady breath. "Yes, everything is fine."

But was it? Austen was only twenty-five in 1888. That would make him seventy-five today. As Calan and I began to dance again, I searched the ballroom, as if Austen might appear. Yet, I couldn't see him as part of the Cliveden Set. Not the Austen I knew in 1888. But *was* he alive? And did he live in London? Perhaps at his old address?

A longing so deep and powerful tugged at me to look for him this very moment, even though I was thirty miles away from the city. But what would I do if I found him? He'd be an old man, and it would shock him to see me again. Nothing good would come from visiting Austen—for him or for me. It was a foolish notion.

When our song came to an end, Calan offered a bow and then handed me over to Papa, who was waiting for the next dance.

As soon as the music began, I fell into Papa's embrace, needing his strength.

"What's bothering you, *ma chérie*?" he asked. "Is it Austen? Mary? Both?"

"Yes." I put my cheek on his shoulder, unsure if I wanted to talk about it all again.

"If I've learned anything, it's that love cannot be rushed," he said, a smile in his voice. "And that if it is meant to be, it usually finds a way to thrive."

I sighed, realizing I did not want to talk about Austen. It was easy for him to say such things, but far harder for me to believe them.

"And," he continued, "as for Mary, is there anyone who might know why she left home, or if it had anything to do with the Freemasons? Someone close to her. A servant, perhaps."

I pulled back from his shoulder as a thought occurred to me.

There was one person who might know—someone Mary had trusted, who knew the ins and outs of her daily life better than anyone else.

Someone who had left our house at the same time as Mary.

"Her lady's maid, Sarah Danbury."

"And you haven't thought to ask her before now?"

"At the time, I thought that Mother was making yet another change in the household staff. But perhaps Danbury was let go because she knew too much."

"There is only one way to find out," Papa said. "But be careful, Kathryn. The truth can set us free, but it can also put us in danger."

I nodded, heeding his words.

I'd already discovered the wisdom in his warning.

15

LONDON, ENGLAND
OCTOBER 1, 1888

The next day, I found myself at 50 Chester Square, an elegant townhome in Belgravia, one of the more affluent districts in central London. The day was overcast, and rain still fell from the dark clouds. To Londoners, the Double Event had just happened the day before, and news was starting to circulate.

My fifteen-minute walk from Wilton Crescent had taken me past several groups of people standing on street corners with newspapers, shaken by the unthinkable. How had the murderer gotten away with *two* killings on the same night? And why had Sir Charles Warren erased the graffito on the wall?

There was a heaviness that permeated the air. Even in our home, the staff whispered about the murders. It was all anyone could think about. With the popularity and subsequent closure of *The Strange Case of Dr. Jekyll and Mr. Hyde*, the public started to question if the killer was a physician like Dr. Jekyll with knowledge of anatomy to accomplish his gruesome tasks. The image of a man in a top hat and overcoat, and carrying a doctor's bag, stalking the dark, foggy streets of Whitechapel, had started to appear on the front cover of all the newspapers.

I knocked on the door of 50 Chester Square and took a deep breath. The owner of the home, Mrs. Windham, was a family acquaintance. She had hired Danbury after she left our house, or so Duffy had told me.

The butler soon answered the door, and I was invited in out of the rain. He took my umbrella and set it on a drying rack and then led me into the parlor.

"My dear Miss Kelly," Mrs. Windham said as she arrived a few minutes later. "What a lovely surprise." She smiled and motioned to one of the chairs. "I've rang for tea. Won't you have a seat?"

I sat opposite her on an ornate chair, perching on the edge as decorum demanded, my skirts tucked properly around my legs, and my corset pinching my waist. I wanted to get the pleasantries over with, but they were a necessity.

"How are you, my dear?" she asked with a friendly smile. She was in her mid-forties and took great pains to deflect the appearance of her age behind a tight corset, expensive clothing, and gaudy jewelry. "I had such a lovely time at your mother's ball several weeks ago. Mr. Maybrick's voice is a dream. What an honor for you to dance with him. I had so hoped my own daughter could join us that night, but she was indisposed. I do hope your mother will invite Mr. Maybrick back again, so that I can introduce him to my daughter. But then again, perhaps you have already stolen him for yourself."

She prattled on and on, and every time she asked a question, I began to answer, but she cut me off and continued speaking.

The butler brought in the tea tray, and Mrs. Windham poured a cup for me and then one for her. She spoke about the Whitechapel Murders, as they were called, but she had no more information than anyone else. I kept my eye on the clock, wanting to be done with the arduous conversation, though I needed to endure it for at least thirty minutes before I could ask to speak to Danbury. It would be rude to cut the visit short before that.

As soon as the clock hit thirty minutes, I gently interrupted my hostess.

"About a year ago," I said, "my mother discharged a maid from her employment, and I've been told she found a place here. I wonder if I may speak to her about a private matter?"

Mrs. Windham's eyebrows shot up. "I hope she's not being accused of something untoward."

"No. Nothing like that. Her name is Sarah Danbury."

"Yes, of course. I know who you're speaking of." She rose abruptly. "I'll call her in."

I also rose. "Thank you, Mrs. Windham."

She nodded and then left the room.

Several minutes passed before the door opened again and Danbury entered, her eyes wide with concern.

"Hello, Danbury."

She nodded and offered a curtsy, though every line of her body communicated her discomfort. The last time I saw her was the night Mary left.

"Please come in and close the door," I said to her.

Danbury slipped inside and shut the door but stood as close to it as she could. "What can I do for you, miss?"

"Please don't be worried," I said as I motioned her closer. "I'm not here to cause trouble. I'd like to ask you some questions about my sister, Mary."

She didn't look relieved or less concerned. If anything, she appeared more upset as her eyes darted around the room. "I don't know anything, miss."

"You don't know why Mary suddenly left our house?"

She swallowed and shook her head.

"You never heard any conversation? Mary didn't mention anything to you?"

"No, miss."

Her behavior told me that she wasn't telling the truth—but why?

I took a step closer, needing her to understand how important her answer was to Mary's well-being.

"Mary is in grave danger. Her very life depends on what you

might know. I need to understand why Mary left my parents' home. I spoke to her, and she said that Father didn't force her to leave, but that she left of her own free will. I don't believe her for a moment. Why would she give up the comfort and safety of her parents' home to—" I couldn't continue. I wanted to know why Mary would take up with a man for safety when she had my father's protection to rely upon. "Please. I must find answers. I fear Mary's life is in danger from the man who is murdering women in Whitechapel."

Danbury's eyes grew wide at that statement. "Is Miss Mary in real danger?"

"Yes."

She glanced around the room again, as if looking for prying ears, and then leaned in. "Please don't tell anyone where you heard this information. I fear for my own life if someone should know."

I frowned, but if the truth was so dire that my sister would hide in Whitechapel, then perhaps Danbury's fears were well-founded.

"Of course I won't," I promised.

She paused, as if second-guessing her decision to share, but then she plunged ahead. "Miss Mary found a book, or something like a book, hidden away in a secret compartment in your father's study. I don't know how she found it, or if she'd been looking for it, but whatever was written in that book terrified and alarmed her. She fretted over it for several days before she confronted your father."

"What was written in the book?" I asked.

"I don't know. Miss Mary wouldn't tell me. I didn't see the book, either. She kept it hidden."

"What happened after she confronted my father?"

"That was the night she left."

"Did she leave of her own free will? Or did my father force her to go?"

"I don't know. I truly don't." She pressed her lips together as sweat beaded on her brow. "The next morning, your mother rang for me. She said that my services were no longer needed. I would be given a letter of reference, and I was to be gone by noon. When

I tried to ask her where Miss Mary had gone, she told me not to ask any questions or discuss anything with the other staff. She threatened to send me away without a reference if I did." Danbury swallowed hard. "I couldn't take that chance, so I didn't say another word until now."

My mind spun with possibilities. "Thank you for answering my questions. I know it was a risk for you to tell me, and I promise I won't get you in trouble."

Danbury nodded slowly, though she didn't look convinced. "Will there be anything else?"

"If you can think of something, please get word to me."

"Yes, miss." Danbury opened the door, clearly eager to see the back of me. "Good day, Miss Kathryn."

I left the Windham's home with my umbrella open and walked back to Wilton Crescent, hardly noticing anything but the thoughts running through my mind.

What kind of book did Mary find that would be so dire as to either send her away or make her choose to leave? And where had Father been hiding this book? Why did he have it to begin with?

The only person who might answer my questions was Mary, but it would be almost impossible to go to her without Austen's help. I couldn't ask for our carriage to take me. Father would find out where I'd gone. But I couldn't ask Austen to take me to Whitechapel again.

I would need to hire a carriage, though I didn't have that kind of money. Father saw to all my expenses, so I would need to sell something.

I was still pondering this when I approached Wilton Crescent. Austen's carriage was just pulling up to the front of his home. We hadn't spoken since returning from Berner Street, and I wasn't sure what I would say to him. I contemplated turning around to walk in the opposite direction, but he stepped out of his carriage and paused when he saw me.

His blue eyes were stormy as he regarded me, and my traitorous heart leapt.

"Hello," I said, swallowing the unexpected nerves racing up my throat.

"What are you doing in the rain?"

"I went to see Mary's lady's maid on Chester Square."

"And did she tell you anything valuable?"

"Yes, but I need to speak to Mary again."

He sighed and glanced at his house before looking back at me. "Get in the carriage. I'll take you."

I stared at him, surprised. "Are you cert—"

"Don't give me time to change my mind, Kathryn." He nodded at Miles, who nodded back, and then Austen opened the door for me.

I quickly walked toward him. He took my umbrella and then offered his hand for me to step into his carriage, but I paused and said, "Thank you."

"You will be the death of me," he said. "I'm certain of it."

I smiled and stepped into the carriage.

I found myself sitting next to Austen once again on our way to Whitechapel. He was stiff beside me as the carriage moved over the cobblestone roads and through the loud traffic of central London.

Two nights ago, the darkness had acted as a buffer between us, and we hadn't needed to speak about the kiss. But in the light of day, it felt like the kiss was staring at me, demanding to be acknowledged and discussed.

How did I bring it up when Austen clearly wasn't planning to address it? He'd spent most of his life ignoring important issues that confronted him, but I couldn't be so blasé. I couldn't pretend it hadn't happened, or that it hadn't affected me so profoundly.

"Are you planning to talk about the kiss?" I asked, deciding bluntness was the best approach to Austen's shifting moods.

His face remained neutral as he stared out the window. "What is there to say?"

"Everything."

The muscles in his cheek twitched before he said, "There is no reason to discuss something that can't happen again."

I leaned back into the seat, trying to control my emotions. He was right. It couldn't happen again. There would be no more kisses, because there was no future for us.

We drove in silence through the rain to Miller's Court. Though it was a small space, and I couldn't avoid touching him, he was hard and unyielding beside me. When the carriage came to a stop on Dorset Street, Austen stepped out and opened the umbrella, then he turned to me, and our gazes met.

From the look in his eyes, I knew he was still thinking about the kiss. I had the urge to return to his arms, right there on the street, to both rekindle the passion and soothe the ache I saw in his gaze.

The ache that was nestled inside my own heart.

Instead, I took the hand he offered and stepped out of the carriage, standing close to him as he held the umbrella over my head and walked me down the passage to the courtyard where Mary's room was located.

I was conscious of his every movement beside me. Every time his arm brushed mine, the way my skirt rustled against the side of his leg, and the way he held his breath at each touch.

My senses heightened, being this near to him again, and the ache grew stronger.

When we came to number thirteen, we stood close so the umbrella protected us both, and Austen knocked on the door.

I took a cautious look up at him, but he stared straight ahead.

"Please don't be mad," I said gently.

He sighed, the tension in his body easing. "I'm not mad, Kate." He looked down at me. "I'm heartbroken."

The door opened, tearing my thoughts from Austen.

I turned, expecting to see my sister, but it wasn't Mary at the door. It was another young woman, probably in her mid-twenties, wearing an old dress and a tattered shawl.

"Can I help you?" she asked in a faint Irish accent as she looked me over with just as much curiosity as I had staring at her.

"Is Mary—Marie Jeanette at home?" I asked.

"Who's asking?"

I opened my mouth to say I was her sister, but then I remembered that Mary didn't want me to tell anyone who I was. "Will she be back soon?" I asked instead.

The woman nodded her head at something behind us. "She's here now."

Austen and I turned as Mary appeared in the passage. She paused at seeing us and then hurried her steps, passing between us as she entered her room. She turned just inside the doorway, frustration in her gaze. "What are you doing back here?"

"I need to speak to you," I said. "I went to see—" I almost said her lady's maid but changed course. "I saw Danbury—"

Mary held up her hand to stop me, glancing out the door before looking at her friend. Finally, she said to Austen, "Wait in the carriage for her. I'll send her out presently."

It was his turn to look between me and Mary—his glance shifting to the other woman—before he nodded and left Mary's room.

"You'll need to step out, too, Dierdre," Mary said to the woman in a voice that sounded more like a Whitechapel accent than the cultured one she'd learned as a child. "I need a bit of privacy."

Dierdre eyed me from head to foot, disdain in her gaze, before she said to Mary, "Don't fret none, Marie Jeanette. I'll just pop into the pub and see if Teddy is around."

Mary nodded as she held the door open for Dierdre. When the other woman was gone and I had entered her room, Mary closed the door and turned to me. "I told you not to come back," she said, pacing to the window to look out before returning to me. "You're putting both of our lives at risk, Kathryn. What if someone followed you?"

I hadn't even considered that possibility. What if Jack had followed me? Or my parents?

I couldn't worry about that now. I needed to tell her why I

had come. "I spoke to Danbury, and she told me about the book, Mary."

My sister's eyes opened wide as her face paled. "What does she know about the book?"

"Then it's true?"

Mary walked to the bed and sat, shaking her head. "She can't know what was in the book. I never told her."

I joined my sister on the bed. "What book did you find? What did it contain?"

She rose again, clearly agitated, and went back to the window. "Joseph might come back—or Dierdre. You need to leave. My neighbor lady asked about you the last time you were here. She suspected you were my sister, because of our red hair."

I recalled that the file on Mary Jane Kelly said that her parents had disowned her, but she was still in contact with her sister. Would her neighbor be questioned after the murder?

"So, you can see it's not safe for you to come here, Kathryn," Mary continued. "I'll have to find a way to explain who you are to Dierdre now, too."

"Who is Dierdre?"

"She is a friend. She stays here, with some others, from time to time, but Joseph doesn't like it. I can't have my friends sleeping on the street when a murderer is afoot, can I? Joseph says he pays for part of this room, so he should have a say, but I told him he can find another place to live if he'd like." She pressed her lips together. "He left early this morning, angry at me. I don't know how I'll make the rent if I don't have his help, but I can't turn my friends away."

She rubbed her hands over her arms and walked to the fireplace, where the embers were burning low. The room was cool and damp and would not hold up against the oncoming winter—but that wouldn't matter, because I would get Mary away from this place before November 9th.

"You didn't leave our parents' house of your own free will, did you?" I asked as I joined her. "You were forced to leave because you found the book and there was something in it that was incriminating? Is that it?"

She stared at me for a moment, her green eyes filled with so many emotions, I couldn't differentiate what she was thinking and feeling.

"Even if I wanted to tell you," she whispered, "I wouldn't."

"Is this about Father?" I asked. "I know he's a Freemason."

Something flickered in her gaze. Fear?

"Is that it?" I asked. "Does this have something to do with the Freemasons?"

"Don't look for answers, Kathryn," Mary begged. "The Freemasons have an innocent enough façade, and I believe that most of them join the Brotherhood with good intentions. But there are members who are formidable and deceitful and cruel, and they use the Freemasons' power as a weapon. There is nothing you can find that will alleviate your curiosity or help in any way."

I stared at her, wanting to heed her words but needing to know what she had found. "What was in the book?"

A movement outside the window made my sister look up quickly. A man was approaching.

"That's Joseph," she said, panic lacing her words. "I don't want him to know who you are. Please. Don't tell him." She looked at my dress, which I hadn't had time to change after paying a call on Mrs. Windham, and shook her head. "He'll never believe you're from Whitechapel. He'll ask too many questions and want to know more about my past."

Dierdre appeared, stepping into the passageway and intercepting Joseph. She drew close to him and whispered into his ear.

Mary watched closely, but I couldn't tell if she was jealous or relieved.

Eventually, Dierdre took the man's hand and tugged him in the opposite direction, and they disappeared onto Dorset Street.

"You have to leave," Mary said to me. "Dierdre can distract Joseph for a time, but he'll be back." She opened the door and looked right and then left. When she turned back to me, she said,

"Please believe me, Kathryn. You do not want to know what I know, or you will end up no better than me. Not even Austen could save you."

She pushed me out the door and then closed it in my face, not giving me the chance to ask her another question or even say good-bye.

Frustrated, angry, and deterred, I hurried through the passage toward Dorset Street and Austen's waiting carriage.

Joseph and Dierdre were nowhere in sight as Austen stepped out of his carriage and helped me in. He tapped on the ceiling, and the carriage pulled away from Miller's Court.

"Did you find the answers you were seeking?" he asked me.

I shook my head as I bit the inside of my cheek and stared out the window. It was infuriating. "At least I know there *was* a book. But she won't tell me anything else."

He let out a weary sigh. "That won't stop you, will it?"

"Of course not." I frowned at him. "Perhaps Mary can't handle the truth, but I've never been afraid of it."

"Even if it puts you in danger?"

"More danger than we're already in?"

He scoffed, but then he softened as he studied me. "What did you learn?"

"That this *does* have to do with my father's involvement in the Freemasons."

Austen's blue eyes filled with anger—or was it frustration? "I was afraid of that."

"Please tell me what you know about them."

"I know that their loyalty to each other exceeds their loyalty to their family." His voice was bitter and tense, and I wondered what experience had given him that edge. "I also know that if the book your sister found has anything to do with the Freemasons, and there was any suspicion that she could use the information against them, that she would be silenced." He took my hand in his—surprising me, even as it brought comfort. "The only reason Miles found Mary is because you had her address from the future."

"I thought you said a private investigator found my sister."

"It doesn't matter. The point I'm trying to make is that Mary disappeared. I don't even think your parents know where she's at. And neither do people in power who might try to silence her. Perhaps your parents are treating her like she's dead because they've told other people that she *is* dead." He stared at me. "Do you understand what I'm saying?"

I stared at him as it was all starting to make sense. "Are you suggesting that my sister's life in Whitechapel is a blessing? That it was a kindness from my parents?"

"It's better than her being killed by the Freemasons."

Neither of us spoke as the carriage entered central London. The rain continued to tap against the roof, and the horse's hooves clopped on the cobblestone. My head was starting to hurt, and I was exhausted in body and soul.

"I'm sorry, Kate," Austen said, his voice heavy. "For everything."

I leaned against his arm, wishing he would hold me but knowing that it wouldn't be wise. His words did bring comfort, though, and despite all the heartache—from everything outside the carriage, as well as within—I knew he spoke the truth.

He *was* sorry.

16

OCTOBER 3, 1938
LONDON, ENGLAND

The Masonic Peace Memorial, the largest Masonic Hall in London, stood on the corner of Great Queen Street between Covent Garden and Holborn. It was a massive art deco structure made of gray stone with a tower on one end and large bronze doors underneath. I'd heard it was built in honor of the thousands of Freemasons who had died in the Great War and had recently replaced an older building.

It was cold, and the sky was overcast as I opened the heavy door and slipped inside the echoing building. Beautiful mosaic tiles created a star design on the floor, while marble pillars flanked either side of the room. A male receptionist sat at a desk near the door, and he rose upon my entry.

"May I help you?" he asked.

I had come to the hall to get answers about my father's involvement in the Freemasons in 1888, since I knew he wouldn't discuss anything with me in person. Mary had warned me that it was dangerous to look for answers, but she'd meant in 1888. Here in 1938, it would be far safer to find what I was looking for—at least, that's what I kept telling myself. Only fifty years had passed since Jack the Ripper let loose his terror on London. If it was a Freemason coverup, as I was more certain than ever that it was, it was likely that there were still people alive who knew who he was and were still hiding his identity.

"I've heard that your research library is open to the public," I said to the receptionist. "I'm wondering if I may have a look around."

"What are you looking for?" he asked as he eyed me from head to foot.

I was wearing a simple navy blue dress with wide lapels and a matching hat. My coat was the same color and hugged tight at my waist. I carried a leather satchel with a notebook and pencils inside. I wasn't sure what he thought about me, but I wasn't concerned.

"I'm looking for information about a family member," I said. "His name was Sir Bernard Kelly. He was a surgeon at King's College Hospital."

"Was?" he asked. "Sir Kelly is still alive."

I lifted my eyebrows, not expecting to hear that news. My father was in his late forties in 1888. I'd assumed he was dead by now. "He is? I—I thought he had passed away."

"He's not in good health," the man told me. "But he's living—at least, he was the last I heard. He doesn't attend meetings any longer, as you can imagine, but we keep an eye on the oldest members of our brotherhood out of respect. I could get you his address if you'd like to visit with him."

"Yes, of course," I said quickly, not wanting to appear heartless, though I had no intention of visiting with my father from my other path. He had no idea I was a time-crosser, and it would only shock his system to see me at his advanced age.

"I'll find it for you as you do your research. Follow me, please." He led me through the building, pointing out the Grand Temple, where the Grand Lodge met, and noting that there were twenty-six smaller temples for the various lodges that gathered in the building.

"Here we are," he finally said as we entered a large, well-lit room with aisles of shelves, boxes, files, and books. "The reference library."

Another man sat at a desk in the library, and when I entered, he rose for introductions.

"I'm Mr. Hornby," he said with a nod. "Here to assist you, Miss . . . ?"

"I'm Kathryn Voland."

"An American?"

"Yes. I work for the Smithsonian Institute, but I'm in London working on a special exhibit with the London Museum."

Both men lifted their eyebrows, but it was Mr. Hornby who said, "That's very impressive, Miss Voland. How may I be of service to you today?"

"I'm looking for information about Sir Bernard Kelly," I said.

Mr. Hornby's eyebrows were still raised. "Sir Kelly? How very interesting. Is this research for your exhibit at the London Museum?"

I shook my head, not wanting to reveal why I needed to find information about my father—or how his connection to Freemasonry might be linked to my sister Mary's exile and, ultimately, how it could be connected to Jack the Ripper. If the Freemasons were hiding Jack's real identity in 1888, I had no reason to think they weren't still hiding it.

"Sir Kelly is a relative of Miss Voland's," the receptionist explained to Mr. Hornby.

"He is," I confirmed. "I'm curious about his connection to the Freemasons for personal reasons."

"Let's see what we can find," Mr. Hornby said as the receptionist left us, promising to find Sir Kelly's address.

I followed Mr. Hornby toward the shelves as he squinted through his glasses, examining the books. "It seems to me that Sir Kelly had quite a history with the Freemasons."

"Oh?"

"Yes, indeed. I'm not surprised you'd be curious about his

involvement with the Brotherhood. He was part of one of the great exploration trips to Israel in 1874 with Sir Charles Warren."

So my suspicions *had* been correct. Father had been in Jerusalem with Sir Charles Warren.

"Sir Warren was an archaeologist, and some say he ushered in the age of biblical archaeology with his work," Mr. Hornby said as he perused a shelf of books. "He made significant discoveries in Jerusalem, specifically concerning the Temple Mount, where King Solomon's Temple was located."

I could hardly believe that my parents knew Sir Charles Warren yet had never mentioned him to me before, especially as his name had become more prominent in the press surrounding the Ripper murders.

Mr. Hornby removed several books from the shelf. "Sir Warren wrote four different books about his discoveries in Jerusalem, and over fifty of his maps were published in what is now known as the *Warren Atlas.*" He brought the books to a table and took one of them out of the pile. "*Underground Jerusalem* was published in 1876, two years after the trip Sir Kelly took with Sir Warren. I think this might be a good place for you to begin your research. But please be careful. There are only two known copies of the book."

"Who has the other one?" I asked.

"It's believed that Sir Warren sent a personal copy to Prince Albert Victor, with his original notes from the trip, but that's only speculation."

"Why are there only two copies?"

"They weren't meant for public distribution," he said. "Just for Masonic reference."

Mr. Hornby opened the book and began to page through it until he came to the place he was looking for. "Here is the account of the group that traveled with Sir Warren in 1874." He stepped back and pulled a chair out for me to sit. "I'll be at my desk if you need further assistance."

"Thank you." I set my purse on the table and smiled at the helpful man.

After he left, I took a seat and pulled the book toward myself, careful not to damage the pages. It was a thick tome with a red cloth cover and gold lettering. If it was one of only two copies that still existed, I didn't want to be the person to ruin it.

Immediately, the name Sir Bernard Kelly jumped out at me, and next to it, Sir Robert Baird—Austen's father.

In 1874, I took a team of amateur archaeologists and Freemasons to the site of the Temple Mount in Jerusalem. Each was intrigued by the work I'd previously done, starting in 1867 with my first trip to Jerusalem, and some were invested financially in the Palestine Exploration Fund. Others had interest in biblical archaeology for various reasons. Several of the team members brought their wives, and we spent many enjoyable days exploring Jerusalem and the surrounding countryside before we began our explorations into the tunnels in the Temple Mount.

Among those present with me in 1874 were Sir Bernard Kelly and his wife, Agatha; Sir Robert Baird, and his wife, Madeline; Mr. William Nichols, and his wife, Polly—

I stopped reading as my mouth fell open, and then I quickly reread the last line. Polly Nichols, the first victim of Jack the Ripper, was on the same trip to Israel as my parents! Father and Mother hadn't once hinted that they knew Polly Nichols after she'd been murdered in Whitechapel—but then, why would they? She was a fallen woman and a murder victim. They wouldn't want anyone to associate them with her. I continued to read, my pulse skipping with both fear and excitement as the pieces of a confusing and heartbreaking puzzle began to fall into place.

Mr. John Chapman, and his wife, Annie, were also in attendance, as were John Stride and his wife, Elizabeth. Thomas Conway was another member of the team, and he brought his wife, Catherine.

I reread the entry three times before I believed what I was seeing. Along with mine and Austen's parents, the Nichols, Chapman, Stride, and Conway families were in Jerusalem with Sir Charles Warren in 1874. Thomas Conway was Catherine Eddowes's common-law husband, and she sometimes went by Conway, though was back to Eddowes at the time of her death.

I could hardly wrap my mind around the information. There was no question that Jack the Ripper was somehow involved in the trip—and that the murders he committed were not random, but were intentional, calculated, and premeditated. He knew exactly who he was killing, but the question remained, why? And why were Sir Charles Warren and the other Freemasons covering up the murderer's identity? Was Jack responsible for the Bairds' murders? And why was my sister a victim, when she wasn't on the trip to Jerusalem? If the pattern was repeated, it should have been my mother who was a victim, since she had been with the team.

But that begged yet another question. Why had all those women ended up in Whitechapel? They were from well-respected families, and none of their husbands had ended up in the poorest district in the city.

There had to be answers to my questions. But I wouldn't get them from my parents in 1888. The only person who might know and might answer me was Austen. His parents had been there—perhaps he knew something. Was he aware that all these families had been with our parents on that trip?

I needed to ask him as soon as possible. Part of me wanted to look for him in 1938, to confront him and demand he tell me the truth. But I couldn't risk being seen by him. I would have to wait until I woke up in 1888 tomorrow.

I scanned the rest of the chapter in the book, but I didn't see anything else of importance. Sir Warren didn't list any other members of his team, nor was there mention of Robert and Madeline Baird's deaths. Instead, he discussed all the technical information about the archaeological dig and the treasures that had been discovered.

After taking up my purse, I found Mr. Hornby.

"Done so soon?" he asked as he rose from his desk.

"Yes. Thank you."

"Did you find what you were looking for?"

"Even more," I told him. "I appreciate your help."

He frowned at me, but then nodded and said, "Any time. Be sure to come back if you need anything else."

I left the Masonic Peace Memorial with more questions than when I had arrived. But at least now I knew there was a connection between the Ripper victims, and that it had something to do with Freemasonry and the trip to Jerusalem fourteen years ago. I just didn't know what it was.

Yet.

I was preoccupied with what I'd learned at the Masonic Peace Memorial as I entered the Lancaster House later that morning. No matter how hard I tried, I couldn't piece all the women's murders together. What could have happened in Jerusalem that led Jack to kill five women fourteen years later in Whitechapel?

"I think I've found them," I overheard Sir Rothschild saying as I entered my office, where he and Calan were speaking. Calan was sitting at the desk, and Sir Rothschild was standing on the other side of it.

"Found what?" I asked as I took off my hat and put it on the hook near the door.

"Good morning," Calan said with a smile as he rose from the desk.

"The paintings," Sir Rothschild said. "It appears that they're in a warehouse in Liverpool. I'm not sure how the mix-up happened, but I've been assured that the shipment will be on the next available train to London, and we should have the paintings by the end of this week."

"That's good news," I said, though the paintings were of little consequence to me.

"Where were you this morning?" Calan asked, changing the subject. "You looked deep in thought when you entered."

I'd been replaying everything I'd learned about the five victims in my mind—yet, nothing made sense. Polly Nichols's husband was a printer on Fleet Street. Annie Chapman's husband was a driver for a wealthy family in Windsor. Elizabeth Stride's husband was a furniture maker and the son of a wealthy property owner. And Catherine Eddowes's common-law husband had been in the military. How had each of those men been involved in the trip to Jerusalem with my parents, the Bairds, and Sir Charles Warren?

"Did you know that each of Jack the Ripper's victims—at least four of them—were on a trip to Jerusalem in 1874 with Sir Charles Warren?"

Calan frowned as Sir Rothschild asked, "Are you serious?"

"Yes, and the only one who wasn't on the trip was Mary Jane Kelly. But her parents were on the trip. You didn't know?"

Sir Rothschild shook his head. "I've never heard that before."

"I just read it in a book written by Sir Charles Warren himself called *Jerusalem Underground*, published in 1876."

"How could this have been overlooked?" Calan asked. "Surely, someone in the past fifty years should have put this together."

"Unless, like everything else, the Freemasons didn't want it known," I suggested. "The gentleman at the Masonic research library told me that there are only two known copies still in existence, and one of them might be in Buckingham Palace, which means they've gone to great lengths to ensure that it wasn't widely known. All the families on that trip had ties to Freemasonry, and if people would have put the pieces together, they might have started to ask questions that the Freemasons didn't want to answer."

"What do you think it all means?" Sir Rothschild asked as he studied me. "Have you come to a conclusion?"

I lifted my shoulders. "Perhaps each of the women had gained information about the Freemasons that put their lives at risk. And Jack was out to silence them for good. Sir Charles Warren was helping him cover his tracks, because he, too, might have wanted their silence." I thought of the book Mary had found in my father's study. Did it have anything to do with the other murders? It was too early to tell, and I didn't want to share too much with Calan and Sir Rothschild until I had more proof.

"That's an interesting theory," Sir Rothschild said as he leaned against my desk and crossed his arms. "But what about this one? What if the women were being killed as punishment to the men who had gone on the trip with Sir Warren? Maybe it didn't have to do with silencing the women, but with threatening the men. Perhaps Jack wanted something from them that he wasn't getting, and he was knocking them off, one by one, trying to tip their hand."

"I hadn't thought about that possibility," I said as I considered the things I knew. My parents had forced Mary out of the house, and she was in hiding. Was it to silence her—or protect her?

"Either way," Calan said, "it's a solid discovery into the case."

"But what remains is the *why*," I said to them, tapping my chin.

The Ripper letters were stacked on my desk, but I'd read enough of them to know that they didn't offer enough clues. I needed to know why Austen's parents died and how the trip to Jerusalem linked all the victims. And the only person who might know was Austen.

"Do you really think you can unmask the man that history has chosen to keep hidden?" Calan asked me. "And, if you did, do you think people would believe you? There are a lot of people who enjoy the mystery surrounding Jack the Ripper, and they wouldn't want to know the truth."

"I don't know," I said with a shrug.

"I need to get back to work." Sir Rothschild sighed and pushed away from the desk. "Keep me posted on what you find, Kathryn."

I nodded as the phone rang and Calan answered.

Walking to the window, I looked out at Green Park. A light rain had begun to fall on the autumn landscape as Buckingham Palace stood in the distance. A thought started to form. If I unmasked Jack the Ripper in 1888, that would mean that his identity would be known in 1938, as well. My grandmother had lived in 2001, and she had mentioned Jack the Ripper once that I recalled. She had said that even in 2001, his identity wasn't known. Would I change history in 1888 *and* 1938 if I shared the truth with the world? And would I lose *both* my paths?

Panic raced up my limbs at the thought. Even if I unmasked Jack, I could never reveal his name. All I might hope to do was protect my sister. But even then, I could simply take her from Miller's Court the night before her murder and send her somewhere far away. If she'd let me.

Yet, that might not be enough. If Jack needed my sister to die to keep his identity a secret, then simply sending her away wouldn't work. He'd always be looking for her.

I needed to learn his identity so I could stop him. Even if that meant forfeiting both my paths. I couldn't live with myself if I had the ability to save Mary and didn't.

17

OCTOBER 4, 1888
LONDON, ENGLAND

I didn't waste a moment the next day. As soon as I was dressed, I walked out of the front door of 11 Wilton Crescent and pulled the ringer for number 12. Brinley answered the door with his familiar calm, though his eyes took on a sparkle for me.

"Good morning, Brinley," I said to Austen's butler. "Is he at home?"

"He's in his study, Miss Kelly. Won't you come in and I'll see if he'll receive you."

I entered Austen's home, and Brinley led me into the parlor, where I waited.

The rain that had been plaguing the city for the past two days had passed, but in its place was a cold dampness that seeped into my bones. I stood at the front window and looked out at the street. Carriages passed and people walked by—and still, Austen didn't come.

I was about to throw my resolve to the wind and storm upstairs to find him for myself when the door finally opened, and he appeared.

His hair was disheveled, and he needed a shave. He hadn't

bothered to put on a coat, and his shirtsleeves were rolled up at his forearms.

Though I'd been prepared to see him, my heart still did a funny little flip, and I had to look down at my hands to steady the nerves that came to life in my stomach. It was getting harder and harder to see Austen, to remember his words to me in the garden and his kisses on Berner Street, and to know that our time together was coming to an end.

"Do you need something?" he asked. "I'm on a tight deadline and have very little time to spare."

Again, his reference to work puzzled me. "What is it that you do?"

"I don't think that's why you've come." He sighed. "What do you want, Kate?"

I lifted my chin and faced him with as much courage as I could muster. "I need to know what *you* know about your parents' murder."

"No."

I stared at him for a moment and then said, "Why not?"

"It's none of your business."

My lips parted as I took a step closer to him. "None of my business? Do you know that the first four victims of Jack the Ripper were on that trip to Jerusalem with our parents?"

He frowned. "What?"

"Polly Nichols, Annie Chapman, Elizabeth Stride, and Catherine Eddowes were all in Jerusalem with their husbands. My sister is the only one of the five who wasn't there. But that means that one woman from each family who was on that trip will be killed by Jack the Ripper. And, if my suspicions are correct, your parents' murder has something to do with the others." I grasped his forearms. "I need to know what you know."

He stared at me for a long time, as if weighing the risk of revealing the truth.

"I can't tell you," he said, his voice low, almost apologetic. "And I don't want you to ask me again."

Anger came over me so suddenly, it took all my willpower not to shake him. Instead, I removed my hands from his arms and balled my fists against my thighs. "Why are you doing this? You know how frustrated I am that my father and Mary won't answer my questions. Why are you so pigheaded and obstinate? You know that all of this has something to do with the Freemasons and the trip to Jerusalem. Yet you refuse to tell me because of your own stubborn, foolish, selfish reasons." Tears stung my eyes, but I was more angry than sad.

He just stared at me.

I took a step back, wiping away my tears, not only because of his stubbornness, but also Mary's. How could I help them if they wouldn't let me? "For fourteen years, you've treated me with anger and indifference. I've tried to understand. Tried to be patient and faithful to our friendship." My gaze slipped to his lips, and I thought of our kiss, and my heart felt like it was tearing inside me. When I lifted my eyes again, I saw anguish in his gaze. "I don't know why you want to hurt me, Austen, but I can't do this anymore. I know that your life has been one injustice after another. I know that you've been wounded, more than anyone should ever be—and I know you're angry that I'm leaving here." More tears fell from my eyes, but this time I didn't wipe them away. "But I've never intentionally harmed you or pushed you away or shut you out. I've never broken your heart."

"You've never broken *my* heart?" he asked, almost incredulous. "Every day I thought about you leaving, my heart broke a little more." He lowered his arms, defeat in his voice. "Until one day, I realized there was nothing left to break."

"What would you have me do?" My voice caught, and I had to swallow before I could continue. "Mary needs—"

"What about before?" he asked. "Before you knew that Mary needed you to save her? You were always going to leave, Kathryn."

"But that was before—" I paused.

"Before what?" he asked.

I pressed my lips together, and for the first time, I was tempted to walk away from Austen and not answer him.

"Before what?" he asked again.

"Before you kissed me," I blurted out, my cheeks growing warm. "Before I realized—"

He took a step closer to me, his voice low. "Before you realized what?"

This was madness. I couldn't stay in 1888, so why was I playing with fire? Why was I about to admit to him that I loved him, desperately?

"I can't keep coming back to you," I said instead, more tears gathering in my eyes as I lowered my gaze. "If you won't tell me about your parents, then I have nothing left to say to you. We both know how all of this will end, so why are we torturing ourselves?"

He remained silent.

"Good-bye, Austen." I didn't bother to look at him before I left him in the parlor and returned to my house.

I hated crying. I hated feeling defenseless and weak.

And I hated that I had walked away from Austen, and I couldn't go back.

I entered our house and closed the door behind me, leaning against it, fighting my tears.

There was no future for us, and we both knew it. If I went back to him but couldn't give him what he wanted—what we both wanted—then it would only hurt more. He'd push me away, I would get upset, and we'd be miserable. I would try to get him to accept what I had to offer, but he wouldn't. And I didn't blame him. If he couldn't have all of me, he didn't want any part of me. It was selfish of me to ask him to settle for less than what he deserved, because I couldn't give Austen forever.

My tears came in earnest as I walked down the hall and entered my father's study. It was the only room in the house the servants didn't bother. And my father wouldn't be home for hours, while Mother was still in bed.

I let my tears fall unchecked as I walked to the window and looked out at the courtyard.

"I don't know how to fix this," I whispered to God. "I don't even know what to pray for."

In the past, I had always told God exactly what I wanted, hoping He'd agree, and it would be done. If things didn't work out how I hoped, they almost always worked out better, and I didn't worry.

But this was different. There was no good solution. No answer that could give me everything I desired. I wanted to save Mary. I wanted to give my heart fully to Austen. I wanted my work in 1938. I didn't want to leave Mama and Papa—but I also didn't want to leave Austen.

As I stared out the window, I realized there was only one thing to do. I had to surrender to God's plan. I wasn't sure what it was, or how it would work, but I was at the end of my own abilities.

A still, small voice whispered in my heart that I would be okay—but I also knew that I would have heartache. Because no matter what happened, I couldn't have everything my heart desired. There was a measure of comfort knowing that God knew what was best for me, though it didn't ease the pain.

The overcast sky opened once again, and rain descended upon London. It ran down the leaded glass windows in little rivulets. I was tired and cold, so I went to a wingback chair and pulled a blanket onto my lap, tucking my feet under me as I sat on the oversized leather chair near the window.

Thunder reverberated through the house, and a moment later I heard Austen say, "I'm leaving London, Kate."

My heart jumped, and my blanket slipped to the ground as I pulled my gaze from the window and found Austen standing at the door.

It was my turn to be surprised and say, "What are you doing here?"

He walked across the study and squatted next to my chair. His face was close to mine, and I could see the specks of gray marbling his blue eyes. He was wearing his overcoat, and he had combed his hair. Slowly, he set his hat on the table next to me and lifted my blanket off the ground to gently lay it back on my lap.

When he was done, he took a moment before he said, "I came to tell you I'm leaving London."

I set my feet on the ground. I wanted to beg him not to leave, yet—why would he stay?

"Where are you going?" I asked, instead.

"To my cottage on Loch Lomond."

"Why are you telling me?" My voice was low. "You've never told me before."

He opened his mouth to speak, but then he closed it again and let out a sigh. "I'm—I wanted—"

I took his hand in mine. "There have never been any pretenses between us. Tell me what you came to say."

The look he gave me was so powerful, my heart felt as if it stopped beating.

"I love you, Kate." He swallowed, and every wall was down as he said, "I'm in love with you. And I'm tired of pretending I'm not."

Tears filled my eyes as the rain tapped against the windowpanes. I placed my hand on his face and ran my thumb over the ridge of his cheekbone.

Austen closed his eyes and pressed against my hand. "I don't expect you—"

"I love you, too," I whispered, unable to keep the truth from him or myself. We both knew how things would end, but that didn't stop me from loving him.

His eyes opened, and he searched my face.

I smiled and nodded, tears falling down my cheeks.

"Kate—" He stood, drawing me up with him, and wrapped me in his embrace.

I clung to him, feeling his heart beating hard against my cheek, drinking in the scent of his cologne, the feel of his arms around me, and the bittersweet pleasure that coursed through me at hearing that he loved me.

"I'm sorry," he whispered against my hair, his voice breaking.

"You're right—you've never hurt me, and I've done nothing but push you away." He pulled back and put his hands on either side of my face, wiping my tears with the pads of his thumbs. "I'm not worthy of your love, but I cherish it, more than you'll ever know."

I placed my hands on his chest and rose on my toes, lifting my face toward his. "Kiss me, Austen," I whispered.

He didn't hesitate and lowered his face to meet mine, capturing my lips with his, covering me with his love. This time, it was not a façade. We had no one to convince that our passion and desire for one another was real.

Pleasure washed over me in warm waves as his kiss deepened, and I offered my heart to his. Tears of joy and sorrow trailed down my cheeks, wetting his hands, until he pulled back.

"Don't cry," he whispered as he took a clean handkerchief out of his pocket and gently wiped my cheeks. "There is no greater pain in this world than knowing that you suffer. I can endure anything but that. I want you to be happy, Kate. And even if that means that you will leave and I'll have to bear more pain, I will endure it. But please, tell me that you'll be happy in 1938."

I knew what he was asking. We both understood that I had no choice. I had to save Mary. But he could endure it if he knew I would be happy.

I would pretend. For his sake. "I'll be happy, Austen," I whispered, the lie sticking in my throat.

He placed his forehead against mine and nodded. "That's all I desire."

"Must you go to Scotland?"

"I won't be gone longer than a fortnight. I have work to do, and it cannot wait. Believe me, I don't want to be separated from you for a day longer than necessary." He took my hand and led me back to the leather chair. I took a seat, and he sat in the chair next to me but didn't let go of my hand. "I want to tell you about my parents."

I'd almost forgotten about our earlier conversation, but I nodded now, encouraging him to continue.

He took a deep breath and shook his head. "I hope I don't regret this, Kate."

"Your secrets are safe with me."

"That's the problem. These secrets aren't safe with anyone." He looked down at my hand and ran his thumb over each finger before he said, "After my parents died, my mother's sister came from New York to oversee my welfare."

"Yes, I know."

"She sent me to Eton, and the first week I was there, I was visited by a guest." He lifted his troubled gaze to mine. "It was Sir Charles Warren."

I blinked several times. "He went to see you?"

"Yes. He told me he was sorry about my loss but asked if I knew anything about my father's work with the Freemasons, or why my parents had been with him in Jerusalem. I told him that I knew nothing, which was true at the time. He became very serious and told me that if I ever found any important papers in my father's collection, anything that had to do with the Freemasons or his trip to Jerusalem, I was supposed to contact Sir Warren immediately—and not tell another soul. Not even my aunt. Then he put his hand on my shoulder and told me that my parents had died heroically, protecting the Brotherhood of Freemasons. He also said that if my father hadn't done what he did, the entire fraternity would have been put in grave danger. I had lost my parents, but their sacrifice had ensured that thousands of other lives were spared. He wanted me to know that when I was ready, I would have a place among the Grand Lodge of Freemasons in London."

I frowned. "What did your father do that was so heroic?"

"I don't know. At least, I didn't know. Not then." He scooted forward on his chair, getting closer to me. "Miles isn't just my coachman. I met him at Eton, and we became friends when we realized that our lives were mixed up with the Freemasons. His father murdered his mother—right before his eyes—but his father was never put on trial because he's a Freemason, and he was spared imprisonment by a Freemason judge and investigator. They're everywhere, and if you're not for them, then you're against them, and your life is meaningless to them."

I nodded, trying to grasp everything he was saying.

"I've investigated my parents' death. I even went to Israel," he continued, "but the Freemasons have done an incredible job covering it up. All I can say for certain is that Sir Warren took several trips to Jerusalem, searching for something important in the Temple Mount. He made maps and excavated countless shafts into the core of the mount. On his trip there with my parents and yours in 1874, they finally found what they were looking for—but my parents died protecting it, and the others brought it back to London.

"What it was, and what happened to it after that, is buried safe within the secrecy of the Brotherhood. I've spent years searching for answers, and I've created many enemies because of it. Men like Michael Maybrick, who suspects my motives." He looked deep into my eyes. "You cannot let anyone know that you're aware of the purpose of that trip to Jerusalem. Not even your parents must know that you know."

"I won't breathe a word," I promised. "But what was it that they found? What could be so important that your parents died protecting it and other people's lives are at risk knowing about it?"

"I don't know, but I suspect that whatever it is, it would uncover the truth behind the Freemasons' power and would have a catastrophic impact on their existence, thereby impacting the English royal crown and who knows how many other countries. It might even cause wars."

I lifted my eyebrows. "That sounds very serious."

"More serious than you can imagine. I'm only telling you this because I'm tired of hurting you, Kate. When you left today, and I knew it was within my power to share this information with you, I had to make a choice. You're an intelligent woman, and I trust that you'll keep this information safe. You might be impetuous and headstrong"—he smiled as he touched my cheek—"but you're not foolish. Please promise me you'll be careful."

"I promise, Austen."

"Good." He lifted my hand and placed a kiss there. "I won't stay longer in Scotland than necessary, and as soon as I'm back, I'll send word to you. But please don't go to Whitechapel while I'm gone."

"I won't. I promise."

He nodded as he rose and drew me to my feet. "Because when I come back, I want to do this again." He lowered his face to mine and gave me another kiss, this one as passionate as the last.

And then he was gone—and I was left with even more questions than before.

18

OCTOBER 15, 1938
LONDON, ENGLAND

The day was clear and bright as I worked on the exhibit in the basement of Lancaster House. It had been eleven days since Austen had left, but I had endured twenty-two days without him. All I could think about were the kisses we'd shared in my father's study on that stormy afternoon and his declaration of love before he'd left.

In 1888, London was still gripped by terror of Jack the Ripper, who was now known by his infamous name. Every newspaper in London, and many around the world, was carrying stories about the four murders, wondering if he might strike again. A vigilante committee had been formed in Whitechapel, and people didn't go out at night if they could help it. I'd upheld my promise to Austen and not returned to Whitechapel other than to volunteer at Toynbee Hall, but I had gone to Bermondsey to the home of Anne Philips, who was Catherine Eddowes's adult daughter. She had been leery answering questions, and I had surmised that she and her mother had not been close. On the contrary, she'd told me that Catherine had only come around when she needed money, and when Anne had given birth to her third child, her mother only agreed to help if Anne paid her.

When I'd asked Anne if she knew anything about the Freemasons or her mother's trip to Jerusalem in 1874, Anne had laughed at the very notion of her mother traveling outside of London.

I had prayed more in the past twenty-two days than I had in all my life. And yet, I had no idea how God would orchestrate my future. Every time I felt panicky or hopeless, I reminded myself that I'd surrendered to His will and that I would trust Him. But it took all my willpower not to fight and push and force circumstances to go my way.

Sunshine poured through the thin windows at the top of the exhibit room, offering a bit of natural light. We'd gathered all the information we could find on Jack the Ripper and borrowed all the evidence from the Crime Museum that we wanted to display. Most of the artifacts were items that the victims had been carrying in their pockets on the nights they were murdered, and because they moved from boardinghouse to boardinghouse, they were many and varied. Bars of soap, combs, silverware, small tins of tea and sugar, pins and needles, and other various sundry items. We also had the piece of apron from Catherine Eddowes, the black bonnet from Polly Nichols, and a pile of clothes that were said to have belonged to Mary Jane Kelly, though I'd never seen them before. The brick façade of Buck's Row was almost finished, and the glass display cases were being assembled. Calan and I were working for hours on end, trying to get everything ready for the grand opening in less than three weeks.

"Did you hear that the paintings have finally arrived?" Calan asked me as we left the lower level to take our lunch break at noon.

"The ones from Scotland?"

"The very same. Bryant is going through them now to make sure all of them arrived safely. They should have been here late last week, but he's happy they're here now."

"Let's go look at them," I said to Calan. "I'm curious to see what all the fuss is about."

We found Sir Rothschild in an empty room on the ground floor with three other men who volunteered in the museum. The room was used as a multipurpose space for events or temporary exhibits. There were four large crates, and Sir Rothschild was standing beside the only one that was open. He held a clipboard in one hand as he directed the volunteers to remove the paintings from the crate. There were three of them already leaning against one wall. Each was a pastoral scene of a beautiful landscape. I wasn't familiar enough with art to know the techniques used, but they were breathtaking. The use of light was so realistic—yet there was a dreamlike quality to each scene. Gilded frames enhanced their beauty, but even if they'd been framed by barnwood, they would have been stunning.

I walked over to the three against the wall and stared at each one.

"Aren't they incredible?" Calan asked me. "All of the artist's paintings were done in Scotland from memory of trips he took to places around the world. I believe these are scenes from the Italian countryside."

"Are all of the paintings landscapes?" I asked.

"Not all of them," Sir Rothschild said from behind me. "There is one portrait amongst them. I'm looking for it now."

Calan and I joined Sir Rothschild as he squinted at the list and then went back to the crate. "Here," he said to one of the volunteers. "It should be the one in the back."

"Who is the artist?" I asked Sir Rothschild.

"His name is Austen Baird," Sir Rothschild said. "And this is the rarest of his paintings. It's called *Kate*."

Austen Baird? *My* Austen?

As the volunteer lifted the painting and turned it around, my heart pumped wildly.

It was a portrait of me in a beautiful green gown with an intricately embroidered bodice of pink roses.

I stared at the likeness, stunned and at a loss for words. Austen was a painter? I'd had no idea. He had never breathed a word of it to me—and, for reasons I couldn't identify, I felt betrayed. Why wouldn't he share something this important with me?

"Good heavens," Calan said beside me. "She looks just like you, Kathryn. And you bear the same name! What are the odds?"

Sir Rothschild looked from the painting to me and back to the painting, his thoughts inscrutable. "It's uncanny," he said. "The hair, the eyes . . . the only difference is the clothing."

"When was this painted?" I asked Sir Rothschild.

Bryant looked at his clipboard and said, "1889."

"So, it couldn't be our Kathryn," Calan said.

"Of course not." My voice shook.

"It's the most beautiful, emotional painting I've ever seen," Sir Rothschild said as he took it from the volunteer and brought it to the wall, where he set it beside the others. He stepped back to admire it. "It is the stunning centerpiece in Baird's collection. There is such pain and heartache in the model's eyes, almost as if the artist was feeling the pain himself."

My heart broke, thinking of Austen painting this portrait the year after I left him. It hadn't happened yet in my other path, but the pain reflected in the portrait was the pain in his heart.

"I would love to know the story behind the painting." Calan sighed. "She must have been the love of his life. There's no other way to capture such a remarkable portrait. But it couldn't have ended well. I asked Mr. Baird about her when I went to his home in Loch Lomond to inquire after this portrait, but he refused to say anything."

"You spoke to him?" I asked Calan.

"Briefly. I was surprised he sold me the painting. It appeared to be very painful for him to let it go. He wouldn't speak of the model." Calan turned to Sir Rothschild. "Do you know anything about her?"

"I know nothing of the model," Sir Rothschild said. "Not much is known of Austen Baird's life."

"How did you come across his paintings?" I asked.

"It wasn't easy since they are unsigned," Sir Rothschild said. "After the Great War, someone began to piece them together under the same artist. For a time, no one knew who the artist was, and then a receipt attached to one of the pastoral paintings from a sale in 1888 was found. It identified the artist's name."

I could only stare, stunned and amazed at what I was learning about the man I thought I knew better than anyone. He'd kept this part of his life a secret from me, too. Perhaps that was what he was hiding in his study, and that was probably what he was doing when he went to his cottage or traveled abroad. The crates he'd sent out of his home the morning I'd come upon him weren't paintings from his parents' collection. They were more than likely commissioned works that he was sending to the buyer. The receipt that had identified him from 1888 could have been the receipt I saw him sign before the movers left.

A yearning grew so deep in my chest, it was a physical pain. I wanted to run to Austen and ask him why he'd never told me. And ask him about the portrait I didn't know he'd painted. But if it was done in 1889, he didn't even know about it yet. I couldn't talk to the Austen of 1888.

But perhaps I could talk to the Austen in 1938.

"He's still alive?" I asked.

"I believe so," Sir Rothschild said.

"Does he live near Loch Lomond?"

"After several paintings were donated to the Royal Museum of Scotland," Calan said, "I began to research and finally found that Mr. Baird had a home in London and a cottage in Loch Lomond. I visited him at his cottage and was able to acquire several more, including the portrait."

"But he still has a home in London?"

"I believe so, but I don't know where it might be."

I had to ask Austen about the paintings.

"Will you excuse me?" I asked. "I'm taking my lunch, and I'll be back as soon as I'm able."

"Of course," Sir Rothschild said. "Take all the time you need."

I was almost out the door when Sir Rothschild stopped me. "I forgot to mention—I've been invited to consult at Versailles at the Musée de l'Histoire de France. I've been putting it off, waiting for this shipment, but now that it's here, I shouldn't delay another day. If I'm gone before you return, please know that I will instruct the staff and volunteers to assist you in any way, and should you need me, you can contact me at the Hôtel Westminster."

"I think we have everything under control," I said, eager to get away. "When should we expect you to return?"

"A week, hopefully no longer."

I nodded. "I'll see you when you return." I didn't want to wait another moment but took the stairs up to my office and grabbed my hat and purse before I left Lancaster House.

I was breaking every rule and risking everything I held dear to look for Austen in this path. It was a foolish, headstrong, and impetuous decision—the very thing I'd promised him I wouldn't do. But after seeing the portrait and witnessing the pain he'd painted into my eyes, my heart yearned to be near Austen. I needed to go to Wilton Crescent. I couldn't explain it.

I just had to see him.

I'd never been so nervous before in my life. I didn't know if Austen still lived at 12 Wilton Crescent or if he'd even be in London. Perhaps he was in his cottage at Loch Lomond or somewhere else entirely.

All I knew was that I needed to go.

It wasn't far from Lancaster House to Wilton Crescent. I tried not to run, but it was almost impossible, even wearing heels. I followed a path through Green Park and then took a left toward my old neighborhood.

The homes looked almost the same as they did in 1888, and the familiarity made me forget for a moment that I was in 1938. Yet the automobiles and the modern street signs were a constant reminder.

Thankfully, it was cold, or I would have overheated as I made my way toward Wilton Crescent. My heart was pounding so hard, I couldn't think straight.

What would I say if I saw him? Fifty years had passed since 1888, and though I looked the same, he would be an old man. Would it be too great a shock for him to see me again?

Would it shock me to see him?

My steps slowed as I caught a glimpse of number twelve, and the foolishness of my decision started to cause more rational thoughts to war within my heart and mind.

I wanted to ask Austen about the paintings. But if I did, I might be tempted to ask him about Mary, too, and that would be far too dangerous.

I paused on the opposite side of the street, realizing that, in this path, I hadn't yet saved Mary. She was the last victim of Jack the Ripper. It wouldn't be until after November 9th that history would change. What version of history did Austen know today? The one in which Mary died and I left? Or the one in which Mary was saved—and I left? But if Mary was saved, why was her name still listed as a victim?

I was suddenly very confused.

Perhaps this was the reason Mama had cautioned me not to knowingly change history. When I saved Mary, everything in this path could change— so drastically, in fact, I might not even recognize it when I woke up here. But how did it work? Was I in the changed history now, or would it change *after* November 9th?

I felt paralyzed on the opposite side of Wilton Crescent as questions and doubt plagued me.

When the door opened to number twelve, panic filled my heart. Yet a quiet voice urged me to stay. I watched as an old man stepped outside of his house, and I immediately knew it was Austen. His body had aged, but he still bore the same movements, even if they were slower. He looked distinguished in a long coat and a bowler hat, and from where I stood, I could see his hair was now gray.

My heart broke as I watched him slowly lock his door. He probably had a servant or two to see to his most basic needs. Gone would be the large household staff, and in their place was electricity, washing machines, toasters, and vacuum cleaners.

Was he lonely?

Or had he found someone else to love? That thought was more painful than all the others.

As he slowly turned, I finally caught a glimpse of his face, and I would have known him anywhere. He was still handsome, though there were lines and wrinkles and age spots on his skin.

He paused as his gaze caught on mine.

The street separated us, but I knew the moment he recognized me. His mouth parted, and he caught his breath. The surprise soon turned to disbelief, and then to sadness . . . and then he smiled.

I thought I would want to run to him, but I didn't. I thought I would have a hundred questions, but no words formed.

Instead, I only looked at him, and he at me.

I swallowed and took a step forward, needing to say something—but he shook his head, the sadness returning—and I paused.

A cab turned the corner and stopped in front of his house, partially blocking him from view.

With one last glance, Austen opened the door and got into the car.

He watched me through the window, but I couldn't move, my heart breaking.

Austen didn't want to talk to me.

The cab pulled away and turned down the street, leaving me alone.

I took a deep breath and then began to walk, tears in my eyes. It hurt that he didn't want to speak to me, but I didn't blame him. It would be too hard for both of us. Seeing him as an old man had been hard. Speaking to him would have been harder.

I should have gone back to Lancaster House, but I needed to talk to Mama and Papa. I needed answers to the questions that had stopped me outside Austen's house.

It took me another twenty minutes to walk from Wilton Crescent to Berkeley Square. My mind was so jumbled and confused, I couldn't keep a single thought straight.

When I arrived at 44 Berkeley Square, I opened the front door and walked blindly up to the parlor.

Mama and Papa were sitting on a settee together. Mama was reading Anne Morrow Lindbergh's latest book, *Listen! The Wind*, about her flight with her husband from Africa to South America across the Atlantic Ocean, and Papa was reading a newspaper. They both looked up at the same moment, surprise on their faces.

"Kathryn!" Mama said. "We weren't expecting you for hours." Her smile faded, and she rose from the settee. "What's wrong?"

I walked across the parlor and sat beside Papa. I placed my head on his shoulder, and I let the tears fall.

Mama sat next to me and took my hand. "What's wrong, Kathryn?"

"I went to see Austen just now."

Papa sat up straighter, forcing me to lift my head and face them.

"What do you mean?" Mama asked.

"Austen still lives at 12 Wilton Crescent," I said. "He's seventy-five years old."

"Kathryn." Papa's voice was full of both a warning and a censure. "What were you thinking? Mama has told you a hundred times not to let one path affect the other. You don't know what kind of trouble you are placing yourself or anyone else in."

"Why did you go?" Mama asked.

"I was impetuous and headstrong." It was what Austen had said to me affectionately in my father's study in 1888, but the truth was, I had tried to push God again.

I told them about the paintings and the portrait Austen had made of me. "I had to see him—"

"Why?" Mama asked.

"I don't know." I shrugged, suddenly unable to remember what had prompted me. "I miss him. I haven't seen him in almost two weeks in my other path."

"So you thought to go to him now?" Mama asked, almost angry.

"When he hasn't seen you in fifty years? What might he be thinking, Kathryn? He is probably shocked and confused and heartbroken."

I wiped my tears, frustrated that I was crying again. "It doesn't matter. He didn't want to talk to me, and I became confused and panicked."

"Why?" Papa asked.

"Because it occurred to me that I haven't changed history yet. What if the history that Austen knows is the history where Mary still dies? I won't change anything until November 9th, but then everything might change." I shook my head. "I don't know. It's just so confusing. I got scared."

"This is why you shouldn't go looking for answers," Mama said. "It's too dangerous, Kathryn. Your paths are so close—closer than any other I've ever heard of. I don't know what that means or what might happen when you change things on November 9th." Her eyes were so sad. "I just wish you wouldn't have to change anything. My mama said that cataclysmic events have taken place when time-crossers have changed history, but I don't know which events happened because of time-crossers. Maybe even wars, I don't know. It's just better to leave things as they are."

"Are you saying I shouldn't save Mary?" I asked, incredulous.

Mama looked at Papa helplessly.

"We can't tell you what to do," Papa said. "But there is a reason why every time-crosser in your mother's family has cautioned the next generation to leave things alone. You have a huge responsibility on your shoulders."

"Do you think changing history could cause a war?" I asked, sitting up straighter. "Could it cause the next World War? If the Freemasons are involved with the Jack the Ripper killings—and I somehow change the outcome of that, or unmask the killer—might it cause World War Two?"

Mama lifted her shoulders. "I don't know, Kathryn. I really don't."

My chest felt heavy, and I couldn't seem to catch a breath. Was it all worth the risk?

When I thought of Mary living in Whitechapel, a victim of the information she had about the Freemasons, the injustice of it all brought air back to my lungs.

Yes, it was worth the risk. I couldn't let my sister die a gruesome death. Not if I could stop it.

I didn't know what would happen. I wasn't sure if it would have a cataclysmic effect on history, but I had to try.

19

LONDON, ENGLAND
OCTOBER 16, 1888

I woke up in 1888 with an ache in my chest that didn't disappear as I dressed in a simple walking gown. Austen was still not back from Scotland, but I wouldn't spend my day waiting for his arrival. After breakfast, I planned to take the carriage to Mile End, not far from Whitechapel, where Catherine Eddowes's ex-husband, Thomas Conway, was reported to live. I still hadn't been able to locate William Nichols, Polly's husband, and both John Chapman and John Stride, Annie and Elizabeth's husbands, had died.

Hopefully Thomas might answer my questions and tell me why all five women ended up in Whitechapel. I had sold a piece of jewelry for funds to hire the cabs that I'd been using, but I was running dangerously low and would need to sell something else soon.

My mother entered my room as Duffy helped me finish my toilette.

"I do wish you'd come calling with me," Mother said as she adjusted her gloves. "I'm running out of excuses for your absences."

"I don't feel like making calls." And I didn't feel like fighting her about it, either.

"Mrs. Kelly?" A maid appeared at the door.

"Yes?" Mother turned to address her.

"There is a caller here to see you and Miss Kelly. A Mr. Maybrick, I believe."

"Michael Maybrick?" Mother asked, her voice rising a notch. "How very interesting."

Michael Maybrick had come to see us? I couldn't stop thinking about what Austen had said about him. Mr. Maybrick suspected that Austen was trying to find answers about the Freemasons, and he'd hinted that Mr. Maybrick was a threat, someone I shouldn't trust. Had he somehow learned that I knew about the trip to Jerusalem? There was no way he could know. I hadn't spoken to anyone about what Austen told me.

Mother turned back to me. "Come, Kathryn. He's asked to see both of us."

"Must I?"

Mother smoothed back a strand of my hair and fastened the top button on my collar. "Of course you must speak to him. Mr. Maybrick is one of the most eligible bachelors in England, and I saw how he admired you when he was here before. I didn't think it would take him this long to call on you, but he's here, nonetheless."

"Surely he's not here to see me."

"Of course he is." She batted her eyes in a playful manner. "I may have dropped the hint that you're quite eligible yourself."

"Mother, you know—"

"Hush, Kathryn. You're running out of time and options. And Michael Maybrick would be the catch of the decade. I don't know what—or who—you're waiting for, but it's time to settle down."

I couldn't look her in the eyes, knowing I might give away my true feelings about Austen if she saw my emotions.

She squinted and put her finger under my chin to lift my gaze to hers. "I know Austen was here a couple weeks ago and that you've been sneaking over to his house."

"I haven't been sneaking," I clarified, quite proud of myself for using his front door.

"Perhaps there was a time when I would have welcomed a union between you," she said, her voice serious as she let go of my chin. "But after—but since—" She paused.

"After the trip to Jerusalem?" I asked her.

Her gaze narrowed, and she nodded for Duffy to leave the room. When my maid was gone, Mother said, "What do you know about that trip?"

"Very little," I said honestly. "I know that Austen's parents died, and nothing has ever been the same."

"Precisely. Perhaps if things had been different, I could encourage you and Austen. But nothing good could come from a marriage with him now."

"Why not? What happened in Jerusalem?" I couldn't help asking. She was the only woman there who hadn't been killed. She must know something.

"What do you mean?"

"How did Austen's parents die? Who else was with you on the trip?"

She took a step back. "Why are you suddenly so interested? You've never wondered before now."

I swallowed my nerves and said, "I know that the women who died in Whitechapel were—"

"Don't breathe another word, Kathryn." She put her hand over my mouth, her voice low and filled with a dire warning. "Not another word." She looked over her shoulder and then back at me. "If you know what is good for you, you will never speak about this again. I was able to save Mar—" Her breath caught, and panic filled her eyes. "Please don't speak about those women. I don't know what you think you know, but nothing is as it appears." She stared at me. "Promise me."

I nodded, my eyes wide.

She lowered her hand and took a step back, inhaling a few deep breaths. "Compose yourself and think carefully about what I just said. Not a word, Kathryn."

I nodded again.

Mother and I left my bedroom, but my legs were shaking. She'd been so fierce and determined. She'd suggested that she'd been able to save Mary, so she didn't know that my sister's life was still in jeopardy. And she'd said that she would have welcomed a union between Austen and me—before Jerusalem. Why not after? If Austen's parents had died heroic deaths, it should be an honor to join our families together.

All I wanted was to get the visit with Mr. Maybrick over so I could go to Mile End and find Thomas Conway to ask him about the trip, despite my promise to Mother. There was too much at stake to not find answers.

As soon as Mother and I entered the parlor, Mr. Maybrick rose from his chair and offered us a slight bow. "It's good to see you again, Mrs. Kelly, Miss Kelly."

After the pleasantries were exchanged, I took a seat beside Mother to face our visitor.

"To what do we owe the pleasure of your visit?" Mother asked.

Mr. Maybrick smiled, his mustache rising slightly. There was superiority and arrogance in his movements as he said, "I will be giving a performance at St. James Hall this Friday evening, and I was hoping your family would attend as my guests of honor."

"We'd love to accept your invitation," she said without hesitation. "How marvelous."

"And, of course," he added, "I would enjoy taking all of you to Café Royal after for a late supper."

Mother's cheeks were filled with color. "We'd be honored, Mr. Maybrick. Simply honored. Wouldn't we, Kathryn?"

The last thing I wanted to do was spend an evening with Michael Maybrick, so I asked the question on everyone's minds in London. "Is it safe to be out at night?"

"Why, Kathryn," Mother said, "what a thing to ask. Everyone knows that it's only the poor who are at risk."

I gave her a look, remembering how she'd reacted when we went to the Lyceum Theatre to see *The Strange Case of Dr. Jekyll and Mr. Hyde*. It was one of the last times she'd gone out to a public place at night, and the only reason she agreed to go now was because of Mr. Maybrick's status.

"You'll be quite safe in my company, I assure you," Mr. Maybrick said with a smile that was far too intimate and familiar.

Mother and Mr. Maybrick continued to chat about the concert, one of many performances Mr. Maybrick would give over the course of October and November. He spoke of his frenzied calendar, often with three or four performances a day, moving from one music hall to the next, from one end of England to the other. He hardly seemed to notice that I remained quiet for most of his visit, anxiously watching the clock, wanting to get to Mile End.

When there was a natural break in the conversation, Mother rose, and Mr. Maybrick followed.

"If you'll excuse me," Mother said, "I need to speak to the housekeeper about tonight's supper, and I'm afraid it can't wait." She turned to me. "Kathryn, you'll see our guest out when he's ready to leave?"

It was a question, but I knew there was only one answer, and I felt sick knowing she was leaving us alone on purpose.

"Of course."

By the look on Mr. Maybrick's face, he'd been waiting for this moment.

"Good-bye, Mr. Maybrick," Mother said, "I look forward to seeing you again soon."

He bowed over her hand, and then she left.

When he turned to face me, there was a pleased smile on his face. "I thought we'd never be alone."

I slowly rose from my chair, uncertain. "I'm not sure I understand your meaning, sir."

He paused, his eyebrows rising high. "Have I misunderstood?"

I frowned. "Misunderstood?"

He advanced again. "The electricity between us is palpable, Miss Kelly. Surely you feel it, too."

I took a step behind my chair, needing something between us. "You forget yourself, Mr. Maybrick. I'm a lady."

"And I'm a gentleman. Clearly we belong together."

I stared at him, stunned. "I don't know what you mean."

He stopped on the other side of the chair, a smile tilting up one edge of his mouth. "From the moment we met, I knew that you were meant to be mine. I've been waiting, biding my time, but I can wait no longer."

"We've hardly spoken," I said. "And we've only seen each other twice."

"Once is all it takes." He started to round the chair, and I left my spot to move toward the door. "Unless your reticence is because of Mr. Baird," he said. "If that's the case, we can remedy that problem."

"I believe it's time you leave, sir," I said, trying to keep my voice level.

He stared at me, his jaw tight. "A thousand women would love to be in your shoes."

I stared back, frustrated at his behavior. "I'd gladly hand my shoes over to anyone who asks."

His scowl turned to surprise and then an arrogant and condescending smile. "I always get what I want."

"Why in the world would you want me?"

"Your family is Freemason royalty, Miss Kelly."

I frowned. "What does that mean?"

"It means that your great-grandfather brought Freemasonry to England, and your family name is greatly revered. I intend to benefit from that connection, and your parents have already agreed to the match."

I lifted my chin. "Then my parents—and you—greatly underestimate me, Mr. Maybrick, because I will never marry you."

And with that, I left the parlor, intent on speaking to Catherine Eddowes's ex-husband.

Mile End was not far from Whitechapel, but the living conditions were a little better. It was home to working-class and lower-class groups of people, mostly immigrants and migrants. I had left home without a word to Mother and hired a cab not far from Wilton Crescent.

When the cab pulled up to a tenement on Bow Road in Mile End, I was still shaking from my encounter with Mr. Maybrick. I couldn't believe my parents would agree to a betrothal without speaking to me—but then again, there were a lot of things they had never told me.

I stared at the run-down building of Mile End with more trepidation than I anticipated. I had promised Austen I wouldn't go to Whitechapel, but was this any better? I was going to approach a man whom I'd never met, on a street I wasn't familiar with, at the height of the Jack the Ripper scare.

But I'd come this far, and I was still angry enough from my visit with Mr. Maybrick to charge ahead.

"Will you wait?" I asked the cab driver, a kind older man with a posy in his hat band. I had just enough money to pay for my fare back to Wilton Crescent.

"Indeed I will, miss," he said as he glanced at the building, worry in the lines of his face. "Be careful."

I nodded, checked the address I'd found in 1938 for Thomas Conway, and then walked down a passageway toward the back of the building to number 5.

Dirty children played in the muddy courtyard while a woman hung wash on a line. Trash was piled up against a wall, and a rotting animal that looked like it might have been a rat lay beside it, filling the air with putrid odors.

I placed my gloved hand under my nose, trying not to gag as I knocked on number 5.

There was a shuffling noise and then the door opened. A middle-aged woman with deep wrinkles and glossy eyes stared at me.

"What do you want?" she asked abruptly in a Cockney accent. "We don't take no charity."

I swallowed my nerves and said, "I'm looking for Mr. Thomas Conway."

The lady frowned. "And who are you? Come looking for a story about Catherine? Well, he won't give it to you unless you pay."

My lips parted in surprise. "I don't have anything to offer."

She nodded at the purse hanging from my wrist. "What's in there?"

"Just enough fare to get home."

"That's what he'll take then."

"But—"

"What's this?" a man asked as he came to the door, scratching his head and blinking away sleep. When he saw me, he sobered enough to lift an eyebrow with interest. According to the reports I'd read in 1938, Thomas had been handsome and charming at one point—but now he was unshaven, overweight, and scarred by time. "And who are you, pretty lady?"

The woman who had answered the door scoffed and went back into the house, tossing a fiery glare in my direction and talking under her breath.

"Are you Thomas Conway?" I asked, aware of the woman hanging laundry, staring at me.

He leaned against the doorframe and looked me up and down, lifting a corner of his mouth in a half smile. "I am, sweetheart. What can I do for you?"

My pulse was thrumming. "May I have a word with you about—about Jerusalem?"

His smile disappeared, and he straightened. "What do you want to know about that?"

I glanced behind me and then said, "May we have a word in private?"

"There ain't nowhere private around here," he said. "And I ain't got nothing to say, anyway." He started to move back into the house, but I took a step forward.

"I can pay you." I took the coins out of my reticule, hoping I could convince the cabby to take me back to Wilton Crescent on credit.

That got Conway's attention. He held out his hand.

"Not until you answer my questions," I said, clutching the coins in my fist.

He worked his jaw for a minute. "What do you want to know?"

I licked my dry lips, hoping he'd share the truth. "I know that Polly, Annie, Elizabeth, and Catherine were all in Jerusalem. And I know you were there, too."

He stared at me, squinting for a second. "Who are you?"

"It doesn't matter. Are you a Freemason, Mr. Conway?"

He hesitated, and I knew he was weighing the wisdom in telling me the truth. He glanced at my fist holding the coins and then leaned against the doorframe again. "I was just a poor, ex-soldier when I joined the Freemasons. I thought they might help me make something of my life. When they called upon me to assist the expedition as a guard and offered to pay my way, I went. Thought it would be a good opportunity for me and Catherine to see a bit of the world."

"Are you still a Freemason?"

He looked down at his worn clothing and then lifted his head in pride. "Not in good standing, as it were. Couldn't afford the dues after a time."

"And what of the others?" I asked. "Was William Nichols a Freemason? Or John Chapman or John Stride?"

Thomas looked right and then left before he said, "Aye, they were all Freemasons, called upon because they had different skills."

"How did each of your wives end up in Whitechapel?" I asked, eager for him to keep talking.

He shrugged and held out his hand. "I need me a coin for what I already told you."

I slightly unclenched my fist, afraid he'd try to take it all, and removed one penny, which I handed to him. "Why were your wives in Whitechapel?"

Thomas put the penny into his pocket and said, "When you're desperate and destitute, it's the cheapest place to live—and to disappear. Polly left William because he had taken up with another woman. Annie left her husband because she couldn't resist the bottle. Elizabeth left her chap because she was disease-ridden and couldn't have children, and it came between them." He shrugged. "Me and Catherine had our quarrels and went our separate ways. She was set up real nice in Woolwich for a time, in a respectable flat, but it didn't take long before I heard she was living in Whitechapel."

"Do you think Jack the Ripper is—"

Thomas's shoulders stiffened, and his face became still. "I don't know nothing about any of that."

"But—"

"I already told you enough." He held out his hand for another penny.

I gave it to him and opened my mouth to ask another question, but he glanced over my shoulder as the shadow of a man fell across the wall. Thomas swallowed hard before he stepped inside and closed the door in my face.

My heart pounded as I turned, knowing there was someone standing behind me.

It was Austen.

"Kathryn, what are you doing here?"

My heart leapt at the sight of him and relief made me feel weak. I ran into his embrace, not caring what the tenants thought of me. I had ached for Austen.

He embraced me, his heart beating hard against his chest.

"What am *I* doing here?" I asked, laughter and joy in my voice. "What are *you* doing here?"

"I was just pulling up to my townhouse when I saw you get into the cab. Miles and I followed you here, but lost you in traffic several times. Thankfully Miles recognized the cab, and we were able to locate you." He looked at the dirty courtyard, a myriad of emotions playing on his face. One was frustration. "You promised you wouldn't come here without me."

"This isn't Whitechapel."

He lifted an eyebrow.

"I'm finished," I said as I tugged him toward the passage. Thomas Conway's door had been firmly closed in my face, and I knew he wouldn't open it to me again. "I have so much to tell you."

I put my arm around his waist and pressed against him as his arm went around my shoulders.

After thanking the cabby for waiting for me and paying him the few pennies I had left, Austen helped me into his carriage.

As soon as the door was closed, I went into his arms.

"Kate," he whispered as he buried his face against my neck.

The carriage began to move, and I wrapped my arms around him, my heart soaring and breaking in the same moment. I couldn't stop thinking about him as an old man with pain in his eyes, a pain I would cause. But I also reveled in the joy we brought into each other's lives here. Now.

He pulled back and slipped a hand up to my cheek, caressing my skin with his thumb. His eyes were shining. "You're so beautiful," he whispered as he lowered his lips to mine and captured them in a kiss.

I had been waiting for this moment for weeks, and it was better than I imagined. All the love I felt for him in the past, in the present, and in the future mingled together in exquisite bliss.

When he finally pulled back, he whispered, "I thought about this kiss every moment I was away from you."

I leaned into his touch, but then I remembered the paintings, and I sat up straight. "Why didn't you tell me, Austen?"

He pulled back and frowned. "Tell you what?"

"About your paintings?"

Comprehension flickered in his eyes. "How did you find out?"

"Sir Rothschild, the keeper of the London Museum in 1938, has just borrowed them from the Royal Museum of Scotland and will be putting them on display."

"They're putting my paintings on display?" he asked with a

frown. "But I've sold them to people all over Europe, ensuring that no one knew my identity. How did they collect them?"

"Someone has been accumulating them through the years. Why didn't you tell me you are a painter?"

He sat back against the bench and ran his hand through his hair. "Why does it matter?"

"Because—" I shook my head in confusion. "Because I'm me, and you're you, and I thought we knew each other."

Austen was quiet for a moment, and then he finally said, "Honestly, it was the last thing I had that no one could take away from me. I was afraid that if people knew, it would be torn from me, too."

My heart ached for him as I sat back on the bench and took his hand into mine. "Is that what you were doing at Loch Lomond?"

He nodded. "I was commissioned to finish a painting for a client in France, and I needed to get it done before the fifteenth. I finished it yesterday, and I left it with my caretakers to mail after the paint dried. I came back to London as soon as I could."

"Why do you paint in Scotland? Why not here?"

"There are too many memories in London. I've tried, but the only place I can truly let my mind go is in Scotland."

"What about that morning when the movers were at your house? I thought you were selling some of your parents' paintings."

"I'd finished the paintings in Scotland and brought them with me to ship to Italy. I don't usually leave my caretakers responsible for shipments, since it's easier to have them sent from London."

"You're extremely talented," I told him with a smile. "Your paintings are stunning."

He returned my smile as the carriage joined a busy thoroughfare. The noise increased as the carriage slowed to accommodate traffic.

"I wish I could have been there when you saw them," he said.

"I do, too." I nibbled my bottom lip, not sure how he would react to my next statement. "I went to see you."

"What do you mean?"

"In 1938. After I saw the paintings."

Austen frowned. "Did I say anything to you?"

"No. You shook your head, as if you didn't want to speak to me."

There was no humor in his eyes as he regarded me, and I wished I knew what he was thinking.

"Why did you go?" he finally asked.

"I missed you, and . . . I wanted to ask you about the portrait."

"Portrait?" He frowned. "What portrait?"

"The one of me."

"I don't have a portrait of you."

"You will."

He studied me again, pain and uncertainty in his gaze. "After you leave, you mean?"

I nodded.

He turned away from me and shook his head. "I'm a fool."

I put my hand on his arm, but he pulled away.

His rejection hurt, and I stiffened.

When he turned back to me, there was so much grief in his eyes, it stung. "Who are we fooling?" he asked. "I keep thinking that by some miracle, you'll choose me, and this will continue. But it won't, will it?"

"I want to choose you," I whispered, my heart thudding with certainty. "But I must save Mary."

Neither of us spoke for a moment, and then Austen let out a sigh and put his arm around me again.

We both knew the truth.

This wouldn't last.

It couldn't.

20

NOVEMBER 4, 1938
LONDON, ENGLAND

It was cold and cloudy as we stood on the airfield at Heston Aerodrome just outside of London. I shivered as Papa handed his suitcase to a flight attendant, who brought it on board the large silver airplane that would take Papa and the Lindberghs from London to Berlin.

"I wish you weren't going." Mama readjusted Papa's tie as he stood before her to say good-bye.

"I won't be gone long," he promised as he placed his hands on her arms and kissed her forehead. "I will be back before you know it."

The Lindberghs had already boarded the airplane, and I caught a glimpse of Mrs. Lindbergh sitting near a window. She had invited Mama to come along one more time, but Mama kindly refused. She didn't want to miss the grand opening of the Jack the Ripper exhibit at Lancaster House, planned for November 7th. At least, that was the excuse she gave.

"I'm sorry I'll miss your big day," Papa said as he turned to me. "But I'll be the first in line to see it when I return."

I stood on tiptoe and placed a kiss on his cheek. "I don't mind that you'll miss the grand opening," I assured him. "Just get back to us safely. That's all I care about."

"And as soon as you get back," Mama added, "we'll book our tickets for home." She looked between Papa and me. "That's the plan, isn't it?"

"Yes." I nodded, knowing that she was eager to return home and leave England and the looming war behind us. It would affect us in Washington, DC, but not like it would if we had to stay in London.

"Good-bye," Papa said as he smiled. "I love you both."

Mama took a step forward, anxiety in her voice. "You promise this is safe, Luc? The threat with Germany is on hold for now?"

He nodded and then drew her into his arms for another hug. "I promise it's safe, *mon petit oiseau*." It was what he'd called her ever since she'd learned to fly. His little bird. "When have you known me to be reckless?"

Mama chuckled affectionately as she pulled back to look at him. "Every day since I met you."

He grinned, and I could see the young, fearless aviator in his smile. The one who had been a daredevil pilot in 1912, perfecting the death dive, flying over Niagara Falls, and stunning his audiences with his aeronautical skills. The pilot Mama had fallen in love with.

The engines of the airplane roared to life.

Papa gave Mama a quick kiss and then sprinted toward the waiting airplane.

Mama and I stepped back to watch the airplane take off, and then we made our way to the car that had brought us to Heston Aerodrome.

"Well," Mama said with a sigh as we settled into our seats. "I knew your father was fearless when I married him in 1912. He's done scarier things before this."

I took her hand in mine as the driver pulled away from the aerodrome and headed back toward London and our next appointment.

"He'll be home in no time," I echoed his promise, "and he'll be full of all sorts of fun stories. He lives for aviation and adventure. I'm thankful he is still able to experience it."

"I am, too, no matter how much it scares me."

We enjoyed a quiet ride into the city and headed toward Buckingham Palace. I'd been looking forward to this afternoon for the past week since Lady Astor had secured an invitation for us to have a private tour of Buckingham Palace. It had been at my request, under the guise of my work with the Smithsonian and the London Museum, but I had an ulterior motive. Mr. Hornby at the Masonic research library claimed that there was a second copy of Sir Warren's book, with his original notes included, in the king's collection, and I wanted to see them. There had to be more to the story than I'd been told, and I was determined to find it.

If I could locate the book.

Plus, it was just the thing Mama and I needed to keep our minds distracted today.

While she was worried about Papa heading to Berlin, all I could think about was Austen and Mary in 1888. In five short days, I needed to save my sister and say good-bye to the man I loved.

I had to blink away the tears thinking about that final farewell. How would I say good-bye to Austen? I closed my eyes, begging God to intervene, or to give me peace about what I was about to do.

He did neither.

The city was busy as we drove toward the palace. I tried to push thoughts of Austen aside and focus on what I hoped to accomplish at Buckingham Palace today, but it was useless. He would be upset with me if he knew what I planned to do, but I was desperate for answers.

Over the past two and a half weeks, Austen and I had spent almost every day together, much to my mother's chagrin. The only night I hadn't been in his company was the night of Michael Maybrick's performance. Mr. Maybrick took my parents and me to Café Royale after the concert, though he spent more time talking to my father than he did to me. I didn't mind, but I knew that my parents were enamored with him, and they'd begun to drop hints that they wanted a union between us. Austen had cautioned me not to be alone with Mr. Maybrick or to share anything I'd learned about the Freemasons. And I had heeded his warning.

As we passed the Marble Arch on the corner of Hyde Park, my thoughts were brought back to 1938 as Mama said, "It was kind of Lady Astor to arrange this tour." She adjusted her gloves and repositioned her hat. "I never dreamed I'd be given a private glimpse of Buckingham Palace."

I smiled at her and forced myself not to worry about what I hoped to accomplish today. If I got caught, there was no way to know what might happen to me. And even if I succeeded, I had no guarantee that I would learn anything useful to help me uncover Jack the Ripper and the Freemasons' involvement.

We circled Wellington Arch and drove down Constitution Hill Road, which cut through Green Park, offering a view of the back side of Buckingham Palace. The honey-colored limestone of the large building looked dull on the cloudy day, but the grandeur of the palace could not be dimmed.

The driver took us around to the front, and we were greeted by the King's guards in their red coats and tall bearskin hats. After showing our invitation, we passed through the gate and drove under the main arch at the front of the building and into the courtyard in the center of the palace. There, the driver parked outside the grand entrance and opened the back door to allow us to exit the vehicle.

Before I was able to thank the driver, the large door opened and a butler appeared in a black tuxedo, white vest, and gleaming white gloves.

"Welcome to Buckingham Palace," he said with a formal bow.

Mama handed him the invitation, but he was clearly expecting us, so he showed us into the impressive entrance hall.

The palace was as glorious as I imagined, with ornate trim work, beautiful paintings, and expensive furniture. Several doors led off from the hall, but which one was the door that would lead me to Prince Albert Victor—or rather, King George VI's—book collection?

Another gentleman stepped out of a door and walked toward us. He was dressed like the butler, but he had a ribbon on his lapel. "Good day," he said. "My name is Mr. Griffin. I presume you are Mrs. and Miss Voland?"

"Yes," Mama said with a pleasant smile.

"It's a pleasure to meet you." He dipped his head and motioned toward a set of red carpeted stairs. "Shall we begin the tour?"

We followed him up to the second floor and into a painting gallery. "The building at the core of the palace was originally built by the Duke of Buckingham in 1703 as a townhome," Mr. Griffin began in a cultured British accent. "In 1761 it was purchased by King George III as a private residence for Queen Charlotte, and over the years, three additional wings were added to make a central courtyard in the middle. Queen Victoria made it the official residence of the monarch in 1837."

"How fascinating," Mama said as we were taken into the throne room, the state dining room, the ballroom, and several galleries on the second level.

"I'm a museum exhibit curator at the Smithsonian Institute in Washington, DC," I told Mr. Griffin after we'd seen several rooms. "And one of my unique interests is in books. Are there any rare collections in Buckingham Palace?"

"There are, indeed," he said with a sparkle in his eye. "I'm also an admirer of rare books. Shall we go to the king's private library?"

"Could we?" I wasn't sure if the book I was looking for would be there, but it was as good a place as any to look.

We followed him to the ground level, and he took us through a door into a different wing of the palace.

"This is the private residence," he told us. "Not many people are given access to this part of the building, but Lady Astor is a favorite of Her Majesty's, and the Queen told me to give you a proper tour." He smiled in a conspiratorial manner. "And what is a proper tour without a peek into the heart of the palace—the library?"

Mama glanced at me, her eyebrows raised high.

We walked down a long gallery before we reached the library. It was a comfortable room, meant for reading, studying, and enjoying the thousands of books on the floor-to-ceiling shelves. Like all the rooms, it was large and spacious, and very formal.

"This is the private collection?" Mama asked, incredulous.

"Indeed," Mr. Griffin said. "These are the books that have been personally acquired by the last five monarchs and their family members. Some are very old and very rare, others are classics, and still others are popular novels, read simply for pleasure or enjoyment. Princess Elizabeth and Princess Margaret even keep their books in here." He smiled fondly when speaking of the young daughters of King George VI and Queen Elizabeth.

"May I have a look around?" I asked.

"Of course. Take your time."

As Mama and the tour guide chatted about the library, perusing some of the shelves, I quickly accessed how the books were organized, and I was relieved to see that they were displayed by the last name of the author. To look for a book written by Sir Charles Warren, I went to the farthest corner of the room to find the Ws.

I had to work quickly, yet I didn't want to draw unwanted attention from our tour guide.

My heart pounded hard when I saw *Underground Jerusalem* by Sir Charles Warren on the shelf, tucked into the corner. It had the same red cloth cover and gold lettering as the one in the Masonic research library.

Gently, I removed the book from the shelf and leafed through it, praying the notes were still inside.

When I was about a fourth of the way through, where Sir Warren named the members of the group who went with him in 1874, a loose leaf of paper stuck out. It was folded in half and yellowed with time, but I could see it was a handwritten note.

With a quick glance over my shoulder, I saw that Mama and Mr. Griffin were deep in discussion about one of the books the guide was holding, so I slipped the note out of *Jerusalem Underground* and set the book aside.

As I scanned the page, I realized it wasn't field notes, but a letter that Sir Warren had written to Prince Albert Victor, shortly after Sir Warren's return from the trip that had cost Austen's parents their lives. As I read the revealing letter, I held my breath.

Your Royal Highness,
May 10, 1874

I'm sure that by now you have heard the distressing news concerning Brother Sir Robert Baird and his wife, Madeline. Their deaths, though tragic, were a necessary sacrifice to ensure the safety of the Book. I have spoken to their orphan, Austen, who is now secured at Eton under the watchful eye of several brothers who will ensure he speaks to no one about what he might know. When he comes of age, we will fold him into the Brotherhood, and he may pick up the work his father left off.

You are probably most concerned about the mission, and that is why I am writing to you. Though it was compromised, Brother Baird gave his life to ensure it was completed successfully. I spent years, not to mention thousands of dollars, searching for the Book. I am happy to inform you that we have finally found it in the Temple Mount and brought it safely to England. I thought it best to separate it among the men on our trip, so it returned in five sections. Each brother will keep his section carefully guarded and has pledged that he will protect it at all costs. I think it best if we keep it separate at this time, until we know the identity of our adversary who tried to take it from Brother Baird and ultimately took his life, instead.

Unfortunately, given the circumstances of the deaths of Brother Baird and his wife, the knowledge of the Book was made known to four of the women on our trip. The only one who does not know the contents of the book is Brother Sir Bernard Kelly's wife, who was ill during much of our time in Jerusalem and was not in the Temple Mount during the incident. Since the other women are not bound to the Oath of the Brotherhood, we cannot be certain of their loyalty or silence. There are plans in place to deal with each of them, should they make trouble.

Once our enemy is defeated, we will commence plans to reunite all five sections of the Book and take it to the secure location you have indicated at WC, where it will remain under the King's guard in perpetuity. I will inform you when this is done.

I remain your faithful and
humble servant,
Brother Sir Charles Warren

"So you see, Mrs. Voland," Mr. Griffin said as he and Mama approached me, "Robert Louis Stevenson was a favorite of King Edward VII, and that is why he has a first edition, signed copy of *The Strange Case of Dr. Jekyll and Mr. Hyde.*"

"What a treasure," Mama said.

I quickly folded the letter and returned it to *Jerusalem Underground* before closing the book and putting it back on the shelf. My heart was still pounding hard after everything I'd read, but I had to pretend to be unaffected.

The book Mary had found, the one that had put her in danger, was most likely one section of the Book Sir Charles Warren referenced. My father had brought it back from Jerusalem, but he was still in possession of it fourteen years later. Which meant that Sir Warren was still looking for the identity of the adversary who took the Bairds' lives. And, if that was the case, was the unknown adversary responsible for killing Polly, Annie, Elizabeth, and Catherine in Whitechapel, because they knew about the Book? Or was it someone working in tandem with Jack? And where was WC? There were a few towns and villages in England with WC for the abbreviation, like Welbourne Common and Wells Cross. Whitechapel could also be abbreviated to WC. But it wouldn't make sense for the Book to be kept there under the King's guard. The King's guard was reserved for royalty, which meant that WC probably stood for Windsor Castle.

"Did you find something of interest?" Mr. Griffin asked.

"I did," I said with a forced smile. "A book by Sir Charles Warren, the man who was the metropolitan police commissioner in 1888 when Jack the Ripper was active."

"Ah, yes," he said with a nod. "The reason you're in London. Some say that Jack knew Sir Warren personally, and it was a cat and mouse game between them. They say that Jack was taunting Warren and that he wanted Warren to lose his job as police commissioner, which is ultimately what happened."

Was Jack taunting Sir Warren? The murders of each woman in Whitechapel had similarities with Freemason rituals and legends. The way in which the victims were killed reflected the ways in which Jubela, Jubelo, and Jubelum were executed. The apron taken from Catherine Eddowes and left under the chalk graffito on Goulston Street might have ties to the aprons the Freemasons wore during their meetings. And the message on the wall had referenced the Juwes. There were other things I'd discovered in my research, clues and evidence that tied the killings to Freemasonry, but had been destroyed, overlooked, or left out of official reports. It was becoming more and more obvious that Jack was sending a message to Sir Warren, one of the most renowned Freemasons in England.

But what did it have to do with the Book?

"Shall we continue our tour?" the guide asked as he motioned for us to precede him out of the library.

Mama glanced at me, questions in her eyes, but I couldn't tell her about my discovery. Not yet.

First, I needed to speak to Mary and beg her to tell me what was written in the Book.

We only had five days left.

21

LONDON, ENGLAND
NOVEMBER 5, 1888

More rain fell on London as Austen and I pulled up to Miller's Court the day after I'd discovered Sir Charles Warren's letter to Prince Albert Victor at Buckingham Palace. I'd gone to Austen immediately and told him what I'd found. He'd called Miles to bring the carriage around, and we now found ourselves outside Mary's lodging, four days before she was supposed to become the last victim of Jack the Ripper.

Austen held my hand as we looked out the window at the dreary scene. It was cold, and the earth had turned to mud. It wasn't fit for man nor beast outside, which meant there was a better chance my sister was at home. But also a better chance that she had company. I wanted to know more about Joseph and how he treated my sister. Yet, if he was in Mary's room, she wouldn't speak to me.

"Tell me again why this couldn't wait?" Austen asked with a frown. "Why being out in this infernal weather is better than being home, near the warm hearth?"

"This may be the last time I get to speak to Mary before we have to force her to leave on the ninth."

"Why not ask her about the book then?"

"Because I don't know how it will work."

"How what will work?"

"Once I change history. How much time I'll have before . . . " I let the words trail off.

"Before you leave and never return?" he asked, his grip tightening ever so slightly on my hand, as if he could hold me there forever.

I didn't want to talk about it again. I hadn't been able to eat anything that morning, and my stomach was sick just thinking about it now.

"You don't have to come with me," I said as I began to pull away from him. "I can speak to Mary on my own."

"I'm coming." He opened the door and stepped out of the carriage before he turned to offer me his hand. His blue eyes were filled with more storm clouds today as he said, "Jack might already be watching Mary, waiting for a chance to strike. I can't risk sending you in alone."

A shiver ran up my spine, and my gaze darted up and down the muddy street. There were only a few pedestrians out, and they weren't paying us any attention.

Austen opened an umbrella over our heads and put his arm around my waist to keep me close.

"None of this makes sense to me," he said, his voice filled with anger, though I knew it was only a mask for his pain and fear. "I don't understand why God would allow any of this to happen."

I didn't, either, and I was trying to believe what Mama and Papa told me, that God had a plan. That His will was better than my own. But none of it made sense to my human mind or heart, either, and I wasn't sure I'd ever understand it.

Miles stayed with the carriage as I lifted my hem and Austen led me across Dorset Street. It had been a rainier autumn than usual, and I was tired of the cold, wet weather. I wanted sunshine and warmth and peace.

And I wanted hope.

The familiar stench of Whitechapel burned my eyes as we

walked through the narrow passage to the back of Miller's Court. Nothing had changed. The small window next to the door at number thirteen was still broken, and a piece of cloth was shoved inside. Some people believed that Mary Jane Kelly let in Jack the Ripper; others speculated that he simply removed the cloth, reached through the window, and unlocked the door. I'd learned that the morning after Mary's death, the door was locked and the cloth was back in place, which meant that Jack had to bother with locking it after he committed the murder.

Another shiver ran up my spine as I tried to push aside the thoughts, reminding myself that this was not how history would play out after November 9th, when I saved Mary from this horror.

Austen knocked on the door, and a moment later, it slowly opened. Mary stood before us, her eyes red-rimmed and swollen from crying.

Instead of looking angry at our arrival, Mary fell into my arms.

"What's wrong?" I asked, reaching up to cradle the back of my sister's head. "Why are you crying, love?"

Austen slowly prodded us into the room and closed the door as I kept my arm around Mary. Without asking, he walked to the fireplace and put a few extra pieces of coal onto the flames to offer more light and warmth.

"Tell me what's wrong," I said to Mary, trying not to shiver from the cold or my concern.

"Joseph left," she said as she wiped at her red nose.

"I'm so sorry, Mary."

"I care for him. He—" She paused and shook her head. "He's been good to me, Kathryn. As good as he can be. He has spared me from the worst sorts of horrors in Whitechapel. And he doesn't ask for much. He helps pay the bills, and he's pleasant to pass the time. He hardly drinks, and he never hurts me." She pressed her lips together and looked down at her red, chapped hands. "He treats me like royalty and tells me he's not good enough for me."

I took her to the bed, and we sat on the edge. I gently moved a piece of her hair off her forehead and put it behind her ear. "What happened?"

"He lost his job," she said, lifting her shoulder. "And he's struggling to get more work. Which means." She took a deep breath. "It means that I need to find another way to pay rent."

I remembered what she'd told me before. That having one man was better than having several, and my throat began to tighten with alarm.

I squeezed her arm, not wanting to act shocked or mortified, but I couldn't help it. My sister wasn't a prostitute, but what choice did a woman in her position have?

"It's not enough being a charwoman," she said almost apologetically. "I can't make the money I need to pay for this room with occasional domestic work. I could go to a boardinghouse, but I'd have to share a room with a dozen or more strangers, and that's not cheap or safe, either."

"We can help," Austen said from where he was still standing near the fireplace. "You don't need to live like this, Mary."

She shook her head. "I can't take your money. People will ask questions."

"We're not going to give you a choice," I told her. I wanted to say that she wouldn't have to worry about it after November 9th, but there was no way I could—unless. "I know why you left home. I know more about the Book."

Mary's gaze came up, and for the first time since I'd entered the room, she really looked at me. "What?"

"I can't tell you how I know, but I've seen a letter written by Sir Charles Warren to Prince Albert Victor. The Book you saw is part of a larger one, split into five sections, and taken out of the Temple Mount in Jerusalem in 1874." I wasn't sure how wise it was to tell her all the details, but I needed her to trust me. "Polly Nichols, Annie Chapman, Elizabeth Stride, and Catherine Eddowes were all on the trip with our parents and Austen's. I think they knew about the Book, and that's why they ended up here, just like you."

Mary's eyes opened wide.

"Austen and I have made plans to take you away from here," I told her. "To get you to a safer place."

"Where?" she asked. "Is any place truly safe from the Freemasons?"

"We're sending you to America," Austen said, taking a step forward. We had talked about what would happen to Mary once we took her away from Whitechapel but hadn't planned to tell her now. "You'll change your name, and I'll see that my aunt finds a place of employment for you in New York City. You'll blend in with all the other immigrants there and have a decent life. It might not be the kind you were born into, but it's a better option than this one."

Mary looked from Austen to me, as if she was weighing her options. As if she was trying to decide which would be a better life. This one—or the one he spoke about in New York.

"You don't have a choice," I told her, wanting to shake her into compliance. "You can't stay in Whitechapel."

She nibbled her bottom lip and looked toward the window with longing.

"Are you in love with Joseph?" I asked.

Tears gathered in her eyes again, and she lifted her apron up to her face. "I'm so ashamed, Kathryn."

"Why?" I asked as I put my arm around her shoulder. "You didn't choose this life. And you've made the best of your circumstances."

"I can't leave Joseph. He'll get back on his feet again. He's looking for a better job, out of Whitechapel." She lowered her apron, her eyes pleading. "He wants to marry me, but he said he won't until he can afford a nice home. He's a good man."

"Listen to yourself, Mary." I frowned, angry and bewildered. "Every time we've been here, you were afraid of him coming back."

"I wasn't afraid of *him*. I was afraid he might find out I had a sister and then ask me too many questions that I couldn't answer."

I was still baffled. "You'd choose to stay in Whitechapel on the unlikely chance that he might make something of himself? You would give up the opportunity to work a decent job in New York? To start over with no threat of the Freemasons?"

"I-I think I do love him."

I was about to tell her how foolish she sounded when I caught sight of Austen, standing quietly, watching us. And it struck me that I couldn't judge my sister. Her love for Joseph was no less important or real than my love for Austen. And if I could, I would give up everything for him. All the plans I'd made in 1938, the modern conveniences I enjoyed, my work at the Smithsonian, even my life with Mama and Papa.

But I wasn't given the choice because I wanted to save my sister.

And now I had to convince her to leave this place. There was no other option.

"I will give you some time to think about Austen's offer," I told her, trying to keep my voice level. "We'll come back in a few days and see what you decide." I'd take her away from this place by force if she didn't come willingly.

Mary nodded. "I will think about it."

"Until then," I said, "I will leave a few coins for you to get by, and I won't take no for an answer."

She threw her arms around me and hugged me tight. Tears came to my eyes as I held my little sister, praying for a miracle.

Austen went to the window and glanced outside. His steady presence gave me the courage to keep going.

"I need to know what is in the Book, Mary."

She pulled away, her green eyes full of apprehension. "Why do you need to know?"

I couldn't tell her that I was trying to learn the identity of Jack the Ripper. So, I said something else that was true, if only a half-truth. "I want closure. I want to know why Austen's parents died and why all the women on the trip, except Mother, were killed. I want to know what is so important to the Freemasons that they'd go to such lengths to protect this Book."

Mary swallowed and shook her head. "If I only saw one-fifth of the Book, I can't imagine what is in the other four parts."

"You can tell us," Austen said. "I lost my parents because of it, and I've spent my entire life trying to understand what could have been so important that they'd give up their lives—give up me—to save it."

Something seemed to break inside Mary as tears came to her eyes. "Anyone connected to that book suffers." She took a deep breath and lifted her chin, wiping away her tears. "But you deserve to know, Austen."

He stood quietly and waited.

"It was a very old book," she said, "perhaps centuries old. At least, the part I saw. It was a record, of sorts, kind of like a ledger. There were names listed, and beside each one was a record of their deeds or misdeeds, like a positive and negative system of what each of those people either owed the Freemasons or had paid—sometimes in money and sometimes in favors. I saw names that shocked me. Rulers and noblemen from all over the world, dating back hundreds of years. And the deeds and misdeeds were not all small or inconsequential, there were assassinations and wars and massacres, things that turned the tide of history. And they were recorded in detail. Vivid, sometimes horrible detail." She shook her head. "If that was just the first part of the Book, I can only imagine what the other four parts contain."

"To be clear, it was the Freemasons who did these deeds?" Austen asked.

"Yes. Powerful Freemasons who committed egregious acts for others. Sometimes they were given money to commit these acts. Other times, they were paid back with lands or titles or with favors."

I stared at her, shocked that a book like that existed, but more shocked that the Freemasons had been behind some of history's most horrific events.

"If the Book is ever made public," Austen said, "it would unravel the entire Brotherhood and take down the Freemasons in one fell swoop."

"Which is why anyone with knowledge of the book is destroyed."

Mary's face was pale as she pleaded with her eyes. "Neither one of you can tell anyone you know about this book. My life was spared because I agreed to disappear. Father took an oath to destroy anyone who might see the Book, but he couldn't kill me. I promised I would never speak of it to anyone or tell anyone who I really am." She turned to me. "The letter I sent you was the one and only time I broke my promise. I knew you couldn't go the rest of your life without knowing that I would be okay. I still don't know how your private detective found me."

I couldn't tell her the truth.

"I'm not truly safe here, am I?" Mary asked, searching my face for answers. "If the four others were found, then I will be found, too. The Freemasons will find me."

"Do you think Jack the Ripper is working with Sir Charles Warren?" I asked Austen. "Is he a henchman for the Freemasons, taking out the women who knew about the Book? Is he doing it for land or money or a favor like the others listed in the ledger?"

"If he is, then why did he wait fourteen years to kill them?" Austen shook his head. "And they didn't all come to Whitechapel immediately upon returning to England after their trip to Jerusalem. It took time for them to get here."

"So you don't think Jack is a Freemason, destroying these women because they have knowledge of the Book?" I asked him.

"I don't know." Austen shrugged. "It's all connected, but it doesn't make sense."

Mary stood as she looked between us. "Am I in danger?"

I took a deep breath, wondering how much to tell her. "Not right now. We have some time. But you need to be ready to leave soon."

"You mean, to go to New York?"

"I think it's your only option, Mary."

She walked to the window, where she looked out at the dirty courtyard, and I knew she was thinking about Joseph. Rain dripped from the eaves of the building and ran down the glass.

After a moment she said, "I'll be ready whenever you tell me."

Relief overwhelmed me, and I joined her by the window to embrace her.

"It'll take a few days to make arrangements," Austen said. "We'll come back for you on the evening of November 8th."

"But you must not breathe a word of this to anyone," I said as I pulled back. "Do you understand? None of your friends, not even Joseph. No one must know that you'll be leaving here."

"I understand the need for secrecy better than anyone," she said quietly. "I've been living this lie for over a year, Kathryn."

I kept my arm around her shoulder, and she laid her head on mine.

"I love you," I whispered.

"I love you, too."

We said good-bye, promising to be back soon, and then Austen led me out of her home and down the passage.

A young woman passed us. She wore a cape with a hood and glanced up at us briefly before she proceeded to Mary's room and knocked on the door.

"Hello, Jane," Mary said a moment later in her Whitechapel accent. "Come in out of the cold, love, and warm yourself by the fire."

My sister's kindness to her friends was heartwarming, and I knew her fear of losing her room was just as much for her as it was for them. I hated to think what would become of her friends once she was in America, but I couldn't worry about them. I could only do so much.

Austen and I were quiet as we left Whitechapel and entered central London on our return to Wilton Crescent. I wasn't sure what he was thinking, but I knew what was occupying my thoughts.

I'd set into motion the final plan I'd ever make for 1888. In just a few days, I would whisk Mary away from Miller's Court and put her on a ship bound for New York City. Then I would say good-bye to her and Austen and go to sleep, and never return to either one of them.

I leaned on Austen's shoulder, and he put his arm around me.

"I've purchased tickets for Mary's travel," Austen said. "I'll have Miles ready to return to Whitechapel on Thursday so we can take her to Southampton to meet the ship."

I sat up, surprised. "You can't help me. I don't know what will happen if you knowingly change history. I don't want to take the risk."

"I won't let you do it alone, Kathryn," he said, just as adamant. "It will be far too dangerous for both of you. Miles and I will help, come what may."

"I couldn't live with myself if you died, Austen."

"You've seen me alive in 1938. It must mean I live."

"I've seen you alive in the *unchanged* version of history. Once we take Mary away, I don't know what will change. You might not be in 1938 after November 9th."

He drew me back into his arms. "It will be my decision, Kathryn. And I will not let you do this alone. No matter how much you protest." He let out a breath, his voice deepening. "Besides, I will have little to live for if you're not here, so it's a risk I'm willing to take."

I laid my head against his shoulder again, a whole new set of concerns weighing down my heart.

I didn't want to live in a world without Austen.

22

LONDON, ENGLAND
NOVEMBER 6, 1938

There was a lot occupying my mind as I worked on the exhibit in the basement of Lancaster house. Austen's words in the carriage only intensified my anxiety and fears for Mary. But it wasn't just 1888 that concerned me. Papa's trip to Berlin was weighing on my mind, as were all the little details I still needed to include in the exhibit. This was my final opportunity to put the finishing touches on the project I had come to London to create.

A dozen people worked alongside me, placing artifacts in glass cases, repositioning signs, touching up a crack that had developed in the façade of Buck's Row, and cleaning the room. I'd spent the earlier part of my day answering questions from the public and the press. This was the first exhibit about Jack the Ripper, and people were curious.

"Are you certain you want to display the pictures of the victims?" Calan asked me one more time as he approached me with a wooden crate. We'd had the pictures framed and were planning to place them in a spot that could be overlooked if people didn't want to see the images. The first four were pictures of the victims' faces after death and were not shocking. The fifth was horrific and showed Mary Jane Kelly in her familiar room, but the body was so mangled and deformed, it was impossible to recognize.

Every time I looked at the picture, I had to disassociate with it. It wasn't my sister. It was a person who had not yet been murdered—and would not be murdered, because I was going to stop it from happening.

"Let's do as we originally planned." I told him. "We'll place a black cloth over the photo of the last victim and tell people that they can look at their own discretion."

Calan nodded and left my side.

I couldn't help but wonder what would happen after November 9th. Would that picture just disappear? I wasn't sure how it would all happen. Would everything be different when I woke up in 1938 after saving my sister? Would I be the only person who knew a different history? When I talked to Calan and Sir Rothschild, would their memory of Mary Jane Kelly have disappeared?

I had no idea, but I was determined to find out.

Sunshine streamed in through the windows at the top of the room, offering us good light to work. Tomorrow in this path would be the official grand opening, and we needed to be ready. Even if I had to work until midnight, I wouldn't leave the museum until every piece of the exhibit was in place.

Sir Rothschild entered the room, and I stole a look to see his response. He had taken a risk in asking me to help Calan, and I wanted him to be pleased.

"Was this what you had envisioned?" I asked as I left the letter case where Jack's famous correspondence was displayed under glass for the world to see. "Does it meet your expectations?"

Sir Rothschild shook his head as he surveyed the room, a smile tilting up his mustache. "My dear Miss Voland, you and Calan have exceeded my wildest expectations. This goes above and beyond what I had hoped for and envisioned for this exhibit. I cannot thank you enough for putting your life in Washington, DC, on hold to be part of this project."

"It was an honor," I assured him.

"I almost didn't ask you to come," he said as he turned to me. "But there was this small voice in my head that kept prompting me. As if this project needed you. And I believe it did."

My lips parted as I realized the truth of his words. If he hadn't invited me to put together this exhibit, I would never have learned the truth about Mary and I wouldn't have had the opportunity to save her. This entire time, I'd been upset with God that He was making me choose, but until this moment, I hadn't realized that it was a blessing in disguise. I *had* a choice because He had allowed me to have a choice.

"Thank you for believing in me and giving me a chance," I said, trying to keep my voice even. "I will always treasure my memories here."

For more reasons than he could possibly know.

"I'll let you get back to your work," he said as he patted my shoulder a bit awkwardly. "It looks like things will be ready for the grand opening tomorrow. And I'm hoping that this new exhibit draws visitors to the art gallery to see Mr. Baird's paintings, as well. It is my special privilege to find such spectacular talent and share it with the world." He smiled at me. "You, included."

"Thank you."

As he left to inspect the exhibit, I thought about Austen's paintings. Whenever I missed him, I went into the gallery to study his work. It was almost as if I was getting to know a new side of him. It was another facet of his personality that intrigued me. I wanted to know more about his painting, but we'd both been so preoccupied with the plans we were making for Mary, we hadn't talked much about his work.

"Kathryn."

I turned at the sound of Mama's voice as she entered the room. It was the first time she'd come to Lancaster House, and I smiled at the unexpected visit.

But the look on her face made me pause. She was pale, and her eyes were glossed over with fear.

My heart began to hammer as I rushed across the room and reached for her hands. "What's wrong? Is it Papa?"

She latched on to me, as if her knees were about to give way, and held on tight. "Yes—oh, Kathryn." She began to weep, and my worst fears jumped into my mind and heart.

People turned our way, curiosity and concern drawing their attention.

I wanted to have privacy, so I led Mama out of the room and across the hall. The basement was empty since we'd closed it off to visitors while we finished the Jack the Ripper exhibit. I found a quiet corner and faced her.

"What happened?" I asked, both wanting and not wanting to know. "Where is Papa?"

It took Mama a moment to compose herself, and she finally lifted her chin to face me. I had always known her to be a strong, thoughtful, and brave woman. But when it came to Papa and her children, her vulnerability showed through.

"They don't know where he is," she said, her voice quivering. "Colonel Lindbergh called me personally, just an hour ago. I came as soon as I could pull myself together."

"What do you mean, they don't know where he is? Where could Papa be?"

"He has been with Colonel Lindbergh and Major Truman Smith for most of his visit," Mama said, "but those two men were invited to a private meeting with other military attaché, and your father said that he would spend the day touring Berlin on his own." She paused as she swallowed. "They were supposed to meet for supper last night, and when your father didn't show, they assumed he was ill or indisposed. But when they went to his room to collect him this morning to fly to a factory in Dessau, he was not in his room, and there was no evidence that he had ever returned to the hotel yesterday." Her voice broke, and she lifted her handkerchief to her mouth as she tried to compose herself.

I wrapped my arms around her, trying to make sense of what she'd said. Papa had never disappeared before. He was responsible and trustworthy. If he said he was going to meet Colonel Lindbergh, then he would have met him. If he was sick or something prevented him, he would have sent word. "Have they checked the hospitals?" I asked.

"They have been looking for him for hours. The American Embassy has been put on full alert, and Colonel Lindbergh assures me that they will exhaust every measure to find your father." Her tears began. "Oh, Kathryn. I knew something horrible was going to happen. I shouldn't have let him go. It was madness to think it was safe to be in Germany at this time."

"You had no way of knowing," I tried to assure her. "No one else went missing. It's not as if a whole airplane of Americans was taken out by the Germans. Perhaps he was walking around the city and there was an accident and at this very moment, he's phoning Colonel Lindbergh to tell him what happened."

"An accident?" Mama asked, her eyes widening. "What if he was hit by an automobile? What if—"

"You can't play that game," I said. "We can't jump to conclusions. We will go insane if we think of all the possibilities. There must be a logical reason that he didn't return to his hotel room last night."

But even as I tried to reassure my mama, I couldn't think of any logical reason Papa would disappear. It didn't make sense. A pit in the center of my gut told me that something was dreadfully wrong.

"May we help?" Calan asked as he appeared just outside the room with Sir Rothschild beside him.

I took a deep breath, not wanting Mama to see how worried I felt. "My father has gone missing," I told them. "He had a free day in Berlin yesterday and was supposed to meet with Colonel Lindbergh last night, but he didn't show. And then this morning, when he didn't arrive for their flight to a factory, they began to look for him. His room was undisturbed, and no one knows where he went."

"I'm so sorry to hear that," Sir Rothschild said as he entered the room. "You need to take your mother home, Miss Voland."

"But—"

"We will oversee the rest of the exhibit," Calan interrupted. "Your plans are in perfect order, and we shouldn't have any trouble executing them. Right now, you are needed somewhere more important."

Mama was in shock, and I knew they were right. She needed me more than the museum staff did. I wouldn't be much help to them, anyway. Not in my current state of mind.

"Perhaps you're right." I nodded as I put my arm around Mama to lead her out of the museum.

"Call us the moment you hear something," Sir Rothschild said.

"We'll be praying for all of you," Calan added.

"Thank you." I tried to smile, to be strong for Mama, but I couldn't force myself to pretend.

We would need all the prayers we could get.

The moment Lady Astor heard about Papa, she came to Berkeley Square and spent the afternoon with us, calling anyone and everyone she knew who might have authority to help. Lord Astor arrived shortly before supper, letting us know he had done the same. None of us could eat a thing.

Calan arrived around eight to let me know that the exhibit was finished and ready for the grand opening tomorrow. I was still in shock and realized I hadn't thought of the exhibit once.

"Are you hungry?" I asked him as we stood in the front hall. "No one touched supper, and I'd hate to see it go to waste."

"I've already eaten," he said, his face filled with concern. "Have you heard anything?"

I shook my head, glancing up the stairs where Mama was sitting in the parlor with the Astors. "Nothing from Germany, though Mama received a call from the US secretary of state today, Cordell Hull. They are aware of the situation and doing all they can to ensure Papa is returned home safely."

"The secretary of state?" Calan asked, his eyes widening. "Do they think someone abducted your father?"

"No one knows, but they are taking his disappearance very seriously. My father is a brigadier general in the US Army Air Corps. He was a flight instructor during the Great War and was instrumental in forming the Air Corps in the 1920s. He not only has classified knowledge, but he's also a high-ranking officer. The world is on the brink of war with Hitler. Something like this is a very serious situation and doesn't feel like a coincidence."

"Who might have taken him, if that's what happened?" Calan asked, quietly. "What would they gain?"

"I don't know." I crossed my arms, wanting something to *do*. I hated all this sitting around and waiting. I was half tempted to fly to Berlin to look for Papa myself.

Calan placed his hand on my arm and gave it a gentle squeeze. "I know your father will come home safely, Kathryn. Don't give up hope."

"I won't."

"And don't worry about the grand opening tomorrow. We can manage—"

"I will be there," I promised. "Papa would want me there."

"Only if you're certain."

I tried to smile, knowing it was the right thing, though I wasn't sure how I would get through the event if Papa wasn't found yet. "I am certain."

Calan left, and as I closed the door behind him—about to face Mama and the Astors again—I longed for Austen. I wanted his reassurance. I wanted to share this burden with him because I knew that he would do everything in his power to help me if he could.

I returned to the parlor, where Mama sat on the chair, another handkerchief in hand. She'd gone through six of them already. Her eyes were red-rimmed, and her face was pale. Even through her tears, I had been impressed with how composed she'd remained all day, though I knew she was a mess inside.

"How is everything at the museum?" she asked me as I took a seat on the chair next to her.

"Good." I smiled. "Calan has everything under control."

She nodded, and I knew she hadn't really been listening, but I didn't blame her.

The telephone rang, and all of us sat up straight. We had brought an extension into the parlor earlier in the afternoon, and Mama reached for it now.

"Hello?" she asked as she sat forward on the edge of her chair, grabbing my hand. "Yes, this is Mrs. Voland."

She was quiet for several seconds, but it was impossible to read the expression on her face.

I glanced at the Astors, who looked back at me, just as eager and nervous to hear who had called. Lady Astor clasped her hands together so tightly, her knuckles were white.

"Yes," Mama said, nodding before she swallowed. "I understand." Her voice cracked, and my heart fell. Mama did not look relieved. Whatever she was hearing was not instilling any confidence in her. "Thank you. I will keep the phone close by."

Her hand shook as she slowly hung up the receiver, but before I could ask her who had called, she lowered her head and began to weep.

"What is it, Mama?" I asked, leaving my chair to kneel in front of her. "Tell me."

Mama took a moment and then inhaled a deep breath before she lifted her head. "That was Major Smith, calling from Berlin. They have not found your father, but they have enough evidence to suggest that he was abducted." She paused again as her breath shuddered out of her body. "No one has come forward with any demands, and the German government is claiming that they have nothing to do with his disappearance. They are assisting the American Embassy with their investigation."

"Who would take Papa?" I asked, angry and frustrated and afraid.

"They aren't sure at this time," Mama said, "but they believe it's an extremist group. They won't know until they're contacted and demands are made." She took another deep breath. "Major Smith has every confidence that your father will remain unharmed. They do not believe this was a random criminal act. Someone took your father with the intent to get something. And until we know what that is, they believe your father will be held captive."

"This is ludicrous," Lord Astor said as he stood and began to pace.

"It's—it's—" Lady Astor shook her head, clearly at a loss for words. "What I do know is that the United States and England will do everything in their power to ensure that Luc is brought home safely."

Mama nodded as she wiped her cheeks with the handkerchief. "Thank you." She rose on shaking legs and said, "I hope you don't mind. I believe I'll turn in for the night. Major Smith said that he doesn't think he'll have any more news for me this evening, and I need to keep up my strength."

"Of course we don't mind," Lady Astor said as she, too, rose. "We'll take our leave, but do not hesitate to call us, even if it's the middle of the night. We will be here as soon as possible."

"Thank you." Mama tried to look stoical as she left the parlor, but I could hear her begin to weep as soon as she entered the hall and went up the stairs.

"We are so sorry, Kathryn," Lady Astor said as she joined me near the chair. "Please know that we are here for you, no matter what you need."

"Thank you." I accepted a hug from her and a smile from Lord Astor.

"We're only a phone call away," she said as we left the parlor and walked down the stairs to the front hall, where their wraps were waiting on a coat-tree near the door.

As soon as they were gone, I went up the stairs and into my bedroom, where I stared out the window at Berkeley Square, shadowed under nightfall. I didn't want to bother Mama, who was in her room across the hall. She would need some time to herself to process everything that had happened. Earlier, we had called my sister, Lydia, in California, but if there was no news to share, it didn't pay to call her again. Hopefully we would have something good to tell her in the morning.

What I really wanted was to go to sleep so I could wake up in 1888 and tell Austen what had happened. I needed his warm embrace to chase away my fears. But it wouldn't be midnight for several hours, and I couldn't cross over until then.

After I put on my nightgown, washed my face, and brushed my teeth, I padded across the hallway to Mama's door and knocked lightly.

"Come in," Mama said.

I opened the door and found her lying on her bed. She was still wearing her dress and hadn't changed into a nightgown. She was holding one of Papa's nightshirts to her face, though it looked as if her tears had stopped.

I'd never seen her so distressed. She worried about us, but she was always our strength in times of trouble. It shook me to my core to see her this upset.

Slowly, she seemed to gather herself and sat up, holding her arms out to me, beckoning me to join her.

I didn't hesitate but climbed into her bed.

And, for the first time since we'd heard the news, I allowed myself to cry.

Mama held me until I fell asleep.

23

NOVEMBER 7, 1888
LONDON, ENGLAND

I had never lived through such a long day before in my life. But if I thought being in 1938 and not having word from Berlin was difficult, it was nothing compared to waiting in 1888. What made it even more unbearable was that Austen hadn't been home all day and no one knew where he had gone.

I spent most of my day pacing, though I tried to stay occupied. I only had two more days in this path, and this was not how I wanted to spend my time. The weather had finally cleared, and the day was bright and warm for early November. I would have preferred walking in the park or taking a drive through the city, but I was confined to our townhouse, afraid to go out, not knowing when I might see Austen next. He knew I was leaving soon. Didn't he want to spend every possible moment with me?

"Your mother sent me to tell you that it's time to get ready," Father said when he opened the parlor door and found me that evening.

"For what?" I asked.

"For a dinner party or something or other."

"I don't plan to go out tonight."

He sighed. "I wouldn't advise you to deny your mother's request today. She's not in a good mood."

"I'm not in a good mood, either." I crossed my arms and stared into the crackling fireplace.

He stood at the door for several seconds and then said, "I hope this doesn't have something to do with Austen. You two have spent far too much time in each other's company lately. I don't like it one bit."

I didn't respond.

He entered the parlor and closed the door behind him.

I finally turned my gaze away from the flames with a frown. Father rarely took the time to address me, unless he was upset.

"I hope Austen isn't preparing to ask for your hand in marriage." His blunt, simple statement made me sit up straighter in my chair.

Austen and I hadn't spoken about marriage because we knew it was pointless. "I'm—"

"It's out of the question." Father planted his feet, as if he was ready to go into battle. "I have other plans for you, and I won't hear of it."

"Why? Austen is a good man, from a good family."

"That doesn't matter—at least not in this situation."

"How could it not matter?" I moved to the edge of my seat. "What does that mean?"

"Austen is not the right man for you. He's headstrong and stubborn and unwilling to yield to common sense. I want you to marry someone who is willing to play by the rules."

I stared at my father for a moment, realization dawning. "He won't join the Freemasons. Is that what you mean? He won't play by their rules, and if he's not for you, then he's against you?"

"You have no idea what you're talking about." His voice became low as his eyes narrowed.

"Austen knows things that you don't want him to know if he's not under a pledge or oath to the Brotherhood. Is that it? Is that what makes him unsuitable for me? You want someone who will bend and comply to your demands. Who can be entrusted with your secrets. Who is willing to toss their daughter onto the street because she knows too much."

Father took a menacing step toward me, his face turning red in an instant. "Who have you been speaking to? Is it Austen? What has he told you?"

My lips parted in surprise at his fury. If I wasn't careful, I might get Austen into the same kind of trouble that Mary had been in.

"He's told me nothing," I said quickly.

He came closer, and I pressed into the back of the chair.

"Have you seen Mary?" Father asked, studying my face for the answer. "Do you know where she is?"

I swallowed. I didn't want to lie—but I couldn't tell him the truth. I shook my head, tasting real fear for the first time.

"I've warned you, Kathryn." He put his hands on either side of the arm rests, his face coming close to mine as he leaned forward. "I cannot protect you if you know too much. Stop looking for answers."

I wanted to tell him I'd already found them, but I didn't want to end up like Mary. I only had two days left, and I needed one of them to help my sister.

"Perhaps you should stay home tonight," he said, standing up straighter while he adjusted the lapels of his coat. "We will give your regrets to the hostess while you stay in your room and think long and hard about what you plan to do with your life. You have a choice, Kathryn. You can keep going down the path you're on and end up like your sister and the others who went to Whitechapel, or you can follow in your mother's footsteps and be silent and compliant."

Was that why Polly, Annie, Elizabeth, and Catherine died? They refused to be silent and compliant. I wanted to ask him, but I didn't dare.

"Go on," he said as he took a step back. "But if I hear that you went to Austen's or that he entered this house, you will not be living here come morning."

I was a twenty-three-year-old woman being sent to my room, and it rankled. But I also knew what my father could do, and I would not test the limits of his patience.

I went to my room, but I didn't go to bed. I couldn't. It was still early, and I planned to see Austen as soon as my parents left. I would send word to him through Duffy.

Austen couldn't come to my house, and I couldn't go to his. But that didn't mean I couldn't meet him somewhere else.

At the appointed hour, I snuck out of my home on Wilton Crescent and walked the ten minutes to Hyde Park and the Statue of Achilles. I'd told Austen to meet me there in the note I had sent with Duffy. I just prayed he would get it in time.

Clouds covered the moon as I made my way along the dark street toward the park. Austen, Mary and I had come here often as children, drawn to the impressive sculpture that stood over thirty feet high. It was on the east end of the park, close enough to reach easily at this time of night, yet sheltered enough that we would have a bit of privacy.

It had grown cold since the sun went down, and a wind had come up, making me pull my cape closer to my body. Though this part of London was relatively safe, I couldn't stop thinking about Jack the Ripper and his next planned victim—my sister. I had no reason to think he'd been watching me, but I couldn't be certain. It was probably a foolish idea to leave the house this late at night. Alone. With only Austen knowing where I planned to go.

I kept my head low as I passed people on the street. It was far too late to be out for social calls. If anyone knew my identity, my reputation would be ruined.

But none of that mattered. I needed to speak to Austen. To tell him what had happened to Papa in 1938 and to make sure all our plans to help Mary were in place.

And, more than anything, I simply wanted to be with him.

I made it to the statue, but there was no one within sight. I had hoped Austen would be waiting for me, though I had arrived earlier than I planned.

The wind whipped the leafless branches of the trees overhead and whistled a low, moaning sound through the park. I shivered as I stood near the statue, on full alert to anyone who might come by. My fingers and nose were cold, so I brought my hands up to my mouth to blow warm air into them.

A lone man entered the park. I watched him closely, but quickly realized it wasn't Austen. My heart began to beat hard as he came closer. I moved deeper into the shadows, praying he would pass by.

Thankfully, he turned on the path and moved out of sight.

My entire body shook as I realized this had been a mistake. I was headstrong, but I wasn't usually foolish, and the longer I stood there, alone, the more foolish I felt.

Twenty minutes passed, and I was about to return home when I saw another man enter the park and walk toward the statue. I knew instantly that it was Austen, and my pulse sped for a different reason as relief and joy washed over me. His stride was so dear, so familiar, I wanted to run to him. But I waited behind the statue until he was within earshot.

"I'm here," I said quietly.

He turned toward the sound of my voice and joined me at the statue. It was then that I noticed he was carrying something in his hands. He set it on the base of the statue and opened his arms to me.

I entered them freely as he enveloped me.

"As soon as I got home and saw your note, I raced to get here," he said. "You shouldn't be alone in the park at any time, but especially not now, when we don't know if Jack has been watching you."

"Father forbade me from going to your house or for you to come to mine. But I had to see you." My voice caught with emotion. "I've wanted to see you all day—to tell you—" I couldn't bring myself to voice the reality of what was happening in 1938.

"What is it, Kate?" He pulled back to study me. And though it was dark, my eyes had adjusted enough to see his face.

"Papa was abducted in 1938." My voice faltered, and I found it harder to tell him than I expected. I relayed everything we'd learned the day before, and when I was done, he drew me into his arms again and held me tight.

"I'm sorry," he said. "I wish I could do something to help you."

"You are. Maybe not there, but here." I clung to him, trying to remember all the little details I could. The smell of his cologne, the feel of his arms, the sound of his voice. "I don't know what I'll do without you."

He tilted my chin up with his finger and placed a kiss on my lips. It was just as tender as all the others, but it held so much passion and longing, it felt different. As if he couldn't get enough.

When I finally pulled back, I asked, "Where were you today? I've missed you."

"I did something that's probably foolish." He let me go and reached for the item he'd set on the statue. "Actually, I know it was foolish. I left last night after I brought you home from Miller's Court, and I just now returned."

He handed me the item, which I quickly realized was a book. A book I would know anywhere.

"It's the book about Queen Elizabeth," I said, quickly opening it and trying to see the pages in the dark. It was the book that Austen and I had read together in the garden as children. The book that had made me want to be a historian. "Austen." I looked up at him, my lips parting in both surprise and delight. "Where was it?"

"At my cottage on Loch Lomond."

"You went all the way there and back to bring it to me?"

He took my hand and walked me to a bench where we sat, out of the wind and in a little alcove of trees. "Do you recall all the hours we sat together reading this book?"

"Of course I do," I said as I ran my hand over the worn fabric cover. "Those are some of my dearest memories. This book made me fall in love with history."

"As I fell in love with you," he said, touching my cheek. "I've always been drawn to your passion and your courage. I could see you living in the Elizabethan period, amid the intrigue at court, like Queen Elizabeth's maid of honor Lady Cecily Pembrooke, who we read about."

I smiled against his hand. "You remember her story?"

"How could I forget? You lit up every time we read about her. I could easily see you in any place and at any time in history," he said, his voice growing sad, "never cowering or bowing down to injustice. That's why the book means so much to me. It makes me feel connected to you through time, somehow. I've never understood it." He paused for a moment, and all the angst and gruffness was gone as he said, "You're timeless, Kate. Whether you're here or in 1938, or in Queen Elizabeth's court, you belong. And I feel honored to know you. To share even a small part of your amazing existence."

His words warmed my heart, and I lifted the book to my chest. "Why did you have this at Loch Lomond?"

"When I left London after my parents died, I didn't take a single thing with me. Nothing. Except this book. I had it with me at Eton and then Oxford, and I had it with me on every trip I took abroad. I leave it at Loch Lomond only because when I'm in London, and you're nearby, I don't need it."

"You took this with you?" I asked, incredulous.

"It reminded me of the happiest moments of my life, of a time that made sense and gave me hope." He ran his thumb over my lower lip. "It connected me to you. No matter where I went."

"Austen," I said on a breath, trying to control my emotions. "What are we going to do?"

"What can we do?" he asked. "We must face the path ahead with courage and faith. Just as Lady Cecily did in 1563. Do *you* remember?"

I smiled and nodded. "But she had a knight in shining armor come to her rescue."

"Did she?" he asked with a smile, taking me into his arms.

"Somehow, I remember that it was Lady Cecily who did the rescuing."

I returned his smile, my heart breaking, knowing that neither of us could rescue the other from what was about to happen.

This was a stolen moment. One I would cherish forever, because there would never again be a night like this.

24

NOVEMBER 7, 1938
LONDON, ENGLAND

My nerves were so raw by the next evening, I could hardly think straight. There had been no news from Berlin. Not even a phone call from Major Smith, Colonel Lindbergh, or anyone from the American embassy. The Astors had come earlier in the day, but seeing that there was nothing they could do, Mama had insisted they leave.

We had called Lydia and spoken to her for over an hour, and then around noon, Mama had told me I needed to leave. She knew I had things to do at Lancaster House to prepare for the grand opening. And, though I didn't want her to be alone, I couldn't deny my need to go to the museum.

As I worked on last-minute touches to the exhibit, I prayed fervently for good news out of Berlin and for a miracle in 1888. Every time I saw something with Mary's name on it, I forced myself to think beyond November 9th. This was not how Mary's story would end. I didn't care what history had to say about it. And I prayed that Austen wouldn't have to suffer for helping me. *I* was the one changing history.

An hour before the grand opening ceremony, I went into the

restroom to touch up my lipstick and smooth down my hair. King George VI and Queen Elizabeth would arrive within half an hour to look over the exhibit before it was opened to the public. They would be on hand for the ceremony, when Sir Rothschild, Calan, and I were scheduled to talk about the history and the collaboration between the London Museum, the Smithsonian, and the Royal Museum of Scotland. It was one of the biggest moments of my career and my life. I just wished Mama and Papa could be there with me to celebrate.

I took several deep breaths, trying to gain control of my emotions so I could get through the next couple of hours. My longing for Austen felt like a gaping hole in my chest. If he could be at my side, things would be a little more bearable. Waiting for news about Papa might not be so hard.

When I left the restroom, I was near the portrait gallery, so I slipped into the long, narrow room to look at Austen's paintings. It still amazed me that he had done this work. If we had more time, I would love to go to Loch Lomond and see his painting studio. Watch him create one of these masterpieces. It was a marvel how he used light to convey the mood of each painting, and how he could transport me to another place and time with his creations.

I stopped in front of the portrait of me. Of all Austen's paintings, this one made me feel the closest to him. I could imagine him brushing each stroke of paint to create my cheeks, my eyes, my lips—almost as if he was caressing them with his fingers now. Warmth filled me at the memories of all the kisses we'd shared in the past couple of weeks.

But then reality washed over me as I thought about all the kisses we would be denied after I forfeited 1888.

Tears stung my eyes, and I had to work valiantly not to cry.

"It's a stunning portrait, is it not?" Sir Rothschild asked as he entered the room.

I blinked several times before I turned to him and smiled, surprised that he'd found me here.

"This is the painting that first caught my eye," he continued as he looked from the painting back to me. "The one that made me interested in Austen Baird's work. I'd already met you in Washington, and when I saw this, I was shocked at the likeness. I was convinced it was you, until I learned that Mr. Baird had painted it in 1889—and it couldn't be you." He chuckled and shook his head. "But it made me curious to see all his other paintings. I had assumed they would all be portraits. I was surprised to learn that this was the only portrait he'd ever painted."

"It is an uncanny likeness," I said, my voice weaker than I liked.

"I'm happy that it is," Sir Rothschild said. "Because it led me to investigate this painter, and I was delighted at what I discovered. Nothing happens by chance. I'm convinced of that."

I nodded, unable to find words to express my agreement.

"And now you're here," he said with a smile. "Not only have you created a spectacular exhibit, but you're able to see this portrait for yourself. I had so hoped you could. It isn't every day that we see a picture of ourselves from the past."

I looked up at him quickly, but he was smiling happily as he admired the portrait.

"I suppose it's not uncommon to have a doppelgänger—is that the word the Germans use?" He chuckled again. "With so many people in the world, both past and present, there has to be others who look like us."

I swallowed my nerves and said, "I suppose so."

"Well." He clasped his hands, apparently ready to move on. "We should prepare to receive the king and queen. They will want a personal tour." He motioned toward the door, and I preceded him out of the gallery.

Thirty minutes later, I was standing beside Calan, just inside the special exhibit room in the basement of Lancaster House when the king and queen were escorted in by Sir Rothschild. They were dressed in formal evening wear, which made me assume they had other plans beyond attending the grand opening. The queen's jewelry sparkled, and the king was boasting a set of ribbons and medals on his chest.

I lifted my chin, determined to enjoy the culmination of weeks of hard work. Meeting the King and Queen of England was an honor I wouldn't waste, even though my heart was filled with the weight of many concerns.

"Your Majesties," Sir Rothschild said, "may I present our lead curator, Mr. Calan McCaffrey from the Royal Museum of Scotland, and our assistant curator, Miss Kathryn Voland from the Smithsonian Institute."

I offered the king and queen a curtsy while Calan bowed.

"How do you do?" I asked them.

"It's a pleasure to meet you," Queen Elizabeth said with a smile.

I rose from my curtsy. "It's an honor to have both of you visit the museum today."

"We've been apprised of the situation with your father," King George said, rocking back on his heels slightly. "And I want you to know that everyone is cooperating to find him as quickly as possible."

Tears threatened again, but I managed to smile. "Thank you."

"Of course."

"Shall we begin the tour?" Sir Rothschild asked as he motioned toward the exhibit.

I walked on one side of King George and Queen Elizabeth, while Sir Rothschild and Calan walked on the other.

"Miss Voland," Sir Rothschild said, "would you like to give a brief history of what happened in 1888 in Whitechapel?"

"Of course."

We'd set up the exhibit in sort of a timeline, starting near the façade of Buck's Row, where the first murder had taken place. "In the early morning hours of Friday, August 31, 1888, the first victim, Mary Ann Nichols, commonly known as Polly, was found here at Buck's Row in Whitechapel."

As we walked through the exhibit, I gave them all the details, though I didn't mention my suspicions about the victims' connection to the Freemasons. I wasn't sure if King George was a member of the Freemasons and how much he might know about the cover-up. I wasn't foolish enough to think that if I cracked the truth open, the Freemasons would let it stay open. Especially if King George was a Grand Master, as Prince Albert Victor had been in 1888.

And even if I did, I would be changing history in 1938, as well, and that was a risk I couldn't take.

The king and queen asked several questions and showed great interest in the exhibit, but when we came to the pictures of the victims, they both declined to look at them.

I didn't want to look at them again, either.

"What a fabulous exhibit," the queen said. "Jack the Ripper has fascinated me since I was a child."

"I've always found it odd," King George mused as he looked at the items found in the victims' pockets. "He has fascinated countless people, yet there have been others before and after him who were much more heinous. Why do you think we are so intrigued by Jack the Ripper?"

"Perhaps it's because he was never caught," the queen offered. "And that he always seemed just out of reach of the authorities. Kind of like a mythical creature. The evidence of his existence was real, but no one could catch him. And then his terror ended as abruptly as it began, causing more speculation about the monster."

"I think you're right," I said. "And the more time that passes, the more his legendary status grows."

We were almost to the letters Jack had written when an aide-de-camp stepped into the room and nodded at them. "Your Majesties? I believe it's time to go upstairs for the ceremony, and then we must be off for your next appointment."

"We do hate to rush," Queen Elizabeth said, "but duty calls."

"Of course." I smiled.

"The exhibit is magnificent," she said. "You have much to be proud of."

"Thank you."

We were ushered out of the exhibit hall and up the stairs to the central room of Lancaster House, where there was more space for people to gather.

The king and queen's presence had not been advertised and was completely unexpected for our guests. Excited chatter filled the room as the royals smiled and nodded. They took their places on the landing of the massive formal staircase where we would address the audience, though neither of them planned to speak.

Even though the room was full, I felt lonelier than ever. I longed for Mama and Papa and for Austen and Lydia and Mary. I even missed Father and Mother, though neither one would approve of me having a career. I couldn't fathom what they would say or think if they knew the truth about my time-crossing. They would be impressed that I'd met the king and queen, though, and that put a smile on my face.

After Sir Rothschild welcomed everyone to the London Museum and gave a special mention to the king and queen, he turned to Calan and me.

"It is with much gratefulness that I introduce our guest exhibit curators, Mr. Calan McCaffrey and Miss Kathryn Voland."

After Calan said a few words, everyone clapped as I stepped up to the microphone and looked out at the eager faces in the crowd. A few people still carried their gas masks in boxes slung over their shoulders, but most people had accepted that Hitler was no longer an imminent threat. I knew differently—especially with my father held captive somewhere in Germany.

I squared my shoulders, knowing he wouldn't want me to cower or back down from this crowning achievement of my career. Both he and Mama had always encouraged me to pursue my dreams and passions, and he would be the proudest of all if he were standing there. So, I pushed forward with the speech I had prepared.

As I spoke about Jack the Ripper and, more importantly, about his five victims, I couldn't help but feel a deep connection with them. Not only because I worked on the exhibit and because my sister was supposed to be the last victim, but because tomorrow, I would thwart his plans and save Mary.

It was late when Sir Rothschild and his wife, Bianca, brought me back to 44 Berkeley Square. All evening, I had hoped to see Mama or one of the Astors arrive with good news, but there had been nothing.

As Sir Rothschild walked me to the front door, I prayed that no news was good news and that they hadn't kept something from me so I could enjoy the grand opening.

"Thank you for everything," Sir Rothschild said again as he stood at the door with me. "We will keep waiting to hear of news about your father. I know that you have things in your office at the museum that you would like to take home with you, but don't rush to gather them on our account. Take your time. We will see you whenever you can come."

I nodded my thanks and then entered the townhouse, closing the door behind me.

Slowly, I walked up the stairs, tired and heartsore. Now that the work of the day was behind me, I was more exhausted than I realized. I just wanted to rest, but to do that, I would have to forget about tomorrow in 1888. And that was an impossible feat.

"Mama?" I asked as I entered the parlor quietly.

She was sitting near the hearth, her elbow on the armrest, her chin in her hand, staring into the fire. Without even asking, I knew that there had been no news.

"Kathryn." She turned and motioned for me to join her.

I knelt beside her and smiled, my love for her as keen as any other emotion I'd ever felt. She represented all that was good and hopeful in my life. She was my connection to the past, the present, and the future.

She touched my cheek and then ran her hand down my hair. "How was it?"

"The king and queen came."

A sad smile tilted up her lips. "I'm so happy for you. I wish I could have been there."

"Any news of Papa?" I asked, almost afraid.

She shook her head and looked back at the fire for a moment. "Colonel Lindbergh called again today, but he had no news to share. They have ramped up their efforts to find Luc, but there is still no communication from whoever took him."

"It doesn't make any sense." I nibbled my bottom lip, trying to think of some reason that someone would want to hold Papa captive.

"Colonel Lindbergh suggests that we head back to Washington, DC," Mama said, "now that your work here is done. He offered to personally escort Papa home as soon as they find him."

"Do you want to leave?" I asked her.

"No." She pressed her lips together and shook her head. "I mean, yes, I long to return home with all my heart. But when your father is ready to come home, I don't want to be an ocean away from him. I want to see him the second I am able. If we go back to Washington, it will be several days at sea for us and then for him. I don't want to spend even one day longer apart than necessary."

My heart broke even more as I listened to her, because I understood the longing she felt to be near the man she loved. The tears I'd been holding back all day came to the surface and fell down my cheeks. I wiped them away, frustrated at how much I had cried the past few weeks.

"I'm so sorry, Kathryn," Mama said as she gave her full attention to me. "In all the chaos of the past two days, I've completely forgotten about what you're facing in 1888 tomorrow."

"When I come back here tomorrow, that will be it," I said, feeling the finality of it. "I won't return to 1888 ever again."

"I know it's hard to imagine, but I do understand." She ran the back of her fingers over my cheek to wipe away another tear. "It gets easier, my love. I promise."

"But you had Papa." I swallowed my pain as I shook my head. "I know you gave up Hope and Isaac, but you didn't have to give up the man you love."

"Not yet," she said as her lips trembled.

"Oh, Mama." I laid my head on her lap to let the tears fall freely. "Papa will come home."

"I know." She lifted my face, and her gaze did not waver as she said, "I have determined to praise God through this storm, Kathryn. To trust Him, even if the darkness overwhelms me. I am not alone, and neither is your father. Wherever he is, God is with him, and that comforts me like nothing else." She placed her hands over mine. "God is not surprised that this happened. He allowed it for a reason, and it's our job to trust that He will use it for our good and His glory. Even if things don't turn out how we hope—" She paused to take a deep breath. "God is good, and His plans are far better than ours."

"What if I don't like His plans?" I whispered, my heart crying out for understanding. "What if it feels unfair or doesn't make sense?"

Peace filled Mama's face as she looked down at me. "Ever since you were little, you've fought for your way. I remember when you were just four, and we were on an afternoon drive. You begged Papa to go as fast as he could, and he humored you on empty roads, but then he had to stop the automobile because there were larger vehicles passing at a crossroad. You became so frustrated that you cried and begged him to keep going. If he'd given in to your demands, we could have been killed. He understood the danger, even if you didn't. I know it's a simple illustration, but it's no different with God. He can see things that are beyond our comprehension, and when He says no, or wait, He is protecting us."

I remembered those drives with Papa, and all the other times I'd felt that my parents weren't allowing me the freedom I desired. And now I felt that way toward God.

Yet, Mama was right. I didn't have full understanding, only God did.

"I think that's why the Bible tells us to trust God and lean not on our own understanding," Mama said with her gentle voice. "Only then will we have real peace."

"Do you have peace about Papa?" I asked her.

"On the surface, I'm anxious and afraid, but in my heart of hearts, there is a peace that doesn't make sense. And I know that's the peace that comes from trusting God."

I pulled myself off the floor and took a seat on the chair next to Mama, ready to talk about something else. "I wish you knew Austen. When Papa comes home, we'll go to the London Museum to tour my exhibit and then you can both see Austen's paintings."

"I can't wait for that day."

"Sir Rothschild said that the portrait that Austen painted of me is one of the reasons why he was first intrigued by Austen's work."

"Isn't it interesting how God pulls all the pieces of our lives together?" Mama asked. "Nothing happens by accident, Kathryn. It's all part of a master plan." She smiled. "You, of all people, can appreciate a plan like that."

I nodded and smiled.

The plan God had put in place for my life wasn't the one I would have chosen for myself, but I would trust Him through the darkest hours and pray that the rays of dawn would bring hope back into my life.

25

NOVEMBER 8, 1888
LONDON, ENGLAND

I looked at my reflection in the mirror as the hall clock struck seven chimes the next day. Mother had insisted that I go shopping with her and had found one excuse after the other to keep me away from home, which made me suspect that Father had told her about Austen.

As Duffy finished styling my hair for supper, I wanted to go to Austen, but my parents were expecting me in the dining room. This would be my last meal with them. My final good-bye. I would miss them, but I'd known for years that I wasn't going to stay. Our relationship wasn't warm or affectionate. On the contrary, I'd always felt more like part of a business than a family. Every decision made was for the prosperity and positioning of the family. And as easily as they had pushed my sister out of their lives, I wasn't too concerned that it would take them long to push memories of me out, either.

Though it didn't make saying good-bye any easier.

It would be a quick supper, and then I would feign illness and sneak out of the house to spend the final few hours with Austen as we went to Miller's Court to save Mary. It was all I could think about.

"You look beautiful," Duffy said as she stepped back to admire her work. "It's a shame that Mr. Baird can't see you like this."

I met her gaze in the mirror, thankful for her loyal support, and smiled my appreciation.

She nodded and then busied herself with putting away my toiletries as I left my room.

I was wearing one of the green gowns that Austen had so often admired. I contemplated changing before we left for Miller's Court, but it wouldn't matter what I was wearing tonight. I didn't need to blend in to save my sister. I had a satchel packed for Mary to take with her to New York, and in it was a fashionable gown she would wear on the ship. I wanted both of us to look our best as we said good-bye to each other in Southampton.

As I drew closer to the downstairs parlor, conversation filtered out, surprising me. A man's voice lifted above the others, making me pause.

It was the voice of Michael Maybrick.

My pulse picked up speed as I began to suspect what my parents had planned. Mother had been anxious all day, and Father had come home early from the hospital. They hadn't told me that Mr. Maybrick was coming, so they intended to surprise me.

If I went into the parlor now, I would be cornered. It wouldn't be a quick supper. It would take hours, and then I'd be expected to entertain Mr. Maybrick long into the evening.

Austen and I planned to get to Miller's Court by nine. From everything I'd researched, there were different accounts as to Mary Jane Kelly's last appearance, but most believed she was killed between one and seven in the morning on November 9th. We wanted to get her away from there after dark so we wouldn't draw as much attention, but not wait too long for the possibility that Jack might be watching. We couldn't risk him following us and knowing where we had sent Mary.

Mr. Maybrick's arrival could potentially change all our plans.

Slowly and as quietly as I could, I turned on my heels and retreated the way I'd come, reentering my bedroom moments after I'd left.

"Did you forget something?" Duffy asked as she looked up from the dress she was brushing.

"I'm suddenly not feeling well," I said, though it wasn't entirely untrue. "I think I might be getting a migraine."

Duffy frowned as she set down the brush and came to me. "You haven't had one of those in a long time."

"I'd like to lie down," I said as I moved toward the bed.

"Shall I help you change into a nightgown?" She pulled the bedding down so I could sit on the mattress.

"Not now. I just need darkness and quiet. Perhaps I'll feel better in an hour or so."

Duffy nodded as she helped me into bed.

It wasn't easy to maneuver in a corset and petticoats, and if I'd had a real headache, I would have wanted to get into my nightclothes, but I didn't have time to change and then try to dress myself afterward.

Hairpins poked my scalp as she pulled the covers up to my chin. "Is there anything I can do for you? Would you like me to get the headache powder?"

"No. I just want some quiet. Please turn out the lights and then give my regrets to my mother."

Duffy paused, uncertainty in her gaze. She wouldn't want to be the one to tell my mother I wasn't going to supper, but she had no choice.

She turned out the lights and then slipped out of my room.

It was dark, and the silence echoed in my ears. I knew that within minutes, my mother would come into my room and demand that I join them, so I needed to be ready. Once she was satisfied that I was unable to sit through supper, she'd leave me for the rest of the night and not check on me.

The clock ticked away the seconds as I lay waiting. My mind filled with dozens of memories of my life in this path, both the good and the bad, and emotions clogged my throat. I would miss it, and not only because I was leaving Austen and Mary. There was a lot I loved about 1888.

Less than five minutes later, my door opened, and a swath of light crossed my bedroom floor. I quickly closed my eyes and did my best to look ill.

"What is the meaning of this, Kathryn?" Mother asked as she strode across the room, the hem of her gown swishing against the carpet.

I moaned just slightly and said, "Please keep your voice down. My head is splitting."

"You've been fine all day. And look at you—dressed for supper. When did this headache begin?"

"Not long ago," I said as I put my hand up to my head, trying to cover my eyes from the hall light. "It hit me like lightning, and I feel sick to my stomach."

Again, I wasn't lying, but my nausea was more from Mr. Maybrick's arrival than from a headache.

"I won't stand for this," she said as her foot tapped the floor. "Mr. Maybrick is in the parlor, expecting to spend the evening with you. He's a very busy man, and his schedule is full of obligations. He finally found a night to join us, and you're not going to be there?" Her voice had raised a notch. "What will I tell him?"

"The truth," I said as I tried to roll over, away from her. My legs got tangled in my petticoats, making it almost impossible, and my corset pinched. "I'm too ill to dine with anyone tonight. I just want to be left alone."

She stood for several moments, breathing deeply, and then said, "Fine. But you will agree to make up for this inconvenience at his leisure."

I didn't respond.

As she left the room, I felt sadder than I expected, knowing that I wouldn't be able to properly say good-bye to her or Father.

I waited for a few minutes, then got up and gathered the things I had been preparing for tonight. It was dark, but my eyes had adjusted, and I knew where everything was located. I had snuck into Mary's room several times that week to pack a satchel for her. I'd hidden it under my bed, so I had to get on my hands and knees to pull it out now. I would wear a dark cloak and bring one for Mary, as well. I had a few pieces of valuable jewelry and took the few that were still in Mary's room and put them in a velvet pouch for her to sell. Austen had already purchased her ticket for New York and had insisted that we didn't need to pay him back, but I didn't expect him to give her money for her other expenses.

As soon as I had everything together, I quietly left my room, praying I wouldn't bump into anyone in the hallway.

The satchel was bulky, and my skirt and cloak were heavy as I maneuvered down the servants' stairs. My pulse was pounding so hard in my ears, I was afraid I might not hear a subtle noise that would alert me to someone's presence. I just needed to get into the courtyard and sneak through the hedge, and then I would be free.

When I came to the door that led into the servants' hall, I knew this would be the hardest place to pass without being seen. The footmen would be walking through with dishes sent up from the kitchen, on their way to the dining room. I had to plan it just right, and then rush through with all haste.

I pressed my ear against the door, and hearing no movement, I opened it slightly just as a man passed through.

Pausing, I waited as sweat dripped down my back.

When he had gone by, I stepped into the hall and ran toward the back door.

The night air was blessedly cool as I stepped outside. But heavy, ominous clouds covered the moon and stars, making it difficult to see.

Thankfully, I knew my way.

As I moved through the garden, the shape of a man suddenly appeared as he stepped onto my path—and without warning, we collided.

I lost my footing and fell on my backside as the satchel flew out of my hands. I let out a startled scream, but it was quickly choked by fear.

The man stared down at me, and my heart sank as I recognized Michael Maybrick.

"Miss Kelly," he said.

"Mr. Maybrick—I-I thought you'd be eating supper."

"I had a feeling that's what you thought." He stood over me, his dark silhouette appearing larger than ever, not offering to help me up. "It looks like you're leaving for an extended visit."

I glanced at the satchel, just out of reach.

"Your father told me that Baird has been taking up a lot of your time lately," Mr. Maybrick continued, "and that if I didn't act soon, I might miss my opportunity. Given our last interaction, I had misgivings about trying again." He looked toward the house and then back at me. "If I'm not mistaken, it looks like I'm about to miss my opportunity entirely. And, if my guess is correct, no one in the house knows you're leaving to meet Baird."

I didn't know what to say, so I said nothing.

He squatted to get close to me, and I backed away.

"I could pick you up right now and carry you away," he said with a strange chuckle, as if he was trying to make a joke, though it sounded too sinister to be funny. "No one would be the wiser."

My entire body trembled at his words. "Wouldn't my parents suspect something if you didn't return to supper?"

"I left as soon as your mother told me that you wouldn't be joining us. They think I've gone home. But I decided to wait out here to see if you would make an appearance." He stood, towering over me again. "You know, it's not safe to be out at night alone. Especially with Jack the Ripper on the loose. There's no telling what might happen to you."

My breath stilled as a new thought filled my heart with terror.

Was Michael Maybrick Jack the Ripper? Had he been working with the Freemasons?

"Cat got your tongue, Kathryn?" he asked as he reached down and picked up my satchel.

I had a choice to make. Every moment I waited was a moment I might lose to save my sister. Whether Mr. Maybrick was Jack or not, I needed to get Mary out of there. I had no proof or reason to think he was Jack, except that he was a Freemason, and his very presence made my skin crawl.

I stood without his help and said, "Please hand that back to me. It is none of your concern what I'm doing or where I'm going."

He stared at me for a moment, and then he slowly held out the satchel.

I took it and brought it close to my chest.

"You're all the same," he sneered. "No better than my sister-in-law, Florence. Sneaking around, lying to the people you're supposed to love. You'll hurt your father, just as Florence has hurt my brother, James. She'll pay, just as you will."

I stared at him, confused and uncertain. Why was he talking about his sister-in-law? And then I recalled the file I'd found in Sir Rothschild's drawer several weeks ago about the trial of Florence Maybrick. She was accused of poisoning her husband just two days from now, and Michael would be the loudest accuser at her trial.

Would he set her up?

"I should tell your father what you're doing," he continued before I could grasp what he meant about Florence. "But I think I'd rather watch you suffer because of your own foolishness. You won't get far, Miss Kelly. None of you do."

And with that portending comment, he strode out of the courtyard, toward the alley.

A shiver ran up my spine as I raced to the hedge.

We needed to get Mary out of Whitechapel immediately.

The moon was hidden behind a bank of clouds as Austen's carriage came to a stop on Dorset Street, not far from Miller's Court. I was still upset from my encounter with Michael Maybrick, though I had chosen not to tell Austen about it. What could he do? We were already on edge because we were about to change history and rescue my sister.

Austen held my hand, and I squeezed his back. "I wish you weren't here with me," I whispered, my pulse racing.

"I would never let you do this alone."

"But you're changing history, too."

He silenced me with a kiss and then said. "I'm fulfilling my destiny, Kate."

I shook my head and took a deep breath. "I pray we can save her."

"She has you, me, and Miles working on her behalf. We will see that she gets out of Whitechapel."

"I hope you're right." I glanced at the ceiling of the carriage for a heartbeat, also hoping and praying that God would forgive me for what I was about to do. I couldn't knowingly allow my sister to die. It wasn't right. I had to believe He understood that.

The street was dark, but people were still walking along the road and conducting business at the grocers, the coffee house, and other buildings nearby. Austen held the door open for me, and I stepped out, staying close to him as we walked toward Miller's Court for the last time. He carried the satchel I had packed for my sister.

Every shadow felt ominous, and every person was a suspect. Was Jack already here? Watching? Miles had brought a pistol and would wait in the carriage, ready for us to leave the moment we got inside.

A man and woman stood in the passageway, speaking in low, suggestive tones. At first, I thought it was Mary, but as we passed, I realized it was someone else.

Austen kept his arm around my shoulder, and mine was around his waist, not only for protection but also reassurance.

When we came to number 13, there was a soft glow through the window. My pulse was racing so hard and fast, I could hear it in my ears. It almost drowned out all the other noises.

Austen knocked on the door as a shadow passed behind us, making the hair rise on my neck. A man walked slowly out of the darkness. He was wearing a peaked hat, like the one I'd seen on Jack on Berner Street. Austen's arm tightened around my shoulder, and his entire body became rigid. He, too, was carrying a loaded pistol. He handed me the satchel and then slipped his free hand inside his coat.

The man passed without a word, walking toward the passageway.

"We need to hurry," I said to Austen, panic raw in my voice.

Austen knocked on the door again.

Was Mary not in her room?

Real terror filled my heart. Had Jack already been there?

A moment later, Mary opened the door, her eyes wide with fear.

Relief weakened my legs as I reached for her. "It's time," I said. "I've brought you clothes to change into."

"I'll wait out here," Austen said. "But hurry."

I entered Mary's room, hating to leave Austen alone but knowing there was no other option.

After I closed the door, I turned to Mary. She clasped her hands together as she paced to her fireplace.

"What's wrong?" I asked. "We can't waste a single moment."

"It's—" She paused and then shook her head. "It's nothing."

"Good." I set the satchel on the table and opened it to pull out the clothing I'd brought for her. "We must hurry."

Mary undressed and folded her clothing, setting it on the chair in a neat pile. I realized with sudden clarity that it was the pile of clothes in the exhibit at Lancaster House.

I pushed thoughts of the exhibit and everything else aside.

Tonight was about Mary.

I had brought everything she'd need, from undergarments to a cape. I helped her change as quickly as I could, horrified at how much weight she'd lost. Her clothing hung on her frame, shocking me because I'd always thought Mary was thin. Now she was skeletal.

As she dressed, I listened for signs that Austen was in trouble or in distress, but everything outside remained silent.

I was sweating by the time we were done, not because the work was hard, but because I'd never been so scared in my life.

"Come," I said as I reached for her hand.

Mary started to lift her clothes off the chair, but I shook my head. "Leave them. Leave everything. It's time to forget about this part of your life."

I stepped over to the lamp, and before I blew it out, I caught Mary looking at her room one last time.

With a quick inhale and exhale, I extinguished her light, grabbed the satchel, and then opened the door.

For a heartbeat, I was afraid Austen was gone—but then he appeared out of the shadows, and I breathed a prayer of thanksgiving.

"Ready?" he whispered.

I nodded and then ushered Mary out of her room as I quietly closed her door behind me.

Austen took the satchel, and the three of us went down the passageway. The couple had left, but a man was walking toward us. Again my pulse skittered, but he passed us without a word.

The carriage was still waiting. Miles jumped off the driver's seat and opened the door for us as we approached.

"Make all haste," Austen said as Mary climbed in first and I followed.

The moment Austen stepped into the carriage and closed the door, I finally let out a breath.

Yet our night had only just begun.

It was almost midnight when our train finally arrived on the outskirts of Southampton. The ship taking Mary to New York would leave at first light, and boarding had already begun at the pier, not far from Southampton Central Railway Station.

I sat on a red velvet bench with Mary as we faced Austen and Miles on the opposite bench. Austen had rented a private compartment, and his coachman had come along for protection. As we'd ridden from London to Southampton, I'd quickly realized they were not merely employer and employee, but friends.

Mary's small hand was in mine, but neither of us spoke as the train began to slow. Weeks of planning did not prepare me for this moment. Or what I might say to her, knowing I'd never see her again.

I was still reeling from the night's events, trying to wrap my mind around all that had happened. Mary had been silent since we'd left Whitechapel. She needed a bath, but her red hair had been combed and styled as best as we could manage. I wondered what was on her mind, and wished she could leave the memories behind as easily as she'd left her clothes.

Austen's gaze was on me as the train began to slow. With Mary and Miles nearby, I could not say what I longed to say. We had already changed history by taking Mary away from Miller's Court, so this wasn't just good-bye to her, it was also good-bye to Austen and to 1888.

I hoped and prayed he wouldn't forfeit his life for helping me. I couldn't live with myself if that happened.

He finally tore his gaze from mine and said to Miles, "I booked passage under the names Mr. and Mrs. Miles Fremont." He took an envelope out of his breast pocket and handed it to Miles. "To keep up appearances, I rented one cabin for you to share. I trust it goes without saying that Mary will have the berth and you'll sleep on the floor."

Miles took the envelope and gave his friend a look that said it was more than unnecessary to tell him.

I sat up straighter on the bench as Mary's hand tightened around mine. "Miles is going with Mary?" I asked.

"I thought it best." Austen turned his attention to me again. "We need to make sure that she gets to her new life safely."

Mary began to tremble as she looked across the compartment to Miles. A man she hardly knew, other than by name and sight.

He looked back at her, his brown eyes softening. "I hope you don't mind the company, Miss Kelly. I will ensure you arrive safely in New York. You have my word."

Mary swallowed and nodded, though there was apprehension in her eyes. I wished there was another way, but knowing that Miles would be with her put my heart at ease.

If only a little.

When the train came to a stop, we were ushered off by a porter.

"I think it's best if we say good-bye to them here," Austen said to me as he handed Mary's satchel to Miles. "Miles will see that Mary gets to the ship safely."

There were still several hours before the ship would leave the harbor, but it would look less suspicious if they went alone.

And I wanted time with Austen to say our good-byes.

I was still holding my sister's hand, so I paused and turned to face her. "There are several pieces of jewelry inside the bag," I whispered. "Hopefully, it will be enough to help you along until you begin to earn an income."

Mary's green eyes filled with tears as she wrapped her arms around me. "I'm going to miss you."

"I'm going to miss you, too." My voice caught. A little over a year ago, I wouldn't have even imagined this night was possible.

"I'll write."

"Perhaps it's safer if you don't," I said. "Miles will get word to us if need be." Though I wouldn't be here to receive it. I couldn't tell Mary that. Not now. Not this way.

Austen put his hand on my back. "It's time."

I squeezed Mary harder. "I love you."

"I love you, Kathryn. Good-bye." She pulled back and looked at Austen. "And thank you. Both of you."

I couldn't bring myself to say good-bye as she turned to Miles.

He offered her a gentle smile and then held out his elbow, like a gentleman would to his wife.

She hesitated for just a moment and then wrapped her arm through his and lifted her head high, looking for all the world like Mrs. Miles Fremont.

Austen and I watched as they walked down the platform and disappeared.

"Do you trust him?" I asked Austen as he put his arm around my waist.

"With my life."

I finally looked up at him as the clock on the platform rang the midnight hour, and the reality of the moment hit me with intensity.

As soon as I fell asleep in this path, I would never come back.

But I didn't have to go to sleep right now. I still had a little more time.

"Where would you like to go?" he asked, his gaze intent upon my face.

"It doesn't matter."

He took my hand and led me down the platform, in the opposite direction that Miles and Mary had just gone.

It was cold, but I didn't mind as we walked along a thoroughfare. I shivered when I thought that at this very moment, Jack the Ripper was supposed to have been approaching my sister at Miller's Court. What would happen when I woke up in 1938 tomorrow? Would everything be different? Would the entire world be changed by one simple adjustment to history?

I wasn't eager to find out.

"I've been through Southampton many times," Austen finally said. "And I've stayed at the Dolphin Hotel. It's the oldest hotel in Southampton, dating back to the 1400s." He put his arm around me as we continued to walk. "Just think, perhaps Lady Cecily could have stayed there at one point."

I smiled at the reference, thinking of the book I'd left in Austen's care after we departed Hyde Park the other night.

"They have some of the best food in the country, and they are open all night," he continued. "I thought perhaps we could get a bite to eat."

I wasn't sure I could eat, but I didn't care where we went.

As soon as we arrived, he opened the door for me, and we were brought to a booth in the corner of the restaurant. Rough timber beams stretched across the ceiling, proof that the building was centuries old. There were more people there than I'd anticipated, but it didn't matter to me. We sat on the same side of the booth, our backs to the room, as we looked out a window toward the dark harbor. Austen kept his arm around me as I laid my cheek against his shoulder.

"I don't want this to be good-bye," I whispered, trying desperately not to cry.

"Neither do I." His voice was gruff with emotion as he took one of my hands.

"What would you do if this wasn't good-bye?" I asked, looking up at him.

"I'd marry you, Kate. And I'd take you away from London."

"Where would you take me?"

"Anywhere your heart desired. But first, I'd take you to Loch Lomond, and I'd keep you all to myself for as long as you'd let me." He kissed me, only stopping when the waitress interrupted us with our food.

We talked about anything and everything and nothing. I tried to savor each moment, wishing it would last for a lifetime.

Neither one of us spoke as the sun started to crest the horizon, and I knew I couldn't put off the inevitable any longer.

"It's time," I said to him, echoing his words to me on the platform. "I must go."

There were tears in his eyes as he ran his thumb over the ridge of my cheek.

He had rented two rooms, and he walked me to mine. Outside the door, he gave me a kiss. It was sweet and tender, full of longing and heartbreak. Our tears mingled and were salty on my lips.

"I love you, Kate," he whispered.

"I love you, too." I kissed him one last time, and then I stepped into my room.

There was no sound outside my door for a few moments, and then I heard his steps as he walked away.

The room was small but clean. I didn't bother to undress but went to bed and lay down. I was exhausted in body and soul. I didn't want to leave 1888, but there was nothing left to do.

So I went to sleep.

26

NOVEMBER 8, 1938
LONDON, ENGLAND

I slowly opened my eyes in my room at 44 Berkeley Square, not knowing what might be different. I must have been crying in my sleep because tears wet my cheeks in 1938, reminding me of all I'd just sacrificed for Mary.

The sun sat low on the horizon as I stared out the window, my heart breaking into a thousand little pieces. Grief hit me in waves, and as soon as I thought I might catch my breath, another memory of Austen or Mary would crash upon me with such force, it would overwhelm me again. The only thing that brought me comfort was knowing Mary had gotten away and, I prayed, lived a long and happy life in New York. Perhaps she was still alive there now. I couldn't visit her, since she didn't know I was a time-crosser, but I could make inquiries.

Nothing brought me comfort where Austen was concerned. I pulled a pillow into my arms and allowed myself to cry for all he and I had lost. Just like Mama had held Papa's nightshirt, I wanted something tangible to hold. Something that smelled like Austen—but I had nothing. He was gone, or at least, the man he had been was gone.

I had nowhere to go and nothing to do today, so I stayed in bed, nursing my sore heart, until I knew Mama would get worried. Every part of my body felt sluggish, and my head pounded. I prayed with all my heart that we would have news of Papa today. Good news that would strengthen me for the days ahead.

Slowly, I got dressed and then left my room to find Mama.

She was in the parlor, the telephone extension within reach.

When she heard my arrival, she stood and rushed across the room to pull me into her embrace.

"I'm so sorry for your loss, Kathryn," she said. "I know what you're going through today. I know how hard this has been for you."

I held her tight, thankful that someone understood.

"We make a fine pair, don't we?" I asked as I wiped my face and pulled back a few moments later. "You, longing for Papa, and me, longing for Austen."

"They say misery loves company, but I don't agree." She shook her head. "I do not want you to feel the misery I'm feeling."

We went to the chairs near the hearth and took a seat. I couldn't think of anything I wanted to do today, but there was one question that was plaguing me.

"Did anything change in the world because I saved Mary?" I asked Mama.

She frowned and shrugged. "I don't know. If you changed something that affected history, then I only know the new version."

"That seems strange and unsettling," I said as I shifted in my chair. "Is Hitler still a threat?"

"Unfortunately, yes."

"And Papa is still missing?"

She lowered her gaze to her hands and nodded.

"And Jack the Ripper only killed four women?"

Mama lifted her face and shook her head. "As far as I know, he killed five women."

I frowned. Would Mama still have all the same memories as before while the rest of the world would only know of the four murders?

"Perhaps I should go to Lancaster House," I said as I stood, "and see for myself how much history changed."

"It might be a good idea for you to get out of the house," Mama agreed. "Take your mind off Austen."

"I'll be home as soon as possible," I told her. "Call the museum if you hear something about Papa."

She smiled and nodded as I left the room.

I took my hat and jacket off the hall coat-tree, and I left 44 Berkeley Square on foot.

As I walked toward Lancaster House, I kept my eyes open to see if anything looked strange or out of the ordinary. But everything appeared as it had yesterday. The buildings were the same, the streets were the same, even the people I passed looked no different. Many of them carried their gas masks, and newspapers on the street corner still boasted similar headlines.

Frowning, I entered Lancaster House through the side entrance, as I had since going to work there. No one seemed surprised to see me, and several people greeted me fondly.

I went to the stairs leading to the basement and was pleased to see that there was a large crowd there to view the new exhibit.

Here, too, everything looked as it had when I left. The brick façade of Buck's Row, the glass exhibit with Jack the Ripper's letters, and even Catherine Eddowes's apron were just as they'd been before.

Slowly, I walked to the corner where we'd hung the photos of the victims—and I stopped short when I saw that there were still five frames on the wall, and the last one was covered with a black cloth.

My mouth slipped open as my heart beat hard. It felt like I was in a nightmare as I slowly walked to the picture. My hand trembled as I lifted the black cloth, not knowing what I might see beneath.

It was Mary's room at Miller's Court, with the same mutilated body on the bed. It was the same picture.

Nothing had changed.

I let out a gasp and stepped back, shaking my head.

Visitors glanced in my direction as I quickly scanned the rest of the exhibit, looking for information about Mary Jane Kelly.

Everything was as it had been. Nothing had changed. Mary's name was in the inquest documents, in the newspapers, and in the coroner's reports. Her general height, weight, and age were all the same. The time she was last seen, the approximate time she'd been killed, and the time her body had been discovered.

Even the clothes that she'd been wearing when I arrived at Miller's Court were in the exhibit.

I couldn't breathe as I stumbled through the exhibit to get into the hall. My mind was jumbled with uncertainty and dread as I climbed the stairs, unsure where I was going. I hadn't eaten that morning, but if I had, I was afraid I might vomit. Cold sweat beaded on my brow as I put my hand to my stomach.

How was it possible that Mary had still been killed at Miller's Court?

Unless . . . I couldn't even accept the thought that came to my mind. Had Miles brought her back to London? Had he been working with Jack the Ripper all along?

Was he Jack? That night on Berner Street, when he dropped us off in the rain, he could have parked the carriage and then met Elizabeth Stride to murder her. That would explain how he knew about the copper's beat and why he was so familiar with Whitechapel.

But Austen assured me that he trusted Miles.

I stopped at the top of the stairs and leaned against the railing for support as possibilities assailed me.

If it wasn't Miles, did that mean that Mary had gone back to look for Joseph?

"Kathryn?" Sir Rothschild appeared, concern on his face. "What's wrong?"

How would I explain everything to him? I couldn't.

He gently took me by the elbow and led me into the nearest room, which happened to be the gallery where Austen's paintings were on display.

Thankfully, we were alone. But my heart was hammering so fast, I thought I might faint.

"What's the trouble?" Sir Rothschild asked me, concern in his face and voice. "You look as if someone has died." His eyes opened wide. "It isn't your father, is it?"

I shook my head, knowing I needed to pull myself together. I took a few deep breaths and then said, "Who was the last victim of Jack the Ripper?"

He frowned as he studied me. "Mary Jane Kelly, of course."

"And when did she die?"

"November 9, 1888."

I pressed my hand to my mouth. "It can't be. I thought I changed everything."

Sir Rothschild continued to study me, and his thoughts were hard to read behind his troubled gaze. Did he think I had lost my mind?

"Perhaps you should go home, Miss Voland," he said and then put his hand on my middle back. "I'll see you there myself. I think the strain of your father's disappearance has been too much."

I shook my head, knowing it was more than Papa's disappearance. Perhaps it would be best if I went home to be with Mama. To figure out where I had gone wrong.

And I knew who I would ask as soon as I could get away.

I would go to 12 Wilton Crescent and confront Austen, no matter how old or feeble he might be.

I needed answers.

Sir Rothschild said very little as he drove me home to Berkeley Square. But what was there to say? My mind was racing with everything I would tell Mama—and then everything I would ask Austen. Surely, he wouldn't be surprised to see me after I learned that my sister had died after all.

Was that why he wouldn't speak to me that day I first learned about the paintings, outside his home? Because he knew Mary still died?

Just thinking about Mary made me shudder with unshed tears as I bit my lower lip, trying to hold myself together until Sir Rothschild left.

"Let me walk you in," he said as he pulled to a stop and turned off the engine of his vehicle. "I'd like to speak to your mother."

I didn't protest as he opened the automobile door for me and put his hand on the middle of my back again as he walked me to the front door. I didn't even bother to take off my hat or jacket as I walked up the stairs, Sir Rothschild close behind, and found Mama in the parlor.

She turned and rose from her chair. "Sir Rothschild, what a nice surprise." But then her gaze landed on me, and her welcoming face turned to concern. "What's wrong, Kathryn?"

I couldn't pretend to be okay when I wasn't. Yet, I couldn't unleash my pain and confusion until Sir Rothschild left.

When I turned to thank him for bringing me home, I paused.

There was something different about his demeanor as he slowly closed the door behind us and then faced Mama and me.

"I think you both need to take a seat," he said, his voice lowering.

I frowned, and when I made no move to sit down, he took a step closer to me and this time pushed me toward the couch.

My fear and uncertainty about Mary turned to discomfort concerning Sir Rothschild and his strange behavior.

I joined Mama, and we both took a seat on the couch. She grasped my hand in hers as she looked up at Sir Rothschild.

"What is this about?" she asked him.

He was wearing his trench coat, but he took off his bowler hat and set it on a nearby table. His movements were slow and decisive.

When he faced us again, he crossed his arms and stared at me. "I believe you and I can help each other, Miss Voland—or should I call you Miss Kelly? Which do you prefer?"

My lips parted as I blinked. "What—"

"We don't have time to pretend." He took a step closer and narrowed his eyes. "When I first saw that painting by Austen Baird, it looked so much like you, I had to do a little research. And what I found surprised me—but not entirely. I learned that Austen's childhood friend and neighbor, the woman he painted in the picture, was named Kathryn Kelly, and it didn't take me long to see you with my own eyes in 1888. I just had to wait outside 11 Wilton Crescent for an afternoon."

"In 1888?" I asked, leaning forward as I stared at him.

"I'm a time-crosser, as well, Kathryn," he said. "My other time is 1888."

Mama's hand tightened around mine, and before I could ask another question, she said, "But you're in your thirties—at least. How do you still occupy two times?"

He frowned, as if he didn't understand her meaning. "I have until my thirty-fifth birthday to choose my path," Sir Rothschild said. "And that date is coming up here very quickly."

"Thirty-five years?" Mama looked truly dumbfounded. "Where is your mark?"

"On my lower back," he said, as if it hardly mattered.

Mama turned to me. "There are other time-crossers out there with different rules. I've never heard of one on the lower back or someone with thirty-five years."

"You don't have thirty-five years?" Sir Rothschild asked, suddenly more curious than he'd been a moment before.

"I only have twenty-five years," I told him and lifted the hair on the back of my head. "My mark is here. Mama's grandmother had her mark on her chest, and she only had twenty-one years."

Sir Rothschild was quiet for a moment, but then he shook his head. "None of that matters right now. I found out who you were in 1888, and I realized that you could help me. But it occurred to me that you didn't know what was going to happen to your sister."

"To Mary, you mean?" I asked.

He nodded. "That's why I invited you to create an exhibit about Jack the Ripper and asked you to come to London. I needed you to realize who your family is in 1888." He narrowed his eyes again. "I've been waiting for today, for this very moment. Because I believe that we both have something the other might want."

I leaned back on the couch, my shoulder brushing Mama's as I waited. What might I have that he wanted? And what did he have that I wanted?

"I've been watching you," he said. "That day when we were in the basement at New Scotland Yard, the moment you saw your sister's name for the first time."

I had been shocked and horrified. But he'd known all along who I was and who Mary was to me. A shiver ran up my spine, just thinking about it.

"I tried to get her away from Miller's Court, but nothing changed. She still died."

"What?" Mama turned to me, her face blanching. "What do you mean?"

"Mary still died," I told her as I shook my head. "I don't know how—or why."

"Maybe you can't change history," Mama said. "Maybe God doesn't allow it."

"But—" I swallowed. "I thought we had free will. That we could choose to change things, even if we weren't supposed to."

"Stop talking!" Sir Rothschild roared. "I don't care about Mary. It was your father's fault that she died. Now I need to focus on you and what I need."

I jumped at his sudden anger, perplexed at the change in his demeanor. "My father's fault?" I frowned. "What do you mean?"

"He wouldn't tell me where the Book is! None of them would!" he yelled, clearly frustrated.

Mama squeezed my hand tight as we stared at him.

"That's what this has all been about." Spittle formed in the corners of his mouth as he raged. "I should have known your father and the others wouldn't give in."

"The Book?" I asked, almost too afraid.

"The Book your father, Sir Bernard Kelly, brought home from

Jerusalem." He paced as he rubbed his whiskered jaw. "I need it. I need to know where it is. None of the other families would cave with threats, and I had to take their women out, one by one. But Sir Charles Warren gathered the pieces of the Book together right after the Double Event when he realized what was happening, before I could get to them, and now it's whole again, hidden away."

Realization dawned, and my heart felt like it stopped. "You're Jack the Ripper."

The look that came over his face made my blood run cold. His gaze was so calculated, so cool, it was the most frightening thing I'd ever seen.

"In another time and place," he said. "But I knew Sir Bernard Kelly wouldn't betray his Brotherhood, even though I threatened to take Mary's life." He paused as he stared at me. "He thought he'd hidden her, though it didn't take much work to find her. But I thwarted his plans, because I still have you. A time-crosser who has a lot more to lose than the rest of them." He walked toward me and bent down until his face was mere inches from mine. "I have someone very important to you in a warehouse nearby."

"Papa?" I asked, my breath catching in my throat.

"Your dear papa wasn't as easy to capture as I had hoped, but the gestapo are just as eager as Hitler to put an end to the Freemasons, so they were told to do whatever I asked of them. And they did."

"Put an end to the Freemasons?" Mama asked, her voice small as she stared at the monster in front of us.

"Hitler knows that the Freemasons support democracy," Sir Rothschild said, "and they are one of the most powerful organizations on the earth. To allow Fascism to rule, we must first destroy the Freemasons. He has started to dismantle their lodges in Germany, Austria, and now Czechoslovakia. But if we have the Book, even a portion of it, we will have enough ammunition to take all of them down. And then Hitler can make his next move."

"You're a Fascist?" I asked him, though I shouldn't be surprised, given his conversations at Cliveden House. "And all of this, even the murders in 1888, were all about taking the Freemasons down for Hitler."

He smiled, pleased with himself, but narrowed his eyes. "I'm giving you just forty-eight hours to locate the Book, Miss Voland. I don't care how you do it. I want it in my hands two days from now. And if you do not present it to me, you will never see your *papa* again."

I started to rise off the couch, to lash out at him, but Mama held me back.

How had I worked side by side with Jack the Ripper for months and not known?

When Sir Rothschild stopped at the door, he turned and said, "And don't try to get the police involved. I have an impeccable record, and I have alibis. Besides that, I have the British Union of Fascists with over fifty-thousand members on my side, not to mention the keen and eager ear of Hermann Göring, the commander in chief of the Luftwaffe, and the second in command in Germany. You do not want to cross any of us." He smiled, though it was cold and lifeless. "Get me the Book in forty-eight hours, or I will not hesitate to kill your papa."

And with that, Sir Rothschild walked out of the parlor and disappeared.

Mama turned to me, her ashen face filled with horror. "He has Luc," she said.

I rose, all my senses firing as I tried to grapple with everything Sir Rothschild had just told us. He was Jack the Ripper! I couldn't remember ever seeing him in 1888, but had he recognized Austen and me on Berner Street? Thinking back, I tried to remember the man I had seen. It had been so dark, but it could very well have been Bryant Rothschild. They were the same height and the same build.

"How will I learn where they are keeping the Book if I don't wake up in 1888 tomorrow?" I asked Mama.

"I don't know." She shook her head, her face filled with panic.

"What if I do wake up there tomorrow? I didn't change history, despite trying. I can't save Mary—" My voice caught as grief choked me, but I had to stay strong for Mama. "But I can still save Papa."

"You knowingly changed history, Kathryn. My grandmother Libby tried to do the same thing, and even though she failed, she still lost her 1774 path."

I frowned as I stared at my mama. "You never told me that."

She lifted her shoulders. "My grandfather Henry was a time-crosser, and he knew his destiny. Libby tried to stop him, but he wouldn't be stopped, because he knew he had to die as a spy in the American Revolution. That's why she couldn't change history. I didn't think it would happen to you, too. Mary didn't know her fate, not like Henry did."

"I have to get the Book," I said as I paced, worrying my bottom lip. My heart was torn in half, thinking about Austen and Mary, but I couldn't dwell on my grief right now. I needed all my energy to find a way to get Papa back.

Yet I still had questions. How did Mary get back to Miller's Court? Was Miles loyal to Sir Rothschild? And what was Sir Rothschild's real name in 1888?

More importantly, how had history not changed when we'd moved Mary far away from the scene of the crime?

"I need to speak to Austen," I said as I came to a stop.

"How? You won't go back to 1888, Kathryn."

"No. I need to speak to the Austen of 1938. Right now."

I began to move toward the door, but she reached out to try and stop me. "Don't go. You can make things so much worse."

"I can't sit here and worry, Mama. I need to *do* something."

I didn't let her stop me, but rushed out of the house and ran from Berkeley Square to Wilton Crescent. I was out of breath when I arrived there fifteen minutes later, and my heart felt like it might burst inside my chest, but I ran right up to the door and rang the bell, then pounded on it with all my might.

I waited as I tried to catch my breath.

But no one answered my knock. I tried again and again, and even shook the doorknob, trying to get in, but nothing.

There was no one at home.

Surely, Austen would know I had questions. He saw me in 1938 and knew I was in London. My sister still died. He'd tried to help me save her. Where was he now when he could tell me what happened?

Unless he had died, as I feared.

I backed away from his house, never feeling more defeated or heartbroken in my life.

I had failed to save Mary, Austen might have died when he tried to help us, and Papa's life was in danger. I wanted to give in to my fear and grief, but I couldn't. I still needed to save Papa. And if no one would help me, I would do it myself.

27

NOVEMBER 9, 1888
SOUTHAMPTON, ENGLAND

Even before I opened my eyes the next morning, thoughts of Sir Bryant Rothschild and Jack the Ripper filled my mind. I groaned as my eyelids fluttered open, not wanting to face the day and all the obstacles in front of me.

I blinked several times, frowning as my gaze took in the dark room around me.

I wasn't at 44 Berkeley Square. I was back in the Dolphin Hotel. In Southampton. My corset was pinching, my hairpins were poking into my scalp, and the sky was not much lighter than it had been when I went to sleep.

Shock propelled me to sit up. I was still in my green gown from last night.

And when I went to the window, I saw a horse tied to a hitching post on the street below.

"What?" I whispered, confused and bewildered.

How had I come back to 1888?

I didn't waste another moment but rushed out of the room and down the hall to Austen's room. I pounded on the door with all my strength.

Austen's door opened, and he stood there fully dressed, his clothes wrinkled and his face in need of a shave. His eyes were red-rimmed, as if he'd been crying. He frowned. "You didn't go to sleep?"

"I did!" I shook my head, still trying to understand what had happened. "I spent an entire day in 1938, but I still came back. How long ago did we say good-bye?"

"Not even ten minutes. What does this mean? I thought you forfeited this path when you changed history."

"I thought I did, too." A faint hint of light lined the eastern horizon through the window, and the morning stars were starting to fade.

"What time is it?" I asked him.

"About six o'clock, I think."

The ship that Mary should have been on wouldn't depart until daybreak. I needed to know if she was still on that ship—or if Miles had brought her back to Miller's Court.

"We have to get to the ship," I said to Austen as I grabbed his hand. "I need to know if Miles took Mary to the ship or if he returned her to Miller's Court."

"Why would he return her to Miller's Court?" Austen asked as he allowed me to pull him into the hall.

"I'll explain on the way," I said, not waiting for him as I rushed toward the steps and the tavern's front door. "Which way to the harbor?"

Austen followed me out, still looking perplexed, but turned left and began to lead me down High Street. "It's about a ten-minute walk this way."

"Then let's run." I lifted the hem of my gown and didn't care if I was breaking every rule of propriety as I began to run toward the harbor.

"What did you mean when you asked if Miles returned Mary to Miller's Court?" Austen asked, running beside me. "Why would you think that?"

"Mary still died," I said, choking on the truth. "When I woke up in 1938, nothing had changed."

"How is that possible?" Austen asked, almost angry.

"I don't know. But I think that's why I came back. I didn't change history." Though, Mama's story about Libby changing history and failing, yet still losing her path, didn't make sense. But I wasn't going to question it right now. All I cared was that I was back in 1888, and I needed to know what had happened to my sister.

"Miles wouldn't have brought her back to Miller's Court," Austen said as we continued to run toward the harbor. "He is the most trustworthy man I know."

"Perhaps he works for Jack."

"Impossible."

"There's more to the story," I said as I explained Sir Bryant Rothschild's connection to the Fascist Party and Hitler and what he hoped to do to the Freemasons. Adolph Hitler wasn't yet born in this path, and Fascism wouldn't be founded until the time of World War I in Italy. But it didn't take much for me to explain both to Austen. "Jack the Ripper isn't a Freemason," I said to him, running out of breath. "He is their enemy. I don't know if he was behind your parents' murder, but I know he wants the Book. He wants to take the Freemasons down." Panic took hold of my heart as I remembered that Miles hated the Freemasons because they had protected his father after he had killed Miles's mother. "Just as Miles wants to see them ruined. Maybe they do work together."

Austen shook his head. "Miles wouldn't allow an innocent woman to be killed, no matter what he believes about the Freemasons."

When we finally got to the harbor, the sky was a little brighter, but several large passenger ships were still docked at the wharf.

"I purchased tickets for them on the passenger liner the *City of New York*." He scanned the harbor and then pointed and said, "There! It's still docked."

We continued down the wharf toward the ship, which looked like one of the newer vessels in the harbor. People were still boarding, so when we approached, I told the steward that we had come to speak to two of the passengers.

"It's very important," I said to the man, knowing that my voice and face revealed the depth of my dismay. "Something that cannot wait."

"We'll be setting sail within the hour," the steward said with sympathy. "So make it quick."

"Thank you." I started up the gangplank with Austen close behind.

"They're in a first-class cabin," he said. "I believe it was room 164 in the bow of the ship."

When we reached the promenade deck, he took my hand and led me toward the front of the ship. We asked a porter where room 164 was located, and he directed us up a beautiful rounded staircase.

Everything in first class was lovely, from the potted ferns to the walnut trim. Part of me was thankful Austen had taken such care to make sure my sister traveled in style, but the other part was so worried Miles had taken her back to Miller's Court that I could hardly see straight.

When we finally reached room 164, I didn't hesitate and pounded hard on the door. "Mary," I said, praying that by some miracle my sister was still in her cabin. "Mary!"

The door finally cracked open, and Miles stood on the other side, blinking away sleep. He was wearing a modest nightshirt, and his hair was disheveled. On the ground behind him was a pallet with blankets and a pillow.

He frowned, clearly confused and alarmed. "What's the trouble?"

"Where is my sister?" I demanded as I pushed open the door.

Mary was in the berth. She sat up, startled, and pulled the covers to her chin. "Kathryn! What's wrong? Why are you here?" She looked toward the small window where the sky was just turning soft pink, obviously sleeping just moments ago. "Haven't we left port yet?"

"Mary!" I cried as I rushed into the room and tripped over the blankets on the floor before falling against my sister with relief. I began to weep. "You didn't die!"

She was baffled as she hugged me back. "Of course not. What has gotten into you, Kathryn?"

It took me a moment to gather myself, but even as I felt relief, more confusion set in. "I don't have much time," I said as I pulled back and righted myself. "But I need to speak to you."

"We'll give you a moment alone," Miles said as he pulled his coat on over his nightshirt and grabbed his pants before he and Austen stepped into the hallway, closing the door behind them.

"What is going on?" Mary asked me as she got out of bed and grabbed her dress.

"There was a murder last night," I told her. "At 13 Miller's Court."

She paused and stared at me. "What?"

I couldn't tell her how I knew, so I said, "Jack the Ripper got into your room and murdered—someone. Someone who looks very much like you, perhaps."

Her expression blanched as she grabbed my arm. "Jane."

"Jane?" I frowned and shook my head. "Who is she?"

"A friend," Mary said. "People always mistook us, and everyone thought we were sisters. Our hair is the same color, and we're about the same height and weight. I was surprised at first, thinking that we might be related. We looked so much alike."

"Why would Jane have been in your room?"

"She came often," Mary said, her voice quivering with emotion. "She was afraid to be on the streets, so I told her that if she couldn't get her doss money, she could always come and stay with me. She was in my room minutes before you came for me last night."

Realization dawned. "She was standing in the passageway when we came, speaking to a man. I thought she was you at first." I rubbed my temples, trying to put all the pieces together. Had Jane been the victim all along? "What were you doing last night before Austen and I came to take you away?"

She lowered her gaze as she said, "I was planning to leave with

Joseph. He'd called on me earlier and said he found a position as a groom in Surrey. He told me to meet him at the Horn of Plenty Pub on Dorset Street at eleven last night. He had some business to attend to first, and then we'd make our way to Surrey, because he had to be to work in the morning." She played with the edge of the blanket and said, "I told him my real name was Mary Jane Kelly. He's the only person in Whitechapel who knew the truth. He also heard that you had visited me a few times, but that's all he knew about me."

That was why she was known to history as Mary Jane Kelly, and not Marie Jeanette Kelly. "You would have left with him?"

"I didn't know when you would come for me, so I'd told myself if you came before I left with Joseph, then it was God's will that I go to America, instead of Surrey. Since you came before I could meet Joseph, I knew what I needed to do."

"You wouldn't have been at Miller's Court last night, either way?"

Mary studied me, and I could see she was confused by my question, but she said, "I would have been heading to Surrey if you hadn't come. So, no, I wouldn't have been at Miller's Court last night."

"And Jane would have gone into your room, even if you weren't there?" I asked, needing to know for certain.

"She did it before," Mary said. "It was one of the reasons Joseph was angry with me. Jane came and went whenever she felt like it. She always promised to pay me for the use of my room, but the money never came."

"And people might have thought it was you," I continued. "If they saw her at night, going into your room."

"Yes. People were always getting us mixed up." She shook her head. "Poor Jane."

I took a seat on one of the chairs in the room and put my face in my hands, trying to breathe normally again. All this time, it hadn't been Mary, but Jane who was Jack the Ripper's last victim. From all reports, the body had been so mutilated, the face included, that they couldn't identify the victim, except for her hair, her height and approximate weight, and the fact that she was in Mary's room.

"I didn't change history," I said quietly to myself, stunned.

"What do you mean?" Mary asked.

The realization hit me hard as I looked up at my sister. I hadn't forfeited this path because I hadn't changed history.

It felt like I had a second chance.

Elation filled me, but it was soon dashed. There was still the matter of Papa being held captive in a warehouse in London in 1938.

A porter yelled, "All visitors ashore," as he passed through the hallway.

It was time to say good-bye to Mary again.

"I'm so sorry about Jane," I said as I gave Mary a big hug. "But you mustn't tell anyone the truth. Everyone thinks you've died, and that's probably for the best. Go to New York and make your life whatever you want. Be happy and do good and don't be afraid, ever again."

She returned my hug, though I could tell she was still a little confused by my sudden appearance and behavior. "I love you."

"I love you, too," I said as I pulled back and smiled.

"Good-bye, Kathryn."

This time I was ready to say good-bye, knowing she was finally safe.

I left the cabin and found Austen and Miles speaking quietly nearby. When Austen saw me, he stood straight, his gaze searching mine.

"All is well," I said to reassure them, though it did little to reassure me.

Austen's smile was so beautiful, it almost brought tears to my eyes.

"I'm sorry to have barged in on you," I said to Miles. "Thank you for caring for my sister."

"It's my pleasure." He smiled, and I knew he meant it, even if he looked confused by my intrusion.

We said good-bye to Miles and then left the ship.

"What happened?" Austen asked me as we walked along the wharf toward land. The smell of fish and wet wood assailed my nose. People passed us on their way to their ships, speaking quickly and excitedly.

"I didn't change history," I told him in a quiet voice, still surprised at the turn of events. "Mary was going to leave with Joseph if we hadn't taken her here. She was never going to be at Miller's Court on the night of November 8th. It was her friend, Jane, who was killed. And because it wasn't Jane who I tried to save, I didn't knowingly change history." My heart broke for Jane and the other four victims. The injustice of it all was senseless. Her name would forever be lost to history. "I'm starting to realize how easy it is to misunderstand history. Something I should have known as a historian."

Austen smiled.

"But I still need to find the Book," I told him.

He put his hand on my arm to stop me. "What do you mean?"

I hadn't had time to tell him about Papa yet, so I did now as we stood on the wharf.

"Sir Rothschild is holding Papa captive in a warehouse in 1938 until I can produce the Book," I said. "I need to know where the Freemasons keep it so I can get it to him in 1938."

"We don't even know where it's at in *1888*," he said. "How in the world will you manage to give it to him in *1938*?"

"I don't know. But I can't give up. The note I read at Buckingham Palace from Sir Charles Warren to Prince Albert Victor said that the Book would be kept under the King's guard at WC—or Windsor Castle. It must be there."

"You cannot go to Windsor Castle and find the Book," he said. "It would be impossible. First, you'd have to know where they kept it, and second, you'd have to get past the guards—*if* they even have it at Windsor Castle. WC could mean any number of places."

I slowly nodded, wishing it wasn't true but feeling desperate. "We must go back to Wilton Crescent so I can speak to my father. Perhaps he'll tell me where the Book is kept."

"Why would he do that? If what you said is true, this Rothschild man threatened each of the families who were in Jerusalem, yours included, with death for the women they loved—and the Freemasons didn't give in to his demands. Why would your father tell you now?"

"Because I know more. I know that it wasn't the Freemasons who killed the women."

"It doesn't matter. The Freemasons are corrupt and ruthless." Austen paused. "Who is Rothschild in 1888?"

"What do you mean?"

"He said he also lived in 1888. So, who is he here?"

"I don't know. His first name in 1938 is Bryant, and since most time-crossers have the same first name in both paths, I would assume his first name in 1888 is also Bryant."

Austen frowned as we continued to walk toward Southampton Central Station. "I don't know of anyone named Bryant."

"I don't, either."

"Are you certain that's his real name in 1938?"

I shrugged. "It's the one he uses."

"We can look for someone with that name here," he said, "and tomorrow when you wake up in 1938, you can see if that's his real name there."

"We still need to go home so I can speak to my father," I reminded him. "To ask him about the Book."

Austen paused again. "I don't think it's a smart idea, Kathryn. Nothing good has come from anyone knowing about that book. And as much as I'd like to see the Freemasons fall, I'm afraid of what might happen if the Book lands in the hands of Jack the Ripper. I don't know anything about the Fascist Party or this man Hitler, but if he's going to lead the world in a war, you could change history by giving Sir Rothschild information about the Book. What if the Freemasons really are keeping power in balance and Hitler has the means to take them down? He sounds like a madman, and if he's against the Freemasons, then they must be doing something right. What would stop him from achieving world domination in 1938?"

I also stopped, but now I needed to sit down. There was a bench looking out at the harbor, so I went to it and took a seat.

Austen joined me.

All I could do was stare at him as I thought through the ramifications of Sir Rothschild getting ahold of the Book. "You're right. I could change history if I knowingly give Sir Rothschild the Book. But I'm so confused now. What if I *am* supposed to give him the Book? What if that's part of history?"

"Helping Mary was a selfless act," he said. "And even if you thought you were changing history, you knew you were doing the right thing. Giving Jack the Ripper and Hitler access to the Book is not the right thing, Kate. I think that's the difference."

"What will I do about Papa?" I asked, trying not to feel defeated or panicked. "How will I save him, if I can't get Sir Rothschild the Book?"

Austen thought for a moment. "First, we'll return to London and search through public records for anyone with the first or last name of Bryant. If we find him, we'll decide what to do next."

"And if we can't find him?"

"You can spend tomorrow in 1938 trying to learn his identity. We have a couple of days to figure this out." He took my hand into his. "We'll free your papa, Kate. I won't rest until we do."

It was a plan—not a perfect one, but it was a start. God had brought me this far, and He'd given me a second chance. I wouldn't waste it being worried.

"What will I tell my parents?" I asked as Austen stood and offered me his hand. "I disappeared last night."

"We'll tell them the truth." He slipped his fingers through mine. "He'll demand that I marry you, Kathryn, but he won't need to force me. I want to marry you, with all my heart."

"And I want to marry you," I said, "but there are so many things still—"

He put his finger to my lips. "God has already worked one miracle. I'm certain He can work others."

I pressed close beside him as we walked to the train station, hoping and praying he was right.

It was almost noon when we finally returned to Wilton Crescent. Austen had hired a hansom cab at Victoria Station, and it dropped us off in front of my parents' home.

Austen stepped out first and then helped me out before paying the cabby.

I stared at the front door of number eleven and wondered what might greet me inside.

"We'll let them know you're well," Austen said as he put his hand on the small of my back and led me to the door, "then we'll both change and head to the Public Records Office to search for Rothschild's name in 1888."

"Last time I spoke to Father, he forbade me from seeing you," I told Austen, pausing just outside the door. "What makes you think he'll allow me to leave with you today?"

Austen turned to me as the cab pulled away. We were standing just outside our homes, but the street was quiet, and it was just the two of us.

"He might try to stop us," Austen agreed, "and I respect your father, but you are a grown woman. You are not obligated to follow his commands. I will do whatever it takes to make sure we find Jack."

"I've been trying to find him for months. How will we do it in two days?"

"At least you know what he looks like, right?"

"Yes." I was very familiar with Sir Rothschild. And, like me, he probably looked the same in 1888 as he did in 1938.

"Then you know more than most."

I nodded and took a deep breath before I opened the front door. No one was in the hall, but I could hear faint voices coming from Father's study in the back of the house.

Austen and I walked in that direction, and when we entered the room, we found Father, Mother, and Michael Maybrick. Mother was seated on the edge of a chair near the window, her handkerchief in hand, as she wept silently. Father and Mr. Maybrick stood near the fireplace, their backs toward the door.

"Do you think he took Kathryn?" Father asked Mr. Maybrick.

"I can't be certain, though I wouldn't be surprised."

"Do you think he killed her, as well?"

"All of the other murders came with fair warnings," Mr. Maybrick said. "I don't think he'll kill her until he knows we won't give in to his demands."

"Why doesn't Sir Warren just arrest him?" Mother asked.

"Because he knows too much!" Father barked.

Mother noticed me and rose to her feet. "Kathryn!"

Father and Mr. Maybrick turned at her exclamation, shock on their faces.

With a cry, Mother rushed across the room and embraced me. It was a rare show of affection, which took me off guard, causing tears to spring to my eyes.

"What is the meaning of this, Austen?" Father asked, his chin rising with anger. "Where have the two of you been?"

"Who cares, Bernard?" Mother asked as she pulled back and turned to him. "She's safe. That's all that matters."

"Her reputation will be in ruins once people hear of this," Father said.

"At least that monster didn't take her and—" Mother's voice broke on another sob.

"I will do right by her," Austen said, standing stiff beside me. "I love Kate—"

"Where were you?" Father demanded again.

Austen glanced down at me, but I put my hand over his to still his response.

Instead, I took a step forward. "I wanted to run away." I couldn't tell them the truth. I didn't want them to know that Mary lived. The world, even my parents, needed to think she'd died. It was the only way she would ever be safe from Rothschild or the Freemasons. “But Austen insisted that we return.”

“You should have stayed away,” Father said, anger making his face red. “And never came back.”

“Bernard!” Mother took my hand. “You don’t mean that. We’ve already lost one daughter. I cannot abide losing another.”

“At least *he* didn’t get her,” Mr. Maybrick said, and I suspected that he wasn’t speaking of Austen. Was he talking about Jack the Ripper? Did they know his identity, and could I get it out of them?

“Have you heard about Mary yet?” Father asked, his gaze clouding with pain.

“Do not repeat it,” Mother said, putting her handkerchief to her lips again. “I cannot bear to hear it again.”

“She was murdered in her bed last night,” Father said anyway.

“It’s all your fault,” Mother hurled at him.

“Quiet.” Father stared at her. “Or you will regret speaking.”

Mother fled the room, weeping, leaving Austen and me alone with Father and Mr. Maybrick.

“Mary is dead?” I asked, trying to look devastated, so they wouldn’t question me.

“Murdered by Jack the Ripper,” Mr. Maybrick said, disgusted. “In the most gruesome way you can imagine.”

Austen put his arm around me, but he asked the men, “Who *is* Jack? Someone you know?”

Father and Mr. Maybrick glanced at each other, and I could see the truth in their eyes. They knew, but they’d never tell.

“This is all about the Book, isn’t it?” I asked scornfully as Austen tightened his hold on me in warning. “Jack wants it, and you refuse to tell him where it is. How many more women will have to die before this stops?”

“You do not know what you speak of,” Father said, caution in his voice.

“She knows about the Book?” Mr. Maybrick turned a cold eye to Father.

"She *thinks* she knows about it," he responded, trying to appease Mr. Maybrick. "But she is only guessing."

"That's good," Mr. Maybrick said as he stared at me, "because if she actually *knew* about it, then we'd have to decide what to do about her."

Austen's hold tightened again, and he took a slight step forward, as if to protect me.

"And what about you, Baird?" Mr. Maybrick asked. "What do you think *you* know about the Book?"

"I want Kate's safety, first and foremost," Austen said. "That's all I care about."

"I suppose this changes our agreement," Father said to Mr. Maybrick.

"I wouldn't want her now." Mr. Maybrick snorted. "I have no taste for used goods."

Austen's entire body tensed, and he took another step forward. I grasped his hand and held him back. "It's not worth it," I said to him.

Mr. Maybrick lifted a corner of his mouth in a sardonic smile and then strode to the door. "I will take care of this mess," he said to Father. "And I know just how to do it."

With that, Mr. Maybrick was gone.

Father lowered himself into the chair behind his desk, and for the first time in his life, he looked old, weary, and defeated.

"You two will be married as soon as I can arrange it," Father said without even looking at us. "Now leave."

I started to speak, but he lifted his hand to silence me.

We walked out of Father's study and stood in the front hall for a moment.

"I'm sorry, Kate," Austen said. "This is not how I wanted our marriage to begin."

"I know." I put my hand over his and nodded. Even though Father had just told me that Austen and I would be married, it was the last thing I could think about now. There were so many other things pressing for my attention. "We'll talk about it later.

Right now I will go up and change, and then we need to go to the Public Records Office."

Austen shook his head. "I'm going to follow Maybrick. I suspect that he knows who Jack is, and if that's true, he'll lead me right to his front door."

I grasped his hand. "It's too dangerous."

"I'll be fine." He smiled. "You saw me in 1938, didn't you? I was still alive."

"I went to your house yesterday to speak to you, but you didn't answer."

"Maybe I knew it was best that we didn't speak." He kissed my forehead. "Get some rest, and as soon as I know who Jack is, I'll be back. I promise."

"Are you sure it's safe?"

"No." He smiled. "But I'll be careful."

I let him kiss me again and then watched as he left the house.

Exhaustion, hunger, and worry plagued me as I started up the stairs. Once all my needs were met, I planned to go to the Public Records Office and start searching for Bryant on my own.

I had to find him.

28

NOVEMBER 9, 1938
LONDON, ENGLAND

My eyes opened quickly the next morning as I woke up at 44 Berkeley Square and tossed my covers aside. Mama would still be asleep, but I couldn't wait to talk to her.

"Mama," I said gently after I entered her room and touched her shoulder, not wanting to startle her.

Her eyes fluttered open, then she sat up quickly. "What's wrong?"

"I didn't lose 1888," I told her. "I was there yesterday."

"What?" She frowned as she blinked a couple of times and readjusted on her bed. "I don't understand."

"I don't, either." I quickly told her that Mary had been planning to leave Miller's Court either way, and her friend Jane was more than likely Jack's victim. It didn't surprise me that Sir Rothschild wouldn't know what Mary looked like, since he was not part of our lives in 1888. "So, I didn't change history."

"But you tried," Mama said, frowning. "When Libby tried, even though she didn't succeed, she still lost 1774."

"She tried to stop Henry from going to Boston," I told Mama. "But he still chose to go. The difference might be that Mary was never going to be killed. It was always going to be Jane. So I wasn't changing anything."

"But you sent Mary to America when she was supposed to end up in Surrey."

"That I didn't know," I said. "So I didn't knowingly change that part."

Mama was still frowning. "I suppose I don't understand all the rules of time-crossing. My mama told me that she saved the life of Virgil Earp using a medical technique that wasn't known in 1861. She thought she had changed history, as well, and that she might lose 1861, but she didn't. It appears that there are loopholes to the rules that each generation is learning as we go." She studied me closely. "But none of this solves our most pressing problem. How will we meet Sir Rothschild's demands? Where would we even begin to look for the Book, and how would we get access to it?"

I took a seat on the bed, ready to answer this question. "It would be impossible. I suspect it's in Windsor Castle, but it's probably hidden cleverly and under guard." I'd been thinking about this all day yesterday as I went through files at the Public Records Office, though every Bryant I found turned out to be the wrong man. "I think I've come up with a plan," I said. "I can't access the Book, but I do know where the letter from Sir Charles Warren is hidden in Buckingham Palace. It confirms that there *is* a Book, and hints at where it might be located. I will tell Sir Rothschild that I have information for him, but that I want to see Papa first. I'll tell him to bring Papa here tomorrow, and between now and then, Austen and I are working to try to find Sir Rothschild in 1888 to see if we can stop him there."

"What will you do if you find him there?" Mama asked.

"I will threaten to unmask him and reveal his name to the world unless he releases Papa."

Mama stared at me, her brown eyes filled with uncertainty. "But you don't know his real name in 1888, and in 1938, no one would believe that Sir Rothschild is also Jack the Ripper."

"That's why Austen and I are working to find him in 1888 and threaten to reveal his name there. I cannot let him hurt Papa."

She studied me and slowly shook her head, though I saw respect in the depths of her gaze. "If you do learn his real name, and you tell the world, you would be forfeiting both paths, Kathryn. I admire your desire for justice and your determination to save those you love, even if it costs you everything."

I wanted to pretend I wasn't scared, or that it was easy for me to make the offer, but I couldn't lie to Mama. "I am praying it doesn't come to that. My hope is that he will let Papa go when I give him information about where the Book is located. I might not be able to get it, but that doesn't mean he couldn't try."

"That's what I am hoping and praying, too." Mama took a deep breath and then said, "What are you planning to do today?"

"I need to find more information on Sir Rothschild here. His address, his connections—anything that might be a clue to help us know where he's keeping Papa. I also want to find out if his real name is Bryant, because if it's not, I'm wasting my time with public records in 1888."

"I'll get dressed and help you." She was about to get out of bed when she stopped and said, "We should go to Lady Astor first. She knows Sir Rothschild. She'll be a good place to start."

I nodded, but added, "Are we doing the right thing by not bringing the authorities in?"

"We're dealing with a man who has not only gone to great lengths to abduct your papa, but he's also responsible for the most famous and gruesome murders in London's history. I fear that if we make him upset, he could be capable of anything—both here and in 1888."

"So we won't tell Lady Astor that we know who took Papa?"

Mama slowly shook her head. "I hope I don't regret this, but I don't think it's wise. Not yet. If you and Austen can't find Jack in 1888 tomorrow, then we'll contact the police here in the morning. We need a little more time."

I hoped we wouldn't regret it, either.

As I got dressed, my thoughts slipped to Austen. He'd come home late the night before and simply sent me a note, through his maid, telling me that he had followed Mr. Maybrick all day but had not yet identified Jack.

After Mr. Maybrick had left our townhouse, he'd gone home, then he'd gone to a café for lunch, and then he'd gone to a cotton exchange building near the waterfront, where Austen had learned that he'd met up with his brother, James, who was a cotton merchant. From there, Mr. Maybrick had gone to a theater and given a performance that evening. After he'd gone back to his home, Austen had returned to his.

Apparently, Mr. Maybrick's comment about taking care of the mess had been a ruse because he hadn't done anything out of the ordinary, leaving us back at square one.

After we dressed and Mama called Lydia to tell her there was no news yet, we hailed a cab and gave the driver Lady Astor's address at St. James Square.

London had gone back to normal after the scare with Hitler in the end of September. Everyone was still wary and concerned about Hitler's plans, but less and less people were carrying their gas masks, and all work on temporary bomb shelters had ended.

Mama held my hand in the back of the cab as we made our way to the Astors' townhouse. I knew she was praying about Papa, about me, and about how we would find answers without risking my life in both paths. I leaned into her strength, offering up some prayers of my own and realizing that no matter what I planned, God was surprising me constantly with His answers.

I hoped He would continue.

When we finally arrived at St. James Square, my entire body was trembling with anxiety. After we knocked on the front door, the butler answered and led us into the parlor. He left to tell Lady Astor that we'd come, and then we waited.

"I'm happy she's home," Mama said as she stood in front of a large painting, looking at it but probably not seeing it.

I paced, trying to think of new ways to deal with Sir Rothschild.

"Oh, my dear Grace," Lady Astor said as she entered the room. "Is there word on Luc?"

Mama turned away from the painting and shook her head no.

Lady Astor's expectant look fell, then she motioned to the chairs. "Have a seat. I'll ring for tea."

"We've come on a mission," I said quickly. "I'm not sure we'll have time for tea."

"Oh?" Lady Astor frowned. "What can I do for you? Whatever it is, I'm here to help."

"How well do you know Sir Rothschild?" I asked without preamble.

She studied me for a second before saying, "I know him about as well as most."

"Is Bryant his first name?"

Lady Astor slowly shook her head. "I don't believe it's his given name, no. Years ago when we first met, he introduced himself as James Bryant Rothschild. It wasn't until he was knighted that he started to go by Bryant."

"James?"

"Yes."

I met Mama's gaze. I'd told her what Austen's note had said the night before. Mr. Maybrick had gone to his brother James's place of employment. Was that a coincidence? But then I recalled the file I'd found in Sir Rothschild's drawer, the one about the murder trial of Florence Maybrick, James's wife. Why was Sir Rothschild so interested in that case? Could it be that *he* was James Maybrick in 1888?

"Why do you want to know?" Lady Astor asked.

"It's a bit of a long story," I said, hedging around the truth. "I was just curious and thought perhaps you could help me."

"Why didn't you ask him yourself?" She was frowning again, clearly suspicious.

"We've had a bit of a falling out," I tried to explain, though it was a vast understatement. I didn't want to alarm her, but I was doing a poor job hiding my emotions. Papa's life was on the line, and Sir Rothschild held the key to his freedom.

Lady Astor's mouth parted, and she took a step forward. "Does Sir Rothschild know where your father is?"

Mama and I glanced at each other, and it was enough to convince Lady Astor.

"He does!" She took a seat, shaking her head. "Oh, dear." She pressed her lips together, regret and pain in her eyes. "I knew he was getting fanatical. He and his wife, Bianca, have spoken to Waldorf and myself on numerous occasions, trying to get us to pledge our loyalty to the Nazi Party, but I refused. I have long feared that he was deeper into the party than I realized and that he might be feeding them information."

"You mean spying?" Mama asked.

"Yes. But I've known them for so long, I thought I was just being paranoid. He was very keen on knowing all about the Lindberghs' and Luc's trip to Germany. When Luc went missing, I had a fleeting thought that he might know something about it, but, again, I pushed it aside." She put her hand to her forehead, clearly upset. When she looked up at us, she said, "I'm so sorry."

"You are not responsible," Mama said. "It's not your fault."

"What did he tell you?" Lady Astor asked. "Where is Luc?"

This was where it got more complicated. Would Lady Astor rouse the police? I had to say something, but I didn't want her to get involved.

"We suspect that he's being held somewhere here in London," I finally said.

"Why?" she asked.

"Sir Rothschild believes I have connections to something he and the Nazi Party want—but I do not." I said the last part very clearly. "That's why he brought me to London in the first place, though I didn't know it at the time."

Lady Astor was quiet for a moment, but she finally said, "I won't even ask what it is. But I am assuming that he spoke to you directly?"

"Yes, and he doesn't want the police involved," Mama added.

"Of course he doesn't." Lady Astor sighed.

"I don't have what he wants," I offered. "But I might know where it is. I am hoping he will agree to meet with us and bring Papa with him so I can see that he's alive and well. Then I'll tell him where the item is, and hopefully it will be enough for him to release Papa."

"Let me know what we can do to help," Lady Astor offered. "I will be there, if you need me."

I shook my head. "I don't think it's a good idea. But if we change our mind, we'll let you know."

"Is there anything else about Sir Rothschild that you can tell us?" Mama asked.

Lady Astor shrugged. "I met him and Bianca at least ten years ago, when he first started to work at the London Museum. As far as I know, he grew up in London and studied in Italy, where he met Bianca and first joined the Fascist movement, probably because of her involvement. He and Bianca live not far from here, on Grosvenor Square. They have no children, and I don't hear them speak of extended family. They tend to be very private people."

Grosvenor Square was one of the most desirable places to live in London in both 1888 and 1938. The only way a man might afford a townhome there was if he was vastly wealthy. Either Sir Rothschild or his wife had family money, or he was getting it some other way, because the modest salary from the London Museum couldn't pay for a house on Grosvenor Square.

"Thank you for your time," I said to Lady Astor.

"Of course." She smiled at us, though there was concern in her gaze. "Don't hesitate to call again, if need be."

We said our good-byes and then exited her townhouse.

The cab had left, but it didn't matter. I knew where we needed to go, and it wasn't far. Just across St. James Square to the London Library.

"Hurry, Mama," I said as I took her hand and led her toward the familiar building. The London Library was housed in the same structure in 1888, and I'd been there many times.

"Where are we going?" she asked.

"To the library to look up newspapers from 1888."

"Why?"

"I have a feeling I know who Sir Rothschild might be there."

"Who?" she asked, curious and surprised.

"A man named James Maybrick."

"Who is he?"

"I don't know anything about him, except that he's the brother of Michael Maybrick, a famous composer that my parents want me to marry—and he's going to become the victim of murder in 1888 tomorrow."

"James Maybrick is going to be murdered?" she asked.

"Yes."

"Who is going to kill him?"

"His wife will be framed, but I have another suspicion. Either his brother, Michael, will kill him because he suspects that James is Jack the Ripper—or it will be suicide. I saw some newspaper articles about the trial in Sir Rothschild's desk drawer."

"But no pictures of James Maybrick in the drawer?"

I shook my head. "At the time, it didn't occur to me to wonder. There were drawings of Florence and Michael, but nothing with James's picture. Now I think I know why. If Sir Rothschild is James Maybrick, he wouldn't want his likeness anywhere near him in 1938."

We entered the cool interior of the London Library, and the smell of musty books met my nose. It was a familiar, welcoming smell, but I didn't revel in it. I needed to find a picture of James Maybrick to know if my suspicions were correct.

A librarian sat behind a desk, and when we approached, he looked up and smiled. "May I help you?"

I forced myself not to speak quickly, but rather to be calm and collected so I didn't arouse his concern. "We are interested in learning about the murder of a man named James Maybrick in 1888."

"Ah"—he smiled and nodded—"a very peculiar and sad story. Mrs. Florence Maybrick was tried and convicted of the murder. She served fourteen years before getting the sentence overturned."

"Do you have any newspapers from that time? I'm specifically interested in learning more about James Maybrick, the victim. Do you happen to have any photos of him?"

"We do, indeed. There's a whole file devoted to the case. Won't you come with me?"

I was both relieved and anxious to hear that there were pictures. If this was the right man, I would tell Austen immediately in the morning, and we would need to find James and confront him. If it wasn't, we would need to keep looking. And we were running out of time.

We followed the librarian to a back corner of the library where tall file cabinets were stored. He went to the one with a large M on the outside and opened the drawer.

After looking through the files for a few moments, he lifted one out and smiled. "Here it is."

It was a thick, promising folder.

"I'll just leave this here with you," he said as he set it on a table. "When you're done, you may leave it here, and I'll return it to the file cabinet." He smiled. "Will that be all for now?"

"Yes. Thank you."

I could hardly wait for him to leave before I went to the table. There were other patrons in the library, some sitting at the tables nearby doing research, some browsing the shelves, and others reading books in chairs by the windows.

"Hurry," Mama said, just as eager as me to know if this was our man.

I opened the folder and saw a newspaper clipping, but there were no drawings. Slowly, I lifted the paper and turned it over, setting it on the front of the folder, and then I stopped.

Right underneath the newspaper clipping was a photo—not a drawing—of James Maybrick.

Mama sucked in a breath, and my legs became weak as I took a seat on one of the chairs.

"Sir Rothschild *is* James Maybrick," Mama said, just under her breath.

"And James Maybrick is Jack the Ripper," I added, fascinated and horrified all at the same time.

The photo of James Maybrick staring back at us was also a photo of Sir James Bryant Rothschild. The same light-colored hair, even the same mustache. The only difference was the style of clothing.

I didn't need to continue to look, so I gently closed the folder and turned to Mama.

"What now?" she asked.

"I'm going to tell Austen what we've learned, and I'm going to confront James in 1888. When I see him there tomorrow, I'm going to tell him to take Papa to Berkeley Square in 1938. If he agrees, I will promise to give him information about the Book. If he doesn't, I'll threaten to reveal his identity to the world."

"Isn't he going to be killed tomorrow?"

"I'll get there before that is supposed to happen." I opened the folder one more time to get the details surrounding his death. "It looks like he died of arsenic poisoning around noon."

Mama put her hand on my arm. "Please be careful, Kathryn. He might die in 1888, but he'll be very much alive here."

"I know. I will be careful. I promise."

She didn't look convinced, but there was little she could do to stop me.

29

NOVEMBER 10, 1888
LONDON, ENGLAND

A light, steady rain tapped against the windows in my bedroom at Wilton Crescent when I woke up there the next morning. Just like the day before, I quickly got out of bed to get dressed. This time, however, I had to ring for Duffy's help, since it would take me too long to dress myself in petticoats and a corset.

Yesterday had felt like an eternity while I waited for the clock to strike midnight in 1938 so I could go back to 1888. Mama and I had spent the day looking through public records, trying to find out if Sir Rothschild owned any buildings, specifically a warehouse in London where he might be holding Papa. But there were no such records. Sir Rothschild didn't even own the townhouse he occupied. Instead, we learned that it was owned by a man from Germany. That had given us hope, so we used the German's name to look up property titles. But we found nothing helpful there, either.

Now, I began to brush out my hair as I waited for Duffy. I didn't know where James Maybrick lived, but it shouldn't be hard to find his address. We needed to get to his house as soon as possible. I had read enough about his death to know that he was complaining of stomach ailments for days prior to his murder and that he died in bed at his home around noon.

When Duffy finally appeared, she looked surprised. "I'm sorry. I didn't think you'd be rising this early, miss."

"Please hurry," I said. "I need to be somewhere as quickly as possible."

She helped me into a simple day dress and styled my hair in a low chignon. She'd barely helped me button up my walking boots, and I was already on my way out.

"Miss, your hat and gloves," she called after me.

I ignored her, not caring if I was properly attired. Instead, I rushed down the hallway to the staircase and came to a halt when I met Father at the top of the stairs.

He gave me a frustrated, disgruntled look and said, "I've arranged for a special license. You and Austen will be wed one week from today at St. Paul's with a small wedding breakfast to follow."

He didn't give me time to respond but continued down the stairs toward the breakfast room.

St. Paul's, Knightsbridge, was an Anglican church just around the corner from our townhome. We'd attended there faithfully since I was a child. It was a beautiful Gothic structure and would make a lovely place for a wedding—if I was getting married in 1888.

There were far too many things to worry about before I could think about that, so I pushed Father's news aside and continued down the stairs and out the front door.

The rain was falling steadier now, and I ran to the townhouse next door and vigorously knocked until Brinley answered.

"Miss Kelly," he said, stepping back to allow me to enter without any formalities. "Come in."

"Is Austen at home?"

"He's just coming down now, miss."

Austen stood at the top of the stairs but quickly descended as Brinley closed the front door behind me and quietly slipped out of the entrance hall.

Austen was dressed, but he hadn't shaved, probably not wanting to waste any time, either. When he met me at the base of the stairs, he took me into his arms without a word.

I melted into his embrace and pressed my cheek against his chest, feeling the reassuring beat of his heart.

He held me tight, as if he didn't want to let me go, and finally whispered, "You don't know how thankful I am that I can still do this."

I closed my eyes, wanting this moment to last forever. But we didn't have much time, so I pulled back and said, "I know who Jack is."

Austen stared at me for a heartbeat before saying, "Is it Michael Maybrick?"

"No. It's his brother, James."

"James—the brother he visited at the cotton merchant's building yesterday?"

"Yes. I've seen his picture, and there is no mistaking that he is Sir Rothschild. I found a folder in Sir Rothschild's desk a couple months ago with information about James Maybrick's death. He is supposed to die at noon today, of an apparent murder by arsenic poisoning. His wife will be arrested and put on trial, with Michael Maybrick as her lead accuser. She'll serve fourteen years, but the sentence will eventually be overturned."

"Do you think she did it?" he asked.

"I don't know. But part of me wonders if he was researching the case in 1938 because he plans to change history and not get murdered here. Either way, we need to find him. I need to talk to him and let him know that if he doesn't release Papa in 1938 tomorrow, I will tell the world his identity as Jack the Ripper."

Austen studied me much the same way as Mama had before he said, "You would be willing to risk changing history and forfeiting this path again?"

"If Papa's life wasn't in danger, I wouldn't risk it. But he *is* in danger, and I cannot let Sir Rothschild get away with this."

Austen nodded, resigned. "I couldn't sleep last night, thinking about you, Kate. Thanking God that I had one more day with you." Sadness and disappointment filled his gaze as he said, "But I can't help feeling that no matter what we do, I'm going to lose you."

My heart fell at his words, and I grasped the lapels of his coat, trying to anchor myself to him, to this moment, and to this path. I wanted to beg him not to say those words, but I couldn't. Because I had the same feeling.

"I'm sorry," I said, since there was nothing else I could say.

"It's not your fault." He hugged me, and I wished his embrace could banish all my fears. But it didn't.

"We need to find James Maybrick."

"I can't believe we're going to face Jack the Ripper." He pulled away and took his jacket off the coat-tree. "I'll never get used to any of this."

"I've faced him countless times," I said. "And each time I recall being alone with him in 1938, I shudder."

"The man has done unspeakable things. I want you to stay close to my side, Kate."

I nodded, not planning to do anything foolish.

At least, not yet.

We took Austen's carriage to the cotton merchant where he'd seen Michael Maybrick the day before. Since Miles was no longer there to drive, Austen's footman maneuvered the vehicle through the busy streets of London.

James wasn't at work, but the clerk gave us his home address.

The carriage drove from the warehouses near the river to Cumberland Terrace in Regents Park. The beautiful white townhomes were similar to Wilton Crescent, with black wrought iron railings around the upper windows and flower boxes on the lower ones.

When the carriage pulled up to number fifty-two, I stared at the nondescript home and wondered what might greet us inside.

Would James be willing to speak to me? It was almost nine o'clock, several hours away from the appointed hour of his death. But had he even stayed home today?

Austen got out and offered me his hand. I was thankful for the simple dress I was wearing, though it was still cumbersome. I didn't care if it got soiled in the dreadful weather.

Neither of us spoke as we walked up to the door, where Austen knocked. He glanced at me with a question in his eyes, giving me one last chance to back away.

I shook my head. There was no backing out now.

A butler answered and allowed us in out of the rain.

"Is Mr. Maybrick home?" I asked the butler.

"May I ask who is calling?"

I hesitated, not knowing if I should give aliases. Finally, I decided Sir Rothschild would be more likely to answer our call if he knew our real identities. "Mr. Austen Baird and Miss Kathryn Kelly."

The butler nodded and led us to the parlor before summoning his employer.

The parlor was well-decorated and comfortable, but the room was cold, and the house was quiet. There was no fire in the hearth and no sound coming from any other room.

We didn't have to wait long before a woman appeared. She was pretty, with blond hair and blue eyes. She carried herself with authority as she said, "Good morning. I'm Mrs. Maybrick. How may I help you?" Her voice was distinctly American with a hint of the south.

I stepped forward. "We've come to see your husband. Is he home?"

She studied me for a moment and then looked at Austen before her gaze came back to me. "May I inquire about your business? My husband isn't feeling well and is in bed."

It surprised me that he hadn't left the house today—unless he wanted to die in this path and was allowing it to happen.

"We really must speak to him directly," I said, my nerves trying to get the better of me. "It's an urgent matter that cannot wait."

Mrs. Maybrick regarded me and then lifted her chin. "I cannot let you see him. He's much too ill, and I fear that if something upsets him, it will be—"

"Leave the room, Flo," a man said from the doorway.

I was startled as my gaze locked on James Maybrick—or, as I knew him best, Sir Rothschild.

It was strange to see him here. He looked pale and bent over a cane.

"You should be in bed, James," Mrs. Maybrick said as she rushed to his side. "The doctor said that the only way to regain your strength is to rest."

"I said leave," he told his wife, his voice cold and unforgiving.

She looked from her husband back to me, curiosity and concern in her gaze, but she didn't argue and took her leave of the room.

"Close the door," he ordered.

She did as he commanded and was gone.

"So," he said, standing straight, no longer in need of the cane, which appeared to be part of a show for his wife's sake. "You found me."

I could hardly believe this was the same man I'd worked with at Lancaster House for the past two months. Or that this was Jack the Ripper. I had so many questions, but I needed to tell him why I'd come. "I want you to release Papa."

A hateful smile tilted up one side of his mouth. "You have the Book?"

Shaking my head, I said, "No one can get the Book. You, of all people, should know that."

"If you don't get the Book to me by noon tomorrow, you can forget about seeing your father alive."

My fists clenched at my sides, and I had to force myself to remain calm. "I can't get you the Book. But I know where it is."

"Tell me now."

I shook my head. "I won't give you the information until you take my father to Berkeley Square. I want to see him. To know that he's alive and well."

"You expect me to believe that you know where the Book is located?" He laughed, but it wasn't a mirthful sound. "I'm not a fool, Miss Kelly."

"Don't you recall the letter I discovered at Buckingham Palace? The one written by Sir Charles Warren to Prince Albert Victor, with information about the Book? I never told you, but he gives the location about where they planned to keep the Book once all the parts of it were brought back together. And since we know that the Book is together again, the letter will tell you where it's at."

Sir Rothschild stared at me. "You're lying."

"I've never been more serious in my life. I have the information, but I will not give it to you unless you take my father to Berkeley Square tomorrow. At noon."

He continued to study me, his eyes calculating. "No police, Miss Kelly. If I see anything out of the usual, I will keep going and your father's body will be found floating in a river in Germany of an apparent suicide a few days later. Think of the shame that it will bring to your family."

I took a step toward him, but Austen reached out to stop me.

Sir Rothschild scoffed again, but then he said, "Do you swear, Miss Kelly? Just you and your mother at Berkeley Square."

I ground my teeth. "I promise it will be just me and my mother. But if you don't bring him to me," I said, tugging against Austen's hold on me, wanting to lash out at Sir Rothschild, "I will not hesitate to reveal that James Maybrick is Jack the Ripper. I have enough evidence to convince the world, both here and in 1938."

He stared at me, his eyes narrowing. "You wouldn't."

"I would. Even if you die here today."

"I'm not dying here today," he said. "The history books claim it's arsenic poisoning and that I have been suffering for weeks. But I haven't touched a bit of food from this house, or my brother's house, in weeks. I've been pretending to feel ill so Florence, or whoever was supposed to poison me, thinks it's working."

"Who do you think it is?" I asked.

"Probably my brother. He's a loyal Freemason, just like our

father." He spat out the word *father* with hatred in every syllable. "I'd take down all of the Freemasons if it meant destroying the one thing my father loved above all others, his Brotherhood."

"But if the history books claim you died here," I said, "you'll forf—"

Austen squeezed my arm and shook his head.

I frowned, but he communicated for me to stop warning Sir Rothschild.

"What?" Sir Rothschild asked. "What were you going to say?"

Realization dawned. When I'd spoken about changing history with Mama while Sir Rothschild was in the room at Berkeley Square, he'd seemed ignorant of the time-crossing rule. Did he not know he was forfeiting 1888 by preventing his death?

I stopped straining against Austen, and he finally let me go. When I looked back at Sir Rothschild I said, "I will see you tomorrow in 1938—with my papa."

"You had better have what I need," he warned.

"I will."

When I opened the door, I found Mrs. Maybrick pacing in the hallway. Behind me, Sir Rothschild began to moan and groan, as if he was in pain. He bent over his cane once again and sat on the sofa, but this time I knew he was faking.

Mrs. Maybrick entered the parlor, her face filled with distress. "James, you must get back in bed."

As she put her arm around him, helping Sir Rothschild to his feet, he gave me one last vicious smile.

30

NOVEMBER 10, 1938
LONDON, ENGLAND

I woke up the next morning with the same determination I had the two days before, but when I went into Mama's room, her bed was empty.

My heart pounded hard as I rushed out of her room and went down the stairs in my pajamas—only to find her in the parlor.

I sagged against the doorframe, my hand over my heart as I caught my breath.

"There you are," I said, entering the parlor.

She sat on the chair near the hearth, but her smile was sad as she greeted me. "I couldn't sleep, worrying about your papa and you. So I thought I'd be more productive if I sat up and prayed through the night while you were in 1888."

"You didn't sleep?" I asked as I entered the room.

She shook her head, but there was more to her sadness this morning. It hung on her like a mantle.

"What's wrong?" I asked.

"News has filtered into London this morning. There is a riot happening across Germany. It was started last night by the Nazis, and the German government is not intervening. Reports are coming in that hundreds of synagogues were destroyed, thousands of

Jewish men have been arrested, and Jewish homes and businesses have been ransacked. The press is calling it *Kristallnacht*, or the Night of Broken Glass."

I sank into a chair near hers, feeling weak and afraid for what was about to come upon the earth. But my fear was nothing compared to the thousands of Jews who had lived through *Kristallnacht*, and the countless others who were fearing for their lives and the lives of their loved ones this morning across Germany.

"Why is the world so broken?" I asked her, tears in my voice.

She gently took my hand. "Because the hearts and the minds of her people are broken. And until we stop fearing our neighbors, and love them as Jesus commanded, there will be war and hatred and anger. Fear has the power to cause an entire nation to rise up and kill her perceived enemies. Just imagine what love could do if we'd let it."

"I spoke to Sir Rothschild," I said.

She nodded, eagerly. "And?"

"He's bringing Papa here at noon—but he made me promise it would just be you and me. No one else."

Mama closed her eyes briefly, and I knew she was trying to control her emotions. She missed Papa more than anything and had spent countless hours praying for his safe return. When she opened them, she nodded. "I'll do anything to get him home."

"I will, too. I think Sir Rothschild will be satisfied with the information I give him. I'll just pray that he can't find it at Windsor Castle." I took a deep breath. "I *hope* he will be satisfied." My hands clenched on my lap as I thought about all that he was getting away with. I hated injustice, especially when it was wrought against the people I loved. "I want him to face the consequences of his actions—both in 1888 and here. He tried to change history there yesterday. I think he might have forfeited his path without realizing it. I plan to find out if he died there."

"Let the Lord deal with Sir Rothschild," Mama said as she took my hand. "I want to return to Washington immediately. As soon as we have Papa."

"Of course." I rose to get dressed, but Mama didn't let go of my hand.

"And when all of this is done," she said. "We'll talk about what you plan to do next."

"I haven't even let myself think that far ahead."

Mama's smile was both sad and hopeful. "I have—and I'm preparing myself to say good-bye, Kathryn."

My mouth parted as I knelt before her. "What do you mean?"

She put her free hand on my cheek. "You're in love with Austen. I think you know what I mean."

"I am in love with Austen," I said as my voice choked with emotion. "But I'm not ready to say good-bye, Mama."

She simply smiled. "I know. I felt the same way when I decided to leave Hope and stay with Papa." Her smile softened. "I shouldn't have said anything yet. Let's focus on today and getting Papa back before we talk about Austen."

I nodded and then rose from the floor to leave the parlor, not wanting to add more anguish to my heart. It was already so overburdened, I was afraid I would crumple into a corner and start to cry and never stop. I wasn't certain that Sir Rothschild would bring Papa to us. And if he did, I wasn't sure if we would survive the encounter. He was a Nazi who had done horrible, terrifying things in two different paths to get something that could change the course of history if it fell into the wrong hands.

He would stop at nothing to get what he wanted, and I was risking everything by telling him where the Book might be located. I wasn't sure it was the right course of action, but I was desperate and prayed that the king's guards would protect the Book.

It was my only hope.

As soon as I had dressed, I left 44 Berkeley Square and returned to the London Library. The librarian greeted me with a smile as he had the day before. "How may I help you?"

"I'd like to see the file on James Maybrick again, if I may." I waited, half expecting him to tell me there was no file on James Maybrick. If James had changed history, then there would be no trial and no newspaper clippings.

The librarian nodded. "Of course. Please follow me."

He took me back to the table I had used yesterday, but when he presented the folder, it was just as thick as the day before.

What did it mean?

As the librarian walked away, I slowly opened the folder, wondering what I might find.

There were just as many newspaper clippings as before, but they contained much different information. James Maybrick had not died at noon on November 10th, 1888, as history had originally stated. Instead, he had died in his sleep, and his body was discovered the next morning on November 11th. His brother, Michael, had still accused Florence Maybrick of poisoning her husband, and it had still gone to trial. But this time, there was no proof of poisoning, and Florence Maybrick did not go to prison.

She'd been spared.

Sir James Bryant Rothschild, also known as James Maybrick, had forfeited his life in 1888. He'd made Jack the Ripper exit history without even realizing it. Which explained why he disappeared so abruptly.

I slipped one of the newspaper clippings into my purse, knowing that Sir Rothschild would never believe me without proof, and planned to return it as soon as I could to the library.

After thanking the librarian, I returned home just before ten, with two hours to wait for Sir Rothschild's arrival.

"He changed history," I said to Mama as soon as I entered the parlor on the main floor.

She was sitting in her chair near the hearth, her eyes closed in prayer, but she opened them when I appeared. "What?"

"Here." I showed her the newspaper clipping and explained everything I'd discovered.

She shook her head in wonder. "This is the newspaper clipping I saw yesterday when we were at the library."

"You don't remember that he was supposed to die at noon, from arsenic poisoning?"

"No."

"But I do."

"That's because you're still a time-crosser," she explained. "I'm not anymore. What I do know is that God's plans cannot be thwarted."

For the next two hours, I paced in the parlor while Mama prayed. If Sir Rothschild didn't bring Papa to Berkeley Square, I would be forced to tell the world about Jack the Ripper—and forfeit my own paths.

When the grandfather clock struck the midday hour, my pulse ticked up another notch.

I strode to the window, but looking out, I could see no one approaching the townhouse.

"Where are they?" I demanded.

Mama didn't answer.

The clock continued to tick. Five minutes passed, ten minutes—and then the front doorbell rang.

Mama rose from her chair, but I ran past her into the hall, down the stairs, and into the foyer, where I tore open the door.

Papa stood on the front stoop beside Sir Rothschild, his hands cuffed.

"Papa!" I cried and rushed toward him.

Sir Rothschild pulled a large knife from his pocket and pointed it at me. "Stay back, Kathryn."

I paused at the sight of the weapon so similar to the one he'd used freely in Whitechapel.

Mama appeared at the top of the steps and cried out in relief. Something sweet and heartbreaking passed between my parents. The longing and love on their faces was the most beautiful thing I'd ever witnessed, though it was bittersweet as Sir Rothschild nudged

Papa into the house and closed the door behind him, keeping his knife in plain sight.

"All of you, into the parlor," Sir Rothschild said, pointing up the stairs.

We did as he commanded, but I could see that it took all of Papa's willpower not to lash out at Sir Rothschild or put his arms around Mama and me. He hadn't shaved in at least a week, and his suit looked as if he hadn't changed since the day he'd been abducted. He'd also lost weight, though it was the least of my concerns. He seemed healthy and whole, and that was all that mattered.

"Sit," Sir Rothschild said to my parents.

They did as he commanded, sitting on the sofa beside each other. Mama took Papa's cuffed hands, tears in her eyes.

"Get the information you came for," Papa demanded, "and then leave us in peace."

Sir Rothschild scoffed. "I'll leave you in peace if the information Kathryn gives me is satisfactory. If it's not, then we have more business to conduct." He tilted his knife to reflect the sunlight from the window, sending a chill up my spine. I'd spent enough time researching the murders he'd committed in Whitechapel in 1888 to know that he was capable of anything.

He approached me, his gaze intent on my face. "Well? What do you have to say?"

Panic overwhelmed me. Would the information from the letter be enough to appease him?

When I didn't answer right away, he yelled, "Stop stalling, Kathryn, and tell me where the Book is."

"What good will it do?" I asked, surprising myself with how bold I felt as I stared at the knife.

"As soon as we take down the Freemasons," he said, as if speaking to a child, "there will be no one to stop us from overtaking Europe—and then the world. I thought I made myself clear." He stared at me and shook his head. "Even if I have to kill you here, I will still come after you and all you love in 1888, so stop stalling."

"You don't know, do you?" I asked him.

He frowned. "Know what?"

"You forfeited your life in 1888."

His frown deepened. "What are you talking about?"

"You can't hurt me in 1888 because you died there. Last night."

His eyes narrowed. "I didn't die there. I refused to let Florence or Michael poison me."

"You changed history. And when we knowingly change history, we forfeit the timeline we try to change." I went to the desk in the corner and lifted the newspaper clipping for him to see. "I went to the London Library today, and I confirmed what I had suspected. You didn't die of poisoning in 1888—you died in your sleep. And Florence wasn't convicted. They could not prove what killed you. But I know."

He tore the clipping from my hand and read it quickly, his face falling with realization.

He stared at thc paper, the knife going limp in his hand. When he finally looked at me, rage filled his face. "You knew yesterday when you visited me, didn't you?" He advanced toward me. "You knew that I was forfeiting my time there."

My heart started to pound as he came toward me.

Papa leapt from the couch, but Sir Rothschild pointed the knife at him. "Stay there, or I'll slit her throat before you take another step."

Panic and anger reverberated off Papa, but he stayed near the couch. For now.

"Why do you hate the Freemasons so much?" I asked, trying to distract him from Papa.

"I've known about Jack the Ripper since I was young," Sir Rothschild said, keeping his knife pointed toward Papa but looking at me. "But I had no idea it was going to be me until last year, when I learned about the Book in 1937. I had discovered that all five women had connections to the trip to Jerusalem because I was fighting against the Freemasons, even in 1887. My father had devoted his life to the Brotherhood, and I despised them and vowed to take them down, as many others have done. I went to Jerusalem in 1887 and met the man who tried to take the Book from Sir Charles Warren in 1874. He told me about each family, and how they had a part of the Book.

"When I came back to London, it didn't take long to realize all the women were in Whitechapel for various reasons. I tried to blackmail the families, but none of them would betray the Brotherhood. So, I followed through with history's plan and brought pain to the Freemasons—the same pain my father inflicted on me when he chose the Freemasons over his own son."

"But did you have a choice?" I asked, horrified. "To become Jack the Ripper?"

"Of course I had a choice," he said with a sneer. "I could have changed history at that time. But in my mind, there was no choice. Hitler must succeed." He stepped closer to me, his voice lowering. "I might not have gotten what I wanted out of them, but when I met you and realized you were also a time-crosser, I knew that I had found another possible solution. I also knew that I was supposed to be poisoned by Florence or Michael, but I wouldn't let history have that satisfaction." He snarled. "Though apparently, history won anyway."

"Drop your knife," Papa said to Sir Rothschild. "There's no need to shed more blood."

In a flash, Sir Rothschild had the knife pointed at me again and he yelled, "Tell me where the Book is, or you will be next!"

A noise in the hall caught all of us by surprise. When Sir Rothschild turned to see what had caused the sound, I darted toward my parents.

The door opened, and police officers began to pour into the parlor before Sir Rothschild could turn right or left.

He glared at me. "I told you no police!"

"I didn't call them—" But my words were cut off as two policemen grabbed Sir Rothschild and wrestled the knife out of his hands. He fought back but was no match for their strength or their surprise attack.

"James Bryant Rothschild," one police officer said, "you are under arrest for the abduction and unlawful captivity of United States Brigadier General Lucas Voland, as well as high treason against His Majesty the King of England."

"This is madness," Sir Rothschild said, fighting to be free. "You will all pay for this. Hitler will personally see that I am vindicated."

He continued to yell threats as they hauled him away.

I turned to Papa, more concerned about his well-being than what Sir Rothschild had to say.

"Are you okay, Papa?" I asked.

He smiled as a police officer took off Papa's handcuffs. "I'm better than ever, Kathryn."

The moment he was free, he embraced Mama.

Tears of joy ran unchecked down her cheeks as she said his name over and over.

"General Voland?" one of the police officers said. "When you have a moment, I have questions for you, sir."

Papa finally pulled away from Mama but kept his arm around her. "What would you like to know?"

"Was Sir Rothschild responsible for your abduction?"

"Yes. I was surprised to see him when he approached me on a street in Berlin, but he told me he was there to consult at a museum."

"He told me he was going to Paris," I said, incredulous. "To consult at Versailles. I had no idea he was in Berlin."

"Why did you go with him?" the officer asked Papa.

"Because I recognized him. I went with him to a café, but by the time I realized I was in trouble, I was seized by several men who I later identified as members of the Nazi party. That same day, I was flown to London with Sir Rothschild, and I've been kept in a warehouse near the river for the past four days."

My heart hurt, listening to him recall his story. As he spoke, I watched another officer lift Sir Rothschild's knife off the ground and carry it away.

When the police officer interviewing Papa seemed to be satisfied, he said, "I'll leave you to reunite with your family and take some time to refresh yourself. But I would like you to come to New Scotland Yard as soon as possible to make an official statement. We will also alert the American authorities that you have been returned safely."

"Thank you," Papa said.

The copper tipped his hat at Papa and then Mama and me and called for his men to clear out.

Papa and Mama embraced again, and then Papa came to me. He drew me into his strong, tender arms and held me tight.

"Thank you, Kathryn," he said, his voice low and gruff with emotion. "Rothschild told me that you visited him in 1888—even though you knew he was Jack the Ripper. He proudly told me several times about the vicious crimes he committed in Whitechapel to try and scare me. You risked everything to have me returned safely to you and Mama. I owe you my life."

"You owe me nothing," I said as tears traced my cheeks. "I would do anything for you."

"I know you would, *ma chérie*."

"Who told the police that he was going to be here?" Mama asked, joining us. "Kathryn and I told no one."

"She told me," an elderly gentleman said as he slowly entered the parlor.

My breath caught as I pulled away from Papa. "Austen."

Mama and Papa turned toward the door and stared at a man who was older than both of them—at least, in this path.

But he didn't look at my parents. He only had eyes for me.

"I've waited fifty years for this moment, Kate," he said with a smile, the wrinkles around his eyes softening and making him look more like his younger self. "I've always wanted to be your knight in shining armor."

With a glad cry, I crossed the room and embraced Austen.

His arms tightened around me, and for a split second, I forgot that he was seventy-five years old. No matter how old Austen was, I fit perfectly into his embrace.

A sound behind me reminded me that my parents were

watching—and they'd never met Austen before. It was strange to leave his arms and turn to face them.

They were both smiling as I said, "Mama and Papa, this is Austen."

I looked up at him, loving that his eyes had not changed. They were filled with affection for me—with just a hint of his former angst.

"Austen, these are my parents, Lucas and Grace Voland."

"It's an honor to meet you, Austen," Mama said as she approached and took his hand. Her eyes filled with tears. "Thank you. For everything."

"It's my pleasure," he said.

Papa shook his hand next. "We owe you everything. Not only for today, but for every day you've been by Kathryn's side."

Austen's gray hair and wrinkles were a reminder of his age, but when he smiled at me, I saw his youth. "I would like to say it has been easy, but I would be lying."

Mama and Papa laughed, and I gave Austen a look, though I couldn't help but laugh, as well.

"I would deny it," I said, "but no one would believe me."

Austen's smile faded, and he grew serious as he regarded me. "It hasn't been easy, Kate, but it has been the greatest honor of my life." He turned to my papa then and said, "I have been waiting fifty years for something else."

"Oh?" Papa asked with a curious frown. "What is that?"

"I know this is all very strange," Austen said, "but seven days from now, I will be celebrating my fiftieth wedding anniversary."

It was my turn to frown at his words.

"Kate and I weren't given a choice by her other father," Austen said, "but I've always wanted to ask for your blessing to marry your daughter."

My mouth parted as Mama reached out and took my hand.

"I married her anyway," Austen said with a mischievous smile, "but I promised her that when the day came, I would officially ask for your blessing."

"You married me?" I asked him.

He turned back to me and nodded. "Nothing could have kept me from it."

"At St. John's?" I asked, my heart warming.

With a shake of his head, he said, "I can't wrap my mind around it, but that hasn't happened for you. Yet."

"No." I could hardly wrap my mind around it, either. I was going to marry Austen in seven days at St. John's. Which meant I would stay in 1888 and leave Mama and Papa on my twenty-fifth birthday. I had time to say good-bye to them and prepare myself for that, but I had a question for Austen now. "Have the last fifty years been good?"

Austen grinned, and it was unlike anything I'd ever seen before. Joy, passion, and love radiated from his smile. "They've been extraordinary."

I returned his smile, overcome with my own happiness. I wanted to be in Austen's arms—young Austen—but I would have to wait until tomorrow.

Papa took a step forward. He placed his hand on Austen's shoulder as if he was a young man and said, "Anyone Kathryn loves is someone we love. You have our blessing." He turned to me and placed a kiss on my forehead. "You have our blessing, Kathryn."

Mama hugged me next, her tears still falling. "I knew it," she whispered with happiness.

When I pulled back, I turned to Austen again, not sure how to ask my next question. "Am I—here?"

He shook his head. "She—you—stayed home today. She wasn't sure if you would want to see yourself as—well, fifty years from now."

"Was she there when I saw you outside Wilton Crescent? The day I discovered the portrait?"

"She was. She watched from an upstairs window, since she knew exactly when you'd be there."

"And when I went to Wilton Crescent the other day? To ask you about Mary?"

"We both knew you would be there, so we made sure we weren't. We knew you would come looking for answers, but we couldn't give them to you. You had to wait until God was ready to reveal everything."

"There is a time for everything," I said, thinking of the Bible verses in Ecclesiastes.

"A season for every activity under heaven," Austen added. "Sometimes, we want to hurry those seasons, but God knows what is best." He turned to Mama and Papa. "It's been almost fifty years since she's seen you. She understands how difficult and strange this is, but she misses you. If you're willing to see—"

"Yes," Mama said with a decisive nod. "Forever yes."

Austen smiled at Mama. "I'll bring her by tomorrow. I'm sure the general would like some time to rest."

Papa nodded his appreciation. "It's been quite the week. We'll be ready to see her tomorrow."

Austen then turned to me. "And you?"

I took a deep breath and shook my head, not fully understanding my choice, but knowing it would be the right one. "I think I'll stay away. I'm not sure it would be a good idea to see myself. It's too . . . odd."

"I don't blame you." He studied me for another moment and then said, "I should go. I don't like leaving her—you—for long."

"I'll walk you out." I followed him to the front hall and stood for a moment with him as he continued to look at me.

He put his hat on and shook his head. "I kept the portrait of you for as long as I could."

Frowning, I asked, "The one you painted in 1889?"

He nodded. "It's strange, but I painted it because I knew it would be used one day to fulfill God's plan. I didn't think I could paint anything other than landscapes, but you'll go back to 1888 tomorrow and tell me all about what's happened. After we're married, I'll begin the portrait and I'll realize it's the easiest thing I've ever painted. It will hang in our cottage at Loch Lomond for forty-nine years until a young man comes to the village in search of my paintings." He smiled. "You'll immediately recognize him as a man named Calan McCaffrey, and you'll insist that I sell him the portrait for the Royal Museum of Scotland. I'll agree—only because I know it's part of God's plan—and because I'll know that I get to see you as a young woman again."

I smiled and shook my head in wonder.

"It does my heart good to see you young," he said. "But I sure do love seeing you as the woman you've become over the last fifty years. I'm blessed that God chose for me to walk this path with you, Kate." He leaned forward and placed a kiss on my cheek. "You're the greatest adventure of my life."

When he pulled back, there were tears in my eyes.

"I'll see you tomorrow in 1888, Austen."

He winked. "I'll be waiting for you."

And with that, he walked away.

31

NOVEMBER 11, 1888
LONDON, ENGLAND

The day was cool, but the sun was bright as I slipped through the hedge between our courtyard and Austen's. My heart was thumping with anticipation and joy, knowing that I would see him again—and knowing all that was in store for us.

I'd spent hours the day before thinking about what Austen had said and what he hadn't. I knew that we would have at least fifty years together, and I prayed for many more after that, but he hadn't told me what those fifty years would contain. Would we have children? Would I continue my work here in 1888? Would we travel?

I could look up those answers in 1938, but I didn't want to. I'd learned that God's timing was best and that He would reveal the answers to me when I needed them. I didn't want to know a moment sooner than necessary.

It was liberating to be free of worry.

I didn't even bother to knock on the back door, but slipped inside and walked down the hall to the breakfast room.

Austen sat at the head of the table with a newspaper before him, while Brinley stood at attention near the sideboard. The smell of fresh croissants, bacon, and eggs wafted with the steam from the serving dishes.

Had it only been two months ago that I entered this same scene after Austen's return from Italy?

Only this time, Austen lowered his newspaper, his blue eyes filled with pleasure and anticipation as he watched for my reaction.

I couldn't help but grin, which caused him to grin.

"Brinley," Austen said as he set his paper down and rose from the table, walking around it to join me. "I thought I told you to put a guard at the door."

"Sir?" Brinley asked.

"A guard at the breakfast room door," Austen said as he gathered me in his arms. "Miss Kelly and I do not want to be bothered."

"Yes, sir," Brinley said with a smile as he slipped out of the room, leaving us alone.

"The news is good?" Austen asked as he held me in his arms.

"The news is very good."

"Your father is safe?"

"Papa is home, in perfect condition, and Sir Rothschild is in jail, where he will most likely stay for the rest of his life." I placed my hands on either side of Austen's dear face. "And we owe it all to you."

He frowned. "Me?"

I stood on tiptoe, not able to wait another moment for a kiss.

He didn't protest or ask for an explanation as he returned my kiss, pulling me close, his hands sliding from my lower back to my upper back and then into my hair, loosening the pins that Duffy had taken great pains to secure.

When he pulled back, he said, "I have so many questions."

"And I have all the answers." I laughed. "At least, I have some of the answers. I don't know everything."

He touched my nose with his, joining in my laughter. "Who are you, and what did you do with my Kate?"

I hugged him again and then said, "I'm famished. Can we eat?"

He grinned and let me go so I could fill a plate with the tantalizing food.

When we were seated, he asked, "What do you mean, you owe it all to me?"

"You came with the police not long after Sir Rothschild arrived. The surprise put him off guard, and the police were able to arrest him with little trouble."

"You saw me again?"

"Yes." I reached across the table and took his hand in mine. "And you told me all about the portrait and how this all came to be."

He frowned, clearly confused.

"You'll understand more later." I couldn't help but smile as I said, "You also told me the best news of all."

He placed his free hand over mine. "What is that?"

"In 1938, we've been happily married for almost fifty years."

Austen was quiet for a long time as he regarded me.

I couldn't read his emotions, so I finally asked, "What? What's wrong?"

"Nothing." He pressed his lips together as emotions overcame him. "I'm just amazed that I get to have breakfast with you every day of my life."

Tears gathered in my eyes, and I left my chair and sat on his lap as I put my arms around him.

"You also told me that I'm your greatest adventure," I said.

He wrapped his arms around my waist and shook his head. "You've always been my greatest adventure, Kate." He looked down as he took a deep breath, and I knew he was collecting his emotions. When he finally looked up at me, he said, "Everyone I've ever loved has left me. When I thought you would leave me, too, a part of me died. The part that has come alive again these past two months. I can't help but be awed that God would promise me at least fifty more years with the woman I adore and love more than anyone else on this planet."

"It's a gift."

"A priceless treasure," he said.

I was quiet a moment as I marveled at that treasure with him, then I wrapped my arms around him. "I know this isn't the way it's done, but my father has secured a special license for us and arranged a date for a wedding at St. Paul's—"

"Yes," he said. "I'll go now, if they're ready for us."

I shook my head in wonder. "We'll have to wait until Saturday."

He groaned as he pulled me closer.

"It's only six more days, my love."

"It feels like a lifetime."

"No." I laughed. "A lifetime is what we have to look forward to after the wedding."

A smile tilted his lips, but then he said, "Will I see you every day until then?"

"You won't be able to get rid of me."

"Is that a promise?"

"That's a promise."

"Then I will find a way to make do."

He kissed me again, taking all the time in the world.

Epilogue

NOVEMBER 11, 1938
LONDON, ENGLAND

Arthritis had settled into my fingers the year before, but that didn't stop me from holding Austen's hand as we walked slowly along Berkeley Square Road, toward the familiar townhouse where I had stayed with my parents fifty years ago. Though it felt like yesterday.

"Do you think this is wise?" I asked Austen as he walked slowly beside me.

"It's up to you," he said with a smile. "Everything from here on out is full of endless possibilities."

"It's strange to be living like the rest of them again," I said with a chuckle. "We knew we had fifty years, but anything can happen now."

The wrinkles around Austen's eyes were a testament to the laughter and joy we'd had for five decades. He lifted my aged hand to his lips and shook his head. "Anything was always possible, my love. But now the real adventure has begun."

I smiled at him, thankful that we'd been guaranteed those fifty years, though life had still thrown us many surprises along the way. Some we cherished and others we mourned.

My smile fell, thinking of our greatest loss.

"Cecily?" he asked, knowing me so well that he could sense the shift in my mood by watching me.

I lifted my face to the sun, not wanting to ruin this special day with the pain from the past. Instead, I allowed myself to smile once again and said her name. "Yes, Cecily."

He squeezed my hand, ever so gently, and nodded at the townhouse up ahead. "Here we are."

I put thoughts of Cecily aside, in the safe place within my heart where she lived forever, and took comfort knowing that her path was extraordinary.

"I'm happy I chose not to be here today as my younger self," I told Austen, my thoughts shifting from Cecily to my mama and papa. "I remember leaving that morning to walk to Lancaster House to visit Jack the Ripper's exhibit one more time before departing for America. I saw it in a brand-new light, knowing who Jack was and knowing that it wasn't the end of mine or Mary's story—but just the beginning in many ways."

"It will be good to see Mary again when she comes to visit," Austen said with excitement.

I nodded. Mary and I had written to each other over the years, once I knew it was safe for us to correspond. She had reimagined her life in ways I hadn't expected, but I applauded. We'd gone to visit her many times, but her upcoming trip to London would be the first time she'd been home since 1888.

I couldn't wait.

"Are you ready?" Austen asked me. "I'm sure your parents are eager to see you."

"Are they?" I laughed and sighed. "For them, it will be a shock. I'm older than both of them! And they just saw me an hour ago—at least, the younger me. I haven't spoken to them in fifty years. But it will be good to see them again. I've missed them fiercely."

"Shall I ring the bell?" he asked.

I nodded, bracing myself.

Austen rang the doorbell, and I took a deep breath, marveling at this strange existence I shared with Mama and all the other time-crossers, Cecily included.

As the door opened and I faced Mama and Papa, tears of joy filled my eyes.

"Kathryn," Mama said, pressing her lips together as she took a step forward to enfold me into her arms.

I let go of Austen's hand and returned her hug, thanking God for the course my life had taken.

There truly was a season for everything, and His timing was perfect.

Historical Note

Like all my TIMELESS books, I love taking real history and exploring all the possibilities. Jack the Ripper has always fascinated me, though I'm not sure why. Perhaps it's because he seems like a mythical monster, with proof of his existence, though he was always just one step ahead of the authorities. Maybe it's because it feels like there was a conspiracy afoot with the Metropolitan Police. Either way, during the fall of 1888, he enthralled and terrified the world, and then he disappeared suddenly into the swirling fog. What better place to put one of my time-crossers!

As always, I'm blown away when I get an idea for a story and then the pieces start to line up while I research. This was the case with *Every Hour until Then*. Before I began my research, I had a vague knowledge of the history, but I didn't know the particulars. My basic story idea was to have Kathryn's sister become the last victim of Jack the Ripper, having no idea at the time that the final victim, Mary Jane Kelly, was the youngest of the five canonical victims, that she had a hidden past, and that the only person she kept in contact with was her sister. When I decided that Kathryn would become my first TIMELESS heroine with red hair, I didn't know that Mary Jane Kelly also had red hair. And when I chose the two timelines, 1938 and 1888, I didn't realize that the final murder happened on November 9, 1888—which was also the date of Kristallnacht in Germany in 1938.

The next thing I needed to determine was what theory seemed most credible and would fit into my premise. In my research, I read several different theories about Jack's identity, though almost all of them are torn apart by a group of people called Ripperologists, who are self-proclaimed experts on the case. During an interview I watched, one Ripperologist was asked if he would ever be satisfied with the truth. His answer was no, because then he would have nothing left to study or speculate about. I suspect that this is why each theory is quickly discarded.

The theory that resonated with me the most came from a book called *They All Love Jack: Busting the Ripper* by Bruce Robinson, which posits that the murders were covered up by the Freemasons. I listened to it on audio (the author does a fantastic job narrating the book), and I was fascinated by his theory and supporting evidence. The book is engrossing (though it does contain expletives and graphic details). The author is a British actor, director, screenwriter, and novelist who collected information on Jack for fifteen years before writing his book. He claims that when he began his research, he had no idea it would lead to the Freemasons, but he discovered that almost everyone involved was a member of the secret society and that all the murders had Freemason rituals tied to them.

Here's where his theory differs from what I've written in my book: None of the victims had anything to do with Freemasonry (as far as I know). They did not go to Jerusalem with Sir Charles Warren, though he was there from 1867–1870 leading the first group of archaeologists into the Temple Mount (and wrote several books about his time there). Mr. Robinson theorizes that Jack was, in fact, a Freemason and that he knew he'd get away with murder because the Freemasons would cover his tracks. In *They All Love Jack*, Mr. Robinson also suggests it was Michael Maybrick, and not James, who was Jack the Ripper, and he lays down a very convincing argument. I chose to use James, because there is another theory that James was the killer, and this worked better into my premise. The James Maybrick theory comes from a diary that was found in 1992 by a man in Liverpool (where James Maybrick lived) and was supposedly owned by a family there. While the diary is convincing, there is a lot of speculation about its legitimacy. Mr. Robinson theorizes that perhaps Michael wrote it to blame James.

Another thing I changed was the date of James Maybrick's death. He died from arsenic poisoning on May 11, 1889 (not November 10, 1888). And he died in Liverpool, not London. But his wife, Florence, did go on trial and was convicted of his murder, though it's known that James took arsenic for medicinal purposes, becoming addicted to it over the years. Another interesting fact is that the letters *FM* were written in blood on Mary Jane Kelly's wall. You can see them in the photos. Some people speculate that the *FM* stands for Florence Maybrick and that either Michael (who may have been spurned by her) or James (who was angry about her infidelity) killed the victims out of their hatred for Florence.

Speaking of the victims, another fascinating book I read was *The Five: The Untold Lives of the Women Killed by Jack the Ripper* by Hallie Rubenhold. It examines the lives of each woman but ends moments before they encounter Jack. I listened to this on audio, as well, and found it to be very helpful in understanding how each of the women ended up in Whitechapel or Spitalfields and how their lives and their culture shaped them. Each one is a sad and difficult story to hear.

One other small detail I changed was that Mary Jane Kelly had been living in her room at Miller's Court about six months before she was murdered (instead of a few weeks, like I claim in my story). And, as far as anyone knows, she was not from a wealthy family in London, but perhaps from a prosperous family in Limerick, Ireland, who moved to Wales when she was a child. Though much of her early years are all speculation, which made her a good fit for Kathryn's fictional sister.

There is so much more about this case, and the Freemason theory, that I wish I could cover in my story. The Book that the

Freemasons recover from the Temple Mount is purely fiction, as was the murder of Austen Baird's parents. I have no preconceived ideas of Freemasonry, and any theories put forth in my story are not proven or substantiated. They are works of fiction, as well.

As always, tying two time periods together presents possibilities and limitations. When I decided on London in 1938, I knew the city was on the cusp of WWII, but that was about all. My only knowledge of that time and place came from the biography *Lindbergh* by A. Scott Berg. I worked at Charles A. Lindbergh's boyhood home for ten years and knew that the Lindberghs had gone to England after the kidnapping and death of their oldest son, but had come back to America when war seemed imminent. Lindbergh had been invited to Germany by the American Military Attaché, Truman Smith, on several occasions to send reports back to Washington, DC, on the German's air power. His last trip was on October 17, 1938, and not November 4, as I claim in the story. No one was abducted on his visits there, either.

The Lindberghs were part of the Cliveden Set, as they'd been dubbed by a journalist, and spent time with the Astors while in England. This group was controversial because of their views on Fascism. Lady Nancy Astor believed that Communism and the USSR were a greater threat to democracy and supported Hitler as a means of keeping Stalin at bay. Lindbergh believed the German airpower was far superior to America's, and he praised Hitler's organization and discipline. I have a lot to say about Lindbergh's opinions, but I won't bog down this author letter with them. Suffice it to say, he was a complicated man.

One interesting fact I learned was that Hitler hated the Freemasons, and this played perfectly into my premise! When I learned that the first documents the Nazis seized upon taking control of France and Belgium were the Freemason records, it gave me the idea for Sir Rothschild's motives. And speaking of Sir Rothschild, who was completely fictional, part of the reason I decided to make Jack the Ripper a time-crosser is because of a statement my editor made a couple years ago. In *When the Day Comes*, book one in the TIMELESS series, Congressman Hollingsworth claims: "Some of history's greatest heroes and heroines were time-crossers. . . . But, there have also been villains, great and small, who have sought to use their gift for personal gain, at the detriment of humanity." And my editor said: "I hope we get to meet them!"

And one final note, before I wrote this book, I didn't realize how often I referenced first floor, second floor, third floor, etc. In England, the first floor is called the ground floor, and the second floor of a building is called the first floor. I learned this when I visited London in 1999, and I was aware of it in my story, but I chose to keep the American terms.

There are many other real people, places, and events peppered throughout this novel. I've tried to keep all of them as accurate as possible while creating a compelling story. I hope I've accomplished my goal. If you've made it this far, it won't come as a surprise that I love history as much as writing. Thank you for letting me share both with you.

Author's Note

Writing a novel about Jack the Ripper hasn't been easy. It's a tough topic, and I'm thankful my phenomenal editor, Jessica Sharpe, was quick to encourage me to tackle this historical event. Her confidence in my story ideas means everything to me. The entire team at Bethany House Fiction is amazing! A special thanks goes out to my editors, Jessica Sharpe and Bethany Lenderink, as well as my rockstar marketing team of Raela Schoenherr, Anne Van Solkema, Joyce Perez, Lindsay Schubert, Rachael Betz, and Emily Vest, and my cover designer, Jennifer Parker. Each of you brings an energy and passion to my books that touches my heart.

A thank-you also goes out to my agent, Wendy Lawton, and the whole team at Books & Such Literary Agency. I also want to thank my mastermind group, Fellowship of the Pen, and my writing friends, both near and far, who encourage me, equip me, and cheer me on with each new book.

And last, but never least, I want to thank my family. My husband, David, makes almost every single meal, keeps the boys' homeschool on track, and makes sure we have clean laundry. More than a doer of household chores, he is my biggest cheerleader and steadfast fan. His support and belief in my writing have never wavered from the moment I told him I wanted to be a writer when we were just sixteen. My daughters, Ellis and Maryn, are my brainstorming network and stand alongside their dad to cheer me on. Ellis is often my first reader and gives great feedback. Maryn steps into the gap for all my other readers and represents each of you when she scolds me for taking my characters through all their trouble. But she also celebrates when they get their happily-ever-after. And my fifteen-year-old twin boys, Judah and Asher, keep things real for me. Whenever I start to think I'm still a young woman and try to keep up with them, they remind me I'm not. In all seriousness, my family is my bedrock and my safety zone. I couldn't write a word without their love and support.

My biggest thank-you is always reserved for my heavenly Father, from whom all blessings flow. I've worked hard to hone my writing skills, but my love and passion for storytelling, and any shred of talent I might possess, are gifts from God that I do not take for granted. It's an honor to write for His glory.

Discussion Questions

1. This story was set in two different eras, and though only fifty years separate them, times had changed a great deal. If you had to pick either 1888 or 1938, which one would you choose and why?
2. The book deals with one of the world's greatest unsolved mysteries, the identity of Jack the Ripper. Have you heard theories about his identity before? Who do you think he was?
3. Why do you think Jack the Ripper continues to fascinate people?
4. In 1938, Kathryn is introduced to the Cliveden Set, a controversial group who saw Hitler without the lens of history. Do you struggle to understand the mindset of some people in the past? Do you fear that we haven't learned from history?
5. Did anything surprise you about 1888 or 1938?
6. Kathryn is determined and sure of herself. She has her life planned out and doesn't want to change midcourse. Do you relate to her? Or do you go with the flow?

7. Kathryn is faced with many difficult choices, but toward the end, she must choose if she wants to see herself as a seventy-three-year-old woman. If given the choice, would you want to see yourself aged?
8. On the flipside, would you like to see yourself young again? How do you think it would affect you?
9. Austen and Kathryn know that they will have at least fifty years together. Do you think you'd live differently if you were guaranteed that much time?
10. Were you happy with how the story played out? Or would you have made different choices?

Read on
for a sneak peek at

Through Each Tomorrow

Book 6 of
the TIMELESS series.
Available November 2025.

1

CHARLES

JUNE 1, 1883
FREDERICKSBURG, VIRGINIA

I had been dreading the stack of envelopes my sister Ada put on my desk all day. I knew there would be bills and late notices, but I hadn't anticipated the letter sitting on top.

"What is it, Charles?" Ada asked as she entered my office and set a cup of coffee in front of me. "Another debt collector?"

Her voice was just as weary as her countenance, and I didn't need to look up to see that she was exhausted. Widowed less than six months after she'd married her childhood sweetheart, she'd come back to the farm pregnant and destitute. The baby wasn't due for another two months, but it was a hot summer day, and she'd been up before sunrise to take care of our mama.

I refolded the letter and smiled as I met her troubled gaze. "I told you not to worry about the bills, Ada. We'll get by."

She put her hand on the back of my head where my time-crossing mark sat just above my hairline. "You don't have much time left, and Cecily needs you more than we do."

I placed my hand over hers. "You and Mama need me, too."

With another sigh, she removed her hand and glanced out at the farm beyond my office window. Her blue eyes had been full of life at one time, but now they looked dull and disillusioned. She was only twenty-six, but she looked much older from her grief.

The farm she surveyed was just as careworn as my older sister. Vibrant before the War Between the States, the property was now a shadow of its former glory. Papa had been a prosperous horse breeder before the war broke out, but he'd died in battle, and then the farm had become a field hospital for Union soldiers during the last Battle of Fredericksburg. The only thing that had survived was the house. I'd been trying to rebuild the farm since I was old enough to hold a hammer, but without money, I had worked in vain, eking out only enough to get by.

"Supper will be done soon," Ada said as she walked to the door, her hand on her lower back. "I'll take a plate to Mama, and then we can eat."

"Is she doing any better today?" I asked, afraid of the answer.

Ada shook her head. "I had hoped the baby would give her something to look forward to." She put her hand on her rounded belly and pressed her lips together. "She hasn't eaten in three days."

This bout of melancholy was the deepest it had ever been. Mama had suffered on and off since Papa's death, but it had never put her in bed before. The weight of her unhappiness had fallen on our shoulders ever since we were children, and though I tried to tell myself it wasn't my fault, I always wondered if things would have been different had I been able to make something of the farm.

Perhaps I finally could.

"I'll check in on her before I come to supper," I said.

She nodded and then left the office. As her footsteps receded down the hall, I unfolded the letter again and slowly rose from my desk chair, wondering if Drew's suggestion was the answer to a prayer I had been afraid to ask.

Whitney Shipping
New York, New York

Charles,

I'm sure you're surprised by this letter, and frankly, I never expected to write it. But something has come up, and I hope you can help me.

I need an English aristocrat. I know that sounds strange. Since you're the only one I know—sort of—I thought I would ask you. Mother has been in a terrible feud with my aunt for years; perhaps you've read about it in the papers. It's become a legendary fight, each one trying to prove that she is the Mrs. Whitney, *the queen of the nouveau riche. They've both built enormous cottages in Newport and ridiculous mansions in New York City. They've thrown elaborate parties, costing hundreds of thousands of dollars, and purchased the most outlandish things to try to outdo one another.*

So, when my aunt informed the New York World *that she was on her way back from Paris with Vicomte Deville, and that she would be entertaining him in Newport for the summer, my mother insisted that I find an aristocrat with higher standing so she could outdo my aunt.*

I know you're not an earl in 1883, but you are one in 1563, and you have all the knowledge and mannerisms of an earl to pull it off for a few weeks. You can even tell Mother your real name from 1563, Charles Pembrooke, the Earl of Norfolk, so you won't mess anything up.

I just need you to show up at a few parties and impress a few of her friends. I'll be there, and we can keep a low profile.

You might wonder why I'd go to so much trouble. The truth is that my parents' marriage isn't doing so well, and I hate to see my mother unhappy. I imagine you can relate. This might be the last summer in Newport before a possible divorce that would shake the foundations of Mother's fragile place in society.

You would be doing me a huge favor—and in return, I'd like to help you. I know your Virginia farm is in dire straits, and I think I can convince my father to invest in it, given the right angle. He's always been an avid horseman, but his shipping business has kept him too busy to pursue his passion. He's in Europe and won't return to New York until September. He has no plans to go to Newport, since he and Mother are not speaking.

I propose that you come to Newport for July and August as Lord Norfolk. Then we will go to New York when Father returns in September, and you can meet him as Charles Hollingsworth, the owner of the Hollingsworth Horse Farm. Mother and Father's social and business lives do not intersect, so neither one will be the wiser. If all goes as planned, your horse farm could be up and running by the beginning of next year—before your twenty-fifth birthday, when you need to make your final decision. If you choose to stay in 1563, you can have someone in place to keep up the farm, so your mother and sister have an income. And, if you choose to stay in 1883, you'll have all the financial backing you'll need.

I must have your answer immediately. If you're willing to come, I will wire you enough money to get to New York, and enough to take care of your mother and sister until your return at the end of the summer. I will meet you in New York to outfit you as the Earl of Norfolk before we head to Newport.

I await your reply,
Drew

I folded the letter again and ran my hand over the stubble of a beard I hadn't shaved that morning. In 1563, I was the Earl of Norfolk, a member of Queen Elizabeth's Privy Council, esteemed and respected. I was the young heir of Arundel Castle, where I had met Andrew Bromley, the carpenter's son. I had recognized the time-crossing mark on the back of his head, and we'd learned that we occupied the same two paths—only, he was the son and heir of a massive shipping fortune in 1883, and I was the destitute son of a widowed mother. Our lives were complete opposites, but because of our time-crossing marks, we had been lifelong friends—even though I'd never met him in person in 1883. This letter was the first correspondence I'd ever received from him in this path.

"You must eat, Mama." Ada's voice filtered into my office from our mother's bedroom across the hall. "You haven't touched anything in days."

I walked to the window and let my gaze wander over the farm. There was so much potential; it was heartbreaking to see the waste.

But it wasn't just Mama and Ada who needed me. I was the only person my younger stepsister Cecily had in 1563. I had a plan to help her, but I wasn't sure it would work, either. Like Drew's plan, there were complications I needed to overcome to ensure Cecily was taken care of if I left her.

It was part of my time-crossing gift. I had to choose which life I wanted to keep on my twenty-fifth birthday next March, and which one I would forfeit.

If I could find a husband for Cecily before then, I would stay with Mama and Ada. If I could secure a financial investor for the farm before then, I would stay with Cecily.

Either way, I had a lot of work ahead of me and not enough time.

Squaring my shoulders, I decided I didn't have much choice. But I wouldn't accept Drew's proposal without a counterproposal.

I wanted something from him in 1563.

I needed to know what was killing Queen Elizabeth, and Drew was my last hope.

But if he agreed, and we weren't careful, asking for his help could land us in the Tower—or worse, on the end of a royal noose.

Gabrielle Meyer is a Christy Award–winner and ECPA bestselling author. She has worked for state and local historical societies and loves writing fiction inspired by real people, places, and events. She currently resides along the banks of the Mississippi River in central Minnesota with her husband and four children. By day, she's a busy homeschool mom, and by night she pens fiction and nonfiction filled with hope. Find her online at GabrielleMeyer.com.

Sign Up for Gabrielle's Newsletter

Keep up to date with Gabrielle's latest news on book releases and events by signing up for her email list at the link below.

GabrielleMeyer.com

FOLLOW GABRIELLE ON SOCIAL MEDIA

Gabrielle Meyer, Author

@Gabrielle_Meyer

@MeyerGabrielle